About the Authors

haron Kendrick started story-telling at the age of leven and has never stopped. She likes to write fast-aced, feel-good romances with heroes who are so sexy ley'll make your toes curl! She lives in the beautiful ty of Winchester – where she can see the cathedral om her window (when standing on tip-toe!). She has vo children, Celia and Patrick and her passions include usic, books, cooking and eating – and drifting into aydreams while working out new plots.

larion Lennox is a country girl, born on an Australian dairy farm. She moved on, because the cows just eren't interested in her stories! Married to a 'very pecial doctor', she has also written under the name risha David. She's now stepped back from her 'other' areer teaching statistics. Finally, she's figured what's nportant and discovered the joys of baths, romance and chocolate. Preferably all at the same time! Marion an international award winning author.

A Cinderella Story

COLLECTION

January 2020
A Modern Cinderella

February 2020
Working with Cinderella

March 2020
Saved by His Cinderella

April 2020
Seducing His Cinderella

May 2020
His Exotic Cinderella

June 2020
A Groom for Cinderella

His Exotic Cinderella

SHARON KENDRICK

MARIONLENNOX

MILLS & BOON

First Published in Great Britain 2020
By Mills & Boon, an imprint of HarperCollins*Publishers*
1 London Bridge Street, London, SE1 9GF

ISBN: 978-0-263-28138-5

This book is produced from independently certified FSC™ paper to ensure responsible forest management.

For more information visit: www.harpercollins.co.uk/green

Printed and bound in Spain
by CPI, Barcelona

MONARCH OF THE SANDS

SHARON KENDRICK

With special thanks to Dr Lloyd Wood—whose passion about oil discovery was contagious and helped make my heroine's father become real.

And to Sarah of Smart Bitches, who inadvertently inspired this story.

CHAPTER ONE

AGAINST her pale skin, the diamond flashed like a shooting star and Frankie gazed at it in wonder. Who would ever have thought it? Geeky, freaky Frankie O'Hara engaged to be married—and sporting a solitaire the size of a blueberry.

Spreading out her fingers, she watched as the precious stone caught the pale November light and glittered it back at her. Her father would have smiled and said that a diamond was nothing but a hard and highly refractive form of carbon—but to Frankie it was so much more than that. It was a symbol. It signified that a man loved her and wanted to spend the rest of his life with her. A handsome, successful man, too. Not the kind of man she'd ever have thought would be attracted to someone like her—not in the million or so years it took to make a diamond.

The low roar of a car disturbed her dreamy thoughts and Frankie blinked with surprise and a slight feeling of panic. Surely Simon wasn't here already? Why, she hadn't peeled a single potato for the celebration meal she'd been planning—and surely the chicken breasts hadn't been marinating for nearly long enough?

She peered out of the window and the breath caught

sharply in her throat as she saw the expensive and gleaming vehicle which was making its way up the drive, spraying little shoals of gravel in its wake.

That certainly wasn't Simon—who drove a comfortable saloon indistinguishable from the many others which dominated the roads of this affluent area of suburban England. The car which was now pulling to a halt in front of the house was sporty, black and powerful and looked as if it would be more at home on an international racing circuit than in this quiet corner of the world. And she didn't have to look at the driver's hard profile to know exactly who was driving it.

Zahid!

Her heart began to pound and Frankie's mouth became parchment-dry. After all, the man in question was pretty close to every woman's fantasy man and he was sitting right outside her house. Zahid Al Hakam—royal Sheikh and King. The man with the hard, hawklike features and the dark, enigmatic eyes.

It was highly unusual for someone as ordinary as Frankie to be friends with an exotic and powerful sheikh, but life often had funny twists and turns along the way. The sheikh's father had been a long-time friend of her father's, so she'd known the Prince of Khayarzah ever since she'd been a little girl—though his visits had tapered away since he had unexpectedly become King. The sudden death of his uncle and his cousin had left Zahid as the heir apparent—with no time in his busy diary to visit old friends in small English towns.

At first, she'd missed his visits dreadfully, before deciding that his absence was probably all for the best—because hadn't she wasted too many hours fantasising about a man who was way out of her league?

She glanced out of the window again. So why had he just turned up out of the blue? And why today, of all days?

She saw him get out of the car—unfolding his long-legged frame with the lithe elegance which always made her think of a jungle cat. He slammed the car door but didn't bother locking it—though, come to think of it, he'd probably stationed his security people at the end of the drive. And besides, who would dare try and steal *his* car?

The pealing of the doorbell galvanised her into life—and as she rushed to answer it she thought that wasn't the only thing which was peeling. The walls badly needed painting. The big house was inevitably showing signs of wear and tear—despite her best efforts to try to maintain the place. And didn't that only reinforce Simon's increasingly urgent suggestion that she sell the family home and the valuable land on which it stood?

Heart still pounding, she pulled open the door and psyched herself up to greet him, praying that she might have grown up and moved on enough not to be affected by him. Five long years had passed since she'd last seen him—surely enough time to give her some kind of immunity against him.

Vain hope. She swallowed, trying to quell the rush of guilty longing which made her heart begin to race as she stared into his stern face. Because was there a woman on earth who could have been unmoved by his presence—even if they had just agreed to marry someone else?

He wasn't how most people expected a sheikh to look—with not a flowing robe in sight—but that was deliberate. Years ago, he had told her that he liked to blend in—like the chameleon who adapted its appearance to its habitat in order to survive. That was the reason why he was fluent in several languages and spoke them like a native. Except that someone as rugged and as powerful as Zahid could never really *blend* in. No matter what he said or wore, he drew the eye and caught people's attention, just as a beautiful bloom tossed on a dusty roadside might have done.

Clad in a beautifully cut grey suit, which showcased the musculature of his magnificent body, he completely dominated the doorway of her house. Eyes like chips of black stone surveyed her from a hawk-featured face, his skin a shade lighter than burnished copper. With that raven-dark hair, he looked like some brooding movie-star of yesteryear, she thought, with a sudden and unwanted ache. He was all stillness and silence—while managing to exude a raw and undeniable animal magnetism.

For some inexplicable reason, Frankie plunged her left hand deep into the pocket of her jeans and a wave of guilt shivered through her. Was she *trying to hide her brand-new engagement ring?* And *why on earth was she doing that?*

'Hello, Zahid,' she said.

Few people—and especially commoners—were permitted to use his first name, but Zahid wasn't thinking about protocol at that moment. For a moment there was complete silence as his gaze raked over her in astonishment. Surely there must be some kind of mistake?

'Francesca?' His eyes narrowed—as if he'd been confronted by a mirage in the middle of the desert. 'Is that really you?'

Frankie tried not to react. *Nobody* called her Francesca. Nobody except him. She heard the familiar way he curled the syllables around his tongue and a stupid little shiver whispered over her skin. It was a name given to her by her glamorous mother who had been hoping for a mini-me and been bitterly disappointed. When the duckling child had stubbornly refused to become a swan, the exotic tag had disappeared and been replaced by the much more workaday 'Frankie' and that was what she'd been ever since. But not to Zahid.

'Of course it's me!' she said, but she wouldn't have been human if she hadn't felt a sudden rush of pleasure at that flash of very grown-up appreciation in his eyes. He'd never looked at her in any way other than the way he might have regarded a faithful retainer. A loyal servant, say—or a pet dog who came running over with its tail wagging eagerly. She knew that her question was an unnecessary one but she wanted to hear how Zahid would answer it. 'Why, do I look different?'

He felt a flicker of something unexpected. Damned right she did. Different didn't even come close to it. Last time he'd seen her, she'd been a tomboyish nineteen-year-old, so nondescript and shapeless that you'd never have noticed her in a crowd. So what the hell had happened in the intervening years?

He studied her closely. The short hair, which used to stick out at odd angles, had been allowed to grow so that now it fell in dark, silken waves down her back. The thick, geeky glasses had disappeared and instead he could see a pair of eyes which were a deep shade of startling blue. And the shapeless clothes she used to wear had been replaced by a pair of snug jeans and a soft oatmeal sweater, which hinted at a body he would never have imagined Francesca possessing.

'What the hell happened to your glasses?' he demanded unevenly.

'Oh, I wear contacts now.' She shrugged. 'Everybody does.'

He wanted to ask when had she developed such an amazing pair of breasts and a bottom which was curvier than a scimitar? He wanted to know when the dramatic transformation from girl to woman had taken place—but he stopped himself by biting back the faintly erotic questions. Because this was *Francesca* he was talking to—sweet, innocent little Francesca—not some potential lover he'd just met at a cocktail party.

Instead, he fixed her with a cool look, which was intended to remind her that although he was a family friend of long-standing he still expected a degree of formality and protocol.

Frankie saw the faint furrow which had appeared on his brow and correctly interpreted it. 'Oh, forgive me! Would you…?' She opened the door a little wider, unable to decide whether she wanted him to go or to stay. Because if he stayed—wouldn't it unsettle her? Wouldn't it risk starting those stupid fantasies again—the ones she used to get whenever he strode into the house? The ones which had always ended with Zahid scooping her up in his arms and starting to kiss her before telling her that he couldn't live without her. 'Would you like to come in?' she finished weakly.

No, he'd driven down from London to stand on her doorstep like a salesman! 'Thanks,' he said drily, and walked into the hallway—a place which was at once both alien and familiar to him. A large and faintly shabby English home with a big, green garden. Yet hadn't this been the one place outside his homeland where he had always been able to kick back and relax? A place where nobody watched him or where there were no indiscreet gossips or the threat of someone talking to the press. Because being the sheikh's nephew meant that you were always watched; always listened to.

Over the years, his father used to bring him here—to talk to the man who had changed the course of his country's history. Francesca's brilliant and eccentric geologist father. It had been his unexpected discovery of oil which had lifted Khayarzah out of the crippling debts caused by decades of warfare—and changed its whole future.

As Francesca shut the door behind him Zahid found his gaze lingering for longer than usual on her unexpectedly blue eyes, remembering seeing her soon after she'd been born. What a mewling little creature she'd been—with her bright red face screaming out from amid a swathe of white blankets. He'd have been, what—thirteen at the time?

He remembered the way she used to waddle up to him as a chubby-faced toddler—unbelievably cute—and the way she'd demand to be carried by him just before she first started school. And hadn't he done as she'd asked? Allowed her to twist him round her little finger in a way which no woman had ever done before, nor since.

He remembered, too, the cold air of neglect and despair which settled on the house when her mother left, pronouncing herself bored with her older, scientist husband. She'd run off with someone richer. Someone who had shown her the finer things in life. The first of the many wealthy lovers who would ultimately dump her before she died in a car crash, a tragedy sullied by the shame of knowing that the car was being driven by a prominent and very married politician.

But Francesca and her father had rallied. They'd formed a tight little unit. The little girl had grown up surrounded by scientists and left largely to her own devices. Consequently, she hadn't gone through the coy teenage years—or the stage of showing off her body with minuscule clothes. In fact, up until this precise moment you would barely have noticed she was a woman at all.

He remembered teaching her how to play cards when she'd been unhappy at school. And actually letting her beat him! He was deeply and instinctively competitive, and it was the only time in his life that he hadn't insisted on winning. It had been worth it just to see the little smile which had briefly illuminated her troubled features.

A voice broke into his thoughts and he realised she was speaking to him. 'Did you say something?' he questioned, shaking his head a little because it was unlike him to be sentimental.

'I was asking what had brought you here, to Surrey.' She tipped her head to one side. 'Or were you just passing?'

For a moment he didn't answer. What *had* brought him here today? The realisation that he hadn't seen her in nearly five years and the faint guilt which had accompanied that thought? He knew that she was alone in the world now—and though he'd always intended to keep an eye on her, life just somehow kept getting in the way. And ever since the unexpected crown had been placed on his head just eighteen months ago the restrictions imposed by his new role had piled down thick and fast.

'I have business in London, so I thought I'd do a detour,' he said. 'To see how you are. Realising that it is quite some time since I last saw you—and that I really ought to do something about it.'

He was looking at her in such an odd and piercing way that Frankie could feel colour stealing into her cheeks.

'Would you…would you like a drink?' she asked, knowing that he rarely accepted any kind of sustenance. She used to wonder if it was because he always had to be careful about someone trying to poison him until her father explained that royals always liked to keep a certain amount of distance about them, no matter where they were.

'Yes, I would.'

'You would?'

He knitted his eyebrows together. 'Didn't you just offer me a drink—or have I started hearing things? And if you offer something, then it's usually expected you'll provide it. Tea, please. Mint—if you have it.'

Nervously, she nodded, wishing that he'd disappear for a moment, leaving her to compose herself. So she could slip her engagement ring off until after he'd gone—thus postponing the inevitable questions she had no desire to answer even though she wasn't quite sure why that was. 'Would you…would you like to wait in the sitting room?'

Zahid frowned. What the hell was the matter with her today? He began to wonder if her dramatic physical transformation was responsible for her odd and rather secretive attitude? 'No. I'll come into the kitchen and talk to you while you're making it—that's what I usually do.'

'Yes.' But usually she didn't feel this odd and prickling kind of awareness fizzing in the air around them. As if something had changed between them and nobody had bothered to warn her about it. 'Come with me,' she said.

Zahid followed her along the chilly corridor, carefully trying to avert his eyes from the rhythmic sway of her bottom and wondering why she was being so edgy. And why she was walking in a way which seemed…

They'd reached the kitchen when he worked out just what the anomaly was and he frowned. 'Is there something the matter with your hand, Francesca?'

She turned round, her heart thudding guiltily against her breast. 'My hand?'

'The one which seems to be glued to your left thigh.'

Was it rude to stand in front of a sheikh with your hand rammed deeply into your pocket? She supposed that it was. And she couldn't exactly potter one-handedly around this vast kitchen making tea, with his clever black eyes watching her, could she? Reluctantly, she withdrew her fingers, aware of the scratch of the stone against the denim and the dazzle of the gem as it emerged into the light.

The feeling of wonderment she'd been experiencing just minutes before his arrival now evaporated into one of acute embarrassment. Stupidly, she found her cheeks colouring as she lifted her eyes to meet his—but finding nothing other than cold curiosity in his gaze.

'Why, Francesca,' he said, with a note in his voice she'd never heard before. 'I don't believe it. You're engaged to be married.'

CHAPTER TWO

BLACK eyes burned into her with a question blazing at their depths and for a moment Frankie felt oddly weak beneath their fierce scrutiny.

'You're getting married?' Zahid queried silkily.

Frankie nodded, her throat parchment-dry, wondering why she was feeling so damned nervous when she should have been feeling *proud.* 'Yes. Yes, I am.'

'When did this happen?'

'Just—yesterday.'

'Let me see. Oh, please don't be coy about it.' His black eyes gleamed with some dark emotion she didn't recognise. 'Come on, Francesca—I thought that all women loved showing off their engagement rings?'

Reluctantly, Frankie extended her hand and as he took it in his she felt the prickle of awareness as the sheikh's warm flesh touched hers. Hadn't there been years and years when she'd dreamt of Zahid holding her hand like this? And yet the exquisite irony was that at last it was happening and it meant precisely nothing. All he was doing was holding her hand so that he could examine an engagement ring bought for her by another man!

Zahid frowned as he studied the gem closely, feeling

her unmistakable shiver as she pulled her fingers away. And hadn't he felt the faintest whisper of something himself? Something which, if he didn't know better, might almost have been the first potent shimmering of desire. Lifting his head, he met her eyes, raising his brows in mocking query. 'But surely this should be a cause for celebration, rather than secrecy?'

The colour in her cheeks intensified. 'Oh, but it is.' *So why had she been hiding the ring from him?* The unspoken question hovered on the air, but even if he'd asked her Frankie doubted whether she would have been able to come up with a satisfactory explanation. Not to him—not even to herself. And as it happened, he didn't ask her.

'So who's the lucky man?'

'His name's Simon Forrester.'

'Simon Forrester.' Zahid pulled out a chair from beneath the large, scrubbed oak table and sat down, spreading his legs out in front of him. Idly, he noticed the unusual and fancy display of hothouse roses which were sitting there replacing the hand-picked sprigs from the garden which she normally favoured. Had 'Simon' bought her those? Was he the reason for the long hair and the junking of her glasses? The incentive to start wearing sexy jeans and a clinging sweater? Had Simon woken her up to all kinds of new experiences, as well as a new way of dressing?

Inexplicably, he felt the souring flavour of distaste in his mouth. 'And what does he do, this Simon Forrester?'

Frankie's smile became fixed. Wasn't this what she had instinctively been fearing—having to give a detailed account? She felt like telling him that it wasn't his place to just breeze in after however long it had been and start interrogating her. But she knew that there was no point. Zahid was used to getting exactly what he wanted—and why on earth *wouldn't* she tell him?

'He owns the estate agency I work in. Remember I mentioned I'd started there, in one of my Christmas cards?'

Had she? Zahid frowned. He was certain she knew that Christmas wasn't celebrated in Khayarzah, but she still insisted on sending him a card every year. And for some reason, he insisted on opening them himself—instead of letting one of his aides deal with it. They were always variations on a theme: images of robins and berry-laden sprigs of holly. Or carol singers singing in snowy villages. And even though he didn't celebrate Christmas, he did find those cards made him nostalgic for the years he spent in England while he was at boarding school.

'Maybe you did mention it,' he said slowly. But it was a surprise. Hadn't he thought she might follow a scientific route, like her father? 'Tell me more.'

Frankie bit her lip. He didn't have a clue what she was talking about! Obviously, he never even bothered to read the chatty accompanying letter she always took the time to tuck inside the annual card. 'Well, Simon runs a very successful company—'

'Not about the company, Francesca—about *him*,' he butted in. 'This man you are proposing to marry. This *Simon Forrester*.'

It wasn't easy when she felt as if he were spearing her with hostile black light from his eyes and spitting out Simon's name as if it were some particularly nasty kind of medicine, but Frankie tried to remember all the things she liked best about her fiancé. Those blue eyes and the way he'd dazzled her with his attention. The roses which he'd had sent to her house, week after week—she, who had never received a bunch of flowers in her life!

She licked her lips. 'He's not the kind of man I would have normally expected to go out with—'

'Really? You go out with many men, do you?' he fired back. 'And then compare them?'

'N-no.' Why on earth was he looking at her so *darkly*? 'That's not what I meant.'

'So what *do* you mean?'

Frankie swallowed as she filled the kettle from the big, old-fashioned sink and put it on to boil. Why was he tying her up in knots with his clever line in questioning and, furthermore, why was he being so…*aggressive*? As if he had some sort of *right* to question her. Resisting the impulse to tell him it was none of his business, she forced her mind back to Simon and an image of his face popped into her mind. She thought of the thick lock of hair which flopped onto his forehead unless he brushed it back, which he did—rather a lot, as it happened. 'Well, he's blond and *very* good-looking.'

Zahid scowled. 'I'm disappointed in you, Francesca,' he said. 'Are you really so superficial that physical attributes matter most?'

'That's rich, coming from you!' said Frankie quietly, before she could stop herself.

There was a short and disbelieving silence. 'I'm sorry?'

'It doesn't matter.'

'Oh, but it does.' His voice dipped to a tone of menacing silk. 'Tell me.'

Frankie met the flash of annoyance which sparked

from his eyes. Why *shouldn't* she tell him? He didn't think twice about foisting his opinion on *her*. 'You're not such an angel yourself, are you, Zahid? Don't you use your so-called "business" trips to Europe and the United States as a cover-up for your affairs with women?'

It would have been laughable if it were not so insulting and Zahid felt a mounting fury that Francesca—whom he had known all her life—could think so poorly of him. As if he were nothing more than some brainless *stud*. 'And just where did you acquire this fascinating piece of information?'

'The gossip columns are always full of your exploits—though I notice that they've tailed off since you became King. But prior to that, you were always being seen with some woman or other!'

'How very naïve you are, Francesca.' With a faint sigh of impatience, he shook his dark head and subjected her to a look of chilly censure. 'Do you really believe everything you read in the papers?'

'I believe the evidence of my own eyes! I've seen enough photos of you with…with…' To her fury and consternation, Frankie found that her breath was catching in her throat and that her mind was now being plagued with images far more vivid than that of Simon's face.

Zahid with a Hollywood hottie gazing up at him, with naked adoration on her face. Zahid being papped with a sexy international lawyer who had been representing one of his rivals in some complicated court case. Except that she was pretty sure it wasn't written into a legal code of conduct that a legal representative should look at her own client's adversary as if she'd like to eat him up for breakfast. 'With all *kinds* of women!' she finished hotly. 'Making you look like some sort of international *playboy*!'

Zahid winced and, to be fair, he conceded that she *did* have a point. He *had* always enjoyed a colourful and varied sex-life until the constraints of his unexpected new role as King had forced him to employ a little more prudence. But even so…

'And you think that's the *only* reason I travel?' he demanded. 'To have affairs with women?'

As his tone of indignation washed over her Frankie forced herself to remember all his humanitarian work. She thought about the money he'd poured into a world peace project and the well-received speeches he had made on the subject. Just because she had experienced the green-eyed monster when she'd seen the photos didn't mean that she should make him out to be some kind of uncaring brute who was only interested in bedding members of the opposite sex.

She shook her head. 'No, of course I don't and I shouldn't have implied that I did,' she said stiffly, tipping boiling water into a pot containing two mint tea bags and glancing up to find his eyes on her. 'But even you wouldn't deny that it's probably one of the perks of being away from all the restrictions in Khayarzah.'

He gave a brief nod. How well she knew him. Or maybe it was just that she was permitted the rare freedom to be able to voice such thoughts because of her long association with his family. And because of the great debt he owed to her father…

'I'm sorry about your father,' he said suddenly. 'And I'm sorry I couldn't get to the funeral.'

Frankie puckered her lips tightly as she picked up the

teapot. Don't show emotion, she told herself fiercely. It's counterproductive because it will only get you upset—and it really isn't done to break down in front of the sheikh, no matter how well you think you know him.

'I understand,' she answered, her voice sounding like a child's squeaky toy. 'You explained in your letter that you had only just acceded to the throne, and that you c-couldn't get away.'

Zahid nodded, remembering back to those troubled days—when the crown he had never imagined he would wear had been placed on his head. 'I couldn't,' he said simply.

'It was good of your brother to come in your place. And that wreath you sent,' Frankie added, with a gulp. 'It was absolutely b-beautiful.'

He heard her voice wobble and he glared, getting up from the table to take the teapot from her trembling hands. 'Here. Let me take that.'

'You can't pour your own tea.'

'Don't be so ridiculous,' he returned. 'I can just about upend a pot of boiling water. Or do you think I have people waiting on me every second of the day?'

'Pretty much.'

A faint smile edged the corners of his mouth. 'Impertinent woman,' he murmured, and as he said it found himself looking into her startled blue eyes as one word leapt out and hung in the air surrounding them. He felt a pulse of heat deep in his groin. *Woman.* He swallowed. He would never have said that to her before. Nor found himself looking at her lips and wondering what it would be like to kiss them—even though they weren't wearing a scrap of make-up. Did *Simon* not like her wearing make-up? he wondered heatedly.

Frankie took one of the mugs of tea and quickly moved away—the fact that it was burning her hand hardly noticeable when measured against the hot burning in her cheeks which had followed that curiously intense moment back then. 'I'll…I'll get some honey,' she said.

Glad to have the distraction of moving away, she walked over to one of the cupboards. Her fingers were trembling as she brought out a half-filled jar and handed it to him, and she watched as he spooned a teaspoonful of honey in each cup, seeing it melt in a golden puddle into the pale green liquid.

He looked up then, a careless question in his eyes. 'So when do I get to meet him?'

'Meet him?' Francesca's heart thudded. Surely he didn't mean what she thought he meant? 'Wh-who?'

'Simon.'

She stared at him, trying to disguise her horror—some instinct telling her that Zahid and Simon should be kept apart at all costs. 'Wh-why on earth would you want to meet him?'

He shrugged and her obvious reluctance to have him do so only fired up his sense of determination that he should. 'Why wouldn't I? My country owes a great debt to your father and I am an old family friend. Since you don't have any senior male relative to look out for you, I consider it my duty to meet the man you are intending to marry.'

Frankie hoped that her face didn't betray her appalled reaction to his suggestion—and not just because he had painted a rather grim image of himself as a "senior male relative". The last thing she wanted was for him to meet Simon—because surely Zahid would make *any* man look hapless in his presence.

'Well, perhaps we can arrange something for the next time you're in town,' she said, with the confident air of someone who knew that tight royal schedules made such casual meetings almost impossible.

'But aren't you seeing him tonight? Aren't you planning to cook him dinner?'

She wondered how on earth he could have known that until she saw him looking at the covered dish of chicken and the little heap of potatoes waiting to be peeled; the box of unopened candles which lay next to them. Perhaps he had been a detective in another life, she thought crossly. 'Yes, I'm cooking him dinner. I'd ask you to join us except that you're probably busy.' She gave a weak smile. 'And I've only got two chicken breasts.'

Zahid almost laughed at the sheer banality of her statement, but the truth of it was that her attitude was firing him up even more. He wasn't used to people saying no to him. And his curiosity had been aroused. What was she trying to hide? 'No woman should have to cook a meal when she's just got engaged—she should be freed from the drudgery of domesticity and left to enjoy the romance,' he said silkily. 'So I'll take you and Simon out to dinner instead.'

'No, honestly—'

'Yes, *honestly*,' he mocked. 'I insist. What's the name of a good local restaurant?'

'Le Poule au Pot is pretty good—but you'll never get a table this late.'

'Please don't be naïve, Francesca—I can always get a table. I'll meet you in there at eight-thirty,' he said implacably, as—pushing away his untouched tea—he got up from the table.

Frankie scrambled to her feet, aware of the sheer power of his body as she stared up into his hawklike features. 'I suppose there's no point in me trying to change your mind?'

'No point at all.' Black eyes bored into her. 'And why would you want to?'

This silky challenge she couldn't—or wouldn't—answer. All she knew was that the thought of subjecting Simon—and herself—to the distracting company of the powerful man she'd known since childhood was filling her with trepidation.

Zahid looked down into her upturned face and those strangely kissable lips, which her tiny white teeth were currently digging into as she turned anxious blue eyes up at him. And in that moment she looked so vulnerable yet so damned *sexy* that he began to wonder whether fate might not have had a hand in bringing him here today.

'Just don't be late,' he added softly.

CHAPTER THREE

'SMILE, baby, and just relax—we're going to have a ball.'

Relax? Frankie swallowed down the acid taste of nerves as Simon eased his car into the last available spot in the Le Poule au Pot's car park. How could she possibly relax, knowing that an evening with Zahid lay ahead of them? Questions had been spinning round in her head all the time she was getting ready. Wondering why the autocratic sheikh was insisting on taking them out to dinner—and what on earth his agenda was. Was it really because he wanted to vet Simon, to see if he measured up and was suitable? And if so, wasn't that an awfully *old-fashioned* point of view?

'I just wish we weren't going out,' she said, her fingers playing nervously with her necklace. 'And having a quiet dinner at home instead—the way we'd planned.'

Simon put the brakes on and shot a quick look at himself in the driving mirror. 'Are you crazy? You're best buddies with some *sheikh*—'

'I wouldn't describe us as "best buddies"—'

'Well, friendly enough for him to invite us out. And you'd rather be sitting in your old kitchen with a home-cooked meal? I mean, what planet are you on, Frankie? *Wait* till I tell everyone that I had dinner with a royal!'

'But you mustn't,' put in Frankie anxiously. 'That's the whole point. You're not supposed to mention it to anyone—it's an infringement on their privacy and they get little enough of that as it is.'

Simon's smile was tight. 'Let's not drift too far from reality, shall we? I don't need lessons in protocol from my secretary.' He gave her knee a quick squeeze. 'Even if she does also happen to be my fiancée!'

She gave him a weak, answering smile but Frankie's heart was pounding as they entered the restaurant and she felt an overpowering feeling of relief when she realised that Zahid wasn't there. Maybe he'd changed his mind about coming, she thought hopefully as they were led to their table. Decided that something more important—or someone very beautiful—had come up. Any minute now and the maître d' would discreetly slide up to their table and tell them that he had been unavoidably detained, and…

'Hello, Francesca.'

She'd been so deep in thought that she hadn't noticed the sheikh enter the room until his silken and faintly accented voice broke into her thoughts. She looked up and there he was, standing in front of their table like some dark god—with Simon springing to his feet as if his long-lost brother had just appeared and for one awful moment Frankie thought that he was actually going to try to *embrace* the sheikh.

But Zahid pre-empted any inappropriate familiarity by extending a cool hand in greeting and an even cooler smile. 'You must be Simon.'

'And you must be Zahid. Frankie's told me *all* about you.'

'Has she really?' Dark eyes were briefly glittered

in her direction as Frankie attempted to clamber to her feet, but a careless wave of his hand indicated that she should remain seated.

'Of course I haven't,' said Frankie. 'And please won't you sit down, Zahid?' she added on a whisper. 'Everyone's staring at us.'

It was true. Even the eyes of the more studiedly cool diners seemed to be drawn irresistibly to the tall man in the impeccably cut suit, whose two burly-looking companions had been seated rather ostentatiously at a table right by the door. Frankie sighed. Even if it hadn't been for his bodyguards, he just oozed power, wealth and a potent sexual charisma which had all the women in the restaurant responding to him. She could see a blonde who'd been shoehorned into a silver dress and who seemed to be wearing most of Fort Knox around her neck was now flashing him a sticky, vermilion-lip-sticked smile.

But Zahid seemed oblivious to the restrained excitement his presence was causing. Instead, he sat down with his back to the room, and as two waiters fussed round them with the kind of speed she wasn't used to Frankie realised that this was the first time she'd actually been out in public with him—and that this must be what it was like all the time. The flattery and deference. His every wish anticipated and granted. No wonder his manner could be so assured and so…so…*arrogant*.

Having refused wine himself, Zahid ordered champagne for a clearly eager Simon and then leaned back in his chair—looking, thought Frankie indignantly, as if he were interviewing them for some sort of job!

'I gather congratulations are in order, Simon,' he murmured. 'You are indeed a lucky man.'

Simon took a mouthful of champagne, followed by

an appreciative glance at the label on the bottle. 'Aren't I just? Although naturally, there were lots of raised eyebrows when we first announced it!'

Zahid slowly curled his fingers over the starched linen surface of the tablecloth. 'Really?' he questioned coolly.

Simon leaned across the table towards him, in a man-to-man kind of way. 'Well, lots of my friends were surprised to begin with,' he confided.

Frankie squirmed. She could guess what was coming and although she didn't usually mind Simon's justifiable boasts about the dramatic effect he'd had on her appearance, something in her rebelled at having *Zahid* hear them. 'Zahid isn't interested,' she said quickly.

'Oh, but Zahid is,' corrected the sheikh archly. 'In fact, he's absolutely fascinated. Do continue, Simon.'

Simon gave a disarming shrug. 'Well, Frankie isn't my usual type. In fact, she won't mind me saying that she looked a bit of a geek when she came to work for me, didn't you, darling?' He shrugged like a man who had found a winning lottery ticket scrunched up on the pavement. 'So I told her to grow her hair, to lose the glasses and wear a few clothes that might show off her body—and suddenly it's "Good Morning, Cinderella!".' He raked the flop of blond hair off his forehead and glittered her the kind of smile which had once made her go weak at the knees. 'And just look at her now!'

Zahid turned his head, taking in the slump of Francesca's shoulders and the look of acute embarrassment on her face. And even though he had been amazed and surprised by her new look, he would not have dreamed of speaking of it in such a way. He certainly would not have boasted about it as if he had been preparing a horse for its first important race. A slow tide of rage began to build up inside him. What kind of a man had she harnessed her destiny to—who would humiliate her in such a way? Some pretty-pretty blond boy who was drinking champagne as if it were cordial!

'Why, you flaunt her as if she were a new toy,' he observed softly.

'And a very cuddly toy she is, too,' said Simon.

Frankie knew Zahid well enough to know when he was angry and he was very angry now. Surely Simon wasn't blind to the nerve which was flickering at his temple, or the way he had started flexing and unflexing his long fingers on the starchy linen tablecloth. Why wouldn't he shut up? Her eyes were beseeching him to stop being indiscreet but he didn't even notice her—instead he seemed transfixed by his royal dining companion.

'Shall we…order?' she questioned hurriedly.

'Yeah, let's.' Simon scanned the menu with the avaricious scrutiny of someone who knew they wouldn't be paying the bill. 'I'll have the foie gras, followed by the duck à l'orange.'

Across the table, Zahid's black eyes met hers and she thought she read in them a mixture of mockery and contempt. She felt like squirming in her seat—or trying to explain that Simon wasn't *always* like this—but instead she just offered the sheikh a polite smile.

'Francesca?' he questioned sardonically.

She wasn't in the least bit hungry, but she could hardly sit there with an empty plate while her fiancé ate his way through a gourmet feast. 'Oh, a salad—and then the fish please.'

'I'll have the same,' said Zahid, snapping shut his

leather menu and handing it back to the maître d'. 'I'm assuming you'll drink wine, Simon?'

'Love to!' Simon beamed. 'Frankie can drive, can't you, darling?'

'Of course I can.'

The drinks and first courses were brought and after he'd seen off most of his foie gras, Simon, now further emboldened by more wine, pushed back his lock of blond hair and smiled at Zahid.

'I'm still not entirely sure how you happen to be such a good friend of the family, Zahid,' he said. 'Something to do with your fathers being friends, isn't it?'

Zahid nodded. There was no earthly reason not to try to engage in conversation with the man—even though something about him was setting his teeth on edge. He glanced over at Francesca, who was picking uninterestedly at a plate of salad, and he found his eyes lingering with reluctant fascination on the creamy swell of her breasts, which was emphasised by the silky black dress she wore.

Swallowing down the sudden stir of lust, he looked at Simon. 'Our fathers were indeed friends—they met at university and maintained that connection throughout their lives. You know that Francesca's father was a geologist?'

'Well, I never met him, of course,' said Simon. 'He sounds as if he was brilliant.' He smirked. 'Though more than a bit batty—a sort of nutty-professor type.'

Francesca looked up, her face flushing. 'Eccentric,' she corrected. 'He was eccentric.'

'He was very brilliant,' said Zahid icily. 'It was through his ground-breaking work into unusual rock formations in the desert that we discovered Khayarzah's first oil well. That discovery brought unimaginable riches to my country at a time when they were badly needed.' His eyes met Francesca's and he held her gaze, giving her a soft smile. 'Leaving us for ever indebted to him.'

Simon swirled some ruby-coloured claret in his glass and took a large mouthful. 'Ah, so that explains why your father gifted him the house and land,' he said smoothly.

Zahid arched questioning eyebrows at Francesca and she rushed in with an explanation—terrified he would think she'd been abusing their friendship by blabbing or boasting about it.

'Simon couldn't work out why we had such a big property in such a wealthy area and no…'

'No money!' finished Simon cheerfully. 'I'm afraid that Frankie is asset rich and cash poor, as we say in the business. It's a common enough scenario—and completely unnecessary, especially when she's sitting on an absolute gold mine. Land round here is worth an absolute fortune—which is why we're putting the house on the market as soon as possible.'

There was an odd kind of pause and when Frankie looked into Zahid's eyes she didn't like what she could see there. Was that disappointment she could read?

'You're selling the house?' he asked quietly.

'It's so big,' she said helplessly, wishing he wouldn't look at her so *disapprovingly*.

'But you love that house, Francesca.'

She bit her lip. Of course she loved it—who wouldn't love it? Much of her past was tied up in the place. It was a very old and beautiful building with a disused laboratory in the grounds, where her father used to work. It also had large and exquisitely laid-out grounds, which looked glorious during every season of the year. But she couldn't afford the upkeep and the garden was much too big for one person to handle—and Simon was unwilling to take it on.

'And it's so expensive to maintain,' she added, though Zahid's grim expression did not soften one bit.

Simon nodded. 'Life will be much easier without it. I've told her that if we give the place a lick of paint and stick a few hanging baskets outside, then we should be able to shift it fairly quickly.' He fiddled with the signet ring on his little finger and winked at Frankie. 'And then we'll be able to move into one of the brand-new houses which are being built in the middle of town. Perfect for us, aren't they, darling?'

'You seem to have it all planned out, Simon,' said Zahid slowly.

Simon nodded. 'You could say that I needed to. Frankie has her head in the clouds a lot of the time—she just needs a little guidance, that's all.'

'And you feel you are just the person to do it, do you?'

'As her fiancé, yes, I do.'

Frankie cringed. She felt like an outsider as she sat there, picking at her food and listening to the two men engaged in an unmistakable sparring match. Zahid was interrogating Simon as if he were a suspect in some major crime and Simon was showing off—it was as simple as that.

It was a strange sensation watching them both—as if she were a spectator at some sort of gladiatorial event. But worse than that, it seemed as if Zahid were holding up a mirror and she was suddenly seeing Simon through *his* eyes.

Her blond fiancé's breezy confidence—which had once so captivated her—now appeared to be more like a conceited swagger. Was that coincidence, she wondered—or was Zahid deliberately winding him up? Needling him with all the wrong questions in order to make him look bad.

But why on earth would he do something like that?

Not that she cared what Zahid's motives were—they, and he, were irrelevant to her life. She *loved* Simon. He was the first real boyfriend she'd ever had—when she'd given up hope of ever finding anyone who cared about her. Hadn't he stepped into her life when she'd most needed someone? Given her a job even though she wasn't really qualified for anything, because she'd spent much of the last few years looking after her sick father. And he'd given her so much more than that, hadn't he? He'd offered her a glimpse of what a normal life could be like—with pubs and restaurants and trips to the cinema. He'd changed her from the geeky young woman who had walked so hesitantly into his life and made her into someone he wasn't ashamed to be seen with. She'd been so grateful for that…grateful to *him*.

Refusing pudding and the brandy which Simon accepted with alacrity, Frankie was relieved when at last the dinner was over and it was time to leave—though she noticed that they weren't presented with anything as vulgar as a bill. She saw one of the bodyguards speaking to the maître d' and assumed that he had dealt with the financial transaction.

'Th-thanks very much, Zahid,' said Simon as he rose unsteadily to his feet.

But the sheikh's attention was focused solely on Frankie. 'You're sure you're going to be okay getting home?' he questioned, with a frown.

'I've only had water all night,' she said.

'It's dark. I can have one of my aides drive the car for you?'

She smiled. How old-fashioned he could be! 'I'm perfectly capable of driving home, thank you, Zahid—and I'm fine in the dark. My eyesight is perfect and it's only just down the road!'

But Zahid wasn't happy. Not happy at all. He watched while Francesca was handed her coat by the cloakroom attendant. It was a cheap-looking thing, in his opinion—and as she slid it over her shoulders it covered up the milky-pale flesh of her arms, which had drawn his eye throughout the meal.

Would Simon be removing the coat and then the dress later? he wondered—and a spear of some unknown emotion shot through him. It made his blood feel thick and his groin heavy. It felt like desire but it was underpinned with something else. Something dark and bitter and unpalatable. Surely… He shook his head. Surely it wasn't *jealousy*? Why on earth would he be jealous of little Francesca O'Hara's lover—when he could have any woman he wanted?

Except that she wasn't so little any more, was she? Not in any sense. Not in height, or… He swallowed. Surely the last time he'd seen her, she'd been completely flat-chested? Or had the slouchy clothes she used to favour done her *no* favours?

'Thanks so much for the meal, Zahid.'

She was smiling up at him now—the curve of her lips putting deep dimples in her cheeks the way it had done all those years ago, and he was hit by a renewed wave of protectiveness.

He found himself remembering the time when, as a lively ten-year-old, she had scrambled into a huge tree looking for a lost shuttlecock and managed to get herself stranded there. He had climbed up into the branches and rescued her, quietening her teeth-chattering fear with a few teasing words of admonishment. And she had put her arms around his neck and clung to him like a little monkey.

He should have been there for her when her father had died. Why the hell hadn't his brother reported back to him that she was vulnerable? And she *was* vulnerable. Even now. Anyone could see that.

He saw Simon giving a young waitress an easy smile, the careless crinkling of his eyes the tell-tale sign of the practised flirt. But Francesca didn't seem to have noticed.

Zahid watched as she buttoned up her thin coat, the ostentatious engagement ring glittering on her finger, and his mouth tightened. A man would have to spend a lot of money to buy a diamond that size, he thought suddenly. A man who was a lot more committed than her pretty-boy fiancé seemed to be.

'You're going back home soon, are you, Zahid?' Francesca was asking.

She was leaning towards him and he caught an elusive drift of her scent—which smelt of rain-washed rose petals—and a distracting shiver began to whisper its way over his skin.

'Mmm?' he questioned distractedly.

She dimpled him another smile. 'I feel so guilty—

we've hardly said a word about you all evening, and I love hearing about Khayarzah.'

'Please don't feel guilty,' said Zahid as he nodded over at one of his bodyguards to indicate that they were ready to leave. 'We shall be meeting very soon and I will tell you everything you wish to know.'

Frankie smiled uncertainly. Was he just making polite conversation? Unlikely. Yet they both knew how uncommon his visits to England were, especially these days. But suddenly, she could see that it was probably a good thing that their paths didn't cross very often. Too much of Zahid Al Hakam could make a woman feel very discontented with her lot. 'What, you mean next year?' she joked.

'No, not next year, but next week,' he corrected silkily. 'I have business in mainland Europe all this week—but after that, I'll come back.'

'Come back?' questioned Frankie nervously, turning her head to look for Simon and wondering what that waitress could be saying to him, which was making him look so engrossed. 'Come back where?'

'Don't look so scared, Francesca—I just meant that we still have a lot of catching up to do.' Zahid's eyes flicked over to Simon, who was now leaning even closer to the young waitress. 'I'm sure your fiancé won't object if I visit you again on my return.'

Like a goldfish, Frankie opened her mouth and shut it again. Because how could she possibly object? Even if Zahid hadn't been a king whose requests could not be turned down from a protocol point of view—she could hardly tell him that she thought it was a bad idea, because she found him dangerous and unsettling as a man. Why, he would probably laugh in her face.

So she nodded obediently and hoped her misgivings didn't show. 'Okay. I'll…I'll look forward to it.'

'So will I,' promised Zahid softly.

CHAPTER FOUR

IN THE days which followed the awkward restaurant meal Frankie tried to convince herself that the sheikh's promise to return must have been made on the spur of the moment. He probably hadn't meant it. It was the kind of flippant thing which people always said when they were leaving— "oh, we must meet up soon"—and then you didn't see them for years.

But she was wrong. One of his aides rang and told her that he would be arriving on Saturday afternoon and that he wished to see her, alone.

Alone?

Uncomfortably, she touched her shiny new engagement ring—as if expecting it to suddenly disappear in a puff of smoke. Her conscience was making her feel slightly awkward and she had been worried what Simon would say. Was it wrong for her to have made an arrangement to see the king?

Nervously, she'd asked her fiancé about Zahid's proposed visit, but it seemed that Simon didn't mind at all. In fact, to Frankie's surprise he seemed inordinately pleased by the idea.

'Maybe he's planning to give you a wedding present—hopefully in the form of some whacking great cheque,' he said, when she told him.

'That's a very mercenary thing to say,' objected Frankie.

'I'm a businessman, sweetheart—being mercenary goes with the territory!' He fiddled with his gold signet ring and shot her a sly glance. 'Maybe you could get him to invest in some property while you're at it? That colossal eyesore at the top of the hill could do with a big injection of Middle Eastern cash.'

'I don't think so.' With a wan smile, she walked out of Simon's office, wishing that she could shrug off the restlessness which had haunted her since the night they'd had dinner with Zahid. Up until that point, she had been relatively contented with her lot. She'd been anticipating being a new wife, with a new life ahead of her—but now everything had changed and, deep down, she knew exactly why. It was all because she had seen the dashing desert king again, after years of absence.

Images of his hawklike features kept flashing into her mind at the most inopportune moments. She had found herself filling up her car at the petrol station and wondering if Khayarzah might have supplied the fuel. Last night she'd even dreamt about him—some stupid, schoolgirlish fantasy which seemed to involve him riding in the desert on one of his favoured black stallions and scooping her into the saddle in front of him…

And this morning she had woken up with her heart racing and an odd, squirmy feeling at the pit of her stomach—plus a terrible feeling of guilt that she could feel that way about him, when she was planning to marry Simon.

She prepared for Zahid's visit with the same care

she'd employed when she'd been growing up and he and his father used to stop by. Nowadays she was rather more efficient at cleaning the house, and the home-made cake which filled the kitchen with the smell of lemons didn't have a great big crater in the centre.

The pale roses which Simon had bought were already dead and so Frankie put on her old raincoat and went outside to look for something to replace them. Although she hadn't dared tell her fiancé, she much preferred home-grown flowers to the forced, hothouse variety—and you could always find something suitable which was already growing in the garden.

Especially *this* garden, she thought as she looked around and breathed in the damp, autumnal air. How she loved this garden—and how she would miss it when she moved into the town house which Simon had his eye on, where they all had nothing but a small, paved 'easy-care' patio area.

The misty atmosphere of the November day had created diamonds on the cobwebs and fallen leaves lay like scattered toffee wrappers on the wet grass. Taking out her pair of secateurs, she began to snip at some of the hips and berry laden branches and soon her basket was half-full. She would cram them in that big copper pot and the dark green foliage and scarlet berries would contrast against it quite perfectly and brighten up the kitchen.

The sound of a powerful engine disturbed her thoughts and, turning round, she saw Zahid's sports car growling its way up the drive before coming to a halt next to her own, rather beaten-up old car.

Frankie watched as he got out—and once again she was reminded of his chameleon-like capacity. Today's look was casual and expensive and very, very compelling. Faded blue jeans clung to his powerful legs and beneath his leather jacket she could see a dark cashmere sweater, which echoed the coal-black of his hair. She let her gaze linger on his stern expression and her heart gave a curious little flutter before her fingers curled tightly around the secateurs she was holding. What kind of a disloyal and horrible woman was she, if the sight of a man who wasn't her fiancé should fill her with an overwhelming sense of excitement? What was the *matter* with her?

Putting her basket down, she went across the damp grass to meet him, her smile feeling forced. 'Hello, Zahid.'

'Francesca.' He looked down at her, thinking how young and *innocent* she looked today. And much more like the Francesca he knew of old, with that big old raincoat and a pair of wellington boots which had seen better days. But the dark, mist-sprinkled hair still hung in a silken fall over her shoulders and her eyes were still that newly discovered shade of blue. And she was no longer young, he thought grimly. Nor innocent. He felt an odd twist of his heart and a sense of anger building inside him, but he forced himself to control it. 'Has Simon recovered after the other night?'

'Yes, he was fine. Had a bit of a headache the next day. He says to say thank you for dinner—and hopes he wasn't out of order.'

Black eyes bored into her. 'Does he always drink that much?'

'Of course he doesn't!' She saw the look of censure on his face and wondered why he had to be so judgemental—had *he* never had a few drinks too many? She supposed he hadn't—for none of the Al Hakam family drank alcohol, did they? 'He was probably just nervous, meeting you. You must be used to that, Zahid—it's not every day that someone like Simon gets to have dinner with a real-live sheikh.'

'Maybe not—but it was naïve and inappropriate behaviour in the circumstances. Especially for a man of—*how* old is he, Francesca?'

'He's twenty-eight—he's hardly about to start drawing his pension!' Frankie frowned when he gave no answering smile. 'Have you come here today just to talk about Simon?'

'Actually, yes. I have.'

She stared at him. 'Well, if we're talking inappropriate—then wanting to discuss my fiancé with me behind his back surely falls into that category? Okay, so he *got a little drunk*—big deal! These things happen sometimes—they probably happen in Khayarzah, if you only knew it!'

'But nobody there would dare to get drunk in front of the king!' Zahid snapped, before drawing in a deep breath, reminding himself that he had come here today with a purpose. Not a particularly palatable one, it was true—but he needed to muster up every diplomatic atom in his body if he was to limit the emotional damage his discovery was going to have on Francesca. 'Shall we take a walk around the garden?'

At this, she smiled. 'Are you sure you wouldn't prefer to go inside, into the warmth? I've made you a cake.'

He felt the unfamiliar stab of guilt. She'd spent the morning making him a cake—just like old times. While he had spent the morning accruing information which would…

'No cake, thank you.' He saw the brief look of hurt which flitted over her pale face and forced himself to breathe out a platitude. 'I'm sorry if you went to any trouble.'

'Not even your favourite lemon?'

'Francesca—' He paused, reluctant to open the can of grotesquely wriggling worms he was in possession of. 'Tell me how you met Simon.'

'Oh, for heaven's sake.' Couldn't he let this go? 'Does it really matter?'

'Yes.' His gaze was steady. 'It matters a lot.'

She stared at him, remembering about what he'd said the other day. Something about it being his 'duty' to meet Simon. And if that was the case, then wasn't he taking duty a little too far? 'Is this another quasi-paternal question?' she questioned.

Paternal? Zahid winced. God help him but he didn't feel in the least bit paternal at the moment—not when those wide-spaced eyes looked so blue and so deep that he felt he might be able to dive into them. 'Just answer the question,' he said unevenly.

She sighed, giving into the inevitable—sensing that he wouldn't give her any peace until she provided him with the information he wanted. 'I met him when he came to the house after my father died.'

Zahid nodded. 'So he knew your father? He came to pay his respects?'

Francesca bit her lip because the next piece of information had never sat very easily with her—even when Simon had explained that people in the business world needed to be outgoing in order to keep themselves afloat.

'Not really,' she said slowly. 'He'd read about his death in the papers and so he came…he came…'

'He came to see whether you needed to sell the house?'

Frankie flushed under the black glare of his fierce scrutiny. 'I suppose so.'

'Like some low-life lawyer chasing an ambulance, touting for business?' The words were out before he could stop them.

Frankie froze. 'Don't you *dare* judge him! How would you know what it's like, Zahid? You're a sheikh and even when your country was broke, you still lived in a palace and had servants all over the place—while Simon has had to fight to make his way in the world!'

'My heart bleeds for him.'

Something about the way he said it made a queer kind of frustration bubble up inside her and for a moment Frankie actually took an angry step towards him, until he halted her with a voice like ice.

'I think you forget yourself!' he snapped. 'I allow you the kind of leeway which I wouldn't tolerate from anyone else, Francesca—but there really are limits.'

'What, so you think you can stand there and insult my fiancé and I'm just expected to take it?'

His eyes lanced her a piercing question. 'You aren't even interested why I've brought the subject up?'

Something in the way he asked it unsettled her enough to hide behind defiance. 'To cause trouble?'

'Funnily enough, my schedule is usually too tight to indulge myself with random acts of interference—especially towards people I care about. I want you to tell me what happened next—after Simon came to see you that first time.'

Frankie was tempted not to reply—or to change the subject completely. But if she had nothing to hide, then why should she shy away from his questioning, no matter how intrusive it seemed? 'I told him that I didn't really want to sell the house unless it was absolutely necessary, and that I needed a job.'

Zahid nodded. 'So he gave you a job, a makeover and a proposal in quick succession and when you agreed to marry him, he somehow persuaded you that it was in your best interests to sell the house?'

Frankie flushed to the roots of her hair. He was making it all sound so…so *mercenary*. As if Simon had *planned* it all. 'These things happen.'

'I bet they do,' he drawled. 'But I'm right, aren't I?'

'Yes, Zahid—I expect you're always right.'

'And you don't think it's slightly suspect behaviour?'

'Why should I? Maybe I'm not as suspicious as you are! Maybe I like to think the best of people! And Simon loves me!'

'Does he?'

Frankie stilled as something in his sombre tone iced her skin with a terrible sense of foreboding. 'Of course he does.'

'How *much* do you think he loves you?'

'What kind of a question is that?' She eyed him warily. 'Enough to want to marry me.'

There was, he realised, no diplomatic way to do this. No way of telling her which wasn't going to hurt her. 'I wonder,' he said quietly.

'Will you please stop talking in riddles? What do you wonder?'

There was another pause. Like the split-second pause

before a marksman fired a bullet from a gun. And then he spoke. 'He's got another woman.'

Frankie's heart began to pound. 'What did you say?' she whispered.

'Simon's got another woman. There's someone else.'

She shook her head, her fingers flying to her cheeks. 'No! You're making it up!'

'Why would I do that?'

'I don't *know*!'

Her face had gone completely white and she swayed so that Zahid's hand automatically went out to steady her, his body tensing. Had he been so brutal with the facts that she was about to faint? Wasn't he supposed to have been diplomatic? Protective? Surely there was a way he could have told her which wouldn't have made her face looked so bleached and transparent.

Uttering a short curse in his native tongue, he bent and scooped his arms underneath her knees, despite her ineffectual protests to push him away. And as the firmness of her young body imprinted itself on his mind he was aware of the blood in his own veins growing hot and heavy. He could feel the curved definition of her thighs beneath his fingers, the soft weight of her breast as she slumped against his chest—and he felt a wave of guilty pleasure as he carried her into the house.

Some of her strength must have returned because by the time he had deposited her on the old sofa in the sitting room, she had begun half-heartedly punching against his chest—and he let her. He crouched down in front of her, holding his palms up in front of him—like a man trying to quieten a fractious horse. 'Francesca—'

Her hands fell like stones into her lap. 'Go away!' she whispered.

'You don't want the truth?'

'It isn't true! Why would he want someone else when he's engaged to me?' *But mightn't that explain why Simon had been so unbelievably cautious about making love to her? Was it really nothing to do with respect for the old-fashioned morals she'd been brought up to believe in? Had the truth of it been that all along he had another woman and didn't find Frankie attractive after all—makeover or no makeover?*

'You want proof?' he demanded.

Recovering some of her composure, Frankie sat up. 'Yes, I want proof! Except you probably haven't got any, have you? This is all because he got a bit drunk and you're making a value judgement because you don't think he's good enough for me!'

'Damned right he's not,' he said grimly, rising to his feet and going outside to retrieve a package from the passenger seat of his car, before carrying it back inside—still hoping that she might have changed her mind and just take his word for it. But one look at her face when he returned—a mutinous expression written on it that he'd never seen before—and Zahid knew that there was no alternative but to show her.

Reluctantly, he pulled out a series of black and white photos and silently handed them to her.

With fingers which felt frozen and a heart which was numb, Frankie looked down at the glossy images in her hands.

There was Simon, locking his car—an innocent enough shot, but if she looked a bit more closely Frankie could see someone standing in the doorway of a house, waving to him. A rangy blonde wearing one of those skirts which only just about covered her knickers.

The next image showed Simon warmly embracing the same woman and Frankie sought refuge in yet more denial.

'She might just be his sister, or a relative,' she croaked.

'Really?' questioned Zahid as she pulled out the third photo. 'Pretty close family, if that's the case.'

This one was the killer. There could be no mistake or misunderstanding about a close-up where Simon appeared to be going for a new world record in how much tongue it was possible to shove down a woman's throat. Frankie shuddered with revulsion as she compared it to all the chaste kisses he used to share with her. But didn't it all make sense now? The reason he'd never touched her had not been because he'd *respected* her—but because he had someone else. Someone he really cared for and desired—rather than someone he just wanted to milk for all she was worth.

With a ragged little cry, she let the photos slip from her fingers, her hurt and dismay making her turn on Zahid.

'You had him followed!' she accused as she felt hot tears of humiliation fill her eyes. 'What right did you have to do that?'

'Francesca,' he admonished softly. 'Aren't you turning your anger on the wrong person here? I did it for your own good.'

'B-but *why*?' Frankie sobbed. 'Why did you do it? Couldn't you have just let me be happy for a while?' she cried as tears of humiliation and shame began to slide down her cheeks.

'You really think you can be happy in a relationship which is based on a tissue of lies? And then what?' he flared, when still she didn't answer. And for a moment, he acknowledged the irony of *him* dishing out advice on relationships. 'You'd have discovered even further down the line how duplicitous he was being—and found yourself even *more* hurt! Is that what you want from your life, Francesca?'

What kind of a question was that to ask her at a time like this? Scrambling to her feet, she pushed him away, her thoughts spinning round and round. But some small and stupid hope was still flickering in her heart, stubbornly refusing to be extinguished. Maybe there was some kind of explanation for it, after all. Something which Simon would explain and then she could turn round to Zahid and tell him that for once in his life he'd been *wrong*! 'I'm going to ask him!'

He shook his head. 'Don't even think about it,' he warned her grimly. 'You'll only regret it.'

But she turned on him—and part of her terrible pain was that Zahid should have borne witness to her humiliation. The man she had idolised for all her life should have seen her made a complete fool of. *That* she regretted.

'So if it's true—and we haven't even established that it is—you think I should just walk away and let him get away with it? Just fade away into the background as if I never really existed and let him get away with making a fool of me?' she raged as a sense of justice and determination began to replace her hurt and mortification.

In that moment she realised that there was going to be no mistake. That the photos told the truth and that Simon had lied to her—but one thing she was sure of was that she was not going to be some sad little *victim*. Especially in Zahid's eyes. 'Obviously, I no longer have a job—so I might as well tell him exactly what I think of him.'

'The job doesn't matter, Francesca,' he grated.

'You don't think so? Well, it might just interest you to know that I need to earn money because I need to eat! Most people do.'

He gave an impatient wave of his hand. 'I can find you a job in the flicker of an eye. I can create some sort of role for you in my organisation and it can be as permanent or as temporary as you like.'

There was a pin-drop silence as Frankie stared at him. What, and make her detachment from reality complete? She could just imagine the hawklike eye he would keep on her if she got involved with his organisation. Governed and bossed around by a powerful man who seemed to have the misplaced idea that his role was to protect her. Long ago, she had abandoned her foolish romantic dreams about him, but wouldn't enforced proximity and hurt pride make her vulnerable to him again?

She would have to watch from the sidelines while he bedded the glamorous women who were his girlfriends—and how would *that* feel? There would be all the disadvantages of being closeted with the devastatingly attractive sheikh—but none of the benefits. She would end up feeling completely invisible because to him she was just Francesca—sexless, safe Francesca who had got herself into a laughable situation with a worthless man and now needed rescuing.

'Thank you, but no, thank you,' she said tightly, walking over to the table and grabbing her shoulder bag. 'I don't know what I'm going to do with my future—but before I make any decisions, I'm going to ask Simon Forrester a few questions!'

As he watched her pull the bag over one slender shoulder Zahid knew that he could have restrained her in an instant—and not by confiscating her car keys. For wasn't there an urgent part of him which wanted to subdue her into forgetting about that worthless creep by simply *kissing* her? He felt the heavy throb of desire as arrogance and a justifiable pride in his methods of seduction told him that he would have succeeded within seconds. He could show her what it was like to be with a *real* man.

But deep down he knew that would be wrong. For all kinds of reasons, Francesca O'Hara was not a woman he was ever going to be able to seduce—and ultimately she was free to do what she needed to do. And it seemed that she needed to go and confront the man who had betrayed her.

A faint smile of admiration curved the edges of his lips as he heard the front door slamming shut behind her, and soon after that came the sound of her old car spluttering into life.

CHAPTER FIVE

'His Royal Highness, the Sheikh Zahid will see you now, Miss O'Hara.' The sleek receptionist indicated the discreet private elevator which was set in the marbled foyer of the luxury hotel. 'If you'd like to go up?'

'Thanks very much.' With a polite smile at the glacial beauty who was the last barrier between her and Zahid, Frankie walked over to the elevator and pressed the button up to the penthouse suite.

Outwardly, she was trying to project a calm and unruffled image, which wasn't easy, given her rain-swept appearance.

It had been quite an afternoon.

Tracking Zahid down hadn't been easy. It had come as something of a shock to realise that she had never actually contacted *him* before. He had mostly only visited with his father—and everything had always been arranged by palace aides. But she knew that his family owned a skyscraper headquarters in a swish central London location, where his brother masterminded the European arm of the Al Hakams' extensive empire.

Eventually, after she had spoken to a series of suspicious-sounding people who presumably okayed it with Zahid himself, an appointment had been made for her to see him. But instead of it being at the company headquarters, they'd given her the name of the hotel where he was staying. The famous Granchester hotel—the kind of place you only read about in the gossip columns of newspapers, or when a Hollywood superstar happened to be visiting town.

The elevator was so speedy that it made her feel a bit sick and Frankie couldn't help but notice that her legs were splashed with icy water from the grim November day. She dabbed at them with a tissue pulled from her bag, but by the time the elevator slid to a halt and she rapped on the door of Zahid's suite she felt even more chewed up with nerves. A feeling which was only increased when she heard his distinctive voice call: "Come!"

Her heart was pounding as she pushed open the door and for a moment she noticed nothing other than the fabulous works of art which lined the walls and the enormous windows overlooking some of the most expensive real estate in the world. The polished floor was as big as a football pitch and strewn with exquisite silken rugs. It was, she realised, the first time that she had ever been in *his* environment, and it was even more polished and intimidating than she'd thought it would be.

And now, walking in from a room which led off the main living area, came Zahid himself—his face unsmiling and not particularly welcoming as he looked at her. Was he angry that she had flung his job offer back in his face the other day? she wondered.

'Hello, Francesca,' he said. His narrowed black eyes were shuttered as he looked at her—taking in the raindrops which glittered like diamonds among the tousled strands of her dark hair. 'You'd better take off your raincoat.'

Frankie saw that she was dripping rain onto the polished wood floor and so she struggled out of her coat, wondering if he might help her. But he simply watched as she removed it and then pointed to a coat-stand which stood next to the door. She cleared her throat as she looped the damp garment over the peg then turned round to face him. 'It was good of you to see me, Zahid.'

There was the faintest elevation of his jet-dark brows. 'I was surprised you wanted to—in view of our last meeting.'

She supposed she deserved that, just as she supposed he deserved an apology for the way she'd reacted to what he told her. Was that why he was being so cool towards her? So *distant*? 'I was very…rude to you.'

He shrugged as if it didn't matter, but, of course, it did—just not in the way she thought. In a funny sort of way he had been glad about her rudeness—because hadn't it stopped him from ringing her to find out what had happened after she'd gone to confront Simon? He'd convinced himself that it would have been all about self-interest if he'd done so. And told himself that he should stay away from her—for both their sakes. Yes, he had opened her eyes to the fact that she had been involved with some pathetic fortune-hunter—but now that she was presumably free of him, it should have no impact on *his* life.

Because hadn't he been disturbed by the rush of lust he'd felt while carrying her into the house? And hadn't the thoughts he'd had about her subsequently made him realise that she had grown up into a subtle kind of beauty—and that it would be better for both of them if he kept his distance from her? Wasn't that the reason why he hadn't helped her with her coat, because he was reluctant to be tempted by her soft scent and even softer skin?

'Don't worry about your rudeness, Francesca—it's forgotten,' he said coolly. 'I probably would have felt exactly the same if the situation had been reversed.'

She watched as he walked across the room. She wanted to protest that such a scenario would never have happened—that Zahid was far too clever to be manipulated as she had been. But somehow the words dried in her throat and it was nothing to do with their relevance. No, it was the sight of him looking like some lithe jungle cat who seemed a little too *elemental* to be at home in these luxurious surroundings.

A silk shirt of palest ivory briefly brushed against the hard contours of his torso and clung like cream to the powerful line of his shoulders. Black trousers hugged at the narrow line of his hips and skated over the cradle of his masculinity. He had loosened his tie and a couple of buttons of his shirt and, catching a glimpse of the dark hair which was arrowing downwards, she felt her mouth dry.

He looked as if he had been engrossed in work and was now relaxing a little. It was a snapshot image of his own, private world—and even more daunting than his physical appearance was the realisation that Zahid had a complete and busy life of which she knew nothing. What was it like being a king? she wondered. Particularly if such a daunting office had been thrust on you out of the blue, as had happened to him. Had it changed him? It *must* have changed him.

Frankie licked the parchment-dry surface of her lips, trying to concentrate on reality, rather than hopeless fantasy. That was yet another great difference between them, she thought. He had a life, and she didn't. Well, not any more—no job, a broken engagement and some broken dreams as well.

He slanted her a questioning look. 'Why don't you sit down, Francesca? Would you like some coffee? Or tea, perhaps?'

'No. No, thanks.' Sitting down felt too relaxed, too informal for what she was about to say—and so Frankie walked over to the massive windows on the pretext of enjoying the view. And for a moment, she didn't have to pretend. There was the London Eye—its massive circle framing the Houses of Parliament and iconic clock-face of Big Ben. 'Oh, wow,' she said.

'Picture-postcard stuff, isn't it?' he offered drily, looking at the stiff set of her shoulders and the hair which today was hanging neatly down her back. Her hand was bare of an engagement ring and she was wearing a navy dress which, despite its plainness, still managed to emphasise every amazing curve of her healthy young body. His eyes focused on the luscious swell of her bottom and her long, shapely legs and he found himself thinking some dark and very erotic thoughts until he reminded himself that this was Francesca. Francesca O'Hara, his childhood friend.

'So is this a social call?' he questioned thickly.

She turned around. Was that his way of saying that he was busy? That he might have sat and drunk tea on *her* territory many times, but on his she was only permitted a very small window in his own busy schedule.

'No. It's not.' He was staring at her, not saying

anything, and once again she felt frozen out. Gone was the ease which had always existed between them, even during that last, emotionally charged meeting.

She had thought that he'd be eager to hear about her confrontation with Simon. But she had been wrong. There had been no phone call to ask what had happened and even now, face to face, there was only a polite indifference as to why she had come today. Here in the luxury hotel suite, she was simply someone from his past. The daughter of an old friend—in the presence of a very powerful, royal personage. And she was probably *wasting his time.*

'So if it isn't *social*, then why exactly are you here?' he queried coolly.

For a moment she felt tempted to make some lame excuse and to walk away, leaving her with her dignity intact and not running the risk of him saying no to what she was going to ask him. Wouldn't that be easier?

But wasn't it exactly that kind of grabbing at the easy option which had made it laughingly simple for Simon to make a fool of her?

'I was wondering if I could take you up on that offer you made?' She noticed that his body had tensed and her words stumbled over themselves to give him a reasonable get-out clause. 'You…you mentioned something about giving me a role within your organisation. But if you've changed your mind, then I quite understand.'

'It's you who seems to have changed your mind, Francesca—since you were adamant that you didn't want any kind of role in my organisation,' he returned silkily. 'Would you care to tell me why?'

She swallowed. It was hateful having to relive scenes she'd sooner forget—and more than a little disappointing that Zahid should have asked her for some sort of explanation. Had she thought that instantly he would become malleable and go along with her wishes as he had done when she'd been growing up? But she was no longer asking him to carry her around on his shoulders or rescue her shuttlecock from the branches of a tree. She needed a far more grown-up favour from him than that.

'I went to see Simon—and he…' Briefly, Frankie closed her eyes as she remembered the ugly showdown. Simon's initial blustering denial and then his sneer when he realised he was cornered. He'd said a few things she would never forget—about the fact that she was about as alluring as a plate of cold porridge and it had been no hardship not to bed her. He told her she was a fool if she thought that Zahid having him followed meant anything other than that the sheikh was an interfering control freak. And that she certainly shouldn't start reading anything into it. That a man like that might play with her for a while and then discard her like last year's calendar.

And she *wasn't* reading anything into Zahid's interference, she told herself fiercely. She hadn't even considered that a man like him might be interested in 'playing' with someone like her. He was simply looking out for her, that was all—the way he always had done in the past.

'He what, Francesca?' prompted Zahid.

'He made me realise that I needed to take a good look at my life,' she said.

And hadn't she decided that her doomed affair with Simon ought to have some lasting effect other than making her feel like a fool and a failure? That it was time to stop letting things *happen* to her and to have the courage to reach out to try to grasp them for herself. Wasn't that the reason why she'd plucked up the courage to come here today—even though her heart had been skittering with nerves from the moment she'd left home?

'I realised that I'd worked myself into a bit of a dead-end,' she continued slowly. 'That my life was going nowhere.'

Curiously, Zahid looked at her, remembering the little girl in her father's laboratory who had been given her own space on the bench, with her own test tubes and an oversized white coat to wear. 'I thought you wanted to be a scientist, like your father,' he said slowly.

Frankie shook her head. 'I was never as talented as he was. But I loved it—that's why I used to hang around the lab so much when I was young. And when he got ill my school work suffered—not that I'd ever particularly been happy at school.' She'd been too easy a target for the cruel-tongued girls who loved to mock the odd-looking child whose flighty mother had brought such shame on the family.

'And then there was the house and the garden to look after,' she added. Life had caught hold of her like a piece of flotsam and she'd allowed herself to drift around until her father had died and she'd found the job with Simon.

She knew that now she had some experience she might be able to get a job in one of the rival estate agencies—but she didn't want one. Not any more. She didn't want to stay in the same small town, but she didn't want to move just for the sake of it. She didn't really know *what* she wanted—just that she wanted something different. Something exciting. Something to make her forget the humiliation of her broken engagement. She looked up into Zahid's narrowed and watchful black eyes.

'I can type and I can file,' she finished. 'I can deal with people and I can problem solve. And I can cook, of course.'

It was an unusual combination, he mused as he studied her. A woman with a neglected scientific talent who was also a great cook. Though when he stopped to think about it—wasn't cooking all about chemistry?

And speaking of chemistry…what about the other kind? The kind which was making him notice the pinpointing of her nipples which were thrusting against the navy dress and turning an otherwise commonplace outfit into something which was demanding to be peeled off. He looked into her wide-spaced blue eyes and felt the sizzle of danger in the air.

'I already have people to cook and to file for me,' he said evenly.

'I realise that.'

'Then what exactly are you asking me for, Francesca?'

She bit her lip, some of her nerve deserting her—until she remembered that if she wanted to take control of her own life, then wasn't this the first step? She had to reach out and ask—not be deterred by the first obstacle which was put in her way. 'I have no idea, Zahid. You were the one who made the offer that you could find me a job, remember? Although perhaps you didn't mean it at the time.'

There was a moment's silence before Zahid walked over to a book which lay open on the walnut writing desk, giving himself time to think. Was she trying to insult him by implying that he had made an empty offer—or was she simply calling his bluff?

He closed the book and looked up, still not saying anything. He could see anxiety vying with bravado on her face. Such a pale face, he thought and in amid his own warring feelings he felt a twist of concern; of the old, familiar protectiveness. Didn't she deserve a break? A chance to get away from the scurrilous Simon and the bad memories he'd helped create?

But it wasn't that easy.

He'd recognised that offering Francesca such an opportunity had been a mistake, for many reasons. It was unheard of in his country for a woman to work closely for a member of the ruling family. Perhaps he could have swung it if he'd been remaining in England for a while, but he wasn't. He was due to go home to Khayarzah within the next few days, and how could he possibly take her with him—a single Englishwoman living within the strict confines of palace life?

But Zahid also recognised that these reservations were all easily overcome and that the main stumbling block was the fact that he had begun to *desire* her with a hunger which at times had overwhelmed him. *And he couldn't afford to do that.*

Since that last meeting, hadn't he been thinking about her in a way which was most uncharacteristic? He enjoyed women and they enjoyed him—but he didn't get hung up about them. Not ever. Sometimes not even when he was thrusting into them and watching dispassionately as they orgasmed around him and squealed their joy. One of his own perceived strengths was emotional detachment and it had always served him well.

Yet for days now he'd been remembering Francesca's firm body and her soft, unpainted lips. The way she made him smile when he least expected it. Those deep blue eyes, which had stared at him from the confusion of his unusually restless and troubled dreams. Even when his sometime Russian lover Katya had arrived the other night—wearing nothing but a fur coat and a pair of tiny, crotchless panties—he had sent her away without making love to her.

Why the hell had he done that?

Wouldn't the best thing of all be for him to send Francesca away, too?

Because Zahid recognised that something had changed between them—and changed for ever. He no longer saw her as simply Francesca, his innocent childhood friend. He saw her now as a woman—a sexy and experienced woman who had just emerged from a bruising experience. And wasn't that dangerous?

Wouldn't she be feeling very natural frustration now that her relationship with Simon had ended? Wasn't there a danger that close confinement might prove too much of a temptation for them both?

He saw her reach out to touch the petals of a spray of orchids with light, tentative fingers and he was just imagining how delicate her touch might be on his aching skin when the telephone rang.

The sound ruptured his reverie. 'Answer it,' he said abruptly.

'But—'

'I said, answer it.'

Frankie's heart was thudding as she walked over towards the bureau and picked up the phone. Should she announce that it was the sheikh's phone? Probably not. It could so easily be the press. 'Hello?'

A woman's sultry and faintly disgruntled voice came down the line. 'Who the hell are you?'

Frankie's fingers tightened around the receiver; she felt fired up by some unknown instinct which had the little hairs on the back of her neck prickling. She wanted to say, "Who the hell are *you*?", but something stopped her and that something was Zahid watching her very closely. 'May I help you?' she questioned politely.

'Sure you can. I want to speak to Zahid.'

There was the briefest of pauses before Frankie spoke. 'I'm afraid that the sheikh is unavailable at the moment.' From the other side of the room, she saw Zahid raise his eyebrows in silent question. 'But if you'd like to give me your name and number, I'll make sure he gets it.'

'My name is Katya,' snapped the voice. 'And he already has my number—tell him to damned well use it!'

The connection was broken abruptly and Frankie replaced the phone, looking up to find Zahid's now inscrutable expression fixed on her. Her heart was thudding fiercely and she wondered who the woman with the sultry voice was.

'Who was it?' he demanded.

'Katya.'

His eyes narrowed. 'You didn't bother checking whether I wanted to speak to her?'

Awkwardly, Frankie wriggled her shoulders. Had she overstepped the mark and allowed her feelings of undeniable jealousy to influence her reaction?

'She sounded slightly…angry,' she explained, in a sudden rush. 'And I thought that the call might be of a personal nature, which you probably wouldn't care to take in front of me. Alternatively, if I'd asked you whether you wished to take the call and you'd declined—then that would have been embarrassing for all three of us. I made a judgement, Zahid—which is presumably the reason you asked me to answer your phone.' Tentatively, she chewed on her lip as he continued to stare at her in that expressionless way. 'Was it the wrong one?'

There was a pause while he regarded her thoughtfully. A bold judgement, he thought as he met the question in her deep blue eyes. And a brave one, too. He saw the sudden flush of colour which had flared into her pale cheeks. Had she guessed that Katya was a lover? An *ex*-lover, he reminded himself as he shook his head.

'No, it was not the wrong one—it was exactly right. I wanted to see whether you could think on your feet and it seems that you can,' he said softly. 'It's a pity you couldn't have been that insightful when you fell into bed with that creep Simon.'

For a moment, Frankie felt close to giving him a confessional, wondering if she should enlighten him about the laughably true nature of her relationship with Simon. But prospective employees didn't suddenly start talking about their sex lives, did they? 'It's easy to be insightful when you're acting for somebody else.'

'Well, you've got yourself a job.'

'I have?'

'Don't look so shocked.' He gave a short laugh because it seemed that she hadn't lost her ability to twist him around her little finger, after all. 'It was pretty much on the cards all along.'

'And what sort…what sort of job will it be?'

There was a brief silence as he allowed the longstanding glimmerings of an idea to float to the surface of his mind. 'My father once kept a diary,' he said slowly. 'Did I ever tell you that?'

She shook her head. 'No.'

'Writing it became a kind of refuge for him,' he continued. 'Particularly in the troubled years during the wars and then when my mother became ill. And it suddenly occurred to me that you might be just the person to type them up for me.'

'But I can't speak your language,' she objected.

'He wrote them in English.' He met her uncomprehending expression and shrugged. 'It ensured their privacy—since most of my people don't speak the language. I've been meaning to make them into a formal record for some time—the difficulty was in finding someone I could trust to do it.' His black eyes gleamed. 'And you, my dear Francesca, will be absolutely perfect for the task.'

Frankie blushed with pleasure—because praise from Zahid felt like the very best sort of praise.

'Does that sort of role appeal to you?' he questioned.

She nodded, trying not to be affected by the silken texture of his voice, but it wasn't easy. 'I'd like that very much.' She hesitated. 'You know, you haven't even mentioned why you're here—in England.'

He thought back to the working breakfast he'd had that morning with England's leading horse-racing experts—and the similar meetings which had taken place in every major city in Europe. With an effort, he switched his attention away from the soft rose-pink of her cheeks and the sapphire gleam of her eyes.

'I've been promoting the new horse-racing track and stadium we've almost completed in Khayarzah,' he said. 'One which will put us firmly on the international equestrian circuit. But this particular trip has also been personal.' He walked over to the window and stared at a rusty barge which was chugging its way down the heavy grey waters of the Thames. He wouldn't have discussed such a matter with anyone else, but his inherent trust in Francesca made him more candid than was usual. And didn't it come as a kind of liberation—to be able to speak his mind for once? 'I needed to meet with my brother,' he said as he turned back to face her. 'To see if he's really been behaving as badly as the media suggest.'

Frankie saw the sudden tension which had tightened his face and she wrinkled her nose in question.

She'd only met his brother Tariq on a few occasions—and one of those had been at her father's funeral, when she'd been too fogged down in grief to be able to think straight.

Like Zahid, Tariq had enjoyed a mixed and fairly liberal upbringing—some of it spent far away from his homeland. But the destinies of two princes could be so radically different…

When Zahid had become King, his life had changed immeasurably—while Tariq was still able to behave pretty much as he always had done. Frankie knew that the younger prince was known for being outrageously gorgeous and had been dubbed 'The Playboy Sheikh' by the more extravagant sections of the western press.

'Why, what has he done?' she questioned.

'That's just the point. He hasn't done nearly enough.' Zahid gave a little click of irritation. 'Well, that's not entirely true, since Tariq possesses the uncanny ability to produce excellent results with the minimum amount of work. He just needs a little reminding from time to time that he is a royal prince with an obligation to his country—and not simply an habitué of the gambling tables and an object of slavish female desire. But let us not talk about that now. You will fly with me to Khayarzah at the end of the week—do you have a passport?'

She nodded, aware how parochial his question made her sound. 'Of course.'

'And we need to get you settled. In fact, we'd better find you a room here.'

Taken aback, Frankie blinked at him. 'You mean I'm going to be staying *here*, at the Granchester?'

Something in the innocent way she framed the question sparked an unwanted hunger deep inside him—so that for a moment Zahid forgot that she was almost like one of the family. Forgot that his groin was not supposed to tighten and throb as he looked at her. Because when her pink and unpainted lips opened like that, he suddenly found he could think of a much better use for them than talking…

Unwanted lust made him tease her—trying to make his arousal go away but wondering idly whether she would respond. *And how would you react if she did? Would you take her in your arms and taste her? Treat you both to a sweet interlude of mutually satisfying sex?*

'Of course you're going to be staying here,' he murmured, shifting his position slightly, which did precisely nothing to relieve the deep ache at his groin. 'You'll need to make a few preparations before we fly to Khayarzah. You'll need a visa. Security clearance—that kind of thing—and it will all have to be done in London. You don't have a problem with that, do you?'

It took a moment for Frankie to answer because her body was responding crazily to the way he was looking at her. She could feel the prickle of her breasts and a strange pooling of heat at the pit of her stomach so that she felt all light-headed, and vulnerable. Was this something he did to all women—made them feel all kinds of stuff they weren't supposed to be feeling—leaving them aching and unsettled and wanting more?

But Frankie was determined to appear professional. He had seen her being made a fool of by her ex-fiancé—and her pride was hurting because of that. She must show him that she could be strong—that she wasn't some vulnerable little girl who jumped every time somebody made a loud bang.

'No, not a problem at all,' she said calmly. 'I'm very adaptable.'

'Good. Then come and meet the rest of my staff. I'll introduce you to my bodyguards and they'll explain a few simple guidelines to you.' He glanced down at her rain-spattered legs and the shoes which didn't quite match the plain blue dress. 'And we'd better organise some clothes for you. You'll need something appropriate to wear—especially in Khayarzah, where it's very hot but women cover their legs and their arms at all times. Something which befits a staff member to the sheikh.'

Frankie looked down at the dress she'd bought specially for this meeting—wondering if he had any idea of all the angst which had gone into choosing the neat garment. 'You mean there's something wrong with what I'm wearing?'

Did he protect her from the truth, or did he give it to her straight? Zahid's mouth hardened. Hadn't she already been lied to enough by one man? And she would never learn about life's harsh realities unless somebody taught her. He looked her straight in the eye. 'There's nothing fundamentally *wrong* with it, Francesca—other than that it's cheap.' He gave her a regretful shrug as he reached out to pick up the phone. 'And I'm afraid I don't do cheap.'

CHAPTER SIX

PLONKING herself down on the bed, Frankie kicked the shoes from her aching feet and fell back against the snowy bank of pillows. It had been a long day. Even longer than yesterday, when she'd travelled back down to Surrey, packed some essentials and locked up the house—ready to embrace her new role as a member of Zahid's staff. Already, her world seemed to have altered out of all recognition. She'd been given a luxurious room in one of London's smartest hotels, a list of all the people who worked for the sheikh—as well as his busy schedule for the weeks ahead.

And today she had been sent off to see a stylist and to acquire the clothes which Zahid had told her were essential for her working trip to his homeland.

She hadn't realised that shopping could be so exhausting—but then she didn't usually buy an entire wardrobe at one fell swoop. The swish store was situated in a side street, not far from the Khayarzah Embassy, and Frankie was put in the hands of an elegant woman who seemed to know exactly the kind of clothes she needed for her forthcoming trip.

The shopping expedition had been so intensive that she'd missed lunch and by the time she got back to the hotel she was too exhausted to bother with room service. So she ate the chocolate which had been left lying on her pillow and lay down on the bed just to rest her eyes.

She must have dozed off because before she knew it she was startled out of some bizarre and fitful dream about telephones by an urgent knocking on the door. Reluctantly, Frankie got up off the feathery mattress and padded across the room to answer it. Still yawning, she pulled open the door to find Zahid standing there with a look of unmistakable irritation on his face.

'I've been calling and calling you—didn't you hear me?'

Still dozy from an unfamiliar daytime nap, she raked her fingers through her tousled hair. 'No, of course I didn't—otherwise I'd have answered.' With difficulty, she stifled another yawn. 'Sorry—I must have fallen asleep.'

'Clearly.' Reluctantly, Zahid found his eyes drawn to her. Her cheeks were flushed and her lashes looked like ebony smudges making spiky shadows on her soft cheek. With her hair spilling down untidily over her shoulders, she looked as if she had just been ravished, he thought—with an unwelcome beat of awareness. But she was wearing an old pair of jeans and an oatmeal-coloured sweater he recognised and he frowned. 'I thought you'd been out shopping?'

'I have. I just got back.' She saw him looking askance at her jeans and shrugged as his gaze travelled over to the still open doors of her wardrobe, where the new clothes could be seen hanging in a neat line. 'They seem almost too nice to wear—does that sound stupid?'

'Yes.'

'Especially when I'm just mooching around the hotel room.'

'Well, stop mooching and start getting ready,' he said coolly. 'We're having dinner with my brother in just over an hour.'

'You're kidding?'

He sucked in a breath of irritation as he glanced at the rumpled bed directly behind her. 'No, Francesca, I am not. And just remember that I'm not paying you to lie around…' Now why had his mind focused on *that* particular verb? Dragging his gaze away from the ruffled duvet, he narrowed his eyes as he spotted a discarded chocolate wrapper lying on the carpet. 'Eating chocolate all day and napping! Be ready in an hour,' he ordered. 'One of my bodyguards will let you know when we're ready to go.'

He slammed the door shut behind him and for a moment Frankie stood staring at it in disbelief. Talk about leaping to the wrong conclusions! He'd made her sound like some decadent couch potato who loved stuffing her face with carbs—when pretty much all she'd eaten all day had been that one, measly chocolate.

But she enjoyed soaking in a scented bath—and afterwards selecting something silken and suitable from her newly acquired wardrobe. The clothes she had been guided towards were fundamentally modest—there wasn't a low neck or a miniskirt in sight. Their beauty lay in the quality of the exquisite fabrics as they whispered delicately over her skin. As she slid on her own bra and knickers she thought that they seemed positively *dingy* in comparison to the quiet opulence of the green silk gown she'd chosen to wear.

One of Zahid's enigmatic-looking bodyguards

rapped at the door at eight o'clock precisely, and Frankie stepped into the corridor to find Zahid just emerging from his own room. He was wearing a suit of pale grey, which served as a perfect foil for his bronzed and dark colouring. But he stopped dead when he saw her and stood completely still—as if someone had turned him to stone.

'Are you…ready?' she asked tentatively, wondering if she had committed some awful faux pas that she wasn't aware of. Was the dress too formal? Her shoes too high? Should she have worn her hair up instead of letting it tumble loosely down her back?

In answer to her stumbled question Zahid nodded—though he wasn't really listening to what she'd asked him. Because, against all the odds—she looked *beautiful*. More beautiful than any woman he had ever seen. Like some princess who had stepped from the pages of one of the old Khayarzah fables his nanny used to read to him as a child.

Her dark hair was glossy, her blue eyes wide and watchful—and the deep green of her dress emphasised the porcelain paleness of her face and soft curves of her body. What must it be like for her, he wondered, to have blossomed as she had blossomed—to have gone from tomboy to temptress in one seamless step? Was she aware of the power which now lay at her fingertips—the power possessed by every woman who could hold a man in her thrall?

Yet *Simon* had been the one to awaken her, he reminded himself grimly. He might have been a duplicitous and money-grubbing creep—but he was responsible for this new, sensual allure of hers. He had been the one who had…who had…

'Is this okay, Zahid?' Aware that his bright, hard gaze was still fixed on her, Frankie brushed her palms down over the silk skirt of her dress and gave him an anxious look. Why on earth was he scowling at her like that? 'The dress, I mean?'

'Are you searching for a compliment?' he queried, more acidly than he had intended—but he was having to quash a reaction to her that he had not intended and did not particularly want. The kind of reaction which would have usually culminated in him peeling her brand-new dress from her body and tossing it contemptuously to the floor, thus ensuring that they would be late for dinner. 'I'm sure you're perfectly aware that it's more than okay and that you look very…agreeable,' he finished.

Her smile was uncertain as she looped a big cashmere wrap around her shoulders. *Agreeable?* Was that supposed to have been a compliment? She wasn't sure—not when he had managed to make it sound like some sort of growled *insult.*

Frankie felt nervous as they went downstairs to the car—a short journey which seemed to involve a lot of high-powered and pre-arranged choreography. Cocooned by a small phalanx of bodyguards, Zahid walked at speed through the lobby—seemingly oblivious to the curious eyes which were darted in his direction—with her tottering on high heels behind him.

A limousine was waiting outside the hotel—its door already open and engine purring—and as Frankie sat back against the squishy, soft leather seat she wondered how all this could have happened—and so quickly. Why, only last week she'd been showing a couple around a new-build and today she was being whisked through central London in a luxury limousine, with a brooding-looking sheikh sitting beside her.

She splayed her fingers out over her lap. He seemed *uncomfortably* close—so that the atmosphere seemed full of his own particular scent. A potent cocktail of raw male mixed with sweet sandalwood and the tang of lemons was now invading her senses. And somehow he was managing to imprint his powerful body onto her subconscious, even though she was pointedly looking out of the car window in an attempt to lessen the impact he was having on her. What on earth was the matter with her? Shouldn't she have been missing Simon—if only a little bit—instead of fantasising what it might be like if Zahid pulled her into his arms and began to kiss her?

'Where...where are we going?' she questioned breathlessly. 'And tell me a bit more about what Tariq is doing these days.'

Zahid watched with interest as she dug her nails into one silk-covered thigh. Much more of that and she would claw tiny holes into that new dress of hers, he thought. 'There's a private members' club next door to The Ivy—and we're meeting him there. He lives in England permanently now.'

'*Does* he? Doing what?'

'He runs the European arm of the family business—but he also has a very successful polo club in the south of England which he bought quite recently.'

Of course he does, thought Frankie as the car coasted past the shining shop lights which lightened the dark November night and drew to a halt in front of a discreet door. She knew that Tariq was a superb and talented polo player, so it followed that he would have a club of his own. The Al Hakam family never did anything by halves.

Inside the private members' club, masses of flowers stood in eye-catching arrangements and a glass lift zoomed them up to a large room which somehow managed to have an intimate feel to it. In one corner, a grand piano was being played softly by an aging crooner who smiled at them as they walked in—and on a nearby table, Frankie recognised a soap-star who was more famous for her chequered love-life than for her work as an actress.

They were ushered towards a small, private dining room and when they arrived Tariq was already seated at the table. It was the first time that Frankie had ever seen the brothers together—and with their dramatically dark good looks, the family resemblance was startling. But the younger brother was wearing faded jeans and a silk shirt—his shadowed jaw resolutely unshaven—and he had an air of slightly disreputable charm, which was at odds with Zahid's rather more formal appearance.

He rose to his feet when he saw them approach and the two men embraced. And then as Tariq let his arms fall away he gave Frankie a smile which she suspected had made many women melt into a puddle at his feet.

'How unusual. It's not like you to bring a woman with you, Zahid,' he observed, his voice a honeyed murmur. 'So who is *this* little beauty?'

Zahid glared at his sibling. 'This is Francesca.'

'Francesca?' There was a pause as Tariq frowned and then his face suddenly cleared as he made the connection. 'Frankie? *Frankie?* I don't believe it! Is that really you?'

'Yes!' She smiled back as he gathered her in a bear

hug and she realised that Zahid had said pretty much the same thing. Which begged the question of how much she had changed. Did she really look that different? She guessed she did. Yet it was funny how you could be altered so radically on the exterior—and yet inside you felt exactly the same…with all those same nagging doubts and insecurities. 'Yes, it's really me!'

'Wow! You look so *different*. Amazing! All pretty, and grown-up. Good heavens…' Tariq frowned. 'You and Zahid, I mean you aren't—'

'We aren't anything,' Zahid snapped, giving his brother another furious glare. 'Francesca is working for me now.'

'*Is* she now? That's quite a bold step.'

'But maybe it's about time. Such an appointment will show the western world that we do take women seriously. And it will pacify some of the more rebellious females back home in Khayarzah.'

Tariq laughed. 'There speaks my brother, the King! How completely ruthless you can be, Zahid.'

'You think so? I prefer to describe myself as a realist.' Zahid shrugged. 'And why not capitalise on opportunity when it comes knocking?'

Frankie bit her lip as she heard herself described as an 'opportunity'.

'Wine, Frankie?' asked Tariq.

'I'd better not—'

'Nonsense. If Zahid wants to show the world he's tolerant and open to the ways of the west, then he should let his pretty guest have a glass of wine even if he doesn't much care for it himself.'

She rarely drank but Frankie suddenly found herself longing for a glass. So many emotional missiles had been hurled at her over the last few days and she still felt a little dazed by it all. Her whole pattern of living had crashed and she hadn't quite got used to the new, rebooted version. She knew that she should be feeling more pain about the end of her relationship with Simon—but the crazy thing was that she didn't. And that in turn made her feel guilty. She kept questioning her own judgment and every time she did it filled her with a feeling of failure. A drink might help relax her.

'Thank you,' she said, ignoring the narrow-eyed look which Zahid sent shooting in her direction. 'I think I will.'

The meal was a mixture of glamour and grit. Frankie was aware that she was in a high-octane atmosphere and being served some of the best food in the capital. But she felt strangely removed from it all—as if she was an outsider, looking in.

Maybe that wasn't so surprising. She was with two members of a royal family and they spent a lot of the evening speaking—and arguing—in their native tongue. Consequently, she found herself sipping at the rich red wine without really noticing and before she knew it she was halfway through a second glass. Her cheeks had begun to burn and Zahid was frowning at her across the table—and suddenly she found herself lost in the judgemental razoring of his gaze. Her tongue snaked out to encircle lips which had suddenly become bone-dry and she could have sworn she saw his eyes darken in response.

'Don't have anything more to drink, Francesca.'

She hadn't been intending to—at least, not until he clipped out that peremptory order. 'Why, are you *ration-*

ing me now?' she questioned. 'This is only my second glass.'

Zahid felt irritated. It had been bad enough that his younger brother was stubbornly refusing to listen to reason and take his advice—without Francesca suddenly throwing her inhibitions to the wind. Why the hell had Tariq foisted that wine on her—and why had she let him?

'You're clearly not used to it. Come on,' he said abruptly, rising to his feet. 'It's time we were going.'

'But I haven't had any pudding!' she protested.

'Wasn't the chocolate you were eating earlier enough to satisfy your sweet cravings?' questioned Zahid acidly.

'But I only had one—and I missed lunch!'

Dark eyes looked positively *frozen* now. 'You can order something from room service when we get back,' he snapped. 'And fascinating as this conversation is, I feel we must deprive my brother of any more of it.'

But Tariq was laughing. 'Oh, please don't let me stop you—I don't think I've ever heard you sounding quite so *domesticated*, Zahid.'

Frankie's feisty mood had evaporated by the time she retrieved her cashmere wrap from the cloakroom, and Tariq slid it round her shoulders with automatic courtesy. Why couldn't Zahid do a gentlemanly thing like that, she wondered wistfully—instead of glaring at her as if she had suddenly become radioactive? She stepped out into the cold night and the drop in temperature was so dramatic that she stumbled a little until Zahid caught her elbow and steadied her.

She could feel his fingers burning through the fine cashmere of her wrap and she saw his mouth grow taut, before he gently manoeuvred her into the limousine as it slid to a halt beside them.

He turned to his brother, his face tense and his voice low. 'Just remember what I said. You are now the brother of the sheikh—the heir. You shouldn't be associated with a woman like that, a woman who is…'

Frankie had been listening intently to their conversation but rather annoyingly he had said the last word in his native language—or rather, he hissed it out like a cornered snake she had once seen at the zoo.

'Who's Tariq going out with who you obviously don't approve of?' she questioned, after they'd said goodbye and the car was pulling away.

'Nobody,' he answered tersely.

'But I just heard you say—'

'Well, you shouldn't have done. You should have blocked the sound out. Don't you know what they say about eavesdroppers?'

'If I'm supposed to be working for you, and if you're supposed to trust me, then don't I need to know these things?'

'Not *now*, Francesca! You will know what I wish you to know and when I wish you to know it. But top of the list of my requirements is an assurance that you do *not* persist with a line in questioning when your sheikh has expressly forbidden it. Do you understand?'

He had never spoken to her like that before. Never. Not once had he ever pulled rank—and Frankie shrank back against the seat of the car as she realised that this was the price she must pay for working for him. She was no longer to be indulged and protected by him—but to be treated as he would treat any other member of his staff. And didn't a stupid and stubborn little part of her suddenly long for some of the slightly indulgent and caring attitude which he'd always shown to her before? 'I think you've made yourself very clear,' she said, in a small voice.

He turned towards her, his mood made sombre by his younger brother's stubbornness—but something in the crestfallen expression on her face wiped the anger clean out of his head and replaced it with something entirely different.

Her lips were trembling and her face was pale. Framed by the soft cashmere of her wrap, the dark green silk of her dress seemed to be straining against the weight of her luscious breasts. And legs. He swallowed down the sudden hot surge of lust. What about her legs? When she crossed them like that, was she aware that the delicate silk moulded against the outline of her thighs and that her shapely ankles would drive any normal, hot-blooded man crazy with desire?

He wanted to kiss her.

He wanted to tear away the silk-satin to see those breasts for himself before tasting their rosy tips. He wanted to slide the dress still further up her legs and make her hot and sweet and wet for him.

He must be out of his mind!

Shifting his position further along the seat, Zahid stared at her with an expression which would have made his sage old advisors back in Khayarzah shiver with apprehension if they'd seen it. But his fury was directed at himself.

What the hell was he playing at?

'Cover your legs!' he bit out.

His furious words crashed in and shattered Frankie's pensive mood and she sat up and returned his angry stare, her eyes bewildered. Her *legs*? Why, there was hardly any of her legs on show—barely even a flash of ankle! Perhaps she *hadn't* been sitting in a way which was very ladylike, but even so—there was no need for him to shout. She leaned forward to tug at her skirt but that didn't seem to please him either.

'Is this the way you behave when you go out for dinner with a man?' he demanded. 'Quaffing wine by the glass and wriggling around in the back of a car with a dress which looks at least one size too small?'

'No! *No!* I told you—I hardly drink a thing. And the dress is a perfect fit! Don't be so old-fashioned, Zahid!'

'But I *am* old-fashioned!' he thundered, before the hypocrisy of his own words hit him. He wasn't *usually* old-fashioned when it came to women, was he? Usually, the more outrageous the outfit, the more he enjoyed it. He thought of Katya the other night, turning up in nothing but her glittery panties and a fur coat and his mouth thinned. He hadn't enjoyed *that* very much, had he?

'We are almost at the hotel,' he said in a cold voice. 'Do you think you can possibly manage to make it upstairs on your own, without stumbling?'

She'd never heard him sound quite so *frosty* before—or so angry—and Frankie puckered her lips together, afraid that she might top off the evening with something unforgivable—like bursting into tears. Had she had made another serious misjudgement, thinking that the answer to her problems had been to grab at this job? Had she really thought that working for Zahid might be some sort of *adventure*?

Well, she had been wrong. Now they seemed to do nothing but rub each other up the wrong way and she would tell him so. She would tell him that she had made a mistake and that she would be staying in England after all. But not tonight. She wanted tonight to end as soon as possible. She would inform him in the cold, clear light of day that it was probably better if she looked elsewhere for a job. 'Of course I can,' she answered flatly.

Their little convoy of cars drew to a halt and they travelled up in the lift together—an awkward little group which consisted of a stony-faced Zahid, a Frankie who was trying very hard not to let her lips wobble and two bodyguards who were built like bulldogs.

And when they reached their floor and Frankie had extracted her key-card, her fumbling fingers somehow prevented her from getting the door open and Zahid plucked it from her with a click of irritation.

For a moment their fingers brushed together and her eyes widened in startled recognition of the sudden warm thrill of that brief, physical contact. Irresistibly, their gazes locked and she saw the sudden darkening of his eyes. For one crazy second she observed the soft parting of his lips and the breath froze in her throat. *Was Zahid attracted to her—as she was to him?* Was he leaning forward as if he was about to *kiss* her?

But then the moment passed and he turned away. Her heart was beating frantically as he swiped the key-card and this time the light went on.

'Ah, I'm getting the green light again,' he said sardonically, unable to resist the sensual taunt—but she made no response to it. And he found himself wondering what he would have done if she had taunted him right back…

Frankie set her face into a frozen little smile. Was he laughing at her? Making fun of her? Her heart gave a painful lurch but she kept her face completely expressionless. 'Goodnight, Zahid,' she said quietly. 'Thank you very much for dinner.'

Her dignified statement filled him with a sudden feeling of guilt and Zahid wasn't quite sure what had provoked it. Perplexed, he watched as she closed the door behind her and he was left standing outside Francesca's bedroom with a distinctly rare feeling of frustration.

CHAPTER SEVEN

ZAHID slept restlessly for much of the night. He was troubled by the stubbornness of his brother and the life he seemed to be leading. But he was troubled by something else, too—and that something was desire.

He opened his eyes. Nothing new there. Desire was as much a part of his life as eating. He had the healthy appetite of a man in his glorious prime and enjoyed sex as much as he enjoyed hunting, or riding—or seeing his beloved falcon soar up into the azure splendour of the Khayarzah skies.

But he had never made the connection between sex and *emotion* before—mainly because the latter did not figure greatly in his life. Early on, he had recognised that it was useful for a king to be emotionally detached. Maybe it was useful for *all* men to be so.

Emotion was messy—and so was depending on only one person—everyone knew that. Wasn't he grateful that his position as King meant that he would never be required to walk such a potentially explosive path?

Pushing back the sweat-damp sheets, he got out of bed and walked naked into the bathroom, where he stood beneath a cold shower. The icy jets of water lashed down onto his tense and overheated body to briefly offer some relief. But not for very long.

His erotic dreams of last night had disturbed him—and they disturbed him still—because this time they were not easily fixed. For once, the dreams had not been of some beauty he'd met at some function, whom he could summon at will and have writhing beneath him before the day was out. Someone with whom he could enjoy a sweet, no strings affair—before kissing them goodbye with a significant piece of jewellery to remember him by.

Because the face which had haunted him all night long had been that of Francesca.

Francesca O'Hara.

He groaned as he lathered soap over his hips, feeling the heavy throb of desire at his groin and praying that the ice-water would quickly dispel these useless fantasies. Because they *were* fantasy. She was *completely forbidden* to him—and he had to force himself to remember why.

He had known her all her life.

Her father had trusted him.

Most important of all, there was no future for her with him—because she was English and he was Khayarzahian. The destinies ordained for each of them were radically different—and she meant too much to him to ever want to hurt her. Because although Francesca O'Hara was an experienced woman of the world with one fiancé already behind her, he respected her too much to offer her nothing but a quick fling.

The thought of Simon robbing Francesca of her precious innocence was enough to kill Zahid's desire stone-dead and abruptly he turned off the shower, towelled himself dry and dressed.

His breakfast laid up on the table beside him, he'd just hit the 'send' button on an email when there was a rap at the door—quickly followed by a soft English voice.

'Zahid?'

'Come in.'

He looked up as the door opened slowly and Francesca stood there, her expression more than a little anxious, wearing some sort of muted grey dress which seemed to have leached all the colour from her face.

'Zahid—'

'You'd better come in and shut the door behind you,' he commanded softly.

She did as he asked, drawing in a deep breath. 'I need to talk to you.'

'Talk away. But at least let's do it in some degree of comfort.' He gestured towards the table which was laid with breakfast, in an alcoved window overlooking the city. 'Have you had breakfast?'

'No. I'm not…very hungry.'

'Francesca.' He gave a slightly impatient sigh as he rose to his feet and walked over to her, taking her firmly by the elbow and steering her towards the table. But he felt the unmistakable tension in her body when he touched her and the answering clamour of his own senses in response. 'On a current showing, you aren't impressing me with your daily diet. All this skipping meals simply will not do. Coffee?'

She wanted to tell him that she was leaving but now he was propelling her into a chair and pouring her a cup of inky-dark coffee and somehow had persuaded her to take a warm croissant from the linen cradle of the bread basket.

Under his fierce gaze, she tore a buttery strip from the pastry and held it in her fingers. 'Zahid, about last night—'

'Yes, I've been meaning to speak to you about last night.'

'You have?''

'Mmm.' He sipped at his coffee and looked at her over the rim of the cup. 'But I'll hear what you have to say first.'

She thought that was a little unfair, but she was hardly in a position to say so. And it was hard to put anything into words when he was sitting right opposite her like that—managing to appear both relaxed and yet supremely powerful. With his fine silk shirt unbuttoned at the neck and his black hair still glittering from the shower, Frankie could have sat looking at him all day. But wasn't that precisely *why* she needed to do the decent thing and hand her notice in, before her stupid desire for him got out of hand?

'It seemed a good idea at the time to accept your offer,' she began. 'But clearly this isn't going to work. Or rather, *I'm* not going to work—at least, not for you. I can't come to Khayarzah, Zahid. I thought I could, but I can't. I'm sorry.'

'What a jumble of words!' He reached for a glass of juice. 'Why not?'

'Because you don't *treat* me fairly!' she objected.

'I don't?' he questioned coolly. 'I fail to see how when I have just bought you an entire new wardrobe and will be paying you a very handsome salary to type up my father's diary.'

'That's not what I meant, and you know it.'

'Really?' He registered her spiky challenge with surprise. 'Then just what *do* you mean?'

She let the untouched piece of croissant flutter onto the plate. 'All that stuff last night about what I was wearing and the way I was sitting—and how I'd had too much to drink, when we both know I hadn't. That was all because you've known me all my life and still treat me like a child!'

'On the contrary,' Zahid said, sitting back in his chair and regarding her with unsettling scrutiny. 'On reflection, the reason I said all those things was because you *aren't* a child any more.'

Now it was her turn to look to him for clarification. Her brow creased in a puzzled frown. 'I don't understand.'

'I think you probably do—if you stop for a minute to think about it. You see, I'm used to thinking of you as a friend—my only real female friend, as it happens.'

The simple accolade affected her deeply and for a moment Frankie was filled with a fear that he was about to snatch it away from her. And suddenly she realised that no job in the world was worth *that*. 'Please don't make it sound as if it's all in the past!' she cried, before she had time to think about the wisdom of her words or that they had poured out so emotionally.

'I have no intention of making it something in the past,' he said, his voice gentling by a fraction. 'It's just that you have grown up into a beautiful and very desirable young woman—and I'm finding it difficult to know how to react to you.'

It was such a stark and honest admission that it took Frankie completely by surprise. She looked at him in disbelief until she found herself blushing and then glanced down at her plate, terrified about what he might read into her embarrassment. Did he have any idea that she had entertained stupid fantasies about him since the year dot?

For a full minute there was silence and when the tension in the air had grown to such a point that she couldn't take it any more, Frankie risked glancing up into his eyes once more.

'I don't know what to say,' she whispered.

And for once in his life, neither did Zahid.

Looking at the morning light as it fell on the dark gleam of her hair, he knew what he *should* say. He should tell her he agreed with her—that it was an impossible situation which he hadn't really thought through. That he hadn't expected desire to rear its powerful head—and maybe it was best if she *did* go. Yet to Zahid that smacked of failure, and he didn't *do* failure—not in any sphere of his life.

Now his gaze skated over the swell of her breasts, which seemed to transform the demure grey dress into a garment of shocking provocation. Wouldn't it be a formidable and life-affirming challenge to resist the temptation she represented? Like the times when he and his brother had travelled into the arid centre of the desert and denied themselves the soft comforts of palace life. Such deprivation had been imposed on them by their elders as a deliberate means of making them strong and tough. Wouldn't this simply be a variation on the same kind of denial?

'I am loath to let you go,' he admitted slowly. 'And the reasons for giving you the job haven't changed.'

'No.'

'But…' He hesitated. Didn't they know each other well enough to dispense with coy hints and get straight to the truth? He gave a rueful shrug of his shoulders. 'We're worried because something has changed and we've discovered that we are sexually attracted to each other.'

At this, she blushed. How *anatomical* he made it sound. 'Zahid!'

'Oh, come on, Francesca—don't play the outraged innocent.' His eyes gleamed. 'It's what we've both been thinking—or are you going to deny this rather inconvenient desire which has flared up between us?'

His black eyes were lasering into her and beneath their intensity she felt positively weak. *Inconvenient?* Was that how he saw it? She shook her head, because surely she could be honest, too. 'No, I'm not going to deny it.'

'The trouble is that you're no longer the innocent little girl I remember,' he observed. 'You're a beautiful and experienced young woman who's just come out of a bruising bust-up.'

Experienced? He thought she was *experienced?* Frankie gave a weak smile in response. Well, of course he did. Why wouldn't he? Most modern engaged women were having fantastic sex with the man they were going to marry. The fact that she and Simon hadn't progressed much beyond 'first base' she'd put down to some pathetic idea that he was a gentleman—never realising that it was because he was enjoying an illicit passion with somebody else. Should she tell Zahid that? Should she come right out and say it?

Zahid, I'm still a virgin.

Wouldn't that make her look like a complete loser?

Of course it would.

He leaned back in his chair, watching the play of emotions which shadowed her face. 'In fact, if it were anyone other than you, I'd be pulling you into my arms and kissing you right now and then dragging you off to the nearest bed before making love to you. But for all kinds of reasons, we both know that isn't going to happen,' he added, with a careless air which his protesting body didn't quite endorse. 'So you see, I completely understand why you don't want to come to Khayarzah. The question is whether or not you would be a fool not to do so?'

His words fell between them like a challenge—and Frankie suddenly felt as if he'd tied her up in verbal knots. Hadn't *she* been the one who had told him that she didn't think the job was such a good idea, after all? And wasn't *he* the one who had somehow managed to turn it around to make her want to reconsider her opinion?

Yet there was enough substance behind his question to *make* her reconsider. Because the truth of it was that it had been a long-time dream of hers to see the land which her father had helped mould with his discovery of its oil. A land which he had visited on many occasions and had enthused about with most uncharacteristic passion.

Frankie had always longed to see for herself the fabulous palace at Mangalsutra, the country's capital—with its beautiful, scented gardens which he had talked about so often. And hadn't she longed to eat some more of those crystallised walnuts she'd once tasted—bought from the colourful and bustling market which was held in the main square of the city?

'I've always wanted to go there,' she said truthfully, her eyes shining as she remembered the stories she'd grown up with. 'My father used to tell me all about the place. He said that in springtime, fields of poppies sprang up overnight—turning the landscape into a scarlet haze. That at night-time the moon was so big that you felt you could almost reach out and lasso it from the sky. And that leopards lived in the high mountains in the east—and sometimes a very lucky traveller might be able to spot one.'

'Well, then.' Zahid listened to the faraway note in her voice—and found himself ridiculously touched by her knowledge and obvious love of his country. So many people dismissed the east as just a prolific provider of oil—as if Khayarzah consisted of nothing but refineries and gilded palaces! The only thing she had got wrong was the leopard—for he'd never known anyone who had seen the elusive creatures which were reputed to live on the eastern heights. But he had no intention of telling her that. Why destroy someone's dreams unless you had to?

He glittered her a cool smile. 'In that case, it seems to be that your destiny intends you to come to my country and see it for yourself.'

It was what she'd always wanted—but the tug in her heart alerted her to an unfamiliar kind of danger. And something in Zahid's now shuttered expression made a feeling of apprehension whisper over Frankie's skin.

CHAPTER EIGHT

HE DIDN'T look so urbane now.

'What's the matter, Francesca?' questioned Zahid softly.

The matter? Frankie stared at him. Did he mean apart from the fact that her heart was racing so fast that she felt dizzy? Or that her knees felt so weak, she was glad she was sitting down? With an effort she quashed the pervasive sense of desire which had hit her the moment he'd emerged from the concealed section situated at the back of his private jet. Because Frankie had never seen Zahid looking like *this* before.

Just before the Gulfstream jet had landed—descending like a silver bird from the darkening blue of the desert sky—he had disappeared to change. The very act of dressing and undressing on the aircraft had seemed an unbearably intimate act and Frankie was ill prepared for the sight which greeted her on his return. Because the sleek and sophisticated royal with whom she'd breakfasted in his penthouse suite seemed to be nothing but a distant memory.

Gone was the urbane image of the man he had been in London—the exquisitely cut Italian suit now replaced by robes of flowing white. She'd seen pictures of him in traditional dress before—but nothing on earth could have prepared her for the impact of seeing the real-life version.

The delicate fabric hinted at the hard body beneath and the blanched colour threw his burnished skin into stark relief. Jet-dark hair was covered by a white head-dress held in place by a dark and intricately knotted circlet of scarlet.

Frankie couldn't tear her eyes away from him. Yes, he was a king—but somehow that seemed irrelevant in the light of his blatant masculinity. He looked almost...*primitive*, she thought as she swallowed down the sudden dryness in her mouth. *Elemental.* As if he had appeared from some bygone age where men were unashamedly men, and women were...

'Nervous?' he questioned drily.

'Not at all,' she lied.

'Then why are you wringing your hands so tightly together? *Relax*.'

Frankie looked down to see that her knuckles were as white as if she'd been on a roller-coaster ride. Because hadn't concerns plagued her during the flight from London? Perfectly legitimate concerns which made her question the wisdom of agreeing to accompany Zahid to Khayarzah.

She would be on *his* territory—and subject to *his* whim. In close contact with a man she desired. He had assured her that he wasn't going to seduce an old family friend—and had said it with a steely resolve that she didn't doubt for one minute. Yet the irony was that his words had left her with a dull and aching feeling of disappointment—even though she knew they made perfect sense.

As the plane came to a halt Frankie unclipped her seat belt. 'I wonder how my appearance is going to go down?' she questioned tentatively. 'Whether your people will approve?'

'I have given up trying to please everyone,' Zahid said in a suddenly harsh tone as he remembered his early days on the throne, and how he had not known whom he could trust. The previous sheikh had been very traditional and Zahid found that most of those old advisors were just as resistant to modernising the country as his uncle had been. 'I must just be true to myself and let myself be judged by my actions.' He stood up and gestured for her to follow him. 'But I am not anticipating many problems when it comes to your appearance—for let's not forget that you have a famous surname.'

'I'm not famous, Zahid,' she protested.

'No. But your father is. His name is taught in our schools as the man who discovered our rich resources. He's a little bit of a national hero—surely you realised that?' He saw the pleasure in her eyes, and a brief smile touched the edges of his lips. 'There will be a delegation waiting to meet me, but you'll soon get used to that. So do as I told you on the plane. Just keep your eyes averted—and walk a few paces behind me.'

She smoothed down the silk tunic top, with its matching narrow trousers. 'And my outfit…is it okay?' she questioned.

Reluctantly, Zahid studied her, allowing his eyes to linger on her youthful form. Cool, practical and decent, her clothes met all the necessary criteria which the country's strict dress-code required. Yet in spite of that they managed to make her look incredibly *sexy*—something he hadn't really been expecting. Was that because it hinted at the firm flesh which lay beneath—or because he knew he could never have her in the way he wanted?

Feeling the unwilling heat of desire begin to build, he turned away. 'It's fine,' he said abruptly as the aircraft steps were lowered. 'Now let's go.'

She followed him out into the cooling air of the Khayarzah evening, to see a row of officials waiting to greet their king. And it seemed that their initial looks of wariness were softened when she was introduced to them and the 'O'Hara' connection was made. Through the butterfly build-up of nerves, Frankie suddenly felt an overwhelming sense of pride in her father and what he had done for this country.

They journeyed to the palace in a sleek limousine and through the smoked glass of their car window she could see tall palms, their fronds dramatically etched against the perfect blue of the sky. The road was long and straight and smoother than any English road she'd encountered. Behind them she could hear the muffled roar of the outriders—and beside her sat Zahid, his powerful body swathed in white silk, incongruously speaking into a mobile phone in his native tongue.

They skirted the main city of Mangalsutra—with its winding streets and jumble of rooftops—until they reached the gates of the palace itself. The immense white marble building rose up before her, fronted by a long, rectangular space of water fringed by palm trees. Turrets and domes and shadowed arches were contrasted against the darkening sky in which she could already see the faint twinkle of stars. Slowly Frankie expelled the breath she had been holding and Zahid must have heard her because he shot her a glance.

'Beautiful, isn't it?'

'It's exquisite,' she answered simply.

And so was she, he thought achingly. Against all the odds—so was she. With those blue eyes widening in wonder and the pert thrust of her breasts filling him with dark and erotic impulses. Would it be so bad if, after a cursory but necessary introduction to key members of his staff, he took her off to his private quarters, stripped the concealing silk garments from her body and laid her bare? If he opened thighs which would inevitably be milky-pale as he thrust hungrily between them?

Angrily, he crossed one leg over another. Had he forgotten where he was? *Who* he was? More importantly, who *she* was?

'Come and meet my staff,' he said unsteadily.

Frankie was taken to meet another line of robed servants, but her senses were too full of all these new experiences to be able to remember many of their exotic-sounding names. And she was preoccupied with watching Zahid—for he was no longer just the long-standing family friend who had always been kind to her, but the leader of a desert kingdom. He was in charge, she realised—and he radiated an impressive kind of power.

Swallowed up by advisors and aides, she watched as solemn-looking men bowed and began briefing him in his native tongue. Someone handed him a sheaf of papers and then a phone began to ring and was passed to him. He seemed to have forgotten that she was there—

for he barely raised his dark head as she left the gilded chamber.

A young girl of about seventeen called Fayruz had been assigned to look after her, and as Frankie was led along a marbled corridor lined with blue and gold mosaic she wondered how on earth she was going to be able to communicate with her. But to her surprise, it transpired that Fayruz spoke good—if slightly tentative—English.

'I learn it at school,' she said shyly, in response to Frankie's question. 'It is my best subject—which is why I have been brought in to assist you while you are here.'

'You're at school still?'

'Oh, yes,' Fayruz offered shyly.

'And then what—university, I suppose?'

There was a pause. 'In my country, women are not encouraged to go to university.'

Frankie frowned. 'You're kidding?'

Fayruz shook her head. 'It's thought women make better mothers than scholars.' She gave a small sigh and then shrugged her shoulders. 'I will unpack for you now.'

'No, honestly—I can do that for myself,' said Frankie, shaking her head in slight disbelief. Women *not encouraged to go to university*? This was much worse than she had imagined.

'Then let me draw a bath for you,' said Fayruz eagerly. 'Please. You must be hot after your long journey and the Sheikh will be displeased if I do not show you Khayarzahian hospitality.'

Frankie nodded, recognising that she must learn to adapt to a different way of living, to graciously accept a slower pace and help when it was offered. And wouldn't it be good to freshen up and relax before dinner? 'Thank you,' she said quietly. 'That would be lovely.'

Lovely turned out to be something of an understatement—because when Fayruz called to say that the bath was ready, Frankie could hardly believe her eyes. A wide, square bath—big as a child's swimming pool—was filled with warm, rose-scented water on which floated fresh petals.

After the servant had gone, Frankie stripped off her clothes and slowly submerged herself in its scented depths, the silky water lapping over her. This was heaven. Bliss. She closed her eyes. The closest she'd ever come to pure indulgence. Lulled by the warm water and the total silence, she relaxed for a while before reluctantly climbing out of the cooling water to get ready for dinner.

Skimming her fingers over the row of silk outfits which now hung in the wardrobe, she picked a long dress of pure white. People often wore white in desert countries, didn't they? And Zahid had been robed in white earlier…

She'd just finished dressing when Fayruz tapped at the door and led her through a maze of intricate corridors to what was described as the 'small' dining room—but this proved to be yet another understatement. It was bigger than any dining room she'd ever seen and decorated lavishly in gold and lapis lazuli. Intricately tooled hanging lamps filled the room with a soft radiance and the scent of cinnamon and sandalwood wafted through the air. The table itself was low and, instead of chairs, there were brocade cushions heaped around it.

At that moment, Zahid swept into the room—a small, accompanying retinue of stern-faced men walking close behind him. Across the exotic room, their eyes met, and Frankie felt a sizzle of awareness warming her skin, beneath the silk gown.

'Hello, Zahid,' she said softly.

Lulled by the soft familiarity of her voice, Zahid slowly let his gaze travel over her. She was wearing white—pure and virginal white—and he felt his body clench with instinctive jealousy. Did she not realise the bitter irony of her choice—she who no longer had the right to wear the traditional hue of innocence? A black tide of rage rose up in him as he remembered that it had been the rogue Simon who had taken her virginity.

He could see his advisors standing, waiting for his command. He had intended to invite them to stay—for their English was certainly good enough. And it might dilute Frankie's undeniable appeal if he was faced with the subtle censoring of his aides. Yet now, on impulse he found himself raising his hand to dismiss them and they filed obediently from the room. Settling himself on a pile of cushions so that his groin was shielded by a thick swathe of his robes, he indicated that she too should sit.

'Your room meets with your approval?' he questioned.

Frankie sank down onto soft brocade. 'How could it not? It's amazing.'

'And you are hungry, I hope?'

She couldn't possibly tell him that her interest in food had been eclipsed by the man sitting opposite her. With an effort, she tore her eyes away from the shockingly sensual outline of his mouth and glanced around the room with the rapt interest of a tourist. 'I'm looking forward to tasting some of your fabled Khayarzahian cuisine,' she answered politely.

Zahid narrowed his eyes. This was not the Francesca he knew, the one whose sharp wit he had always secretly admired. Why, she sounded like one of the many visiting ambassadors who regularly mouthed their platitudes!

'Then let us begin,' he said, nodding to the silent servants who were standing unobtrusively at the sides of the room and who then began to bring dishes of food in.

Frankie could only pick at the gleaming rice studded with pistachios and the dried fruits and soft cheeses—though she enjoyed the slightly fizzy date juice which Zahid called *Nadirah*. And all the time she tried to keep her eyes fixed on the plate in front of her, not daring to raise her face to his—fearful of what he might read in her eyes.

'You seem very…nervous tonight,' he observed softly. 'Or is there some special reason why you won't look at me?'

Reluctantly, she lifted her head to find his ebony stare burning into her like dark fire. She wondered how he would react if she told him the truth—that she longed for him to take her in his arms. To kiss her and never stop kissing her. All the things he'd told her weren't going to happen were all the things she *wanted* to happen. She forced her lips into the upward curve of a smile. Maybe a variation on the truth would suffice. 'I can't quite get used to seeing you here, being a king.'

Zahid nodded. Hadn't it taken time for *him* to get used to wearing the crown—to being the ruler of all he surveyed and the inevitable intoxication which came with it? Yet power came at a price, too—particularly when it came out of the blue.

When the plane carrying his uncle the king and his only son had crashed during a storm, Zahid had been crowned the new king—a role he had never expected, nor particularly wanted. But it was a role he was determined to fulfil to the best of his ability, even though many had looked on him suspiciously. He was still working hard to earn the faith of the key palace advisors—and push forward his agenda to modernise the country. But it would take time to get consensus and to earn the trust of the government and the people of Khayarzah. But that kind of trust had *always* existed between him and Francesca—and he didn't ever want to jeopardise it. 'But I *am* a king and have been for some time,' he said softly. 'You knew that. So nothing has changed, Francesca.'

Frankie stared into the gleaming depths of his ebony eyes. 'Yes, intellectually I knew all that. But seeing it for myself is a little dazzling—the robes and the palace and the servants. I'm used to seeing a more casual version of you back in England.'

He picked up a grape and ate it. 'If it makes you feel any better, it's pretty strange for me to have a woman sitting here like this.'

'But there must have been women here before,' she probed.

'Very occasionally, yes—of course—but they are always married women, accompanying their husbands. Never…' *Never a woman whose scent of rose and jasmine was filling his senses.* 'A single woman,' he finished unevenly.

'So no.' Go on, she urged herself fiercely. *Say it!* Acknowledge the reality of his life instead of your own wishful fantasy version of it. 'No girlfriends?' she finished, as carelessly as she could.

He shook his head. 'Certainly not—for I would consider that disrespectful. I indulge my very natural appetites when I am abroad, never here, and always in the utmost privacy. One day, of course, I will marry. And then my bed will be shared by my….wife.'

The question she'd asked and the answer she'd dreaded now caused her pain, but somehow Frankie's polite smile didn't slip. 'You seem to have your future all mapped out.'

'Of course. It comes with the territory.' He shrugged. 'Though in a way, it is easy for me. I do not have the luxury of choice—for it is my destiny. I will take a wife of pure Khayarzahian stock and thus ensure the continuation of the noble bloodline.'

'But isn't that a little…*old-fashioned*?'

He ate another grape, his teeth biting into the flesh, and a little rush of juice sweetened his mouth. 'More than a little—but I do not take issue with that. I am, as has been acknowledged many times, an old-fashioned man. It is the way things are here and, besides, much of modern life is flawed—you know that as well as I do, Francesca.'

'So you don't resent it?' she questioned, as some vital need to know drove her on. 'The fact that for you there *is* no choice—that you must take a bride who is expected of you, rather than choosing one of your own free will?'

His eyes glittered as he leaned back against the mound of brocade cushions. 'There is no point in railing against the inevitable. And choice can be a poisoned chalice,' he added softly. 'It inspires greed and makes people discontented with their lot. Couples seek perfection in relationships, something which is simply not possible—and when that perfection fails to materialise, they go looking for it elsewhere. Look at your divorce rate in the west and ask yourself whether choice is such a good thing.'

It was not the answer that Frankie had secretly been hoping for—for wasn't it true that deep down she had *wanted* him to rail against his fate? To shake an angry fist at the empty air and admit that he longed to follow his heart. But he had done the very opposite and had sounded as if he meant every word of it. She bit her lip as she stared down at her hands, which lay clasped in her lap. Because surely she wasn't stupid enough to consider herself a candidate for his heart?

'And besides,' he continued softly, 'I will make sure that my bride is beautiful, as well as suitable—so it will be no hardship to spend my life with her.'

The truth hurt, she realised—it hurt like crazy.

She raised her head to look at him. His face was illuminated by the light from the lamps and his high cheekbones cast angled shadows upon his burnished skin. And suddenly she wanted the evening to end and to be alone with her aching heart in the privacy of her room. 'Am I supposed to wait until you retire—or am I allowed to go to bed now?' she asked.

Silently, Zahid cursed her question, wondering if it was as innocent as it sounded—for he knew a million women who would have asked it with something other than sleep on their minds. 'You are tired?' he queried coolly.

'Very.' She kept her voice brisk, knowing that this was how it was going to have to be. She was going to have to remain crisp and bright and professional—and bury all those stupid romantic dreams once and for all. 'It's been a long day.'

'Indeed it has.' Gracefully, he rose to his feet in a shimmer of silk, shaking his head emphatically at one of the servants who immediately stepped forward. He rapped out an order in his native tongue before gesturing to Francesca. 'Come, I will take you there myself.'

Smoothing down her tunic, Frankie scrambled to her feet. 'There's no need for you to do that, Zahid.'

'There is every need—for you will only lose yourself in the vast corridors of my palace,' he drawled, without stopping to ask himself why he had not let the servant accompany her.

Their footfall and the soft swish of Zahid's robes brushing over the marble floor were the only sounds to be heard as they made their way through the long passageways. That and the loud thunder of Frankie's heart as she followed him.

She forced herself to register landmarks along the way even though the arching pillars and intricate mosaics all looked very similar. And then Zahid came to a halt by her room and turned, his eyes glittering ebony in the dim light.

'Here we are. Safely delivered to your door.'

'Thank you very much.' But she didn't feel *safe* as she stared up into the hawklike features and the lash-framed shards of his black eyes. She felt…what? As if danger and excitement were shimmering in the air around them, as tangible as any aura. One step and she could be in his arms, locked in the powerful circle of his embrace. And wasn't that what she yearned for—the culmination of all those years of wistful longing?

Afterwards, she wondered if she communicated something of her desire to him—for why else did he lift his hand to her cheek and lay it there, like a blessing?

'Goodnight, Francesca,' he said softly.

'Goodnight,' she whispered back. The warmth of his hand against her skin was beguiling and she turned her head, just by a fraction—but enough for her lips to graze against his palm. It hadn't been intentional—or at least, she didn't think it was—but it was enough to make him expel a sudden, shuddering breath of air.

'Are you trying to test my resolve?' he demanded unsteadily, but he left his hand exactly where it was and he could feel the warmth of her breath against his skin as she mouthed a single word.

'No.'

Slowly, his thumb began to trace the trembling outline of her lips. 'I'm not sure that I believe you.'

'I'm no…no…liar, Zahid.'

'No.' He knew that. But suddenly he wanted her to be. He wanted her to be devious and manipulative so that his conscience would allow him to pull her into his arms and start making love to her. He wanted her to be *something*—something other than this fresh-faced and blue-eyed girl he'd known for ever, who was making him feel a desire he had no earthly right to feel.

He gave a low laugh as he tilted her face upwards, but his mood was dark as well as anticipatory for deep down he knew this was wrong. *And shouldn't he be the one to stop it—stop it now, before it was too late?*

'Zahid?'

Her tentative question crept into the stillness of the night and hung there.

'Maybe we should stop torturing ourselves and just

give into the inevitable,' he bit out. 'Because what's the point of fighting something neither of us has the heart to fight?' And without giving her a chance to respond, he pulled her into his arms and drove his mouth down on hers in a kiss which had been much too long in the waiting.

Caught off guard by the heated pressure of his lips, Frankie swayed, but he pulled her even closer, so that she could feel the hardness of his body and the wild beat of his heart through the silk of his robes. She should have been daunted by all that unashamed masculinity—but somehow she wasn't. How could she be when he was kissing her with a passion which was overwhelming her—*swamping* her with a rush of pure pleasure? Simon had never made her feel like *this*.

She felt both weak and strong—any lingering doubts vanquished by the sheer potency of Zahid's hungry male body as it pressed against hers. It was as if she'd accidentally fallen into a stream and been taken up by a powerful current—then finding that she was too helpless to fight against it. *And she didn't want to fight against it. She wanted this, and more of this. More of him.*

'Z-Zahid.' With another breathless moan, Frankie reached up—wanting to tangle her fingers in the thick darkness of his hair. But his head was covered and as her fingers met the barrier of his headdress they halted there—unsure of what to do next.

Zahid froze. The soft yielding of her body was intoxicating—but a woman touching his headdress was a rare enough action to make him jerk back and stop kissing her. He only ever made love in western clothes, he realised—and the irony of that didn't escape him.

For once he would not have the tiresome unzipping of trousers and unbuttoning of shirts—because the loose form of his silken robes would allow him almost instant access to her…

And for once it was not going to happen…

Reaching up, he caught hold of her hand and pulled it away from his head, aware of the pulse which hammered so frantically through the delicate skin at her wrist. What had he been *thinking* of? Did all the noble pronouncements he'd made about women at dinner count for nothing?

Yet as he stared down at the disappointed trembling of her lips he recognised how easy it would be to take her. One swift and seamless de-robement and he could be deep inside her, driving into her moist warmth and spilling his seed. Was she as easy as this for all men? he wondered, his mouth tightening with fury.

'This wasn't supposed to happen!' he ground out as he took a step away from her.

Distractedly, she nodded—aware of the soft pooling of desire which was making her feel as weak as a kitten. 'No, I know it wasn't,' she whispered. 'B-but—'

'No buts, Francesca,' he put in fiercely. 'Definitely no buts.' With an angry growl, he opened the bedroom door, his hands infinitely more gentle than his words.

'Just go to sleep,' he said roughly—and with that, Zahid pushed her inside the gilded bedroom and firmly closed the door behind her.

CHAPTER NINE

'SO WHERE exactly are we going?' Frankie injected what she thought was just the right amount of polite interest into her voice as she sat back in the passenger seat of the enormous four-wheel drive.

To hell and back, thought Zahid grimly. Sharply, he turned the key in the ignition and eased away into the shining brightness of the desert morning. 'To the new horse-racing stadium, so that you can see it for yourself before you start work on the diaries. I want you to give me your opinion on how well you think the women's facilities are being catered for—as honestly as only you can, Frankie.'

Great, thought Frankie, blinking her eyes furiously behind the welcome covering of her shades, not knowing if she was trying to hold off tears or tiredness. You get rejected by yet another man and spend a long sleepless night thinking about him—and then he tells you that your day will be spent inspecting the 'women's facilities' at Khayarzah's new racing track. It really didn't get much worse than that, did it?

'Fine with me.' Forcing a neutral smile, she risked a glance at the hawklike profile and hard, unsmiling lips. 'Why are you driving—and not one of your chauffeurs?'

Zahid's hands tightened on the steering wheel. Why did she think he was driving? Wasn't it obvious? To give him something to do other than give into the temptation of finishing off what they'd started last night. Something to look at other than the soft temptation of her lips and thinking about where on his body he would like them to be placed. He glanced in his mirror to see the dark shape of the security car behind, which was shadowing them.

'I like to drive. Especially in the desert. The roads are flat and straight and you can put your foot right down in a way you can't do anywhere else in the world.'

'Right.' Frankie settled back in her seat. Think positive, she told herself. Don't let him realise that you're hurting, or that you can't stop thinking about the hot brush of his lips and the way he made you feel when he held you in his arms last night. She forced herself to concentrate on the road ahead. 'Well, I quite like driving myself—so maybe later on, I can have a go.'

There was the split second of a pause. 'I'm afraid that won't be possible,' he said pleasantly.

'Really? I'm sure that as Sheikh you can get me emergency cover on your car insurance, Zahid.'

He bit back a reluctant smile. 'It's nothing to do with the insurance. It's a very powerful machine.'

If she hadn't been feeling so pent-up and rejected she might have just let that go. But now Frankie was pleased to have something to concentrate on other than the fact that for the first time in her life she was experiencing an intense kind of frustration.

'Fortunately I passed my driving test on the first attempt,' she said sweetly. 'And not just the section for "delicate little women who shouldn't be allowed behind the wheel of a big car".' A new sense of determination filled her. 'So I'd like to have a go at driving, if that's all right with you.'

'Actually, it is not,' he said, flexing his fingers as he anticipated her reaction to his next statement. 'I'm afraid women aren't allowed to drive in my country.'

This time the pause was longer. 'You *are* kidding?'

He shot her a glance. Today she was wearing a tunic and trousers in ice-blue—a cool and untouchable contrast to the hot question which burst from her lips. 'No, I'm not.'

'Women aren't allowed to drive?' she verified, and when he gave a terse nod she raked her fingers back through her hair in agitation. 'Why not?'

Zahid's hands tightened around the steering wheel. He had brought her here to type his father's diaries—not to challenge him or the laws of his land!

'Don't ask me, the laws have been in place for decades.' Frankie's lips fell open as she turned her head to look at him.

'I keep thinking that you're going to come out with some sort of punchline and tell me that it's some kind of joke.'

'I know it seems outdated to you—and to me in fact. But the previous sheikh was not a moderniser. His view—which is still shared by many—was that men and women should not mix freely. At the moment it's just the way things are.'

'I realise that now—and I assume that's the same reason you won't let women go to university.' She saw him nod his head before turning on him angrily. 'But *why* would you stop women from mixing freely with men?'

'Because it is felt that women need to be protected.'

'From who—or what, exactly?'

'From men, of course—and from themselves!'

'And you call that protection?' Frankie shook her head. 'Some people might reasonably describe it as a kind of prison.'

'It depends on your point of view.' Zahid put his foot down on the accelerator. 'Proximity equals sex—and sex before marriage isn't always a good thing. You should know that better than anyone, Francesca—since the man to whom you gave yourself is no longer a part of your future. What a waste of time *that* was.'

If he hadn't made her so angry then she might have told him that he was leaping to false conclusions. As it was, his arrogant statement so irked her that she turned the accusation on *him*.

'So you go away on your foreign trips and have as much sex as you want, on the clear understanding that you will one day return home to marry a Khayarzahian virgin?' she demanded as a hot little spear of jealousy lanced through her like a sabre.

He shrugged. 'I am now the king,' he said quietly. 'And that is what is expected of me.'

And despite knowing that he was a victim of his own circumstances, Frankie could not bite back her burning sense of injustice. 'Meaning that it's one rule for men and another for women?'

He looked in his rear mirror. 'I'm afraid so,' he answered, softly. 'And it has always been that way, no matter how much the feminists might protest.'

Frankie stared out of the window as the car shot along the long and straight desert road and tried to quell her rising tide of indignation. What century did he think he was he living in?

'Well, if men and women should not be mixing freely in Khayarzah—then why on earth did you bring me here?'

Behind his shades, Zahid's eyes narrowed as the roads became fringed with towering date trees, and he slowed down to pass a horse-drawn cart which contained sacks of rice. He felt the familiar flicker of lust licking at his groin. 'You think I haven't already asked myself that very question and realised that I was mistaken in doing so?'

'In what way mistaken?' she flashed back.

For a moment, he didn't answer. But was there any point in pretending, after what had happened last night? One stupid little kiss which had dominated his thoughts ever since, no matter how hard he tried to push it aside. One kiss which had made him wonder whether there was any point in holding back any more. One kiss which had kept him hard and aching all night long and which was making him hard right now… 'Thinking that I could resist you. That resisting you would be a useful test in self-control.'

'But you *did* resist me,' she pointed out. 'So you've passed your stupid test.'

He gave a short laugh. 'I can't believe I'm having this conversation with you.'

'Neither can I.' But even as she said it Frankie realised that it wasn't quite true. Because despite the fundamental disagreements which lay at the heart of their heated discussion, she was aware of an intimacy which existed between her and Zahid, which had never been there with Simon. Was that because she'd known the sheikh for so many years that she felt she could be *herself* with him, no matter how huge the differences in their circumstances? Because she'd known him as a *person* before this inconvenient sexual attraction had reared its seductive head?

'Look over there,' he said suddenly. 'We are skirting the outskirts of Calathara, which is our second biggest city—famous for its diamonds and carpets and the sweetest oranges on the planet. And if you look carefully you'll see the stadium in the distance.'

She was relieved to be able to change the subject and as they approached the stadium it was difficult not to be impressed by the amount of money and work which had clearly been poured into the new building. A gleam of chrome and glass rose up to greet them and Frankie studied the sleek design as she stepped from the car to greet the now-familiar deputation which awaited them.

Walking just behind Zahid, she marvelled at the state-of-the-art racetrack, whose lush grass track curved like an emerald snake—made all the more startling by its stark desert location. She'd once gone to a Boxing Day race meeting in England with her father—but the racecourse had been nothing like this.

Here, no expense had been spared. Not anywhere. Everything was brand-new and the very best that money could buy. There were dining rooms and function rooms—as well as fabulous facilities for the horses and their jockeys. The women's section was separate and lavish, filled with beautiful containers of showy orchids, and there was a dazzling array of French perfumes and soaps in the washrooms.

In one of the executive dining rooms, they drank strong, sweet coffee from dinky little cups and ate cake which had been flavoured with honey and cardamom. And Frankie thought how animated and proud Zahid seemed as they sipped at their coffee.

'I want to make this track part of the international circuit,' he said. 'And for the Khayarzah Cup to be one of the most treasured trophies of the twenty-first century—on a par with the prizes offered at Ascot and Cheltenham and Melbourne.' He put down his cup and looked at her. 'So what do you think of it?

'I think it's superb.'

Zahid gave a satisfied smile. 'It is, isn't it?'

'I also think it's a contradiction.'

His eyes narrowed. 'I'm sorry?'

Frankie wondered whether she would have been saying all this if he'd come into her room last night and made love to her. Would she have been quite so keen to find fault if that had been the case? But it wasn't *fault*, she told herself fiercely. It was a legitimate opinion—and one which he had asked for.

She clasped her hands together. 'You're hoping to attract an international clientele?'

'Of course. It won't work without one.'

'Well, I can tell you right now, Zahid, that independent women will not tolerate being forbidden to drive. How are you proposing they get around?'

'There will be taxis. Chauffeurs.' He gave a soft laugh. 'Show me a woman who doesn't like having a driver—though I doubt you will be able to produce one.'

Impatiently, she shook her head. 'You're missing the point. Women may like being chauffeured around but they will see the driving ban as completely unreasonable. They won't want their liberty being curtailed.'

'Then let them stay away!'

'Meaning their powerful husbands might stay away, too—and then where will you be? You won't have successful horse races if you're playing to an empty stadium!'

Zahid tensed. Why had he thought that bringing her out here was a good idea? It was supposed to be as a favour to *her*—to give her a break after the demise of her disastrous relationship. And yes, he had tailor-made a job for her, but for that he expected her unquestioning loyalty. He certainly hadn't expected to have to endure a tirade of criticism. A nerve flickered at his temple. 'You are perfectly entitled to your opinion, Francesca. Just don't expect me to agree with it.'

'So you only employ people who tell you what you want to hear?' she suggested softly.

Zahid stilled. Enough was enough! Why, he was according her all kinds of privilege and yet she could not show him even a modicum of common courtesy! He stood up.

'Let's go,' he said abruptly.

She knew he was angry, but she didn't care; she was angry herself—she just wasn't sure why. Or maybe she was and she didn't want to admit it.

She heard him saying something terse in his native tongue to the bodyguards who had followed them and then, having made their farewells to the various dignitaries, the two of them made their way to the car in complete silence.

As the car pulled away Frankie stared out of the window at the startlingly clear line of the distant horizon and deep blue of the desert sky. She saw the sizzle of heat shimmering off the sand and wondered why her heart felt as if it had been plunged into ice-water.

Beside her, Zahid simmered with unspoken rage as he drove and she was aware that she was witnessing a very royal *sulk*. Well, let him sulk! And did he really have to drive that fast?

'You're driving very fast, Zahid.'

'And?'

She bit back a smile at his unashamed arrogance—and yet that made her even angrier. She didn't *want* to smile. She wanted to… Her fingertips strayed to her mouth.

'Don't bite your nails, Francesca.'

'Why, are women forbidden to do *that*, as well?'

He swallowed. She really *was* outrageous. Feisty and fearless and not afraid to say what was on her mind. Shifting a little, he tried in vain to dispel some of the dull ache he felt deep in his groin. He was aware of her own body language, which was making her sit so rigidly in the passenger seat, even if he hadn't been able to detect the steadily escalating sexual tension in the air around them.

Out of the corner of his eye, he could see her cross one slim and silk-clad leg over the other and, no matter how hard he tried, he couldn't prevent himself from imagining her naked. What would her nipples be like? he wondered distractedly. Like tiny, puckered rose-buds crowning a soft and creamy breast? Or large pale pink discs which he could slowly encircle with his tongue?

His erotic imaginings proved too much and suddenly the barriers he had erected between them came tumbling down. His fingers gripped the steering wheel as his mind and his body went to war. Who was he trying to protect by not making love to her—when she was clearly a feisty woman who had made it plain that she despised inequality?

She didn't *want* protection. She wanted him.

And he wanted her.

He glanced in the driving mirror to see the tail-car behind them and as he pressed down hard on the accelerator he saw it begin to retreat until it was nothing more than a tiny black dot in the distance.

He drove with a new sense of purpose, the powerful vehicle eating up the undemanding miles of the desert road, until at last he turned left, down a small track lined with tall cacti, and Frankie was certain that she could see the distant gleam of water in the distance.

Her forehead creased in a frown and she felt the sudden prickling of her skin. 'Where...where are we going, Zahid?'

He recognised that it was a loaded question—and he was careful not to be evasive as he slowed the car down. She should have the opportunity to reject him, even if he knew, deep down, that she wasn't going to.

'I have my own, private house nearby. It's where I go to escape sometimes.' He paused, meaningfully. 'I thought you might like to see it.'

Something in the silky darkness of his tone washed over her senses and Frankie's heart began to hammer as she recognised the unmistakable desire which underpinned his question. This wasn't a guided tour of one of his properties he was offering—his intention was made perfectly clear by the hot sparking of his black eyes.

For a moment she felt intensely vulnerable—but the feeling quickly melted away as she recognised that this opportunity might never come again. That this was the culmination of all her dreams. She bit her lip. She had wanted Zahid for as long as she could remember—and years of wistful fantasy now stood a chance of coming true.

'I'd love to see it,' she said steadily.

CHAPTER TEN

THERE was no finesse. No honeyed words which preceded a leisurely and sophisticated seduction. There was barely even time to take in the surprisingly modern building—for no sooner had the door of Zahid's private house closed behind them than he pulled Frankie into his arms. For a moment, his hands framed her face as he looked down into the wide-spaced blue eyes and the high colour which was splashed over her cheekbones.

'Francesca,' he grated. 'God help me for doing this.'

'Then God help me, too,' she whispered.

And then they were in each other's arms and kissing as if it had just been invented. Only for Frankie, maybe it just had—because no kiss could ever have prepared her for *this*. Her arms wrapped themselves tightly around his neck and she clung to him like some kind of rampant vine while their mouths locked and their tongues played intimate little dances. With a groan, he pulled her closer into his body. She could feel the hot throb of his need pressing urgently against her and, although she should have found it daunting, it did nothing but make her wriggle her body impatiently against his.

With an effort, he tore himself away from her and saw the dark bewilderment in her eyes.

'What is it?' she whispered.

He shook his head. 'Not here. Come with me. I want to do this properly.'

Properly. It was a word steeped in both sensuality and formality and Frankie gave a shiver of anticipation as he took her hand in his and led her into a room off the main area which was dominated by an enormous bed. She was dimly aware of an extraordinary light from outside—which was quickly muted when Zahid pressed a button recessed into one of the walls and blinds floated down to blot out the day.

'Now…' Lifting his hands, he tangled his fingers in the satin spill of her dark hair and could feel the soft butt of her breasts as he pulled her close to kiss her again. And it was torture. The sweetest and most exquisite torture he could imagine. If it had been anyone else, he would have taken her swiftly and left the slow love-making until afterwards, when his urgent hunger had been satisfied. But he did not want to take her like that. Not Francesca. He wanted to do it slow and he wanted her naked. To see every glorious inch of her.

'Let's rid ourselves of these damned clothes, shall we?'

Frankie's heart was racing as he brushed his lips negligently over hers. Half of her was afraid to let him go—terrified that he might change his mind and decide that his wretched self-control was more important than this. But the old familiar nerves which she had been dreading had so far failed to make an appearance. 'Oh, Zahid,' she whispered. 'Yes, please.'

With one movement and the swift gleam of a smile,

he tore off his headdress—to reveal the familiar raven-blue gleam of his hair. 'Lift up your arms,' he said unsteadily.

Where were all those paralysing insecurities now? she wondered. Banished by the urgency of her desire for him, that was where. She did as he commanded, so that he was able to skim off her tunic, and then the silken trousers were removed in one fluid movement. She realised that her mediocre bra and panties were on show and that maybe this was the point where she should have felt self-conscious. Yet the hot look of approbation which glittered from his eyes made her thrill with a potent kind of pride and suddenly she forgot the fact that she was wearing chain-store underwear.

Impatiently, he pulled off his own clothing and suddenly Frankie felt a wave of shyness as she realised that he was completely naked beneath it. The robes fell to the ground in a whisper and her cheeks flamed as she saw the hard, lean body and the proud evidence of his arousal.

'You like what you see?' he murmured.

Too dazed to speak, she nodded her head, even though she was certainly no expert. But she liked what she saw in Zahid's body—all burnished skin covering honed and powerful muscle. More importantly, she liked the man inside it—in spite of his outrageously outdated attitudes and cavalier air.

Her skin and her body felt as if they were on fire as, impatiently, he pushed aside a cashmere throw and drew her down onto the smooth, satin surface of the bed.

'Zahid…' She closed her eyes as he peeled off her bra and panties and brought her close to his naked body.

'Mmm?'

'It's…' His fingers were tiptoeing over her breasts—teasing the achingly aroused and puckered nipples and then letting his palms spread deliciously over them, covering them like a warm blanket.

'What is it, *anisah bahiya*?' he murmured. 'Is it like a little piece of heaven that we have found here on earth?'

'Yes, *yes*—that's exactly it! Oh! Oh!' Now his lips were on her breasts and his fingers were snaking their way down over her belly as the feeling of warmth grew into one of molten heat.

She should have felt shy when he touched her where she most longed to be touched, but how could she be shy about entering the little piece of heaven he had so rightly described? And should she be touching *him*? What would a man like Zahid expect from his lover?

Tentatively, her fingertips reached down to brush against his manhood. It felt like silk and steel, she thought, before her hand was swiftly removed from his flesh as if she had been caught pick-pocketing.

'No, *anisah*,' he murmured regretfully as he kissed each finger in turn. 'Not this time—for you have made me so aroused that I do not trust myself. I am like a novice in your arms and if you touch me again like that, it will all be over.' It was, he realised with a sudden start, the most intimate thing he had ever said to a woman. But his thoughts reminded him of one vital omission and he reached into the cabinet beside the bed to extract a condom, stroking it on with a strange and unmistakable reluctance. And there was a conversation he still needed to have with her…

He moved over her, his arousal pressing provocatively between her thighs, but he forced himself to say what he knew he owed her, even if it meant that the mood might be destroyed and the moment lost for ever.

'Francesca...'

Her eyes fluttered open in question; she was terrified that he might be about to change his mind. 'What?'

'It is not the right time to say this—and yet if I wait, it will be too late.'

'S-say what?'

'You...you do not expect this to lead to something permanent?' he questioned unevenly. 'Because it can never be. You do realise that?'

Frankie stared up into the shifting shadows of his face, momentarily cursing his sense of timing. The heartbreaking words left her in no doubt of his feelings for her, but that didn't change a thing. 'Of course I don't. I just want...' What did she want? To feel as other women felt? To experience pleasure with a man she had always adored? Should she tell him the secret she had kept buttoned up inside her? She looked up at the bowed outline of his lips—so close that she could feel the warmth of his breath on her face.

And if she told him, then what? Would he stop? Yes, she realised, with an instinct she instantly trusted. He *would* stop. Even if it took a supreme effort of will which would defeat most men—Zahid would somehow manage it.

'What do you want, Francesca?' he murmured.

No. She would not tell him. At least, not yet. 'I want...*you*.'

'Then you shall have me.' His lips grazed hers as he moved over her, his fingers moving between her thighs to part her moist flesh in readiness. Grasping his manhood, he brushed provocatively against her honeyed heat. 'You shall have me right…*now*.'

Urgently, he thrust inside her—but the warning bells rang too late. It happened before Zahid properly realised what was happening—before his disbelieving senses could piece together all the facts. The brief barrier. The momentary resistance to his deep thrust before he broke through into a place of such sweet, wet tightness that he groaned aloud. The tiny whimpering sound of pain she made confirmed his worst suspicions but by then it was too late and anger melded with passion and became an unstoppable mix.

'Zahid!' She gave a soft gasp as he tightened his hold on her.

'Relax,' he instructed throatily as he began to move inside her. 'Let go.'

'Oh, Zahid,' she said again, more brokenly this time.

He'd never known love-making like it—even though it tested every reserve he possessed. Time and time he held back from giving into his orgasm—determined that her first time would be memorable for the right reasons. Or at least *some* of the right reasons, he thought grimly as his fingers gripped the satin of her thighs to drive into her even deeper.

Her head turned wildly against the pillow as she began to make soft, moaning sounds—and when at last he sensed the change in her, he drew back to watch it happen. Saw the slow arching of her back and the rosy flowering over her breasts. Heard the fevered entreaty gasped from her parted lips as her orgasm captured her.

Even before her spasms had stilled, he sensed the inevitability of his own release and felt it like nothing he had ever felt before. Everything paled in comparison to those fleeting moments of pure pleasure. Every milestone of his life, every battle fought and victory won—he would have traded them all for this one moment of delicious weakness with Francesca O'Hara.

But afterwards, when his body had begun to quieten, his thoughts began to race. Slowly, he withdrew from her—taking a moment to compose himself before turning her towards him, steeling his heart against the trickle of a tear which slid down her cheek.

It was long moments before he could bring himself to speak and when he did, his words shot out like bullets. The only woman he had thought he could trust—and she had deceived him in the most fundamental way of all.

'So,' he said heavily. 'Are you going to give me some kind of explanation?'

She heard the sudden coolness in his voice and Frankie's heart sank as some of her joy began to evaporate. Couldn't the interrogation wait? Couldn't he just let her revel in this feeling—let her enjoy the sense of warmth and closeness she was experiencing right now? Surely she was allowed to spin out her hopeless fantasies about her dark and brooding lover for just a little longer.

'You mean about—'

'Please don't make it worse by playing games with me, Francesca. It seems you've done enough game-playing to last a lifetime.' Angrily, he wiped away the tear which shimmered on her cheek and which seemed to reproach him. Why hadn't she told him before it was too late? 'You know exactly what I mean.'

'About me being…' Her voice tailed off because the

word seemed like an unwanted intruder and the dark look on his face filled her with trepidation.

'A virgin. A *virgin*!' He shook his head in disbelief as he rolled away from her, reaching down to grab the cashmere throw, which had tumbled to the floor during their love-making and thrusting it at her, not wanting to look at her pink and white nakedness. He saw her move one milky thigh to reveal the secret, dark fuzz of hair and felt the rapid escalation of his heart. 'Cover yourself up!'

Frankie was grateful for the blanket, tugging it over herself with trembling fingers as she stared at him with apprehensive eyes.

'Why didn't you tell me?' he demanded.

'Because I knew you would stop if I did—'

'Damned right I would have stopped!'

'And I didn't want you to,' she said, in a small voice.

Her wide-eyed honesty took him aback and almost made him melt, until he reminded himself of what she had done and the repercussions of her actions. 'You didn't have sex with Simon?' he queried, then gave a short laugh as he realised the ridiculous nature of his question. 'Clearly not, as I've just discovered for myself.' He looked at her, trying to steel himself against the softness of her lips and the blue temptation of her darkened eyes. 'The question is, why not?'

She felt as if she were on a witness stand—suddenly expected to mount her own defence with little or no preparation. And her only defence was the truth, Frankie realised—even if it opened her up to the charge of being too trusting and too vulnerable.

'Because I was...*nervous* whenever Simon touched

me.' Awkwardly, she wriggled her shoulders. 'I sort of...*froze*.'

'You didn't act very nervous just now.' And she certainly hadn't frozen.

She swallowed but the candid question still sparked from his black eyes. Did he want her to spell it out for him, detail by cringe-making detail—and inflate his already over-inflated ego into the bargain? Did she admit that she'd been stupid enough to get engaged to a man who hadn't made her feel a modicum of what she felt for the brooding sheikh? That she had only just discovered what real passion and desire could feel like?

'You made me feel relaxed,' she said simply. 'No, maybe that's the wrong word. You made me feel...' She gave another rueful shrug of her shoulders—for surely there was no place for coyness now. 'Wanton, I guess. Which he never did. He told me that day when I went to see him that I was basically...frigid. And I believed him.' She stopped while Zahid said something very profound in his native tongue, her heart beating hopefully as he pulled the cashmere throw over him as well, so that she could feel the heat from his body as he drew closer. 'Anyway, maybe I should be grateful that we didn't have sex.' Her voice wobbled a little. 'Not if he was sleeping with somebody else at the time.'

Zahid gave a ragged sigh as he stared at the ceiling, cursing the man who had hurt her and cursing his own hot-blooded impetuosity. How bloody complicated life could be at times, he thought. The best sex he'd ever had and it had been with his oldest friend—who had now wasted her virginity on him and given him a whole new layer of unwanted responsibility towards her. Was this not the most impossible of all situations?

'You know what kind of man I am, Francesca,' he said furiously. 'As King, I will be expected to marry a virgin—but it will have to be a woman from my own culture,' he ran on hastily, in case she should think that she now qualified for the position. 'Not a foreigner.'

Frankie was glad that he was looking at the ceiling because otherwise he might have seen the hurt which had criss-crossed over her face. How unwittingly cruel he could be. Did he think she was now angling for marriage, simply because he had been the first man she'd had sex with? Did he imagine that she had withheld the information from him in order to put herself in a powerful position?

But it took her only moments to compose herself. Why *should* he feel guilt about what had just happened, when in a way—she *had* misled him? Yet she hadn't kept quiet about her innocence because she had some form of agenda. She had done it because she'd wanted Zahid more than anything else in the world. She had wanted him to be the man to introduce her to the world of sex. And she had done it because she…well, she *liked* him. That was all. Surely that was something which could be celebrated instead of regretted?

Beneath the superfine cashmere, she stretched her glowing body and the movement made him turn his head to look at her, his eyes narrowing as she gave him a tentative smile.

'I don't want to fall out about it,' she said softly, and with that she reached out her hand to cup the jut of his jaw. She could feel the rasp of new growth there and traced her thumb over his lips, not surprised when he caught it between his teeth and gave it a tiny nip.

'Neither do I,' he growled.

'So couldn't we…couldn't we forget it ever happened?'

'Are you crazy?' The absurdity of her statement stirred him into action and he rolled closer, pulling her against his warm and newly aroused body. And then he sighed. 'No, you're just inexperienced—and in a way, it's a bit of a pity that you've started with the best.'

She bristled at the implication behind his words. 'You mean that no lover will ever match you?'

That hadn't been what he'd meant at all. He'd meant that sex rarely felt this good—especially given that it was her first time. He wondered why that was, before quickly dismissing the thought. The whys and wherefores were irrelevant—it was the facts they had to deal with. And the fact was that he had just made love to his sweet virginal Francesca and he wanted to do it again.

'I doubt it,' he told her honestly.

'Why, you arrogant—'

He silenced her with the brush of his lips. 'Arrogance is sometimes the truth, *anisah*,' he said sombrely.

When he spoke like that—how could she resist him? When his black eyes looked as deep and as dark as ink and she just wanted to write her name with them…

'Oh, Zahid.'

'Zahid, what?'

She shook her head, shrugged her shoulders helplessly so that the throw slipped down. 'I don't know,' she whispered.

And neither did he. All he could think about was the distracting softness of her warm breasts and her evocative feminine scent, which seemed to have invaded his senses. His lips brushing against her shoulder, he slid his fingers between her thighs as he gave into a temptation he had no desire to resist. Why mar this beautiful experience with troublesome questions which could easily wait?

Lowering his mouth onto hers, he gave a low moan as his kiss blotted everything except the hungry clamour of their bodies.

CHAPTER ELEVEN

THE finger which was stroking circles on her belly suddenly stilled and Frankie made a little sound which was midway between pleasure and protest.

'That's nice,' she whispered.

'I know it is. Too damned nice.' With a quick and disbelieving glance at his watch, Zahid saw that it was two hours since they had left the racing stadium. Two hours which hadn't been scheduled into his busy itinerary, which had been spent exploring her sweet body. With an effort, he pushed aside the covers and forced himself to get out of bed and away from the warm lure of her arms. For a woman who was new to sex she had certainly embraced it with enthusiasm. He had never imagined that she could be so deliciously *imaginative.*

'We can't lie around in bed any longer, Francesca—my bodyguards will be wondering what the hell I am doing.'

His mouth hardened. Actually, they would probably have a pretty good idea of what he was doing, he realised—and it was his own stupid fault. He had broken all the rules by bringing Francesca to his private house and spending the whole afternoon making love to her.

'Zahid—'

'Not now. We'd better get dressed and on our way.' Brutally, his words cut across hers—he was terrified that she might make another breathy little sound, which would compel him to start exploring her hot and tight little body yet again. He stared down at her, naked on his bed. Dark hair spilled over her shoulders and her creamy thighs were parted indolently—and with a small groan he swallowed down his rising lust and backed away. 'Will you stop tempting me?' he demanded.

'But I'm not doing anything!'

Now was not the time to explain that she was managing to make him more aroused than he could ever remember feeling before. Because how could he possibly explain something he didn't understand? Instead, he forced his mind to practicalities. 'I'm afraid that we're going to have to wait until we get back to the palace to shower—if you can bear to.' Because they might as well have taken out a full-page advertisement in the *Khayarzah Times* if they suddenly reappeared with damp hair and flushed faces. Even if it meant that the return journey would be perfumed with the distinctive scent of sex. 'Francesca, will you *please* get up?'

Reluctantly, Frankie did as he asked—acutely aware of the fact that she was stark-naked in front of a man she'd known all her life. It felt strange to be getting dressed in such a bizarre setting—and stranger still to see Zahid, his back now averted, hurriedly pulling on his robes.

Locating her bag and finding a nearby bathroom, she freshened up as best she could. But when she returned to the bedroom, it was to find Zahid looking grim—and suddenly, her heart sank with a sense of dread. Was he going to tell her something she suspected he'd felt all along—that he'd just made the biggest mistake of his life?

'So...what happens now?' she asked in a small voice.

Expelling a sigh, he shook his head. If it had been anyone but Francesca, it would have been easy. He could have kissed and dismissed her with a promise to look her up when he was back in London. And then put her on the next plane home and forgotten all about her.

But it wasn't anyone else—and the very fact that it was Francesca was what made the whole situation so damned difficult. He had brought her here to give her a chance to forget her problems back in England—and had promptly added to those problems a hundredfold, by seducing her! *And to make matters worse, she had given him her virginity—the greatest gift a woman could give her lover. Wouldn't that make her clingy—even clingier than new lovers so often were?*

He needed to play it down. To show her that nothing need change. That their friendship could remain intact, if they handled it properly. 'We might be able to manage the situation,' he said slowly. 'If we are very careful.'

Frankie looked at him, fearing the worst—for she had seen the calculating expression which had suddenly hardened his features. 'Manage it?' she echoed cautiously.

He stared at the soft pink face she'd just washed and knew that he had to be straight with her. 'We've just crossed a forbidden line by making love,' he said.

Lips pursed, she nodded, even though he made it sound as if they'd committed some sort of *trespass*. 'I realise that.'

'And I ought to send you back to England straight away—for both our sakes.' He saw her face working as she tried desperately not to react to his words and he found himself wondering if his own reaction was mirroring hers. Could she sense his own reluctance to do that?

'But the thing is, that I don't want to send you back.'

A new note of hope entered her voice. 'You don't?'

'No. I want you to type up my father's diaries as planned.' He swallowed. 'And I want to carry on making love to you.'

'You…do?'

'Of course I do,' he growled. His eyes met hers, and he felt another urgent leap of desire as he registered her quick rise in colour. 'Isn't it crazy for us not to enjoy each other for a little longer?'

Frankie's cheeks burned and her heart raced. She agreed with every word he said, yet she wished he hadn't approached it quite so cold-bloodedly. Couldn't he have just pulled her into his arms and told her between urgent kisses that he couldn't bear to let her go—rather than making it sound like something which was on the agenda at a board meeting?

But Frankie recognised that it was an indication of Zahid's sense of decency that he was not blinding her with emotion, or trying to sway her with more glorious sex. He was putting an offer on the table into which nothing should be read. He was offering her a brief interlude—to be enjoyed by them both while it lasted.

What was there to think about?

'It might be crazy,' she whispered, 'but what's wrong with a little craziness from time to time?'

With a moan, he pulled her towards him—brushing his mouth over hers as if he had been starved of contact for days instead of mere minutes. He felt the thunder of his heart and the urgent hardening of his groin as her soft breasts pressed against him. 'We're going to have to be discreet at all times—because my servants are all-seeing,' he warned softly. 'We must not flaunt our affair in front of them, for that would also be disrespectful to them.'

And what about me? wondered Frankie with a touch of desperation as he whispered his lips over her hair. Did her feelings matter less than those of the servants?

But she recognised that she must not waste precious time wishing for the impossible. She must enjoy what was on offer and applaud Zahid's honesty towards her. He might not be giving her the fairy-tale version of a love affair, but at least he wasn't lying to her—and surely that was showing her respect of the most fundamental kind?

'Come on,' he said, with one last, lingering kiss. 'We'd better go.'

He reached down to press the remote control and the automatic blind floated back up over the window. Frankie blinked, realising that the exceptional brightness she'd noticed before was due to the reflection of sunlight on water. Walking over to the window, she peered out and in the distance she could see the shimmer of water and the unexpected lushness of green foliage.

'Is that a river?' she questioned, in surprise.

He went to stand beside her, his hand lingering briefly on the curve of her bottom. 'Indeed it is—we call it the Jamanah river, which means "silver pearl".' He looked down and shot her a mocking look. 'I suppose you thought that all desert kingdoms were entirely without water?'

'I try to avoid generalisations like that.' Frankie screwed up her eyes as she tried to remember back to her geography lessons. 'Does it happen to have its source outside the country?'

'Bravo,' he affirmed softly. 'It's what is known as an exotic river and it flows from the neighbouring country of Sharifah.'

'Isn't that the one you had all the wars with?'

He raised his eyebrows. 'Bravo again, Francesca. How on earth did you know that?'

'My father told me, of course. He was very interested in Khayarzahian history.'

'And you've remembered it all?'

'Most of it.' She smiled to herself as they left the house and got into the car. Of course she had remembered it all! Didn't she used to collect and store up facts about Zahid like other girls used to collect Barbie dolls? Because hadn't it always fascinated her, to learn what she could about the dark sheikh she so adored and the land which was so precious to him? 'I have a very retentive memory,' she said primly.

His gaze flicked over her. 'You are a surprising woman in many ways.'

'That sounds awfully like a compliment.'

'That's because it is,' he murmured.

Frankie glowed with pleasure as he started up the engine and in that moment she couldn't ever remember feeling happier. Bathed in the warm afterglow of sex, it was easy to forget that Zahid had warned her about any long-term hopes or dreams about their relationship.

Along the way, he pointed out landmarks and the country which she'd grown up hearing so much about slowly came to life. His voice lulled her with tales of battles fought by his ancestors as they drove along the straight and dusty road through the desert, while the sun set like blood on the sand which surrounded them.

It was only when they arrived back at the palace that a subtle change occurred in him. As soon as the ornate golden gates had clanged shut behind them he went from lover to King. His expression became as remote as the distant mountains and the closeness which she'd experienced in the car all but disappeared. There was no brief pressing of flesh or brush of skin against skin as they parted. No honeyed words of affection. Instead, his tone was clipped and flat.

'I must go to speak with my advisors,' he said. 'So I'll leave you with the opportunity to rest after your afternoon in the heat. Before dinner I'll show you the diaries and where you'll be working—so that tomorrow you may begin. How does that sound?'

'That sounds fine,' she answered awkwardly, aware of the formality which had suddenly entered his voice.

And that was that. Nothing more. He was gone with not even a secret shared look or smile to remind them of the intimacy which Frankie now remembered with almost painful clarity. Was it really possible that just a couple of hours ago she'd been naked in his arms and thrilling to the brand-new experience of being made love to? Yet now he was turning away from her as if she were a stranger.

She was standing watching him walk away when Fayruz appeared, as if she had been summoned. And maybe she had, thought Frankie. Probably all the palace machinery had started whirring the moment the sheikh had driven them into the palace forecourt.

At least there was enough time for Frankie to take

extra-special care in dressing and, after she'd dismissed the servant, she looked at the array of silk clothes in her wardrobes. What had Zahid said to her, in one of those quieter moments when his lips had grazed over hers and made her shiver with longing? That her eyes were the most beautiful blue he had ever seen—bluer even than the precious mosaic stones of lapis lazuli which studded the walls of his palace?

His words made her choose a tunic and trousers in deep sapphire blue and she twisted her hair up into a knot on top of her head. It was a bold look and one she wouldn't usually have dared try—but having a man like Zahid purring compliments like that did wonders for a woman's confidence.

Fayruz came to collect her an hour before dinner and took her to where Zahid was waiting in the palace's ancient library. It was an exquisite gilded room, lined with the most beautiful books she had ever seen.

His black eyes were watchful as she walked in, but the faint curve of his smile was unmistakable, even to her. Frankie might not have been the most experienced woman on the block, but she could tell that her lover approved of her appearance. She stood before him as he dismissed Fayruz, wondering if he might quickly pull her into his arms and murmur his appreciation. But the complete absence of softness on his face made her feel nervous.

Nonetheless, her mounting nerves were suddenly subdued by the sight of the intricately inlaid box which stood on a nearby table and which he opened to reveal a neat stack of leather notebooks inside.

All thoughts and worries about her relationship with Zahid were forgotten in the light of this tangible slice of history and Frankie reached into the box with eager care, gently withdrawing the nearest volume.

The pages were a little dry but completely intact and the flowing handwriting was—thankfully—extremely legible. Some pages were full of closely written script, while others—clearly written in times of great trouble or stress—were more bald and succinct. How her father would have loved to have seen these, she thought as her gaze skimmed over them.

After a few minutes she remembered where she was and she looked up to find Zahid watching her with a curiously intent look in his black eyes.

'I gather you like what you see,' he observed.

'I do—and I can't wait to start,' she said.

And at this, Zahid gave a rueful smile. Had he thought that she might be difficult to deal with—having had time to reflect on her sexual awakening? Imagining that she might become demanding—or start behaving inappropriately? Yet there was none of the limpet-like looks he'd anticipated—nor any soft reproachful comments that he hadn't kissed her.

No, she was currently picking up another volume of his father's work and looking as if she would like to sit down at one of the nearby tables and begin reading it from cover to cover right now! It was the first time in his life that he had ever been overlooked by someone deep in a book!

'Are you not hungry, Francesca?' he questioned drily.

Blinking, she glanced up from the diary. 'Hungry? Yes, of course I am.'

'Then perhaps you could bear to endure having dinner with me before losing yourself in my father's work.' He arched her a sardonic look as he saw her reluctantly close the book and he smiled as he saw a glimpse of the earnest schoolgirl she had once been. 'You can start transcribing first thing in the morning. Come on, let's go and eat.'

Frankie felt a sense of unreality as she walked beside him through the marble corridors. In those few moments she felt so close to him and yet so far apart. If it had been anyone but Zahid, then wouldn't they have laced fingers together and walked along, hand in hand? She now knew his body intimately and yet she had not so much as touched him since they'd returned to the palace.

But they ate in the same dining room as the previous night—which at least gave her the comfort of familiarity. Exotic platters of food were brought in and, although she ate some of the delicious morsels, Frankie was sure that she didn't do them justice. How could she, when Zahid was sitting opposite her and driving every thought from her head other than how it had felt to be made love to by him? Was it the same for him—or did one woman simply blur into another, the sexual experience forgotten once it was over?

'You're very quiet, Francesca.'

It sounded more like an observation than a question and she gave a little shrug. 'Am I?'

'In Khayarzah we have an expression— "if you give me your thought, I will give you an almond".'

'In England we say—a penny for your thoughts. Yours is much more poetic.'

'And do you like almonds?'

'I love them.'

'So?' His gaze roved over her questioningly.

'Who's Katya?' she asked suddenly.

His eyes narrowed. 'Katya?'

The question she had buried now came bubbling to the surface. 'The woman who rang that day in London, in the hotel. The one who was very sniffy with me.'

Zahid frowned. He wanted to tell her that Katya was none of her business, but something in the way she was biting her lip made him relent—and he *had* asked. 'Just a woman.'

Just? Somehow Frankie kept her expression ambiguous, wondering if she too was *just* a woman. Would someone one day refuse to let *her* speak to the sheikh when she telephoned—some smart and confident female who was currently the star in his firmament? She saw the future flash before her eyes and felt her heart sink. 'I can't think that any woman would care to hear herself described like that.'

'Okay, perhaps that wasn't the most diplomatic way to put it. She's a Russian model I had an affair with. Satisfied?'

It wasn't the best word to use in the circumstances and Frankie hated the next stupid and insecure question which seemed to blurt from her lips. 'And was she… was she very beautiful?'

He smiled at the predictably feminine response. 'No, she was as ugly as an addax.' He saw her lips wobble and lowered his voice. 'She was a model, Francesca—ergo, she was beautiful. But it's over. The affair is over—it's been over, ever since I became Sheikh. And anyway, why are you doing this, *anisah*—and why now? We're not going to spoil a beautiful affair with petty jealousies, are we?'

She shook her head, trying to ignore the dark claws of envy which were scrabbling at her heart. And hard on the heels of envy came the even more paralysing feeling of fear, even though Zahid had done nothing but speak the truth. This *was* an affair—nothing more, she knew that because he'd told her that right from the start. If she wanted more from the relationship, then not only would she be disappointed, but she would risk ruining what they already had. Somehow she dredged up a smile and hoped it looked more convincing than it felt. 'No, of course we're not.'

'Good. I am very pleased to hear it.'

So she played her part of being the polite guest rather than the jealous lover—and began asking him about the eastern mountains and the fabled leopards which lived there. And it wasn't until tiny little cups of thick, sweet coffee had been brought to the table that she slanted him a look.

'Zahid?'

'Mmm.' Steeling himself against another bout of female possessiveness, he arched his dark brows in question.

'What's an addax?' she asked.

'It's a desert antelope—famous for its ugliness.' He smiled with a sudden, comfortable indulgence. Her sense of humour and quickness of mind stimulated him, but not nearly as much as the soft thrust of her breasts. 'Go to bed, Francesca,' he commanded, in a soft and urgent tone. 'And I will join you as soon as the moon has risen.'

CHAPTER TWELVE

THE soft light of dawn crept through the shutters of her bedroom and, lazily, Frankie stirred beneath the rumpled sheet, her legs willingly trapped beneath the weight of the sheikh's hair-roughened thigh. 'Don't go,' she murmured—a request which seemed to have become a morning ritual.

'I have to go, *anisah bahiya*.' Zahid's voice was regretful, but resolute. 'Don't make this any harder for me than it already is.'

'But I thought that's what you liked…' Her fingers drifted down to tiptoe over the heavy throb of his arousal.

'Witch!' With a low growl, he grazed his mouth against her bare shoulder. 'If I leave it much later, then the servants will be up and if I am seen leaving your rooms…'

His words tailed off, but still he could not quite bring himself to move away from the warm circle of her embrace, or to still the fingers which were stroking between his thighs. How inexplicable was that? Three weeks of sharing her bed every night had proved a curiously potent addiction for a man who was usually averse to constant female companionship. Hadn't he once said to his brother that to eat dinner with the same woman two nights running was to define boredom? And hadn't Tariq given an odd kind of smile and agreed with him?

Frankie bit her lip. 'And would it be the end of the world if your servants *did* see you?'

'Of course it would. But, more importantly, it would be the end of your reputation,' he said fiercely, brushing the silken spill of dark hair away from her cheek. 'And I don't want that.'

Frankie swallowed. 'And what if I told you that I don't care about my reputation?'

'Well, you should.' Her words were the spur he needed and he got out of bed and began to pull on his robes with an economy of movement. 'Your name is respected in my country and I don't intend for that to change, Francesca. And if word got out that you were sharing my bed—that is exactly what would happen.'

She nodded as she met the determination which glittered from his black eyes and knew that to object would be pointless. 'If you say so.' She yawned as he leaned over the bed and tugged the sheet over her.

'I do. Now go back to sleep and I'll see you later.'

And with one last brief and charismatic smile, he was gone, leaving Frankie to drift in and out of sleep before it was time to get up and make her way to the library.

It was an oddly restful place to work. Scented by fragrant roses which stood on her desk and with most of the windows shuttered against the brilliant sunlight outside; she always experienced an immense feeling of peace when she walked into the vast book-lined room each morning.

As happened every day, breakfast had been laid out for her on a table overlooking the palace gardens. Mint tea, a dish of iced oranges and a selection of the very sweet pastries which the Khayarzah people loved.

She ate a little, then went to the desk and pulled out one of the diaries from an inlaid box which was hundreds of years old—something which had stopped being remarkable, because most things in the palace were ancient and beautiful. What *was* remarkable was how quickly she had settled into such a rarefied existence. Instead of being intimidated by her cloistered desert life, she had quickly settled into the exotic world of Khayarzah as if she had been born to it.

Being surrounded by priceless antiques didn't faze her—and neither did the presence of the noiseless servants who seemed to haunt the palace rooms and corridors. She'd quickly become used to luxury and comfort and taking long walks in the manicured gardens during the hours of daylight, while Zahid went about his kingly tasks.

And if she spent most of the day alone—she made up for it in the evenings, when Zahid would usually join her for dinner. Afterwards, they would sometimes sit playing cards—just as they'd done all those years ago. Only these days he no longer let her beat him. These days she had to really *try* in order to win. And that wasn't terribly easy when sexual tension seemed to sizzle in the air around them.

Sometimes, there were nights when Zahid needed to attend some glittering social function and then she would read up on the history of Khayarzah—curled up on an embroidered sofa in one of the less intimidating salons.

'You don't mind being left alone?' he'd asked her

one evening, appearing in the doorway in shimmering robes of muted silver.

Of course she'd minded but, recognising that complaining wasn't going to get her anywhere, she'd shaken her head. What choice did she have but to put up with it? It simply wouldn't be done for him to turn up at a formal function with a foreign woman by his side. 'Not at all. I'm used to my own company.' And she had seen him nod his dark head with satisfaction, pleased with her reply.

But by night it was a different story. When the moon was high in the star-spangled Khayarzahian sky, he would come to her room and silently ravish her in the warm, scented darkness. Heart hammering like a piston, she would lie awake waiting for him—naked and eager beneath Egyptian cotton sheets as she heard the soft whisper of his clothes sliding to the marble floor. And then he would join her on the bed, his hard, virile body hot and hungry, his kisses full of urgent passion. He would make love to her for most of the night until their bodies were exhausted—slipping away only when the milky light of dawn turned the sky a pale apricot colour.

Leaving Frankie to drift off into a dazed sleep. So that sometimes when she opened her heavy eyes in the morning she would wonder whether perhaps she had dreamt the whole thing.

The diaries helped. Having a legitimate reason to be in the palace gave her a sense of purpose and stopped her thinking about what she would do when the affair was over. Because the thought of leaving Zahid was too painful to contemplate. She couldn't imagine it—didn't want to imagine it. Much better to remember what it felt like when he made love to her, when his clever tongue licked all the way up her thigh and then…then…

Frankie closed her eyes with erotic recall. Memories of his love-making always overwhelmed her, but she was aware of something else happening. Something dangerous, deep inside her heart. Because in tandem with the physical flowering of her body had come a new and unwanted emotion and somewhere along the way she had fallen in love with the hawk-faced king. The caring friendship she'd always felt had grown into something much bigger and infinitely more powerful.

She loved him.

Would he be horrified if he knew how she felt?

Frankie stared down at the diary which lay open on the desk but none of the words registered. Of course he would! He'd be more than horrified. Love wasn't on the agenda and it never had been. He'd told her that in no uncertain terms. This was all about sex—great sex, it was true—but nothing more than that.

'I'm not paying you to sit there daydreaming, you know.'

A mocking voice broke into her thoughts as Zahid walked into the library and Frankie looked at him, her heart melting as she stared into the black glitter of his eyes.

'Sometimes I can't help daydreaming,' she defended softly.

'About?'

About the way you hold me when your body is deep inside mine. About the way you kiss me when it's all over. About how much I'd love to stay here, by your side, for ever. But such words could never be uttered. They were forbidden—just as driving was forbidden and showing affection towards each other in public. And being found in bed together. So, with an effort, Frankie scrambled together her thoughts and gestured towards the open leather journal in front of her. 'About your father's diary—it's a fascinating document.'

'In terms of content, you mean—or just generally?'

'Both. A diary is better than an autobiography, don't you think? Much more personal.'

Zahid nodded. 'An intimate glimpse into someone's life, you mean—as well as their thoughts?'

'Well, yes.' She could understand why nobody outside the family had ever seen them before—for they were almost painful in their intimacy. 'Things I already knew, I now see differently. It makes me realise how difficult it must have been for you all, with the war and everything.' She hesitated, wondering whether this was a forbidden subject, too. Perhaps it was, since they had never talked about it. 'And then, when your mother became ill.'

Zahid's face tightened with a sense of inevitability. But maybe he should have realised that by giving her access to his father's work, he would be opening up a part of himself which he had always kept locked away. For a man so fiercely self-contained, it was a disturbing thought that she was delving beneath the surface of his life and seeing into the hidden depths. But this was Francesca, he reminded himself—a woman who knew him almost better than anyone. He could say things to her that he wouldn't for a moment contemplate saying to another.

'It wasn't easy—especially as my father found it difficult to juggle everything,' he admitted. 'As well as my mother's illness, he was busy helping my uncle repair the country after so many years of war. And there was too much going on for him to devote much time to his two lively young sons. It was one of the reasons why Tariq and I spent some of our education in boarding school in England—something which gave us a taste of a very different life. It was far worse for Tariq of course, for he was younger and he…he never really got a chance to know our mother.'

He'd never been quite so forthcoming before and Frankie hesitated, afraid that more questions might make the familiar shutters come down. Yet her need to know overrode her natural caution. 'It must have been a terrible shock for you, when your uncle died.'

There was silence for a moment. Nobody had ever asked him that. His feelings had never been discussed—for his accession to the throne had been a given. And mightn't the natural doubts he had experienced at the time have been interpreted as weakness if he had dared express them?

'It was an utter shock,' answered Zahid simply. 'But the worse thing was that *his* son—the rightful heir—was with him at the time. They should never have been allowed to travel together—and normally they wouldn't have done. But the light over the mountains was fading, there was only one available plane and the decision was made that they should go on the same flight.' He paused. 'And in that split second, their destiny was decided.'

Zahid's face hardened as he remembered the broken pieces of the aeroplane lying in pieces on the ground. His own father had not long died and then he had to cope with these two new deaths in quick succession—followed by a sombre crowning as he was made King.

He had never wanted to be King and yet he could not have admitted that to anyone. And in time, he had grown into the role which he had at first resented. A role which still carried with it strict boundaries, which he must ensure he never forgot.

'I'm so sorry,' said Frankie.

He looked at her, her words breaking him from his reverie and bringing him back to the present. Reminding him with an unwelcome shock of just how very un-kinglike his current mode of behaviour was. He had taken his oldest friend as his lover and at times he had expressed concern about what he was doing to her reputation. But what of his?

Wouldn't his people be appalled if they realised that he was cavorting with a western woman within the palace walls? And could he really hold himself up as some kind of national moral guardian, when he was rejecting all the values which the Khayarzahian people held so dear?

His eyes were drawn to her face—to cheeks the colour of the palest rose and eyes which were bluer than the desert sky. He found himself remembering how sweetly her arms opened for him every night, and how eagerly her body welcomed him. All the pleasures of the body he had taught her, she had embraced with enthusiasm. How he would like this affair to continue—to carry on, just as they were.

But he was not being fair—not to her, and not to his people. Unlike his brother Tariq, he was not a gambling man—but he knew enough about odds and probability to realise that if they continued being lovers, then eventually they would be found out. And then what?

His mouth hardened. He needed to talk to her—and

not in bed where the distractions of her delicious body might cause his resolve to waver. Nor here, where the unseen servants might read their body language even if they could not understand their words. Somewhere away from the palace—a place which she had previously talked about—he needed to say to Francesca the words she deserved to hear.

He glanced at her from between narrowed eyes. 'Today, my diary is almost empty and I had been intending to catch up on some paperwork. But instead, I shall order the kitchens to make us up a picnic and we will go out somewhere for lunch. Somewhere quiet. Would you like that, Francesca?'

Startled by the unexpected and unfamiliar invitation, Frankie felt the leap of excitement. 'I'd absolutely love it.'

'Good. Then it shall be done. We shall be alone.'

'You mean…your bodyguards won't be there?' she ventured, in surprise.

'They will keep their distance,' he said softly. 'Now let me go and organise it.'

They set off just before midday and Zahid drove the big Jeep through the stark terrain. But Frankie was too excited to concentrate on the journey—even when he said that they were heading for the foothills of the eastern mountains. Her father had once told her that it was one of the most beautiful places on earth—and that you could know true peace in a place like that. Yet peaceful was the last thing she felt as she glanced at the sheikh's hard, hawklike profile and the faint shading of new growth at his jaw.

She was aware of an undeniable feeling of excitement building and building inside her—and she couldn't quite work out why. Was it because this was the first time they had done anything remotely normal—like a *real* couple? And did such an action mark a new openness in Zahid's behaviour towards her?

'See up there is the mighty *Nouf* mountain,' Zahid said softly as they drove towards the massive peak which dominated the landscape. 'Where the mountain's shadow and the rare waters which trickle from the top make fertile the land beneath. Where the peaks look purple in the sunset and where falcons soar in the thermal winds.'

'Oh, but it's beautiful,' she breathed.

Her genuine awe made his heart ache as he realised that what he was about to do was not going to be easy. Zahid stopped the car and turned to her. 'Come, we will take our food and our drink and sit in the shade of the rocks awhile—for you must be thirsty.'

Her throat *was* dry, but the sweet, iced melon juice he poured into one of the silver cups which they unpacked from the picnic basket quickly refreshed her. Zahid drank deeply and then put his own cup down, removed hers from her suddenly nerveless fingers and took both her hands in his own.

'I need to talk to you,' he said.

Something in the tone of his voice unsettled her. 'That sounds ominous,' she joked, but a little shiver of apprehension began to whisper its way down her spine.

'Does it?'

'Yes.' She watched as his face became shuttered and her sense of trepidation mounted. 'Why did you bring me here today, Zahid?'

He traced a butterfly circle on her palm with the tip

of his finger and then looked up at her. 'We need to talk about the future.'

She felt the flare of both hope and fear in the sudden leap of her heart as she stared into the dark gleam of his eyes. 'D-do we? What about it?'

'None of this has been as I planned it,' he said suddenly. 'I never planned—foolishly, as it happens—to take you as my lover. I told you back in England that I thought I could resist you—but now it seems that was an arrogant and unrealistic assessment of my own will power.'

In spite of all the intimacies they had known in bed, she found herself blushing at his growled admission. 'Yes.'

'Of course, if you had told me that you were a virgin, then I *would* have resisted you.' There was a heartbeat of a pause. 'But you didn't tell me, did you?'

'No.' Frankie bit her lip—because now she could definitely hear *reprimand* in his voice. 'No, I didn't.'

'And once I'd possessed you, it was too late,' he added. 'For by then I was ensnared.'

She looked at him, unsure of how to respond. Was that supposed to be a compliment, or some kind of territorial boast? 'Ensnared?' she echoed.

'You don't like the word? Would captivated suit you better?'

She nodded, still not certain where any of this was leading. 'Maybe.'

He gave a short laugh. How refreshingly honest she was. And how beautiful. All that sweet promise which could never be his. Soon, her delicious, scented body would no longer grace his sheets at night. With any other woman, it would have been a simple matter to dispatch her—but surely Francesca deserved the truth. 'Maybe you want me to say that I love you?' he questioned quietly. 'As I think you love me.'

She felt her stomach twist itself up into little knots because words of love weren't usually accompanied by a heavy weariness of the voice. And there was something dark written on his face which was filling her with foreboding. 'Not if it isn't true.'

'Because I do,' he said, as if she hadn't spoken. 'You see, I do love you, my *anisah bahiya*.'

Her lips were trembling so much that her stammered response was barely audible. 'You *d-do*?'

Grimly, he nodded his dark head. 'Yes. Unfortunately, I do. And it's because I love you that I'm afraid I have to send you away from here.'

CHAPTER THIRTEEN

THERE was a dense and heavy silence while Frankie's emotions took a trip on some demented roller coaster, which rocked her to the core. 'You say you love me, yet you're sending me away?' she whispered.

Zahid nodded, determined that the sapphire swim of her eyes would not sway him. Didn't she realise what such an admission of love had cost him? 'I have to.'

Perhaps pride should have stopped her from interrogating him—but what price pride when her whole future lay at stake? 'I don't understand.'

'You will if you think about it, Francesca. The longer you're here—the more I risk compromising your reputation. You say you don't care about such a thing, but I do. More than that, we both risk getting deeper and deeper into a relationship which has no future—not now and not ever. I must marry a woman from my own country,' he said bitterly. 'I told you that at the very beginning and nothing has changed.' Except that he had behaved like an impetuous and thoughtless fool and they would now both pay the price for that behaviour. 'I must take a wife—or two—maybe even three.'

The bizarre conversation they were having now took

on an even more surreal aspect. 'Three?' she echoed as she snatched her hand away from his. 'Three wives?'

He met the disbelieving blue blaze in her eyes. 'I am allowed four by law, although I doubt whether I—'

'Zahid, *please*!' Frankie interrupted and her sorrow was replaced by an indignant kind of fury. 'Please don't stand there and make out that we have no future because you're following some kind of *moral* code—and then add that you're going to take what amounts to almost an entire football team of wives!'

He guessed that now was not the time to point out that her numbers were out by about seven. He reached towards her again but she shook her head, stepping back from him as if he were contaminated. 'Francesca—'

'Don't touch me.' She was aware that her eyes were swimming with tears but she didn't care. 'Why did you bring me here today—so far from the palace? Why didn't you just tell me back there?'

Because he had wanted to avoid someone overhearing exactly the kind of scene they were having now. The kind of scene he'd never had with a woman—because no woman had ever got this close to him before. And if he was being honest, hadn't he thought that he might win her round with kisses and soft caresses? Hadn't there been a stupid, unrealistic part of him which had hoped that she might agree to continue their affair back in England? With him visiting her as often as he could—showering her with gifts and luxuries as if that might in some way compensate for his absence?

But he could not do that, he recognised. Not to Francesca. He could not offer her so little because that would devalue the kind of person she was. And it would sully what they had both shared.

'I'm sorry,' he said simply.

'Don't—*don't* apologise,' she said fiercely. 'I'm not some kind of *victim*, Zahid. So will you please take me back to the palace now? And then I'd like to return immediately to England.'

Zahid tensed up, for he was unused to anyone laying down furious demands like this—yet even he could see that she had a right to be angry. But surely they needn't part on terms of such bitterness. Couldn't they end this affair the same way they'd started it—consumed and comforted by the act of love?

'You can, of course, return to England,' he said smoothly. 'And my jet will take you there, but I'm afraid that we'll have to go via Morocco.'

Suspiciously, she stared at him. *'Morocco?'*

'Indeed,' he said, with a shrug. 'I have a friend named Raffaele de Ferretti—we go back a long way. I've arranged to spend the weekend with him in Marrakech and he's expecting us. We will leave tonight.'

'Do I have any choice?'

'I'm afraid not.'

Zahid began to pick up the picnic hamper. He had planned to surprise her with a trip to the exotic north African city. But that had been when he'd thought their affair could continue without consequence. Before he'd been forced to acknowledge that something between them had changed…

But pride would not let him turn up without the woman he had told his Italian friend about on the phone last week. And surely she wouldn't be able to resist him, when the two of them were sharing a luxury suite in a romantic *riad*?

The journey back to the palace was completed in

silence and when they arrived Frankie went straight to her suite of rooms to pack. At least she wouldn't have to wear any more of these stupid tunics with their matching narrow-legged trousers, she thought—until she sat down on the edge of the low divan and bit her lip.

She *liked* wearing those silky-soft tunics—whose very qualities of concealment meant that a woman could feel curiously liberated when she had them on. It made quite a change not to have to worry about whether your bottom looked big or whether you were showing too much cleavage, or sitting in a ladylike fashion.

She was still sitting there, gulping down the threat of tears, when a perplexed-looking Fayruz arrived to tell her that the car was waiting to take them to the airport and the servant turned to Frankie with a troubled face.

'You are leaving Khayarzah?' she questioned.

'I'm afraid that I've got to go back to England, Fayruz.'

'But…'

The girl's words tailed off miserably but Frankie knew it was inappropriate to ask what was troubling her. She *knew* exactly what was troubling her, because she was experiencing similar feelings of misery herself. Fayruz didn't want her to go—and Frankie herself didn't *want* to go. But she had to. The dream she had always nurtured had come true and Zahid had told her that he loved her. And hot on the heels of that wonderful revelation had been her banishment from his kingdom. How on earth could she tell the young servant *that* without compromising the king and breaking down in floods of tears?

So she embraced Fayruz and said goodbye, promising to send her an English dictionary when she arrived home. And then, with one last look round, she went out to the car, where Zahid was seated in the front, in the passenger seat.

He gave her only the most cursory of greetings and spoke to his driver all the way to the airport. And even though that didn't surprise her, it didn't stop her from hurting.

Even on the lavishly appointed Gulfstream jet, Zahid sat working at a table some distance away from her and Frankie wondered if he was going to ignore her the entire weekend. How was he going to introduce her to his Italian friend? *Hello, this is Francesca—you're very welcome to speak to her, but I'm afraid I won't be doing the same.*

The plane landed in the warm spiciness of the Moroccan night, where the indigo sky was peppered with bright stars. Immediately, they were whisked through passport control—but when Frankie raised her head after putting away her passport with trembling fingers, it was to see Zahid subjecting her to a narrow-eyed look.

'You've never been to Morocco before, have you?' he questioned.

She shook her head. 'Never.'

Another wave of unwanted guilt washed over him at the sight of her pinched and unhappy face. Had he done that to her? Brought her out here to heal the pain of her broken engagement and then ended up hurting her much more? And himself, he realised. He was hurting with a pain he'd never experienced. 'It's a very beautiful city,' he said heavily. 'As you will discover for yourself in the morning.'

Frankie tried to concentrate on the loveliness of her

surroundings and the pleasure of this brand-new experience as their car drove them through the walls of the ancient city.

The place where they were staying was stunning. It was situated right in the very heart of Marrakech and not far from the hustle and bustle of the lively market they called the Medina. Here, in their *riad* was a perfect blend of Middle Eastern opulence with every modern convenience you could ever want. There was a massage room and sauna—as well as a floodlit courtyard swimming pool, which glittered gold and turquoise in the moonlight.

And a sumptuous suite with an enormous, low bed.

She stood looking down at it as if it had been covered with a writhing nest of vipers and then Zahid turned to look at her.

'We could have our first full night together,' he said softly.

'We could—but it isn't going to happen.'

'Francesca—'

'I can't,' she said simply, because she was only just about holding it together as it was. Imagine if he kissed her—if she let him enter her body again after everything which had happened? 'I'll sleep on that divan over there.'

'You don't have to.'

'Yes, I do. You're much too tall to be comfortable on it.'

'Very well.' His voice was cool, remote. 'If that is what you wish.'

'It is.'

But that didn't stop her heart from aching as she lay sleepless in the small hours while Zahid slept, his hawklike face looking oddly soft in sleep as it lay, pillowed by his forearm.

Raffaele arrived next day with his fiancée—but Francesca was too exhausted from lack of sleep to meet them until dinner. She spent most of the day reading while Zahid worked and they communicated with a cool politeness she found far more distressing than the row they'd had in the desert.

Unfortunately, she fell asleep while she was supposed to be getting ready—and so by the time she stumbled downstairs the others were already assembled on the rooftop terrace, drinking from heavy red goblets and nibbling at pistachios.

Zahid's face was a mask of disapproval as she walked onto the terrace.

'You are late,' he said.

Frankie shot him a reproving glance. 'Zahid, aren't you going to introduce us?'

Zahid made no attempt to hide his frown. Was there no *end* to her stubborn behaviour? he asked himself angrily. She had refused to share a bed with him and now she was *late*. 'This is Raffaele de Ferretti, a business colleague, and this is his fiancée, Natasha—'

'Phillips,' butted in the woman with silky-looking hair and a rather anxious look on her face.

'This is Francesca,' Zahid said.

'Hello,' said Francesca, and smiled—even though it seemed to take a monumental effort to do so. Just as it took an even bigger effort to get through the meal without breaking down. Especially since Raffaele and his fiancée were clearly on some sort of high. The air was heavy with the sexual tension which seemed to flow between them and which made even more mockery of Frankie's own life and her situation with Zahid.

By the time the evening was over and she and the sheikh were back in their suite, she stared at him as he closed the door.

'Count me out for any further encounters like that,' she said quietly.

'We have a whole weekend to get through,' he objected coldly.

'And I'll spend it in the suite.'

'You can't do that.'

'Oh, but I can.' She stared at him, defying him to challenge her. 'I can do exactly as I please, Zahid. I'm a free agent, aren't I?'

And that was that. Frankie stayed in their suite for the rest of their stay and Zahid presumably made excuses for her absence—because as soon as was decently possible the whole miserable visit was cut short.

'Get your clothes packed,' he bit out. 'We're leaving.'

'What, now?'

'Yes. Now.'

The journey to the airfield was spent with Frankie biting on her lip and trying desperately hard not to break down in front of him. But it wasn't easy. It felt as if someone had punched a hole in her heart and left it aching and empty. When would this feeling go? she wondered distractedly. How long did it take for love to die?

Their limousine drew up onto the tarmac and she was wondering how they would endure the long flight ahead when, to her surprise and consternation, Zahid said goodbye.

'Goodbye?' Sheer panic made all the blood drain

from her face. 'But I thought…I mean, aren't you supposed to be flying to London with me?'

'I was,' he corrected and he looked deep into her eyes, feeling the painful twist of his heart as he registered the whiteness of her face. 'But I've changed my mind. I don't think we need endure any more of this painful charade.'

'Zahid—'

'No, Francesca. Maybe it's best this way. Let's just try and retain some of the good memories, shall we?' he questioned bitterly—because much more of this and he would do something unforgivable. Like break down in front of her. And what good would that do? It wouldn't actually *change* anything.

The aircraft steps were lowered and Frankie was suddenly stricken by an overwhelming sense of fear as she stared up into the harshness of his shadowed features. He was going! He was going and she might realistically never see him again. In all the years which lay ahead, this might be her last glance at his beloved face. Because she realised something else, too. That their friendship of so many years had been irreparably shattered by the end of their affair. And that hurt almost more than anything else.

She took a tentative step forward, not knowing what she was going to say but knowing that she needed to touch him one last time. Just to feel the warm brush of his skin…

'Zahid?'

'What?' He could read the unbearable sadness in her eyes but he kept his distance, knowing that if they touched he would be lost. Instead, he shrugged. 'What can I say, other than that I'm sorry?'

'S-sorry?' The lump in her throat was threatening to choke her. 'You mean you regret what has happened?'

Zahid's mouth hardened. Yes, of course he regretted it—because their affair had given him a taste of a paradise he sensed he would never know again. But the tentative buckling of her rose-pink lips made something inside him melt and revise his opinion. For how could he regret something which had given him so much joy, and fulfilment? He shook his head. 'Of course I don't regret it,' he whispered. 'I'm just sorry that I can't offer you anything more.'

'Zahid.' Her eyes were now brimming with tears and she wanted to blurt out that she would be satisfied with whatever he *was* able to offer her. That she would be contented to be his London mistress if she could continue being his lover—no matter how short and how snatched his visits might be. But Frankie knew that was not the answer. Wouldn't she become increasingly dissatisfied if her sheikh tossed out ever smaller scraps of his time, until there was no respect or love left between them? Far better to part now, while the memories were sweet—no matter how much it hurt to do so.

'Zahid,' she said again, knowing that there was something she needed to tell him—even if it meant that she made herself even more vulnerable in the process.

'What?' he questioned grimly.

Say it, she told herself fiercely. Say it so that he will never be in any doubt of the truth. 'I just want you to know that I love you, my darling. I love you so much.'

Zahid flinched, for it was like having his heart pierced with the sharpest of all swords. 'I know you do,' he answered softly. 'Just as I love you. Now go. Go before…'

She nodded as she heard the sudden break in his voice. ‘Goodbye, my love,’ she whispered.

‘Goodbye, Francesca.’ He turned on his heel and began to walk away from her, scarcely aware of the aide who appeared and informed him that a jet was being fuelled for his return journey to Khayarzah. All Zahid registered was the sight of Francesca’s plane as it took off into the star-filled Moroccan sky and he stood watching it until it had disappeared.

And only then did he board his own plane with a heavy heart—before going straight to the washroom and locking the door.

For there were very few places where a king could cry.

CHAPTER FOURTEEN

'WILL there be anything else, Your Royal Highness?'

Zahid stared at the aide who was standing in front of him with a questioning look on his face and realised that he had been lost in thought. That he had sat through an entire meeting to discuss the opening of the new horse-racing track and that most of it had gone right over his head. Again.

This could not go on.

Flexing and then unflexing his long fingers, he shook his head. 'No, there will be nothing else.'

'We still need to discuss the opening ceremony,' reminded the aide delicately.

'I said, not *now*,' snapped Zahid and could not miss the unmistakable glance which shimmered between his two closest advisors. They were wondering what the hell was the matter with him lately. Why he seemed to have the attention span of a fly and why nothing seemed to bring him pleasure.

Hadn't he been wondering the same thing himself?

Abruptly, he stood up—a movement which brought the assembled group leaping to their feet. And bitterly Zahid recognised that it was a sign of ignorance if you failed to acknowledge what, deep down, you knew to be the truth. Because the reason for his discontentment and heavy heart was as clear as the bright Khayarzah morning.

He missed Francesca.

He missed her in a way that he imagined a man might miss his limb if it had been torn from his body, leaving him shocked and bleeding.

Hadn't he thought that it would be easy? That by doing the right thing by his country, he would soon forget about the sapphire-eyed friend who had burrowed her way into his heart? Somehow, he had imagined that duty would bring some kind of consolation, in the form of some sort of peace of mind. But duty had so far failed to deliver.

Hadn't he done everything he could to stop himself from thinking about her? Thrown himself into every task with a fervour which had astonished his palace staff—as if sheer hard work might provide him with some kind of sanctuary? And when that had failed, hadn't he taken his horse and ridden him in the cool of the desert evening—ridden him harder than he could remember riding for years? But physical exhaustion, sweat and dust had done little to alleviate the terrible emptiness which filled him like a vacuum.

The other night, his brother Tariq had even called from London, on some flimsy pretext—but Zahid had known immediately that the subtext was to enquire how he was. Did that mean that word had got back to him that the ruling sheikh was out of sorts? And did such rumours not threaten to bring instability to Khayarzah? Maybe the ridiculous irony of the whole sorry mess was that the right thing might turn out to be the *wrong* thing?

His face darkened with rage, and the thought that he could be harming his beloved country was enough to spur him into immediate action. Gathering together his aides, he told them that he was making a short trip to England—and by the following day his Gulfstream jet was touching down outside London.

The black car he always used when visiting the country had been brought to the airfield and, after briefing his bodyguards, he set off on the familiar roads towards Francesca's Surrey home, just as dusk was descending.

Fairy lights twinkled in garden bushes and blazed from the windows of the houses he passed—so that the usually subdued suburban roads seemed to resemble some sort of carnival. And then he remembered that it was December, and Christmas—when the whole of the western world seemed to come alight with colour and joy. He glanced down at his watch to read the date.

December twenty-fourth.

The night before Christmas.

Zahid narrowed his eyes. Wasn't that a big deal? When stockings were hung at the ends of beds and carols sung in churches, and, for some European cultures, a feast of fish eaten at midnight? Wasn't this the time when families came together to celebrate and to remember? Close units united against the outside world…

For a moment, a terrible wave of longing washed over him and he almost turned back—until he remembered that Francesca had no family with which to sit around a festive table. She was as alone as he was…

But as he turned into the familiar driveway and flashed at the following bodyguards to instruct them to lay in wait by the gates he almost collided with a saloon car which was roaring in the opposite direction.

And in the driving seat, his face tight with fury, was Simon Forrester.

Zahid had only met Francesca's fiancé once—but once had been enough to remember the sullen curl of his mouth and the handsome, pampered face. He felt something like a dark rage twisting in his gut.

What the hell was he doing here?

Screeching to a halt in front of the house in a spray of gravel, Zahid leapt out of the car and strode up to the house—hammering on the door until it opened and a startled looking Francesca stood blinking up at him. He saw the colour drain from her face and the tip of her tongue dart out to moisten those petal lips. She looked as if she had just seen a ghost. Or was that guilt he read on her face? he thought grimly.

'What the hell was that creep Forrester doing here?' he demanded.

Frankie's senses were in disarray, her heart beating so loudly that it threatened to deafen her as she stared at her Sheikh lover. *Ex*-lover, she reminded herself bitterly. And ex for a good reason. Because a man who wanted four wives and who would always be a desert sheikh in the most traditional sense of the word was not the right kind of man for her. She just had to keep convincing herself of that.

She swallowed. 'You can't just turn up out of the blue, sounding like some B-rated detective, Zahid!' she protested. 'Why…why are you here?'

'Why do you think I'm here?' His voice was unsteady as he stared at her and noticed the deep shadows beneath her cheekbones—and how loose the pale sweater and jeans looked on her narrow frame. 'To talk to you.'

Frankie's heart gave a flare of hope which she did

her best to ignore as she reminded herself of how many nights she had wept into her pillow over him. 'You mean you want to interrogate me about who I'm seeing?' she demanded.

'So you *are* seeing him?'

'Oh, for heaven's *sake*!' A ragged sigh of inevitability escaped from her lips. She knew that she was going to listen to what he had come to say—for how could she turn him away? But one thing was for sure. She was going to be strong. Very strong. The last time he had seen her she had been on the brink of tears and now she needed to show him that she could cope perfectly well without him. 'You'd better come in.'

He noticed that she didn't offer him tea and she didn't take him to the kitchen with its warm range and faded comfort either. He followed her into the room where he'd carried her on the day she'd discovered her fiancé's duplicity, and once there she looked at him with a proud expression on her face.

And Zahid felt the sudden unfamiliar shimmering of apprehension. Surely there could only be one reason why she could look so secure?

'You are back with him?' he questioned, unprepared for the savage lurch of his heart.

'Of course I'm not *back* with him! Do you really think I am as shallow as that?'

'Then why is he here?'

She could see the angry fire spitting from eyes which were narrowed into onyx chips. She thought that if Zahid were suddenly called upon to take a part in the pantomime which was playing to packed houses in the local theatre, he would have made a superb fire-breathing dragon.

'Actually, he was here on a mission,' she said. 'He'd heard I was back from Khayarzah and he came asking for his engagement ring back.'

Zahid remembered the Englishman's furious expression as their cars had passed at the end of the drive and, instinctively, he glanced at her bare hand. 'Which you gave to him?'

'Well, I would have done, if only I could find the damned thing.' She read the question in his eyes and shrugged. 'I seem to have mislaid it somewhere around the house. At any rate, it's missing, and when I told Simon he demanded that I give him the twenty-five thousand pounds he'd paid for it.'

Zahid stilled. 'But you didn't, did you?'

'Are you kidding?' Frankie gave a short laugh. 'Even if I *had* that kind of money—there's no way I would have given it to him. I asked him to produce a receipt which he should have had for a sum that big but, of course, he couldn't—because the ring's a fake.' She met his eyes with a challenging look. 'Something which you knew all along, didn't you, Zahid?' she questioned quietly.

Unexpectedly, Zahid's mouth quirked into a wry half-smile. How she surprised him. Time after time, Francesca O'Hara pulled something different out of the bag to remind him of how complex and remarkable she really was. 'I didn't *know*, not for sure—fakes are increasingly sophisticated these days, and only an expert can truly tell the difference. But looking at his behaviour towards you, he didn't give the impression of someone who would spend thousands of pounds on a ring.' His eyes narrowed. 'What did he say?'

'Oh, he blustered. Made threats—all of which

I ignored.' And it had felt good to stand up to him, Frankie realised—something which she would never have done in the past. She stared at Zahid, realising how much she had grown, and how much she had learned by being his mistress. She'd discovered that once you'd had the courage to tell a powerful king a few home truths, then standing up to a blustering small-town estate agent had been simple. 'I told him to go ahead and sue me!'

'Bravo, Francesca,' he said softly.

The gentling of his voice was her undoing. No longer able to seek refuge in the subject of a worthless ring, Frankie looked at him, some of her bravado leaving her. If he was here with some valiant attempt to show that they still could be friends, well, she didn't want to hear it. She wasn't ready to be friends with him again. Not yet. Maybe not ever… Swallowing down the ever-present hint of heartache, she looked at him. 'So what really brings you here today, Zahid?'

Sapphire light gleamed from her eyes and Zahid found himself lost for words as their gazes clashed. He realised that he could growl at her. He could pull her into his arms and kiss away that fierce look on her face. He could promise her a king's ransom in the truest sense of the world.

But some bone-deep instinct told him that none of these would work, not in the long run—because Frankie was not a woman to be bargained with or bought, or seduced into his way of thinking. He wanted her in every sense, he realised—but most of all he wanted her to come to him *of her own free will.*

He said the words which once would have sounded like an admission of weakness. 'I've missed you.'

I've missed you, too. I've missed you more than I

thought it was ever possible to miss someone. But acknowledging that wasn't going to change anything, was it? He was still unable to offer her any kind of future.

Forcing herself to ignore the plaintive tug of her heart, Frankie shrugged.

His face darkened when she made no response and so, reluctantly, he was forced to elaborate—his words a growled statement. 'And I can't seem to stop thinking about you.'

Still she said nothing, nor gave any indication that she liked what he said—and suddenly Zahid realised the true meaning of the word courage. In his youth, during a spell in the Khayarzahian army he had fought bloody battles and known real hunger. He had slept beneath the stars in the most inhospitable parts of the desert, untroubled by the threat of the scorpions and snakes nearby. His physical daring was admired and feared in equal measures by his compatriots, and it was said that there was no more intrepid rider than Zahid Al Hakam.

But did he have the kind of courage to tell this woman what lay almost buried at the bottom of his heart? An admission which would make her realise the immense power she had over him?

'I told you that I loved you, Francesca,' he said. 'But that I couldn't marry you. And I guess I thought that I would get over it. You know, like a head-cold, or a broken leg. But the truth is that I haven't. If anything the feeling is worse—'

'Worse?'

Had that been the wrong word? he wondered dazedly. Had he implied that it was somehow a *bad* feeling, this love he felt for her? But it *was* a bad feeling, he recognised. A negative and destructive one—if this love was not allowed the room and the right to grow and mature.

'My life is empty without you,' he admitted. 'I gave you up because I wanted to fulfil all the demands made of me by my country. But I now know I cannot rule without the woman I love beside me. And that is the truth.'

That did get a reaction. Francesca shook her head and bit down on her lips, like someone who had just witnessed something distressing.

'Please don't, Zahid,' she whispered, her voice now perilously close to tears, despite her determination not to break down in front of him. 'That's not the point. You *may* love me—as you must know that I love you—and that's rather wonderful. Because love is. But it doesn't actually *change* anything, does it? And I can't be your wife because I'm not Khayarzah born—'

'I will have the law changed,' he said arrogantly. 'For I am the king and I can.'

She carried on as if he hadn't interrupted her. 'And I certainly can't contemplate sharing you with three other wives—'

'But you will be my *only* wife!' he declared savagely. 'For I have decided to renounce all my rights to take any others—this is what I have come here today to tell you! I will not rest until you are my wife. *My only wife.*'

Frankie could see what that statement had cost him, just as she could see the passion which had animated his dark and hawklike features. And even though her heart swelled up with an overwhelming wave of love and longing, she forced herself not to be swayed by his emotional declaration. Because short-term gain would inevitably produce long-term pain.

'It won't work.'

'Why not?'

'Because it's not enough, my darling,' she said, her voice soft and trembling with emotion.

His eyes narrowed. 'What do you mean, it's not enough?'

She swallowed. 'I can't...I can't live in a country where I'm not even allowed to drive or women are discouraged from going to university.'

There was a long and disbelieving silence. 'You come to me with no dowry—and I accept that without a murmur,' he declared. 'I renounce my rights to other women and tell you that you will be my only love—and *still* it is not enough? You are now asking me to change yet more laws of my land before you will consent to be my bride?'

She shook her head. 'Of course I'm not. This isn't some kind of bidding war we're engaged in! I'm not asking you or telling you to do anything—just explaining what I must be true to. And I must be true to myself. You've made me grow as a woman and as a person, Zahid. I am no longer the innocent and naïve person who was duped by Simon. And while I thank you for that from the bottom of my heart—it is also something of a double-edged sword.' She sucked in a deep breath. 'Because I can't now take a step backwards. I can't do something which I think is fundamentally unsound—and I can't live in a country where women are second-class citizens—no matter how much I love the man who leads that country.'

Silence hung heavily in the air as Zahid said nothing—for her words were too important to be answered without him giving them careful consideration. He turned and walked over to the French windows which overlooked the big garden which had so fascinated him during his growing up. Such a green and lush oasis it had always seemed to the boy from the desert. But there was no green today. Everything looked black and white. The frost was thick and the bare branches of the big trees looked as if they had been daubed in bleached and glittering brush strokes.

He sighed. Surely everything *was* black and white—in more ways than one? Francesca had had the temerity to tell him what he knew was frequently on the minds of many—sentiments which had been growing stronger over the years. For hadn't he read the outraged leader pages in western newspapers—and once, in New York, come face to face with some banner-waving women who had been demanding equal rights for women?

Was he not guilty of hypocrisy—taking western lovers as and when it suited him, while keeping the females of Khayarzah shackled in the past? Yet there was a solution. And Francesca had made him see that such a solution would be possible. It would be difficult to change, and painful, too—but change was part of life and to try to stop that was as futile as King Canute trying to turn back the tide.

And did he have a choice? Could he bear the thought of going through his own life without his strong and sapphire-eyed Francesca beside him? The woman who had shown him what it meant to love?

He turned to face her. 'The legislation cannot be changed overnight,' he warned.

She heard the promise in his voice and knew that she had to meet it halfway. 'But I know that you wouldn't drag your feet, just for the sake of it.'

Zahid smiled. There! She had done it again. By voicing her confidence and her trust in him, she had made it morally impossible for him to do anything but obey her!

'I will drag my feet on nothing,' he growled. 'Especially not this.' And he strode across the room and pulled her into his arms, his eyes blazing as he looked down at her. 'I love you, Francesca O'Hara—you and only you, for the rest of my life. You are the only woman I have ever truly wanted and ever shall want. You have captured my heart and my soul and my body—and I am asking you once again, will you marry me?'

'Oh, yes, my darling,' she said softly, her fingertips moving to trace the outline of his sensual mouth. 'Yes and yes, and a thousand times yes.'

For a moment Zahid just enjoyed the unfamiliar sensation of pure contentment and the sudden warmth which flooded through his veins until his heart felt as if it were on fire. Remember this moment, he told himself fiercely. Remember it for as long as you draw breath. He brushed aside the dark lock of hair which had fallen over her cheek and, lowering his head, he began to kiss her.

EPILOGUE

IT WASN'T, as Zahid remarked to Francesca on their wedding night, the most straightforward of unions. For the sheikh and his English bride began their married life with more challenges than most newly-wed couples had to contend with. But they had always known it would be that way.

First, there was the challenge of getting his country to accept a western wife who was also a commoner, rather than someone of noble blood who had been born and reared there. But here Frankie was at a definite advantage. Her late father had been known and adored by the people of Khayarzah—and her own obvious love of the culture shone through in all she did and said.

She charmed them by adopting a traditional Khayarzahian wedding gown for the emotional ceremony which took place over four days. And then proceeded to amaze them by saying her vows in flawless Khayarzahian—the product of her hard and ongoing work on the tricky language, for she was determined to be fluent one day. But mostly she was accepted because the people saw how deeply their king loved her. As she loved him. It was as clear as the night-time moon, they said.

So they named her Queen Anwar, which meant 'rays of light'. And the single wedding day photo which was issued to the world's media showed the two of them gazing rapt into each other's eyes, as if nothing outside that moment existed for either of them.

The second challenge was getting such a traditional male-led society to accept that changes were needed and that they *were* going to be made. The move to allowing women to drive and to attend universities didn't happen overnight, but it *did* happen, albeit very slowly. It came too late for Fayruz to go to college in her own country—but Frankie felt a fierce determination that the bright young girl should fulfil her intellectual potential. Thus, with her husband's blessing, the new queen sponsored her former servant to attend Cambridge University, where she excelled in both her degree subject of Middle Eastern politics, and on her college swimming team.

The final challenge was Frankie's alone. It meant saying goodbye to a way of life she had always known in England—and embracing a brand-new one in a desert land which was radically different. But that was no hardship for her, not even for a single second. Her father had taught her how to love Khayarzah, and she had loved Zahid from the very first moment she had known him. She would have walked to the ends of the earth for him.

In fact, she would do anything to make her beloved husband happy—and when he confided that he was worried about Tariq and the life he was leading, Frankie suggested inviting his brother to Khayarzah for an extended stay. Whether or not that would happen, who could say? Because Frankie knew that the future was like a handful of pebbles dropped to the ground—you never knew where they were going to fall.

Her only disappointment was in never seeing one of the fabled leopards, which her father had told her so much about—although she lived in hope. And Zahid regularly took her for a picnic in the lush foothills of the eastern heights, just in case. The place where they'd had their furious row—where their future had seemed so bleak and hopeless—had become their own, special place.

It was there that she told him that she was pregnant. And where one day—a month before she gave birth to their beautiful black-haired twins—he withdrew a slim leather box and handed it to her.

'What's this?' she questioned, with a smile.

'Why not open it and see?'

The chain was fine and gold and from it hung a glittering, stream-lined charm. A sleek animal, captured in mid-leap, its elegant body studded with diamonds and onyx—its eyes two rare and gleaming emeralds.

'Why, it's a leopard,' she said slowly as she held it up to the light and looked up at him with shining eyes.

Zahid's smile was tender as he took it from her and put it around her neck, fastening the clasp and then touching his lips to her neck in a lingering kiss. He moved round to pull her into his arms as the fertile swell of her belly pressed against him.

'Indeed it is. It's a way of saying that if reality doesn't always give you what you want, sweet Francesca—then you must reach out and create your own. Just as we have done.'

It was also, he knew, yet another way of telling her how much he loved her.

* * * * *

CROWNED: THE PALACE NANNY

MARION LENNOX

CHAPTER ONE

Dr Elsa Langham disappeared after a car accident four years ago. Mrs Elsa Murdoch took her place.

The invitation had been sitting on the table all day, a taunting reminder of her past.

> The International Coral Society invites Dr Elsa Langham, foremost authority on Coral: Alcyonacea, to submit a paper at this year's symposium in Hawaii.

The ICS hadn't kept up with her change in direction. Eight-year-old Zoe was asleep in the next room, totally dependent on her, and Dr Elsa Langham was no longer an acclaimed authority on anything.

She read the invitation one last time, sighed and finally dumped it in the bin.

'I don't know why they're still sending me invitations,' she told the skinny black cat slinking out from under her chair. 'I'm Mrs Elsa Murdoch, a mother to Zoe, an occasional student of starfish to keep my scientific hand in, and my cats need feeding.'

She rose and took a bowl of cat food to the back garden. The little cat followed, deeply suspicious but seduced by the smell of supper.

Four more cats were waiting. Elsa explained the terms of their tenancy as she did every night, fed them, then ignored five feline glares as she locked them up for the night. They knew the deal, but they didn't have to like it.

'At least you guys go free every morning,' she told them. 'You can do what you want during the day.'

And so could she, she told herself. She could take Zoe to the beach. She could study starfish. She could be Mrs Elsa Murdoch.

Until a miracle happens, she thought to herself, pausing to look up at the night sky. Not that I need a miracle. I really love Zoe, I don't mind starfish and I'm incredibly lucky to be alive. It's just…I wouldn't mind a bit of magic. Like a rainbow of coral to appear in our cove. Or Prince Charming to wave his wand and take away my debts and Zoe's scars.

Enough. The cats weren't interested in wishes, and neither was anyone else. She smiled ruefully into the night, turned her back on her disgruntled cats and went inside. She needed to fix a blocked sink.

Where was Prince Charming when you needed him?

The little boy would live.

Prince Stefanos Antoniadis—Dr Steve to his patients—walked out of Theatre savouring a combination of triumph and exhaustion. He'd won.

The boy's mother—a worn-looking woman with no English, but with a smile wide enough to cut through any language barrier—hugged him and cried, and Stefanos hugged her back and felt his exhaustion disappear.

He felt fantastic.

He walked into the scrub room, sorely tempted to punch the air in triumph—and then stopped dead.

This wasn't fantastic. This was trouble.

Two months ago, King Giorgos of the Diamond Isles had died without an heir. Next in line to the throne of the Mediterranean island of Khryseis was Stefanos's cousin, Christos. The only problem was, no one could find Christos. Worse, if Christos couldn't be found, the throne belonged to Stefanos—who wanted the crown like a hole in the head.

In desperation he'd employed a friend who moved in diplomatic circles and whose discretion he trusted absolutely to search internationally for Christos. That his friend was here to tell him the news in person meant there must be a major problem.

'They told me you've been opening a kid's skull, chopping bits out and sticking it back together,' his friend said with easy good humour. 'How hard's that? *Seven hours…*'

'I get paid by the hour,' Stefanos said, grasping his friend's hand. But he couldn't make himself smile. 'What news?'

'From your point of view?' As an investigator this man was the best, and he knew the issues involved. 'You're not Crown Prince of Khryseis.'

'Not!' He closed his eyes. The relief was almost overwhelming.

It hadn't always been like this. As a boy, Stefanos had even dreamed of inheriting the throne that his almost pathologically shy cousin swore he didn't want.

But that was in the past. King Giorgos was bound to have sons, and if not… Christos would just have to wear it. Almost twenty years ago, Stefanos had moved to the States to pursue a medical career. His dream since then had been to perfect and teach surgical techniques, so wounds such as the ones he'd treated today could be repaired in hospitals less specialised than this one, anywhere in the world. 'So you've finally found Christos?' he asked, feeling the weight of the world lift from his shoulders.

'Sort of,' his friend said, but there was something in his face which made Stefanos's jubilation fade. His expression said that whatever was coming wasn't good.

'Christos is dead, Steve,' the man said gently. 'In a car accident in Australia, four years ago. That's why you haven't been able to find him.'

'Dead.' He stared at his friend in horror. 'Christos? My cousin. Why? How?'

'You know he left the island soon after you? Apparently he

and his mother emigrated to Australia. Neither of them kept in touch. It seems his mother held his funeral with no fuss, and contacted no one back on Khryseis. Three months after he died, so did she.'

'Dear God.'

'It's the worst of news,' his friend said. He hesitated. 'But there's more.'

Stefanos knew it. He was replaying their conversation in his head. His friend's first words had been, 'You're not Crown Prince of Khryseis.'

Christos had been first in line to the throne, followed by Stefanos. But Christos was dead. Therefore it had to be Stefanos. Unless…

'There's a child,' his friend told him.

'A child,' he said numbly.

'A little girl. Christos married, but his wife was killed in the same accident. Their child survived. She was four when her parents were killed. She's now eight.'

Stefanos didn't respond. He was staring at his friend, but he was seeing nothing.

He was working on groundbreaking surgical techniques. His work here was vital.

A child.

'Her name's Zoe,' his friend said. 'She's still living in Australia with a woman called Mrs Elsa Murdoch, who seems to be employed as her nanny. But, Steve…'

'Yes?' But he already knew what was coming.

'Christos's death means the child takes the Crown,' he said gently. 'Zoe's now the Crown Princess of Khryseis. That means you're Prince Regent.'

Stefanos still didn't answer. There was a chasm opening before him—a gaping void where his career used to be. He could only listen while his friend told him what he'd learned.

'I've done some preliminary checks. From what I gather of the island's constitution, you'll be in charge until Zoe's twenty-five. The island's rule, and the consequent care of your cousin as Crown Princess, lies squarely on your shoulders. Now…do you want me to find an address for this woman called Elsa?’

CHAPTER TWO

ROYALTY was standing on Elsa's beach.

Sunlight was shimmering from the surface of a turquoise sea. The tide was at its lowest for months. Their beach was a mass of rock pools and there were specimens everywhere.

They'd swum far out to the buoy marking the end of shallow water and a pod of dolphins had nosed in to check them out. They'd dived for starfish. They'd floated lazily in the shallows; floating eased the nagging ache in Elsa's hip as nothing else could. Finally they'd made each other crowns out of seaweed pods, and now Queen Elsa and her consort, Princess Zoe, were marching back to the house for lunch and a nap.

To find royalty waiting for them. Royalty without seaweed.

For a moment Elsa thought she'd been out in the sun too long. The man was dressed like a prince from one of Zoe's picture books. His uniform was black as night, tailored to perfection. His slick-fitting suit was adorned with crimson epaulettes, tassels, braid and medals. His jacket and the top collar of his shirt were unbuttoned, but for some reason that made him look even more princely.

A prince trying to look casual?

Uh-oh. Her hand flew to her seaweed crown and she tugged it off as icy tendrils of fear crept round her heart.

Royalty was fantasy. Not real. Zoe's father had always been afraid of it, but his stories had seemed so far-fetched that Elsa had deemed them ludicrous.

'Look,' Zoe said, puzzled, and the eight-year-old's hand clutched hers. Zoe had only been four when her parents died, but maybe she remembered enough of her father's paranoia to worry.

Or maybe the sight of someone dressed as a prince on a Queensland beach was enough to worry anyone.

'I can see him,' Elsa said. 'Wow. Do you think he's escaped from your *Sleeping Beauty* book?'

'He's gorgeous,' Zoe said, relaxing a little as Elsa deliberately made light of it.

'He must be hot,' Elsa said cautiously.

'Do you think he came in a carriage like in *Cinderella*?'

'If he did, I hope it has air-conditioning,' Elsa retorted and Zoe giggled.

Good. Great. Zoe giggling was far more important than any prince watching them from the sand dunes.

She would not let anything interfere with that giggle.

'Maybe he's looking for us,' Zoe said, worry returning. 'Maybe he's from Khryseis.'

'Maybe he is.' Neither of them had ever been to Khryseis, but the fabulous Mediterranean island was part of Zoe's heritage—home to the father who'd been killed when she was four. According to the Internet, Khryseis was an island paradise in the Mediterranean, ruled up until now by a King who was as corrupt as he was vindictive. Zoe's father, Christos, had spoken occasionally of the old King's malice. Now those stories came flooding back, and Elsa's fears increased accordingly.

The man—the prince?—was walking down the sandy track towards them, tall, tanned and drop-dead gorgeous. Elsa stopped and put down her pail. She held Zoe's hand tighter.

A lesser mortal might look ridiculous in this situation but, despite his uniform, this man looked to be in charge of his world. Strongly built, aquiline features, dark hooded eyes. Cool, authoritative and calm.

And then he smiled. The combination of uniform, body and smile was enough to knock a girl's socks off. If she had any socks that was, she thought, humour reasserting itself as she decided it was ridiculous to be afraid. She wiggled her toes deep into the sand, feeling the need to ground herself.

Oh, but that smile…

Down, she told herself fiercely. Hormonal response was exactly what wasn't wanted right now. Act cool.

She met the man's gaze and deliberately made herself match his smile. Or almost match it. Her smile was carefully that of someone passing a stranger. His smile, on the other hand, was friendly. His gaze dropped to Zoe—and his smile died. That always happened. No one could stop that initial reaction.

Instinctively Elsa tugged Zoe closer but Zoe was already there. They braced together, waiting for the usual response. Try as she might, she couldn't protect Zoe from strangers. Her own scars were more easily hidden, but Zoe's were still all too obvious.

But this wasn't a normal response. 'Zoe,' the man said softly, on a long drawn-out note of discovery. And pleasure. 'You surely must be Zoe. You look just like your father.'

Neither of them knew what to say to that. They stood in the brilliant sunlight while Elsa tried to think straight.

She felt foolish, and that was dumb. She was wearing shorts and an old shirt, and she'd swum in what she was wearing. Her sun-bleached hair had been tied in a ponytail this morning, but her curls had escaped while she swam. She was coated in sand and salt, and her nose was starting to peel.

Ditto for Zoe.

They were at the beach in Australia. They were appropriately dressed, she thought, struggling for defiance. Whereas this man…

'I'm sorry I'm in uniform,' he said, as if guessing her thoughts. 'I know it looks crazy, but I've pulled in some favours trying to find you. Those favours had to be repaid in the form of attending a civic reception as soon as I landed. I left as soon as I could, but the media's staked out my hotel. If

I'd stopped to change they might well have followed me here. I don't want Zoe to be inundated by the press yet.'

Whoa. There was way too much in that last statement to take in. First of all... Was he really royal? What was she supposed to do? Bow?

Not on your life.

'So...who are you?' she managed, and Zoe said nothing.

'I'm Stefanos. Prince Regent of Khryseis. Zoe, your grandfather and my grandfather were brothers. Your father and I were cousins. I guess that makes us cousins of sorts too.'

Cousins. That was almost enough to make her knees give way. Zoe had relations?

This man's voice had the resonance of a Greek accent, not strong but unmistakable. That wasn't enough to confirm anything.

'Christos didn't have any cousins,' she said, which was maybe dumb—what would she know? 'Or...he always said there was no one. So did his mother.'

'And I didn't know they'd died,' he said gently. 'Zoe, I'm so sorry. I knew your father and I knew your grandmother, and I loved them both. I'm very sorry I didn't keep in touch. I'm so sorry I wasn't here when you so obviously needed me.'

Elsa was starting to shake. She so didn't want to be shaking when Zoe was holding her hand, but it was happening regardless.

She was all Zoe had. And—she might as well admit it—for the last four years Zoe was all she'd had.

'You can't have her.' It was said before she had a chance to think, before her head even engaged. It was pure panic and it was infectious. Zoe froze.

'I'm not going with you,' she whispered, and then her voice rose in panic to match Elsa's. 'I'm not, I'm not.' And she buried her face against Elsa and sobbed her terror. Elsa swung her up into her arms and held. The little girl was clutching her as if she were drowning.

And Stefanos...or whoever he was...was staring at them

both in bemusement. She looked at him over Zoe's head and found his expression was almost quizzical.

'Good one,' he said dryly. 'You don't think you might be overreacting just a little?'

She probably was, she conceded, hugging Zoe tighter, but there was no room for humour here.

'You think we might be a bit over the top?' she managed. 'Prince Charming on a Queensland beach.' She looked past him and saw a limousine—a Bentley, no less, with a chauffeur to boot. Overreaction? She didn't think so. 'You're frightening Zoe. You're frightening me.'

'I didn't come to frighten you.'

'So why did you come?' She heard herself then, realising she was sounding hysterical. She knew Zoe's father had come from Khryseis. She knew he'd been part of the royal family. What could be more natural than a distant relative, here on official business, dropping in to see Zoe?

But then there was his statement… *I've pulled in some favours trying to find you.* He'd deliberately come searching for Zoe.

Prince Regent… That made him Prince in charge while someone was incapacitated. The old King?

Or when someone was a child.

No.

'Zoe, hush,' she said, catching her breath, deciding someone had to be mature and it might as well be her. 'I was silly to panic. Stefanos isn't here to take you away.' She glared over Zoe's head, as much to tell him, *Don't you dare say anything different.* 'He comes from the island where your papa grew up. I'm sorry I reacted like I did. I was very rude and very silly. I think it's time to dry our eyes and meet him properly.'

Zoe hiccuped on a sob, but there'd been worse things than this to frighten Zoe in her short life, and she was one brave little girl. She sniffed and wiped her eyes with the back of her hand and turned within Elsa's arms to face him.

She was a whippet of a child, far too thin, and far too small.

The endless operations had taken their toll. It was taking time and painstaking rehabilitation to build her up to anywhere near normal.

'Maybe we both should say sorry and a proper hello,' Elsa said ruefully, and Zoe swallowed manfully and put a thin hand out in greeting. Clinging to Elsa with the other.

'Hello,' she whispered.

'Hello,' Stefanos said and took her hand with all the courtesy of one royal official meeting another. 'I'm very pleased to meet you, Zoe. I've come halfway round the world to meet you.'

And then he turned his attention to Elsa. 'And you must be Mrs Murdoch.'

'She's Elsa,' Zoe corrected him.

'Elsa, then, if that's okay with Elsa,' Stefanos said, meeting her gaze steadily. She had no hand free left to shake and she was glad of it. This man was unsettling enough without touch.

So… She didn't know where to go from here. Did you invite a prince home for a cup of tea? Or for a twelve course luncheon?

'You live here?' he asked, his tone still gentle. There was only one place in sight. Her bungalow—a tired, rundown shack. 'Is this place yours?'

'Yes.'

'Can I come in and talk to you?'

'Your chauffeur…'

'Would it be too much trouble to ask if you could ring for a taxi to take me back into town when we've spoken? I don't like to keep my chauffeur waiting.'

'There's no taxi service out here.'

'Oh.'

Now what? What was a woman to say when a prince didn't want to keep his chauffeur waiting? She needed an instruction manual. Maybe she was still verging on the hysterical.

She gave herself a swift mental shake. 'I'm sorry. A taxi won't come out here but we have a car. It'll only take us fifteen minutes to run you back into town. I'm not normally so…so inhospitable. It's the uniform.'

'I expect it might be,' he said and smiled, and there it was again, that smile—a girl could die and go to heaven in that smile. 'I don't want to put you to trouble.'

'If you can cope with a simple sandwich, you're welcome to lunch,' she managed. 'And…of course we'll drive you into town. After all, you're Christos's cousin.'

'So I can't be all bad?' It was a teasing question and she flushed.

'I loved Christos,' she said, almost defensively. 'And I loved Amy. Zoe's mama and papa were my closest friends.' She managed a shaky smile. 'For their sake…you're welcome.'

The house was saggy and battered and desperately in need of a paint. A couple of weatherboards had crumbled under the front window and a piece of plywood had been tacked in place to fill the gap. The whole place looked as if it could blow over in the next breeze. Only the garden, fabulous and overgrown, looked as if it was holding the place together.

Stefanos hardly noticed the garden. All he noticed was the woman in front of him.

She was…stunning. Stunning in every sense of the word, he thought. Natural, graceful, free.

Free was maybe a dumb adjective but it was the thought that came to mind. She was wearing nothing but shorts and a faded white blouse, its top three buttons undone so he had a glimpse of beautiful cleavage. Her long slim legs seemed to go on for ever, finally ending in bare feet, tanned and sand coated. This woman lived in bare feet, he thought, and a shiver went through him that he couldn't identify. Was it weird to think bare sandy toes were incredibly sexy? If it was, then count him weird.

But it wasn't just her toes. It wasn't just her body.

Her face was tanned, with wide intelligent eyes, a smattering of freckles and a full generous mouth with a lovely smile.

Breathtakingly lovely. Her honey-blonde hair was sun-kissed, bleached to almost translucence by the sun. There was no way those streaks were artificial, for there was nothing artificial about this woman. She wore not a hint of make-up, except the remains of a smear of white suncream over her nose, and her riot of damp, salt-and-sand-laden curls looked as if they hadn't seen a comb for a week.

Quite simply, he'd never seen a woman so beautiful.

'Are you coming in?' Elsa was standing on the veranda, looking at him with the beginnings of amusement. Probably because he was standing with his mouth open.

'Is this a holiday shack?' he managed, forcing his focus to the house—though it was almost impossible to force his focus anywhere but her. The information he'd been given said she lived here. Surely not.

'No,' she said shortly, amusement fading. 'It's our home. I promise it's clean enough inside so you won't get your uniform dirty.'

'I didn't mean…'

'No.' She relented and forced another of her lovely smiles. 'I know you didn't. I'm sorry.'

He came up the veranda steps. Zoe had already disappeared inside, and he heard the sound of running water.

'Zoe gets first turn at the shower while I make lunch,' Elsa explained. 'Then she sets the table while I shower.'

It was said almost defiantly. Like—don't mess with the order of things. She was afraid, he thought.

But… This woman was Zoe's nanny. She was being paid out of Zoe's estate. He'd worried when he'd read that—a stranger making money out of a child.

Now he wasn't so sure. This wasn't a normal nanny-child relationship. Even after knowing them only five minutes, he knew it.

And the fear? She'd be wanting reassurance that he wouldn't take Zoe away. He couldn't give it. He watched her face and he knew his silence was being assessed for what it was.

Why hadn't he found more out about her? His information was that Zoe's parents had died in a car crash four years ago. Since then Zoe had been living with a woman who was being paid out of her parents' estate—an estate consisting mostly of Christos's life insurance.

That information had him hoping things could be handled simply. He could take Zoe back to Khryseis and employ a lovely, warm nanny over there to care for her. Maybe this could even be seen as a rescue mission.

This woman, sunburned, freckled and barefoot, standing with her arms folded across her breasts in a stance of pure defence, said it wasn't simple at all. Mrs Elsa Murdoch was not your normal nanny.

And… Christos and Amy had been her best friends?

'I'm not here to harm Zoe,' he said mildly.

'No.' That was a dumb statement, he conceded. As if she was expecting him to beat the child.

'I just want what's best for her.'

'Good,' she said brusquely. 'You might be able to help me. There are a couple of things I could use some advice over.'

That wasn't what he meant. They both knew it.

'Did you know Zoe's the new Crown Princess of Khryseis?' he asked, and she froze.

'The what?'

'The Crown Princess of Khryseis.'

'I heard you. I don't know what you mean.'

'I think you do,' he said softly. 'Your face when I said it…'

'Doesn't mean a thing,' she whispered. 'I'm tired, confused and hungry, and your uniform is doing my head in. Come in and sit down while I make lunch and take a shower. But if you say one word—one word—of this Crown Princess thing to Zoe before we've discussed it fully, you'll be off my property so fast you'll leave your gold tassels behind. Got it?'

'Um…got it,' he said.

'Right,' she said and turned and marched inside, leaving him to follow if he felt like it. Or go away if he felt like it.

Her body language said the second option was the one she favoured.

The moment he got inside he took his jacket off. He pulled off his tie, undid the next two buttons of his shirt and rolled up his sleeves.

It was a casual gesture of making himself at home and it rendered her almost speechless.

Outside he'd seemed large. Inside, tossing his jacket on the settee, rolling up his sleeves, taking a slow visual sweep of her kitchen-living room, he seemed much larger. It was as if he was filling the room, the space not taken up with his sheer physical size overwhelmed by his sheer masculinity.

He was six one or six two, she thought. Not huge. Just…male. And more good-looking than was proper. And way too sexy.

Sexy. Where had that word come from? She shoved it away in near panic.

'This is great,' he said, and she fought for composure and tried to see the house as he saw it.

It was tumbledown. Of course it was. There was no way she could afford to fix the big things. One day in the not too distant future Zoe might be able to go to school and she could take a proper job again and earn some money. But meanwhile they made do.

'Where did you get this stuff?' he asked, gesturing to the room in general. 'It's amazing.'

'Most of it we found or we made.'

He gazed around at the eclectic mix of brightly coloured cushions and faded crimson curtains, the colourful knotted rugs on the floor, lobster pots hanging from the ceiling with shells threaded through to make them look like proper decorations, a fishing net strung across the length of one wall, filled with old buoys and huge seashells. There were worn pottery jugs filled with flowers from the garden; bird of paradise plants, crimson and deep green.

'You found all this?' he demanded.

'I used to have an apartment at the university,' she told him. 'Small. My parents left me this place and I came here at weekends. I'm a marine biologist and we…I used the cottage as an occasional base for research. Zoe's parents were what you might call itinerant. They had a camper van and most of what they owned was destroyed in the accident. So Zoe and I scrounged what we could find, we made a bit and we filled the rest by beachcombing.' She met his gaze full on, defying him to deny her next assertion. 'Zoe and I are the best beachcombers in the world.'

'I can see you are,' he said. He paused. 'You're a marine biologist?'

'Yes.' She faltered and tried for a recovery. 'Very part-time until Zoe goes to school.'

'Zoe doesn't go to school?'

'I home-school her here at the moment.'

'So meanwhile you're living off Christos's life insurance.'

She'd opened the refrigerator and was lifting out salad ingredients. She froze.

She didn't turn around. She couldn't. If she had he might have got lettuce square in the middle of his face. What was he suggesting?

'That's right,' she said stiffly. 'I'm ripping Zoe off for every cent I can get.'

'I didn't mean…'

'I'm very sure you did mean.' Finally she turned, carefully placing the lettuce out of throwing range. 'What is it you want of us, Mr Whoever-The-Hell-You-Are, because there's no way I'm calling you Prince. I don't know why you're here but don't you dare imply I'm acting dishonestly. Don't you dare.'

'I already did,' he said, holding his hands up as if in surrender. 'I'm sorry.'

'So am I.'

The door swung open. Zoe appeared, looking wary. The

little girl was in clean T-shirt and shorts. Her hair was a tangle of dark, wet curls. She was far too thin, Elsa thought, trying to see her dispassionately through Stefanos's eyes.

She was so scarred. The burns had been to almost fifty per cent of her body, and twenty per cent of those had been full thickness. She'd had graft after graft. Thankfully her face was almost untouched but her skinny little legs looked almost like patchwork. Her left arm still needed work—her left hand was missing its little finger—and there was deep scarring under her chin.

She'd protect this child with her life, she thought, but protection could only go so far. This man was part of Zoe's real family. She had to back off a little.

'Okay, it's my turn for the shower, poppet,' she said, trying to make her voice normal.

'You sounded angry,' she said, doubtful.

'I'm crabby 'cos I'm hungry.' She tugged Zoe to her in a swift hug. 'I'll have a shower in world record time. Can you set the table and talk to…Stefanos. He's your papa's cousin. He knows all about Khryseis. Maybe he could show you exactly where he lives on the Internet. We have pictures of Khryseis bookmarked.'

And, with a final warning glance at Stefanos, she whisked herself away. She didn't want to leave at all. She wanted to bring Zoe into the bathroom with her. She wanted to defend her with everything she had.

Zoe, Crown Princess?

Zoe had far too much to deal with already. If Stefanos wanted to take on part of Zoe's life, then he had to contend with her. Zoe's life was her life. She'd sworn that to Zoe's mother, and she wasn't backing down on it now.

She couldn't. She was so afraid…

CHAPTER THREE

Zoe set the table while he watched her. The little girl was watching him out of the corner of her eye, not meeting his gaze directly. Table done, she turned to a corner desk holding a computer. The machine looked like something out of the Dark Ages, big, cumbersome and ugly. She checked the Internet, waiting until the Khryseis information downloaded—seemingly by slow-boat from China.

But finally the websites in Khryseis were on the screen. By the look of the bookmarks, she and Elsa spent a lot of time browsing them.

He tentatively showed her where he lived on the island—or where he'd lived as a child. She reacted with silent politeness.

He checked the other bookmarks for the island. They were marine sites, he saw. Research articles about the island.

Worth noting.

'So you and Elsa spend a lot of time studying…fish?' he ventured and got a scornful look for his pains.

'Echinoderms.'

Right. Good. What the hell were echinoderms?

And then Elsa was back. Same uniform as before—shorts and faded shirt. She was tugging her curls back into a ponytail. Still she wore no make-up, and without the suncream her freckles were more pronounced. Her nose was peeling and her feet were still bare.

She walked with a slight limp, he noted, but it was very slight. A twisted ankle, maybe? But that was a side issue. He wasn't about to focus on an ankle when he was looking at the whole package.

She was so different from the women in the circles he moved in that her appearance left him stunned. Awed, even.

He'd implied she was dishonest. There was nothing in this place, in her dress, in anything in this house, that said she was taking advantage of Zoe. His investigator had shown him Christos's financial affairs. If they were both living totally on Christos's life insurance…

'How much outside work do you do?' he said, carefully neutral, and Elsa pulled up short.

'You mean how much of my obviously fabulous riches are derived from honest toil and how much by stealing from orphans?'

He had to smile. And, to his relief, she returned a wry smile herself, as if she was ordering herself to relax.

'I'm not accusing you in any sense of the word,' he assured her. 'What's in front of my eyes is Zoe, in need of your care, and you, providing that care. Christos's life insurance wouldn't come close to paying for your combined expenses.'

'You don't know the half of it.'

'So tell me.'

She shook her head. 'I'm sorry, but Christos never spoke of you, as a cousin or as a friend. As far as I know, neither Christos nor his mother ever wanted to have anything to do with anyone from Khryseis. How can my finances have anything to do with you?'

'I do want to help.'

'Is that right?' she said neutrally. She shook her head. 'I'm sorry. Look, can we eat? I can't think while I'm hungry and after a morning on the beach I could eat a horse.'

She almost did. There was cold meat and salad, and freshly baked bread which she tipped from an ancient bread-maker. She cut doorstop slices of bread and made sandwiches. She poured tumblers of home-made lemonade, sat herself down, checked Zoe had what she needed—the sandwich she'd made for Zoe was much smaller, almost delicate in comparison to the ones she'd made for herself and for him—and then proceeded to eat.

She ate two doorstop sandwiches and drank three tumblers of lemonade, while Zoe ate half a sandwich and Elsa prodded her to eat more.

'Those legs are never going to get strong if they're hollow,' she teased, and Zoe gave her a shy smile, threw Stefanos a scared glance and nibbled a bit more.

She was trying to eat. He could see that. Was his presence scaring her?

The idea of frightening this child was appalling. The whole situation was appalling. He was starting to have serious qualms about whether his idea of Zoe's future was possible.

Except it must be. He had to get this child back to Khryseis. Oh, but her little body…

It didn't take his medical qualifications to realise how badly this child was damaged. The report he'd read had told him that four years ago Christos, his wife and their four-year-old daughter had been involved in a major car accident. Christos had died instantly. Amy, his wife, had died almost two weeks later and Zoe, their child, had been orphaned. No details.

There was a story behind every story, he thought, and suddenly he had a flash of what must have happened. A camper van crashing. A fire. A death, a woman so badly burned she died two weeks later, and a child. A child burned like her mother.

He knew enough about burns to understand you didn't get these type of scars without months—years—of medical treatment. Without considerable pain.

He'd arrived here thinking he had an orphaned eight-year-old on his hands. On *his* hands. She'd seemed like one more responsibility to add to his list. Her nanny was listed as one Mrs Elsa Murdoch. He'd had visions of a matronly employee, taking care of a school-aged child in return for cash.

His preconceptions had been so far from the mark that he felt dizzy.

Despite the man-sized sandwich on his plate, he wasn't eating. The official reception had been mid-morning, there'd been canapés, and he'd been watched to see which ones he ate, which chef he'd offend. So he'd eaten far more than he wanted. Elsa's doorstop sandwich was good, but he felt free to leave the second half uneaten. He had a feeling Elsa wasn't a woman who was precious about her cooking.

Actually…was this cooking? He stared down at his sandwich and thought of the delicacies he'd been offered since he'd taken over the throne—and he grinned.

'So what's funny?' Elsa demanded, and he looked up and found she was watching him. Once more she was wearing her assessing expression. He found it penetrating…and disturbing. He didn't like to be read, but he had a feeling that in Elsa Murdoch he'd found someone who could do just that.

'I've had an overload of royal food,' he told her. 'This is great.'

'So you wouldn't be eating…why?'

'I'm full of canapés.'

'I can see that about you,' she said. 'A canapé snacker. Can I have your sandwich, then?'

He handed it over and watched in astonishment as she ate. Where was she putting it? There wasn't an ounce of spare flesh on her. She looked…just about perfect.

Where had that description come from? He thought of the glamorous women he'd had in his life, how appalled they'd be if they could hear the *perfect* adjective applied to this woman, and once more he couldn't help smiling.

'Yep, we're a world away from your world,' she said brusquely.

What the…? 'Will you stop that?'

'What?' she asked, all innocence.

'Mind reading.'

'Not if it works. It's fun.' She rose and started clearing dishes. He noted the limp again but, almost as he noted it, it ceased. Zoe was visibly wilting. 'Zoe, poppet, you go take a nap. Unless…' She paused. 'Unless Stefanos wants us to drive him into town now.'

'I need to talk to you,' he said.

'There you go,' she said equably. 'I mind read that too. So, Zoe, pop into bed and we'll take Stefanos home when you wake up.'

'You won't get angry again?' Zoe asked her, casting an anxious look across at him.

And he got that too. This child's mental state was fragile. She did not need angry voices. She did not need anyone arguing about her future.

This place was perfect for an injured child to heal, he thought. A tropical paradise.

He had another paradise for her, though. He watched with concern as Elsa kissed her soundly, promised her no anger and sent her off to bed.

There was no choice. He just had to make this…nanny… accept it.

She washed.

He wiped.

She protested, but he was on the back foot already—the idea of watching while she worked would make the chasm deeper.

They didn't speak. Maybe the idea of having a prince doing her wiping was intimidating, he thought wryly, and here it was again. Her response before he could voice his thought.

'An apron beats tassels for this job any day. I need a camera,' she said, handing him a sudsy breadboard to wipe. 'No one will believe this.'

'Aren't you supposed to rinse off the suds?'

'You're criticising my washing? I'm more than happy to let you do both.'

'I'm more than happy to do both.'

She paused. She set down her dishcloth and turned to face him, wiping her sudsy hands on the sides of her shorts.

She looked anxious again. And territorial.

And really, really cute.

'Why the limp?' he asked and she glanced at him as if he was intruding where he wasn't wanted.

'It's hardly a limp. I'm fine. Next question?'

'Where's Mr Murdoch?' he asked, and her face grew another emotion.

'What?' she said dangerously.

Uh-oh. But he couldn't take the question back. It hung between them, waiting for an answer.

'My researchers said Zoe's nanny was a Mrs Elsa Murdoch.'

'Ms,' she said and glared.

'So never a Mrs?'

'What's that to do with the price of eggs?'

'It's merely a polite question.'

'Polite. Okay.' She even managed a…polite…smile. 'So where's your Princess?'

'Sorry?'

'I'm Mrs so there has to be a Mr. I believe I'm simply reversing your question. Is there a matching Princess?'

'Why would you want to know that?'

'Exactly,' she said, and smiled—a smile that confounded him as she turned back to her washing. Only there was nothing left to wash. She let the water out and wiped the sink with care. She waited for him to dry the last glass, then wiped his part of the sink as well, as if it was vital that not a speck of anything remained.

This woman confounded him—but he had to focus on their future. He must.

'Zoe's needed back on Khryseis,' he said, and Elsa's hand stilled mid-wipe. She couldn't disguise the fear sweeping over her face.

'She stays here.'

'I believe I'm her nearest living relative,' he said mildly. 'As such I can challenge your guardianship.'

She didn't move. Her hand seemed suddenly to be locked on the sink. She was staring downward as if there was something riveting in its depths.

'Oh…' He couldn't mistake the distress on her face. 'No!'

But it had to be said. Like it or not, the stakes were too high to allow emotion to hold sway.

'I'm her cousin,' he said, gently but as firm as he needed to be. 'It's obvious you're struggling to care for her. I can…'

'You can't.' She whirled to face him at that. Her voice was low enough not to disturb Zoe, but loud enough to make him feel her fury. And her fear. 'She's been with me for four years. I'm her godmother and her guardian. Her mother was my best friend and I promised Amy I'd care for her. Her father was a colleague and I loved him too. You…did you know any of them?'

'I knew Christos.'

'Yeah, close family,' she mocked. 'He never mentioned you. Not once. He said royalty on Khryseis was a shambles, the King was concerned only with himself, the King controlled all three of the Diamond Isles and the original royal families of each island were helpless. Christos was frightened of the royal family. He came here to escape what he saw as persecution. He hated them.'

Okay, he thought. Stick to facts. Get over this patch of ground as fast as possible and move on.

'King Giorgos gave Christos a dreadful time,' he told her, keeping his voice as neutral as he could. 'Christos and his mother left Khryseis when he was seventeen. Did he tell you he was first in line to the crown of Khryseis's original royal family?'

'No.'

'He was. That's why Giorgos made life hell for him. He made life hard enough for me and I was only second in line. So we both left and made our lives overseas, but when Giorgos died…'

'Giorgos is dead?'

'Without an heir. So Christos should be Crown Prince. It's taken weeks to get this far. To find he was dead. No one on Khryseis knew he'd died.'

'His mother wasn't well when her son died.' He could see facts and emotions swirling, fighting for space as she took in his words. 'I guess… I imagined it was up to her to tell others if she wanted. But she was frail already, and her son's death made things… Well, she died three months later.'

'So Zoe lost her grandmother as well.'

Her eyes flew to his. She hadn't expected that response, he thought, and wondered what she had expected.

'Yes,' she whispered. 'Thank you for recognising that. It did make things much harder.'

'So then you stepped in.'

'There was no one else.'

'And now we have a mess,' he said, choosing his words with care. 'Yes, Christos hated the royal family, but it was King Giorgos he feared and Giorgos's line is finished. The three Diamond Isles have splintered into three principalities. As Christos's only child, Zoe's the new Crown Princess of Khryseis. She'll inherit full sovereign power when she's twenty-five but until then, like it or not, I'm Prince Regent. Whether I want that power or not, the island's desperate for change. The infrastructure's appalling but I only have power for change if Zoe lives on Khryseis for at least three months of every year. Otherwise the power stays with an island council that's as impotent as it is corrupt. Elsa, she has to come home.'

She didn't say a word.

She was a really self-contained woman, he thought. He'd shaken her out of her containment but he'd done it with fear of losing Zoe. She had her self-containment back now, and he had no idea what was going in her head. He wouldn't be privy to it until she decided to speak again.

She poured two tumblers of water. She walked outside—

not limping now, he thought, and found he was relieved. He could cope with an injured child—but not an incapacitated nanny as well. There were two ancient deckchairs on the porch. She sank into one of them and left it to him to decide whether to sit on the other.

The chairs were old and stained and the one left vacant looked to be covered in cat fur.

His trousers were jet-black with a slash of crimson up the side. Ceremonial uniform.

'It brushes off,' she said wryly, not looking at him. Gazing out through the palms to the sea beyond.

He sat.

'You have a cat?' he asked, feeling his way.

'Five,' she said, and as he looked around she shook her head.

'They won't come near when you're here. They're feral cats. Cats are a huge problem up here—they decimate the wildlife. Only Zoe loves them. So we've caught every one we can. If they're at all approachable we have them neutered. We feed them really well at dusk and again in the morning. We lock them up overnight where we feed them—in the little enclosure behind the house. That way they don't need to kill wildlife to eat. Apart from our new little black one, they're fat and lazy, and if you weren't here they'd be lined up here snoozing their day away.'

'You can afford to feed five cats?'

Mistake. Once again she froze. 'You're inordinately interested in my financial affairs,' she said flatly. 'Can you tell me why they're you're business?'

'You're spending Zoe's money.'

'And you're responsible for Zoe how? You didn't even know she existed.'

'Now I do know, she's family.'

'Good, then,' she said. 'Go talk to Zoe's lawyers. They'll tell you we put her money in a trust fund and I take out only what's absolutely necessary for us to live.'

'And the cats?'

She sighed. 'We catch fish,' she said. 'I cook the heads and innards with rice. That's my cat food for the week. So yes, I waste rice and some fish heads on our cats. Shoot me now.'

'I'm not criticising.'

'You are,' she said bluntly. 'You said I'm struggling to care for her. Tell me in what way I'm struggling?'

'Look at this place,' he said before he could stop himself—and her simmering anger exploded.

'I'm looking. I can't see a palace, if that's what you mean. I can't see surround-sound theatre rooms and dishwashers and air-conditioning. I can't see wall to wall carpet and granite bench tops. So how does Zoe need those?'

'It's falling down.'

'So if it falls down I'll rebuild. We have isolation, which Zoe needs until she gets her confidence back. We have our own private beach. We have my work—yes, I'm still doing research and I'm being paid a stipend which goes towards Zoe's medical costs, but…'

'You're paying Zoe's medical costs?'

'Your investigator didn't go very far if he didn't find that out. Her parents hadn't taken out medical insurance,' she said. 'In this country the basics are covered but there have been so many small things. The last lot of plastic surgery was on her shoulder. The surgeon was wonderful—that's why we used him—but he only operates on private patients so we had to pay.'

'*You* had to pay.'

'Whatever.'

'You can't keep doing that.'

'Try and stop me,' she said, carefully neutral again. She'd obviously decided it was important to keep a rein on her temper.

'Where does that leave you?'

'Where I am.'

'Stuck in the middle of nowhere, with a damaged child.'

She put her drink carefully down on the packing case that served as their outdoor table. She rose.

'You know, I'm not enjoying myself here and I have work to do. I correct assignments online and I try to do it while Zoe's asleep. When she wakes we'll drive you back into town. But meanwhile… Meanwhile you go take a walk on the beach, calculate cat food costs, do whatever you want, I don't care. I believe any further dialogue should be through our lawyers.'

And she walked deliberately inside and let the screen door bang closed after her.

CHAPTER FOUR

SHE was true to her word. She wouldn't speak to him until Zoe woke up. He took a walk on the beach, feeling ridiculous in his ridiculous uniform. He came back and talked for a while to a little black cat who deigned to be sociable. Finally Zoe woke, but even then Elsa only spoke when necessary.

'I'll give you the address of my lawyer,' she said.

'I already know who your lawyer is.'

'Of course you do,' she said cordially. 'Silly me.'

'You're being…'

'Obstructive?' she said. 'Yes, I am.'

'What's obstructive?' Zoe asked.

'Not letting your cousin Stefanos have what he wants.'

'What does he want?'

'You might ask him.'

Zoe turned to him, puzzled. 'What do you want?'

'To get to know you,' he said, refusing to be distracted by Elsa's anger. 'Your papa was a very good friend of mine. When he left Khryseis we didn't write—he wanted a clean break. I should have made more of an effort to keep in touch and I'll be sorry for the rest of my life that I didn't. That he married and had a little girl called Zoe…that he died…it breaks my heart that I didn't know.'

'It makes you sad?'

'Very sad.'

But apparently Zoe knew about sad—and she had a cure.

'When I'm in hospital and I'm sad, Elsa tells me about the fish she's seen that day, and shells and starfish. Elsa keeps saying the sea's waiting for me to get well. She brings in pictures of the beach and the house and the cats and she pins them all over the walls so every time I wake up I can see that the sea and this house and our cats are waiting for me.'

His gaze flew to Elsa. She was staring blankly ahead, as if she hadn't heard.

But she had heard, he thought. She surely had.

And he knew then… As he watched her stoical face he realised that he was threatening her foundations. He was threatening to remove a little girl she loved with all her heart.

He'd never thought of this as a possibility. That a nanny could truly love his little cousin.

He'd come here expecting to meet Mrs Elsa Murdoch, paid nanny. Instead he'd met Elsa, marine biologist, friend, protector, mother to Zoe in every sense but name.

After the shock of learning of Zoe's existence, his plan had been to rescue his orphaned cousin, take her back to Khryseis and pay others to continue her care. Or, if Zoe was attached to this particular nanny, then he could continue to employ her to give the kid continuity.

It had to be option two.

Only if he broached it now Elsa might well lock the door and call the authorities to throw him off her land.

So do it when? He had so little time.

'I need to go back to Khryseis tomorrow,' he told Zoe and glanced sideways to see relief flood Elsa's face. 'Elsa's said she'll drive me into town now. But I've upset her. She thought I might want to take you away from her, and I'd never do that. I promise. So if you and Elsa drive me into town now, can I come and visit again tomorrow morning?' He looked ruefully down at his ceremonial trousers—now liberally coated in cat fur. 'If I'm welcome?'

'Is he welcome?' Zoe asked Elsa.

'If you want him to come,' Elsa said neutrally. 'Stefanos is your cousin.'

Zoe thought about it. He was being judged, he thought, and the sensation was weird. Judged by an eight-year-old, with Elsa on the sidelines doing her own judging.

Or…it seemed she'd already judged.

'If you come you should bring your togs,' Zoe said.

'Togs?'

'Your swimming gear—if you own any without tassels and braid,' Elsa said, still obviously forcing herself not to glower. 'As a farewell visit,' she added warningly. 'Because, if you really are Zoe's cousin, then I accept that she should get to know you.'

'That's gracious of you,' he said gravely.

'It is,' she said and managed a half-hearted smile.

The drive back to town started in silence. Elsa's car was an ancient family wagon, filled in the back with—of all things—lobster pots. There was a pile of buoys and nets heaped on the front passenger seat, so he was forced to sit in the rear seat with Zoe.

She could have put the gear in the back, he thought, but she didn't offer and he wasn't pushing it. So she was chauffeur and he and Zoe were passengers.

'You catch lobsters?' he said cautiously.

'We weigh them, sex them, tag then and let them go,' she said briefly from the front.

'You have a boat?'

'The university supplies one. But I only go when Zoe can come with me.'

'It's really fun,' Zoe said. 'I like catching the little ones. You have to be really careful when you pick them up. If you grab them behind their necks they can't reach and scratch you.'

'We have lobsters on the Diamond Isles,' he told her. 'My friend Nikos is a champion fisherman.'

'Do you fish?' Zoe demanded.

'I did when I was a boy.'

They chatted on. Elsa was left to listen. And fret.

He was good, she conceded. He was wriggling his way into

Zoe's trust and that wasn't something lightly achieved. Like her father before her, Zoe was almost excruciatingly shy, and that shyness had been made worse by people's reaction to her scars.

Stefanos hadn't once referred to her scars. To the little girl it must be as if he hadn't noticed them.

The concept, for Zoe, must be huge. Here was someone out of her papa's past, wanting to talk to her about interesting stuff like what he'd done on Khryseis when he was a boy with her papa.

She shouldn't be driving him back into town. She should be asking him to dinner, even asking him to sleep over to give Zoe as much contact as she could get.

Only there were other issues. Like the Crown. Like the fact that he'd said that Zoe had to return to Khryseis. Like crazy stuff that she couldn't consider.

Like asking a prince of the blood whether he'd like to sleep on her living room settee, she thought suddenly, and the idea was so ridiculous she almost smiled.

He was leaving tomorrow. He'd stopped talking about the possibility of Zoe coming with him. Maybe he'd given up.

She glanced into the rear-view mirror and he looked up and met her eyes.

No, she thought, and fear settled back around her heart. Prince Stefanos of Khryseis looked like a man who didn't give up—on anything.

The township of Waratah Cove had two three-star hotels and one luxury six-star resort out on the headland past the town.

Without asking, she turned the car towards the headland and he didn't correct her.

Money, she thought bleakly. If she could have the cost of one night's accommodation in this place…

'Can you stop here?' Stefanos asked and she jammed her foot on the brake and stopped dead. Maybe a bit too suddenly.

'Wow,' Zoe said. 'Are you crabby or something?'

'Or something,' she said neutrally, glancing again at Stefanos in the rear-view mirror.

'Your nanny thinks I spend too much money,' he said, amused, and she flushed. Was she so obvious?

'Elsa's not my nanny,' Zoe said, amused herself.

'What is she?'

'She's just my Elsa.'

My Elsa. It was said with such sureness that he knew he could never break this bond. If he was to take Zoe back to Khryseis, he needed to take them both.

He had to get this right.

'So why did you want me to stop here?' Elsa asked.

'Because the ambassador to the Diamond Isles leaked to the media that I was coming here,' he said bitterly. 'That's why I had to find myself a uniform and attend the reception. I've already had to bribe—heavily—the chauffeur they arranged for me so he wouldn't tell anyone my location. I imagine there'll be cameramen outside my hotel, wanting to know where I've been, and I don't want a media circus descending on Zoe. I can walk the last couple of hundred yards.'

'Maybe you should check your trousers,' Elsa said, and there was suddenly laughter in her voice. 'Cat fur isn't a great look for a Royal Prince.'

'Thanks very much,' he said, and smiled.

And, unaccountably, she smiled back.

Hers was a gorgeous smile. Warm and natural and full of humour. If he'd met this woman under normal circumstances…

Maybe he'd never have noticed her, he thought. She didn't move in the circles he moved in. Plus he liked his women groomed. Sophisticated. Able to hold their own in any company.

She'd be able to hold her own. This was one feisty woman.

He needed to learn more about her. He needed to hit the phones, extend his research, come up with an offer she couldn't refuse.

Unaccountably, he didn't want to get out of the car. The

battered family wagon, loaded with lobster pots, smelling faintly—no, more than faintly—of fish, unaccountably seemed a good place to stay.

He thought suddenly of his apartment in Manhattan. Of his consulting suite with its soft grey carpet, its trendy chrome furniture, its soft piped music.

They were worlds apart—he and Mrs Elsa Murdoch.

But now their lives needed to overlap, enough to keep the island safe. The islanders safe.

Zoe safe.

Until today he'd seen Zoe as a problem—a shock, to be muted before the islanders found out.

Now, suddenly that obstacle was human—a little girl with scars, attached to a woman who loved her.

They were waiting for him to get out of the car. If he left it any longer a media vehicle might come this way. One cameraman and Zoe would run, he thought, and it'd be Elsa who ran with her.

Elsa wasn't family. It wasn't her role to care for Zoe.

Forget the roles, he told himself sharply. Now he must protect the pair of them. He climbed from the car and tried to dust himself off. He had ginger cat fur on black trousers.

Suddenly Elsa was out of the car as well, watching as he shrugged on his jacket.

'Do your buttons up,' she said, almost kindly. 'You look much more princely with your buttons done up. And hold still. If a car comes I'll stop, but let's see what we can achieve before that happens.'

And, before he knew what she intended, she'd twisted him round so she could attack the backs of his legs and the seat of his trousers.

With a hairbrush?

'It's actually a brush Zoe uses for her dolls,' she told him, sweeping the cat fur off in long efficient strokes. 'But see—I've rolled sticky tape the wrong way round around its bristles. It's very effective.'

He was so confounded he submitted. He was standing on

a headland in the middle of nowhere while a woman called Mrs Elsa Murdoch attacked his trousers with a dolls' hair-brush.

She brushed until she was satisfied. Then she straightened. 'Turn round and let me look at you,' she said.

He turned.

'Very nice,' she said. 'Back to being a prince again. What do you think, Zoe? Is he ready for the cameras?'

'His top button's undone,' Zoe said.

'That's because it's hot,' he retorted but Elsa shook her head.

'No class at all,' she said soulfully. 'I don't know what you modern day royals are coming to.' She carefully fastened his top button while he felt…he felt… He didn't know how he felt; he was only aware that when the button was fastened and she stepped back there was a sharp stab of something that might even be loss.

'There you go, Your Highness,' she said, like a valet who'd just done a good job making a recalcitrant prince respectable. 'Off you go and face the world while Zoe and I get back to our cats and our lobster pots.'

And she was in the car, turned and driving away before he had a chance to reply.

His first task was to get his breath back. To face the media with some sort of dignity.

His second task was to talk to the hotel concierge.

'I need some extensive shopping done on my behalf,' he said. 'Fast. Oh, and I need to hire a car. No, not a limousine. Anything not smelling of fish would be acceptable.'

Then he rang Prince Alexandros back in the Diamond Isles. As well as being a friend, Alexandros was Crown Prince of Sappheiros, and Alex more than anyone else knew what was at stake—why he was forced to be in Australia in royal uniform when he should be in theatre garb back in Manhattan.

'Problem?' his friend asked.

'I don't know.'

'What don't you know?'

'The child's been burned. She's dreadfully scarred.'

There was a sharp intake of breath. 'Hell. Is she…'

'She's okay. It's healing. But my idea of leaving her on the island… She'll have special needs.'

'You were never going to be able to leave her anyway.'

'I don't have a choice,' he snapped. 'You know I can't leave my work yet—I can't break promises. But there's a nanny. A good one. A Mrs Elsa Murdoch. She's not like any Mrs Elsa Murdoch I've ever met.'

There was a lengthy silence on the end of the phone. Then, 'How many Mrs Elsa Murdochs have you met?' Alexandros asked, with a certain amount of caution.

Uh-oh. Alex and Stefanos had known each other since they were kids. Maybe Alex had heard something in his voice that he didn't necessarily want to share.

'Just the one,' he said.

Another silence. 'She's young?' Alex ventured.

'Yes.'

'Aha.'

'There's no aha about it.'

'There's a Mr Elsa Murdoch?'

'No.'

'I rest my case,' he said. 'Hey, Stefanos, like me, you've spent so much of your life pushing your career…avoiding family. Maybe it's time you did a heads up and noticed the Elsa Murdochs of this world.'

'Alex…' He couldn't think what to add next.

'You want something more?' Alex asked. 'Something specific? If not…my wife's waiting for me. Not a bad thing for a prince to have, you know. A wife. Especially if that prince needs to care for a child with injuries.'

'This isn't a joke.'

'I don't believe I was joking,' Alex threw back at him. 'Okay, so this Mrs Elsa Murdoch… You want to tell me about her?'

How had he got himself into this conversation? He didn't have a clue.

'I'll leave you to your wife,' he said stiffly.

'Excellent,' Alex said. 'I'll leave you to your Mrs Elsa Murdoch. And your little Crown Princess. Steve…'

'Yes?'

'Take care. And keep an open mind. Speaking as a man who's just married…it can make all the difference in the world.'

Elsa lay awake far into the night, staring at a life she'd never envisaged. A life without Zoe.

She'd never thought of it.

Four years ago she'd been happily married, full of plans for the future, working with Matty and her good friends and their little girl.

One stupid drunken driver—who'd walked away unscathed—and she was left with nothing but the care of Zoe.

Up until today she'd thought Zoe depended totally on her. Up until now she'd never really considered that the reverse was true as well.

Without Zoe…

No. She couldn't think it. It left a void in her life so huge it terrified her.

He'd backed off. He'd said he was leaving tomorrow.

Zoe's needed back on Khryseis.

She reran his words through her mind—she remembered almost every word he'd uttered. He hadn't backed off.

Zoe's needed back on Khryseis.

She was Zoe's legal guardian. But if it came to a custody battle between Elsa, with no blood tie and no means of giving Zoe the last operations she so desperately needed—or Stefanos, a royal prince, a blood relative, with money and means at his disposal, able to give her every chance in life…

What choice was there?

She felt sick and tired.

A letter lay on her bureau. She rose from her tumbled

sheets—lying in bed was useless anyway—and read it for the thousandth time.

It was an outline of costs for cosmetic plastic surgery to smooth the skin under Zoe's chin and across her neck.

She'd sold everything she had. There was no money left.

Stefanos.

Not if it meant losing Zoe. Not!

Who was she protecting here? Herself or Zoe?

Damn him!

She should be welcoming him, she thought. Knight on white charger with loaded wallet.

Not if it meant giving up Zoe.

To watch them go…

To watch him go.

Where had that thought come from? Nowhere. She did not need to think he was sexy. The fact that he was drop-dead gorgeous only added to her fear. She did not need her hormones to stir.

They were stirring.

She walked outside, stood on the veranda and stared into the dark.

Prince Stefanos of Khryseis. Cousin to Zoe.

A man about to change her life.

A man about to take her child.

Fifteen miles across the water, Stefanos was doing the same thing. Watching the moonbeams ripple across the ocean. Thinking how his life had changed.

Because of Zoe.

And…Elsa? A barefoot, poverty stricken marine biologist of a nanny?

He had a million other things to think about.

So why was he thinking of Elsa?

It was mid-morning when he arrived and they hadn't left for the beach yet. There was a tiny seeping wound under Zoe's arm. It was minuscule but they'd learned from bitter experience to treat small as big. This was a skin graft area. If it extended Zoe could lose the whole graft—an appalling prospect.

Elsa had found it while she was applying Zoe's suncream and now she was hovering between wait and see or ring the local medical centre and get it seen to now.

Only it was Sunday. Their normal doctor would be away. Waratah Cove had a small bush-nursing hospital, manned by casual staff over the weekend. Less experienced doctors tended to react to Zoe's injuries with fear, dreading under-treating. If she took Zoe in, she'd be admitted and transferred to hospital in the city. Simple as that.

And they were both so weary of hospitals.

Her worry almost made her forget Stefanos was coming—but not completely. The sound of a car on the track made her feel as if the world was caving in, landing right on her shoulders.

She hated this. She just hated it.

She tugged a T-shirt over Zoe's scarred little body and turned to welcome him. And almost gasped.

This was a different Stefanos. Faded jeans. T-shirt. Scuffed trainers.

Great body. Really great body.

A body to make her feel she was a woman again.

She had to do something about these hormones. They were doing things to her head. She'd married Matty. His picture was still on the mantel. Get a grip.

'Hi,' he said, and smiled at the two of them and Elsa couldn't resist. She had to smile. It was as if he had the strength to change her world, just by smiling.

'Hi,' Zoe said shyly and smiled as well, and Elsa looked at Zoe in astonishment. Two minutes earlier the two of them had been close to tears.

Stefanos's smile was a force to be reckoned with.

'I thought you'd be at the beach,' he said, and then he looked more closely—maybe seeing the traces of their distress. 'Is something wrong?'

'We thought we wouldn't go to the beach this morning,' Elsa said repressively. Zoe loathed people talking about her injuries. She'd had enough fuss to last one small girl a lifetime.

Stefanos had never mentioned her scars. Maybe he hadn't even noticed. Or…not.

'Why not?' he said gently, and suddenly he was talking to Zoe, and not to her. As if he'd guessed.

'There's a bit of my skin graft come loose,' Zoe said.

Once again it was as much as Elsa could do not to gasp. Zoe never volunteered such information.

She'd had the best doctors—the best!—but almost every one of them talked to her and not to Zoe. Oh, they chatted to Zoe, but in the patronising way elders often talked to children. For the hard questions—even things like: 'Is she sleeping at night?'—they turned to her, as if Zoe couldn't possibly know.

So what had Stefanos done different?

She knew. He hadn't treated her as an object of sympathy, and he'd talked directly to her. Simple but so important.

'Whereabouts?' Stefanos asked, still speaking only to Zoe.

'Under my arm at the back.'

'Is it hurting?'

'No, but…it's scary,' Zoe said, and her bottom lip wobbled.

'Can I ask why?'

'Elsa will have to take me to hospital and they'll make me stay there, and I don't want to go.' Her voice ended on a wail, she turned her face into Elsa's shirt and she sobbed.

'Zoe,' Stefanos said, in a voice she'd not heard before. Gentle, yet firm. He squatted so he was at her eye level. 'Zoe, will you let me take a look? I don't know if I can help, but I'm a doctor. Will you trust me to see if I think you need hospital?'

He was a doctor?

There was a loaded silence. Zoe would be as stunned as she was, Elsa thought.

You still can't have her, she thought, her instinctive response overriding everything else, but she had the sense to shut up. The last thing Zoe needed was more fear.

Because, astonishingly, Zoe was turning towards him. She was still hard against Elsa but he'd cut through her distress.

'You're a doctor?'

'Yes.'

'But you're a prince.'

'People are allowed to be both.'

'My papa was a doctor,' she said. 'But a doctor of science. He studied shellfish.'

'Did Christos get his doctorate?' he said with pleasure. 'Hey, how about that. I wish I'd known.' Still he was talking to Zoe. 'Your papa and I used to be really good friends. He taught me where to find the best shells on Khryseis. Only I always wanted to find the pretty ones or the big ones and he wanted to look for the interesting ones. Sometimes he'd pick up a little grey shell I didn't think at all special and off he'd go, telling me it was a Multi-Armpit Hairy Cyclamate, or a Wobblysaurus Rex, or something even sillier.'

Zoe stared in astonishment—and then she giggled.

You could forgive a lot of a man who could make Zoe giggle, Elsa conceded. And…a man who could make her giggle as well?

'Will you let me see what the problem is?' he asked gently, and Zoe lifted her T-shirt without hesitation. Which was another miracle all by itself.

And here was another miracle. He didn't react. Zoe's left side was a mass of scar tissue but Stefanos's expression didn't change by as much as a hair's breadth. He was still smiling a little—with Zoe—and she was smiling back. His long fingers probed the scar tissue with infinite gentleness, not going near the tiny suppurating wound but simply assessing the situation overall.

He had such long fingers, Elsa thought. Big hands, tanned and gentle. She wouldn't mind…

Um…whoa. Attention back to Zoe. Fast.

'What sort of medical supplies do you have here?' he asked, still speaking only to Zoe, and Elsa held her breath.

This was a question every doctor or nurse she knew would address to her, but this whole conversation was between the two of them.

'We have lots of stuff,' Zoe volunteered. 'Sometimes when I'm just out of hospital the nurses come here and change my dressings. It costs a lot though, 'cause we're so far out of town, so Elsa keeps a lot of stuff here and she's learned to do it instead.'

'Well, good for Elsa.' And, dumbly, Elsa found she was blushing with pleasure. 'Can I see?' he asked.

'I'll get it,' she said and headed for the bathroom—and even that was a minor miracle. For Zoe to let her leave the room while a strange doctor was examining her… Definitely a miracle.

She didn't push it, though. She was back in seconds, carrying a hefty plastic crate. She set it down and Stefanos examined its contents and whistled.

'You have enough here to treat an elephant,' he said. 'You don't have an elephant hidden under a bed somewhere, do you?'

Once again Zoe giggled. It was the best sound. It made her feel… It made her feel…

No. She would not get turned on because this man made a child giggle.

Only she already was. She was fighting hormones here as hard as she could. And losing.

It had been too long. You're a sick, sad spinster, she told herself, and then rebuked herself sharply. Not a spinster. She glanced across at the mantel, and Matty's face smiled down at her from its frame. Sorry, she told him under her breath. Sorry, sorry, sorry.

'You know, I'm sure I can fix this.' Stefanos's words tugged her attention straight back to him. 'Zoe, if you and Elsa trust me… I think all this needs is some antiseptic cream, a couple of Steri-Strips to tug it together—see, it's at the end of the graft so we can attach the strips to good skin on either side and tug it together. Then we can pop one of these waterproof dressings over the whole thing and you could even go swimming this morning. Which, seeing I brought my bathers, is probably a good thing.' He grinned.

And Elsa thought, I'm in trouble here. I'm in serious trouble.

But they were moving on. Stefanos rose and washed his hands with the thoroughness of a surgeon. Then he lifted Zoe carefully—being mindful of where her scars were without Zoe noticing he was mindful, Elsa thought. He sat her on the kitchen table and proceeded to do his stuff.

He was skilled. She just had to see those fingers gently probing. She just had to listen to him chat to Zoe, distracting her as he worked. He was so careful, so precise, and she thought of all the doctors who'd treated Zoe over the past four years and she thought this man was a blessing.

This man wanted to take Zoe away.

This man was Zoe's cousin—a prince.

This man was a doctor, with all the skills needed to take care of her.

She was a marine biologist with nothing.

He was applying the waterproof dressing now and he glanced over his shoulder to say something to her. And he saw her expression. She'd tried to get it under control but he could see—she knew he could see.

'There's nothing to be afraid of, Elsa,' he said gently and she thought, You don't know the half of it. Nothing to be afraid of? When he was threatening to turn her world around?

'I... You came here to talk,' she said, and it was really hard to get her words out.

'I came here to swim,' he said. 'Are there any other problems to sort before we swim? Nothing I can treat? Ingrown toenails? Snakebite? Measles?'

Zoe giggled again and wriggled down from the table. She was totally at ease now, completely relaxed in his company.

He couldn't take her away, she thought frantically. Zoe would always want her. Wouldn't she?

There's nothing to be afraid of, she told herself, but she knew she was lying.

There was everything to be afraid of. Everything she held dear.

But for now…it seemed they were going for a swim.

CHAPTER FIVE

THE swim was glorious, fun and deeply scary.

Glorious in that the weather gods had decided this was another day out of the box—brilliant sunshine but not too hot, the water cool enough to refresh but not so cold they couldn't stay in for as long they wanted, turquoise-clear so they could see everything on the bottom.

Fun because Stefanos made it fun. He twisted and turned under the water, teaching Zoe new tricks, tickling her toes on the sandy bottom, making her play as a child should play. As Zoe had been unable to play.

She'd been isolated for so long. She should be with other children, but there were so many complications. Twice Elsa had tried to send her to school but each time she'd ended up with a major infection and back in hospital.

So if it couldn't be a bunch of kids whooping and hollering around her, Stefanos was definitely next best. He was a fabulous swimmer and he knew how to make Zoe laugh.

Of course he was and of course he did, Elsa thought, with what she recognised as dumb and irrational resentment. She loved that Zoe was falling for Stefanos's charm, but she was also fearful of it.

She was fearful of falling for Stefanos's charm herself.

Because he was…gorgeous. She'd seen him yesterday in full royal regalia and thought he was gorgeous then. She'd seen him this morning in his jeans and T-shirt and thought he was just plain yummy. Now, clad only in his board shorts, she could hardly keep her eyes off him. Lean and tanned, every muscle delineated…

He was a doctor, for heaven's sake. He must spend his life indoors. Where had he got those muscles?

He was scaring her. Not only because of what he'd suggested yesterday—that he take Zoe away. Not only because of his effect on Zoe. But because of his effect on her.

Mathew had been dead for four years now. Her friends told her it was time to move on.

She'd never had the slightest urge to move on, until right now. And now…what her body was telling her, what her hormones were telling her, felt like a betrayal.

'Mathew, Mathew, Mathew,' she murmured over and over, and because Zoe was perfectly safe with her big cousin, because Stefanos's sole desire seemed to be to make the little girl laugh, she left them to it, stroking strongly out across the entrance to the cove.

She put her head down and swam as she never swam, for it wasn't safe to do this when no one was here to watch Zoe. She'd always gloried in swimming. It was her quiet time. Her time of peace. She was swimming now, hoping her head could settle, so her jumbled thoughts could somehow untangle, so she could find the strength to stand up to this unknown prince and his terrifying charm.

She lost track of time. She swam and swam and finally when she raised her head she realised Zoe and Stefanos were out of the water, standing on the beach and watching her.

And that felt strange too. That this man was watching her…

She caught a wave back to the beach, surfing in with the agility she'd always gloried in. The sea had always been her escape. It could be again, she thought. If the worst happened. If he took Zoe away…

They strolled down the beach to meet her. Her wave washed her into the shallows, she wiped her eyes and looked up to find Stefanos standing above her, smiling, holding out his hand to tug her up.

She nearly didn't take it, she was so disconcerted. But that'd be petty. Zoe was standing beside him, beaming, waiting for her to stand.

She took his hand, he tugged her up and she came up too fast.

She stumbled and he steadied her. Which was a tiny gesture—Prince steadies Elsa—and why the feel of his hands on her waist should have the power to totally disconcert her she didn't know.

'You're beautiful,' he said and she was disconcerted all over again.

'Do you…' She fought for breath and took a while finding it. 'Do you mind?'

'I'm only speaking the truth.'

'Right,' she said and headed up the beach fast. She grabbed her towel and disappeared underneath. At least here she could get her face under control.

Beautiful?

Matty had thought she was beautiful. Until then no one. After him no one.

She wasn't even wearing a bathing suit. Neither she nor Zoe did. They both wore shorts and T-shirts. It'd be unfair for her to wear pretty bathers when Zoe had to wear scar-covering clothes. And she had scars herself—nothing like Zoe's, but bad enough.

And besides, she thought grimly, she was mousy. She'd always been mousy and she always would be mousy. Mathew had thought she was beautiful because he'd fallen in love with her mind. He'd been academically brilliant and he'd loved that she could keep up with him. Her intelligence was a turn on.

But her body? Not so much that he'd ever said. Beauty was in the eye of the beholder and in Mathew's eyes she was his brilliant wife.

Matty.

Dammit, why wasn't he here? And…why was he starting to fade? It was terrifying that when she thought of him now the image that came straight to mind was the photograph on the mantel. Photographs were becoming the reality, and reality moved on, whether she willed it or not.

All this she thought under her towel. All this she thought while she rubbed her hair dry.

'Zoe and I think your hair will dry faster in the sun.'

His voice made her jump. They'd followed her up the beach!

You're not being paranoid? she demanded of herself, and she knew that she was.

'It's lunch time,' Zoe said, puzzled. 'You never take this long to dry your hair.'

And I never have a Prince of the Blood waiting to see when I'll come out from my towel, she thought, but what the heck, there was no choice.

She emerged. She wrapped her towel around her hair and she checked on Zoe. Another surprise. She was wrapped sarong-style in her towel.

'You're dry.'

'Stefanos dried me,' she said. 'And he was really careful of my scars.'

Once again, a jolt. Here was another adult with the responsibility and skills to help her look after this injured child.

If he lived down the road she'd welcome him with open arms.

He lived on the Diamond Isles. Khryseis. A world away from her world.

'Lunch,' he said, smiling at her, and there was a trace of sympathy in his smile that said he understood her turmoil. He couldn't help it, he couldn't stop it, but he understood.

How could you understand? she thought. You're not having her. You're not!

What had he said? *There's nothing to be afraid of.*

Did she believe him?

No way.

* * *

Lunch was the same as yesterday, only Zoe ate more without being prodded. Then Stefanos disappeared to his car and returned with a box.

Cherries! She'd seen them in the shops last week. They'd been twenty dollars a small box, and they'd still been hard, not fully ripened. These were almost the size of golf balls, deep burgundy, shining and luscious.

Stefanos was looking smug—deeply pleased with the fact that her jaw and Zoe's jaw had dropped to somewhere round their ankles. 'The concierge at my hotel knows someone who flies up here from wherever cherries grow,' he told them. 'They're hot off the plane.'

Twenty dollars wouldn't pay for transport from the airport, Elsa thought. How much had these cost?

'They're not to be wasted,' he said severely, and Zoe needed no further prodding. She popped one into her mouth really fast.

'They're not just for eating,' he told her, lifting two pairs of cherries, each pair joined at the stem, and looping them over Zoe's ears. 'Cherry earrings are my favourite accessory.'

'You wear them too,' Zoe said, and he promptly did.

A prince was sitting at her kitchen table wearing cherry earrings.

Her foundations were getting shaky.

'Have a cherry,' he said kindly. 'They go off fast, I hear.'

'Not in range of us, they don't,' she said and ate a cherry and then another. And then...why not?...another.

'I'm up to nine already,' Zoe crowed. Zoe was showered and shiny clean, her face was flushed with pleasure and she was popping cherries in with an enjoyment Elsa had never seen. For four long years, for operation after operation, this little girl had been cheated of her childhood. And now... Stefanos had arrived and joy was flooding in.

Without warning, tendrils of fear wound their way round her heart yet again. But this time it was different. It wasn't just the fear of Zoe being taken away. It was stronger. Maybe Stefanos could give Zoe a better life than she could. If he cared for his little cousin and loved her and made her laugh… What right did she have to stand in his way?

'You're not eating,' he said gently and draped cherry earrings on her as well. 'There. We're the cherry family—Mama Cherry, Papa Cherry, Baby Cherry.'

She smiled and ate another cherry but there were icicles forming inside. She'd only ever wanted what was best for Zoe. If this was what was best…

'Let me show you what else I have in my car,' he said, watching her face. He could see her terror, she thought. This man saw things she didn't want to reveal to anyone.

Maybe it was the man himself who terrified her the most.

'Presents?' Zoe said hopefully and he grinned.

'Exactly,' he said. 'Coming right up.'

'This is exciting,' Zoe said.

'It is.' She was desperately trying to match Zoe's pleasure. Outwardly succeeding. Inwardly failing.

And then he was back, carrying suitcases, one soft blue leather, the other pink.

Suitcases. A wave of nausea swept over her so strongly that she rose and made a move towards the bathroom.

Stefanos dumped the suitcases and stopped her.

'Elsa, no,' he said softly. 'I told you before, you have nothing to be afraid of.'

'You're taking Zoe away.' She hadn't meant to say it. To say it in front of Zoe was unforgivable, but her terror was too raw, too real for her to disguise it.

'I do need to take Zoe to Khryseis,' he said, still in that gentle, reassuring tone that must surely be a learned bedside manner. *Yes, we are going to elongate your ears and swap your legs for your arms, but trust me, I'm a doctor.*

'Trust me,' he said now, as Zoe rose, her panic matching Elsa's. 'I want to take you both to the Diamond Isles. Zoe is the Crown Princess of Khryseis. Khryseis needs Zoe, and Zoe needs you. So I need you both. Thus I'm asking if you'll both come home with me.'

* * *

It was important—really important—to get her expression right. Zoe was staring at her and she'd seen terror. Stefanos was Zoe's cousin. This was Zoe's life, not hers. She had to get fear off her face and show courage.

'You…you scared me,' she managed at last, and to her relief her voice came out calm. 'I saw the suitcase and I thought you might be wanting Zoe to go away today. She doesn't even have a passport.'

'It will take a few days to get the documentation through.' His gaze was holding hers. 'Zoe, I think I frightened Elsa,' he said, rueful. 'How can we stop her being scared?'

You could go away, Elsa thought, but she knew Zoe wouldn't say that. Zoe was entranced with her big new cousin, and why shouldn't she be?

Stefanos was a prince, Zoe was a princess, and he'd pulled Zoe onside simply by acting as if the two of them needed to reassure her. Prince and princess together.

'Hey, Elsa, it's okay,' he said and reached to take her hand. His hold was strong and firm and…reassuring? How could touch be reassuring? How could his touch warm her when she was so cold she was beginning to shake?

She should pull away.

She couldn't.

'Does Khryseis have a beach?' Zoe asked, and Elsa knew right then that this was a done deal. 'Elsa likes beaches,' the little girl told her cousin. 'We looked at Khryseis on the computer and Elsa said she bet there were more fish than we could count. And more starfish.'

'Starfish?' he said, bemused, and his hand was still holding hers. She should pull it away, but how could she? How could she find strength to pull from such a touch?

'The real name for starfish is echinoderms, or asteroidea,' Zoe was saying importantly. 'They have two stomachs. They use one stomach to digest food while the other stomach turns inside out to pull its food in. But the really cool thing is that if they lose an arm they can grow another one. If I was a starfish I could grow another finger. And if you find just one leg of a starfish still joined to just a little bit of its body, a whole new starfish can grow. How cool is that?'

'Really cool,' he said, sounding stunned.

'It's what me and Elsa are working on,' she told him, sounding about twenty years older than her eight years. 'And the Internet says Khryseis has some really weird starfish.' She turned to Elsa, her eyes shining with small girl excitement. 'Elsa, can we go?'

No, she wanted to scream. No!

Instead she took a deep breath. She tried a tug on her hand but it wasn't released.

'Sweetheart, maybe we could work things out so you could go,' she whispered. 'I need to work.'

Zoe's face fell. 'I can't go without you,' she said, her bottom lip wobbling. 'I'd be scared.'

So would I, Elsa thought, but once again she held her tongue.

'I need you both to come,' Stefanos said. He was watching the two of them, focusing as much on Elsa as he was on Zoe. The pressure on her hand remained. Was he trying to warn her? she wondered. It didn't feel like that. It simply felt as if he was feeding her…strength. It was a crazy concept but it seemed the only one that would fit.

'That's why I've brought two suitcases,' he told them. Finally he released her hand. He'd set the suitcases on the floor and he flipped one open.

From the top he lifted a shiny new laptop computer. She'd seen these advertised. They were worth…a tenth of Zoe's next operation?

'This is for you,' he told her, setting it on the table. 'Whether you decide to come or not. You work from home. Why can't that home be on Khryseis?'

Because…

There was no because. She couldn't think of one, apart from the fact that the thought left her terrified.

She glanced at the mantel. Mathew's face smiled at her. Steadied her.

There must be a because.

Because my husband is buried here? Because this is where my grief is?

That wasn't a good because.

Because this guy in front of me makes my body react as I don't believe it's ever reacted?

Well, that was something she needed to dismiss. How weak a because was that?

Because I'd have no control over Zoe's life? Because people would stare at her scars? Because, as a royal, she'd be on display, and it could well destroy her?

Here at last were valid reasons, but before she could voice them Stefanos had lifted parcels onto the table.

'These are for you,' he said softly to Zoe. 'Because you're one of the bravest young women I've met. Because I know how much your body's hurt over the last four years, and I know how beautiful you are, inside and out. I'm so sorry I wasn't here for you when your parents died but I am now. These are to make you even more beautiful than you already are.'

Zoe looked uncertainly at Elsa—and then tentatively unwrapped the top parcel.

It was a pink blouse. It had tiny buttons shaped like butterflies. It had soft puffed sleeves designed to reach Zoe's elbows. A tiny white mandarin collar was designed so the top buttons could stay open, but the collar itself would stay high. Just high enough to hide the scars.

And there was more.

Elsa had searched for clothes like these, as far as her budget could afford it. She'd even tried making them. That was a joke, trying to learn dressmaking from an instruction manual. To say her attempts had failed was an understatement.

But after one night Stefanos had found these. There were three pairs of trousers, capri style, like long shorts, one red and white, one a lovely soft blue and one a deeper shade of pink. There were four more blouses, each with the same soft high collar. There were hair ribbons to match, and pretty sandals and a couple of dainty bracelets. There was an exquisite lilac party dress with white lace and a vast bow at the back. It came with a lilac choker with stars embroidered in white.

Within minutes Zoe was surrounded by a sea of clothes. She looked up at Elsa and her eyes were shining.

'They're beautiful,' she breathed. 'Can I keep them?'

What sort of question was that? There was no way she could refuse this gift. She just wished, so badly it hurt, that she'd been in a position to give these to her herself.

'They might not fit,' Stefanos warned, casting Elsa a thoughtful glance and then directing his attention back to Zoe. 'I had to guess sizes, but I've organised a dressmaker to visit you this evening and let them out or take them in as you need. We can change anything too—she has my authority.'

'And my authority?' Elsa whispered.

'I hope you'll agree,' Stefanos said gravely and met her gaze and held.

What was she thinking? 'Of course I agree,' she said shakily. She hugged Zoe and managed a smile. 'They're lovely. Your cousin has been wonderfully generous.' She bit her lip. 'But you're not my cousin, Stefanos. I can't take the laptop.'

'It's part of a debt,' he said softly. 'I owe you so much.'

'You owe me nothing.'

'I loved Christos.'

'He was my friend too.'

'No,' he said, and suddenly he was almost stern. 'You don't understand. Christos was my family. That I didn't know he was dead…that Zoe has been alone for so long…it touches my honour. I'm asking you to take this and it doesn't begin to repay the debt I owe you.'

It touches my honour… It was a quaint phrase. Old-fashioned.

He meant it—absolutely.

'I…' She took a deep breath. If they were going to talk about old-fashioned… 'Then it's my honour to care for Zoe,' she said, and she tilted her chin. 'Zoe is not related to me by blood, but I'm her godmother and her guardian. I won't let that go.'

'I'm not asking you to,' he said evenly. 'I'm asking for you to give Khryseis a chance. I'm asking you to come with Zoe—as her nanny as well as her guardian—and if you do this then you *will* be paid. I want you to help me introduce her to her birthright.'

'And then come home without her?'

'No,' Zoe said. She'd been examining her pile of clothes with joy, but this wasn't a child who could be bought. She looked at the clothes with longing and then pushed them away. Suddenly panicking. 'I don't want them if I can't have Elsa.'

'You can have Elsa,' Stefanos said evenly. 'I'm asking you both to come.' He smiled at Elsa, ignoring her obvious panic, simply smiling at her as if he understood what she was thinking; she was being slightly foolish but he wasn't about to threaten her.

His smile lied, she thought desperately. This man was a prince, about as far from her world as it was possible to be. He was accustomed to having his charm work for him. He thought now that he simply had to smile and shower gifts and he'd get what he wanted.

'Do you know what a royal nanny earns?' he asked, and she caught her breath.

'I don't want to know.'

'Now that's just dumb,' he said. 'Knocking back a fabulous job because you haven't heard the terms? I rang a couple of friends last night. They have nannies in Europe and they kindly rang a couple of the top agencies and asked. What's the going rate for the best nanny in the world? they asked.'

And he gave her a figure.

She gasped. She stared across the table at him and he smiled back at her. 'That's what I'm offering,' he said softly. 'Starting today.'

She could be paid for doing what she loved? Caring for Zoe?

But this… This could never be about money. Because she did what she did for Zoe for love; for nothing else.

'Elsa, Zoe needs to come home anyway,' he said gently. 'I'm sorry, but it's not negotiable. I've also talked to people here in Social Services and to lawyers from your Family Court. I have more chance at success in gaining custody than you might think. The court would look at what Zoe stands to inherit. They'd look at the home I'm prepared to give her. The consensus is that she should have the right to learn about Khryseis. It's her heritage.'

He turned to Zoe and spread his hands. 'Zoe, your father was the Crown Prince of Khryseis and you're now the Crown Princess. If you agree, I'd like to show you the place where your papa grew up. I'd like to introduce you to an island that I know you'll love, to live in a palace that's exciting, to see what your father's life could have been if he'd lived. I'm asking Elsa to come as well, and I'd like you both to consider Khryseis as a place to live.' He glanced at Elsa and then glanced away. Her emotions were written on her face, she thought.

'I'll sign legal documents with international legal authorities,' he said, and now he was speaking directly to Elsa. 'We need Zoe for at least three months a year.'

'For ever?' Elsa whispered.

'Until Zoe's old enough to know whether she wishes to accept the Crown,' he said and suddenly he sounded stern. 'It's her birthright, Elsa, and neither of us have the right to take that away from her.'

She was close to tears—but she would not cry. Not in front of Zoe. Zoe was taking her cues from her—to disintegrate on her own behalf would be cruel.

And he knew what she was thinking.

'Hey, it's not so bad. You could think of it as a holiday.' He took her hands again. Strong and warm and sure. 'You've been on your own for so long, Elsa. Will you let me share?'

She would not cry. But the feel of his hands…

You've been on your own for so long…

That was what it felt like. Four long years of fighting to get Zoe the medical treatment she needed, fighting to keep her own career viable enough to put food on the table, fighting to forget the ache in her hip and to stop the grey fog of depression and loneliness taking her over.

A holiday in Khryseis. Three months a year?

If she said yes, she'd lose Zoe.

'You won't lose her,' Stefanos said, strongly and surely. 'I promise you that. I've spent the last eighteen hours finding out exactly what you've done for Zoe. The money you've spent. Your own money.'

Her eyes flew to his. Distress gave way to indignation. 'How did you find that out? Who are you to…?'

'To enquire? I have friends in high places, Elsa. So does Zoe now. In future she'll have the best medical treatment money can buy.'

Anger, fear, anguish… They were a kaleidoscope of her emotions. But they should be her emotions. Not Zoe's. This was Zoe's future and she must not deny her.

Her own terror had to be put aside.

'What do you think, Zoe?' she asked, feeling inordinately pleased when she got her voice right. 'Stefanos is offering us an initial three-month holiday on his island while we see what it's like. It's been…it's been a shock, but I don't think it's something we should be scared of. His island looks really beautiful on the Internet.'

'It's *your* island, Zoe,' Stefanos said, gently but firmly.

'So let me get this right,' Elsa said, opening the laptop to give her something to look at rather than Stefanos's face. He saw too much, she thought. He knew how scared she was and he was sympathetic. But still he was determined.

She couldn't afford to be seduced into doing what was wrong for Zoe.

Seduced? It was the wrong word but it was the one that popped into her head. Because…because…

Because he was too big and too male and too sexy and she'd

been alone for far too long. It felt dangerous to even be in the same room as him.

Maybe *he* should be worried, she thought dryly. If he knew what this scary, ridiculous part of her was thinking…

Nanny jumps prince…

Whoa.

Well, at least that pulled her out of the fog, she decided, fighting an almost hysterical desire to laugh. Maybe she ought to focus on slightly more…realistic issues.

'Let me get this straight,' she said again, and watched him smile. How much of what she was thinking was obvious? To her fury she felt a blush start, from the toes up.

'Christos…Zoe's papa…should have been Crown Prince of Khryseis,' she managed, staring fiercely down at the laptop as if she was totally absorbed in its keyboard. 'How come the King wasn't his father?'

Stefanos nodded, still serious. 'Potted history? The Diamond Isles were principalities for hundreds of years,' he told her. 'Then the Prince of Sappheiros invaded the other islands and declared himself King. Subsequent armies kept the islanders under iron rule, and his line continued as long as there was a direct male heir. Six generations later, King Giorgos died without a son. The islands have continued supporting their own royal families, even though they haven't been able to publicly acknowledge them, and now they can take their rightful place. Giorgos's death meant Christos was heir to the throne of Khryseis. Under the old rule, men and women inherited equally. Therefore Zoe inherits after Christos. As her closest adult relative I'm Prince Regent until she can take the throne at twenty-five. Currently the island's being run by a council set up by Giorgos. They're corrupt and useless. The only way for us to unseat them is for Zoe to come home and for us to take over.'

'Us?'

'I was thinking me,' he said, suddenly converting from history lesson to the personal. 'But in the long-term…' He smiled at her, considering. 'Maybe you can find a way to be useful as well.'

'Useful?' The concept made Elsa gasp. What was she letting herself in for? This man…this *prince*…was moving way too fast, and she had no idea where he was going. 'Like how?' And then as he paused as if he wasn't sure how to answer, she decided this was deeply scary and a girl had to set some limits.

'Can we get some ground rules in place?' she ventured, searching wildly for some way to ground herself. Employment as a palace nanny… What did she know of such a job? What did royal nannies do?

In the absence of a job description, maybe she ought to list her own.

'Ground rules?' he asked, quirking one eyebrow. Again he seemed to be on the verge of laughter, and the sensation made her feel crazy.

'No washing, no ironing and definitely no scrubbing the stairs on hands and knees,' she said wildly, while he and Zoe looked on with astonishment. 'No attending royal banquets and sitting at the bottom of the table where I don't know anyone. Neither will I wear a calf-length uniform with a starched collar and *Nanny* embroidered on the front. Nor will I curtsey or walk out of Zoe's presence backwards. No shoe shining, no…'

'But we do still need to go,' Zoe said, cutting into a tirade that was getting…well, more than a bit irrational.

Elsa paused. She looked at Stefanos's hiked eyebrows—both of them were hiked now. His lips were twitching.

Maybe she was being just ever so slightly over the top.

She struggled for calm. Hysteria wasn't what was needed, she told herself severely. Nor was treating this as a crazy joke. She needed to stay practical and focus on Zoe—regardless of whether or not Stefanos was laughing at her.

In her short life Zoe had faced her parents' deaths, and then more hospitals and doctors and paramedics and social workers than Elsa wanted to think about. Almost all of them talked over her head. It made Zoe mad, but usually she became quiet and passive.

Not now. She'd been listening to Elsa in astonishment, but with an attention more suitable to one twice her age. Now she turned to Stefanos and frowned.

'Elsa doesn't have to do all that stuff, does she?'

'No,' Stefanos said definitely. 'I think Elsa's been reading too many fairy tales.'

'But there really is a palace?'

'There really is a palace,' he said and smiled at her. 'And you really are a princess.'

He'd hooked Zoe, Elsa thought frantically. Just because he had a smile to die for.

Just because he was logical, thoughtful and he sounded as if he cared. Just because he was smiling at Zoe now with kindness and also the trace of a challenge, convincing her that this could be some sort of magical adventure.

He was glancing at her with a quizzical look that was kind as well as knowing.

How could he be kind? What did she know of the man?

What did she know about the island?

'What…what medical facilities are on the island?' she managed, trying valiantly to sound grown-up, sensible and in control. Or at least as grown-up, sensible and in control as Zoe.

'Zoe will have me to care for her,' he told her, matching her tone. 'And there's specialist backup in Athens.'

'There are no paediatricians on Khryseis?'

He hesitated. 'Education has hardly been King Giorgos's concern,' he admitted at last. 'In fact he's actively discouraged it. Even I haven't been able to work there. Giorgos wouldn't permit me to practice medicine on Khryseis, so I've built my career elsewhere.'

'There are no medical facilities at all?' she asked incredulously.

'There's one elderly doctor and a midwife. Up until now the fishermen have taken really ill islanders to Athens.'

'You're kidding me.'

'Sadly, no.'

'And…and now?'

'And now we go back to the island and think about the future from there.'

'You'll get more medical staff?'

'That's one of my first priorities. The island's not big enough to support a huge range of specialties but there will be good basic medicine with fast transfers to Athens at need.'

He hesitated. 'Elsa, you will be looked after,' he said, gently but strongly. 'You both will. So no, Elsa, you will not be asked to scrub stairs or polish silver. You'll be on the island as Zoe's friend and as her nanny, for as long as you wish to stay. I'll ask nothing more of you. This isn't a trap, Elsa. I promise you. No strings.' His face broke into another of his magical smiles. 'Our island's lovely, Elsa. Zoe. We can work things out. The three of us. Please?'

His smile caught her and held. Demanding a response. How could she resist an appeal like this?

And, despite her fears, a tiny trickle of excitement crept in.

She had no idea where this man was coming from—or where he was going—but his smile was mesmerising. And as well as that…

She and Zoe had eaten sandwiches for lunch almost every day for four years. She'd had to chop wood to cook and to heat their water. Wood-chopping jarred her hip so much that sometimes it was hard not to just give in. But there was never the choice of giving in.

But now…Stefanos was offering them a home in a palace on an island in the Mediterranean. He was offering her a well-paid job. She'd have no more money worries. No wood-chopping. Did he realise how enticing it sounded? This man might appear seriously sexy but right now it was the lack of wood-chopping that was more seductive.

'I do need to keep my research skills up,' she muttered, fighting to sound practical and reserved and wary.

'Of course. I see you doing the same things you're doing now. With Zoe.'

'Home-schooling?'

'We can get a tutor. Zoe, you'll need to learn Greek.'

'I already know Greek,' Zoe said proudly.

'You already know…'

'Christos spoke Greek to her as a baby,' Elsa told him, feeling a bit smug herself as she noted his astonishment. 'We figured it was part of who she was, so we've kept it up.'

'Elsa speaks it now too,' Zoe added, 'and we both read it. There are two old Greek ladies in Waratah Cove. We visit them once a week and talk with them, and Elsa does their shopping and says it's payment for our lessons. If we went away I'd miss them.' Her face clouded. 'And the cats. How can we go away without our cats?'

'Yeah, the cats,' Elsa said, as if it was a challenge.

He grinned at that. 'That's one more thing fixed. Zoe, open the blue suitcase.'

She opened it. Fascinated. To display cat food. Bulk cat food. A suitcase of cat food.

'So we're supposed to open the suitcase and come home when they need a refill?' Elsa said and she couldn't help sounding waspish.

'That's fixed too,' he said, his grin teasing her to smile with him. 'There's a guy who works round here tending gardens, doing odd jobs. I've arranged for him to visit every night at dusk, feed the cats, lock them up, then let them out at dawn. In perpetuity. And if any other stray comes along then he's to do exactly what you'd do. Take it in, get it neutered, tell it the house rules. He can even do your two Greek ladies' shopping if you want. Now… Any more objections?'

'My…my house?' Elsa stammered.

'I told you, he does gardens and odd jobs. He'll maintain this place as long as we want.'

'You found this guy when?'

'The concierge at the hotel earned his keep last night,' he said, and grinned again. 'He brought his wife in to help. His wife knows you and knows what you need. So there you go. Local knowledge and my cash.'

'Yeah, your cash,' she said, breathless. 'We can't take it.'

'See, what you don't understand is that you can,' he said. 'Zoe's a princess. You're nanny to a princess. Are there any other problems?'

'The medical facilities…'

'I'll be there and, as I said, there are fast flights to Athens. Until we get other medical facilities organised we can cope.' He took her hand again and held, and with his other hand he took Zoe's. 'Khryseis needs a team,' he said. 'A royal team. Prince Regent, Princess Zoe and Nanny Elsa. Do we have it?'

'Yes,' Zoe said.

There were no arguments left. The only one that was still swirling round and round in her mind was, I don't want to be a nanny to your prince.

But that was dumb. She glanced at the mantel where Matt still smiled.

Definitely it was dumb.

He glanced to where she'd looked. Saw what she'd been looking at.

Didn't ask a question.

'It'll be fine,' he said softly, and the pressure on her hand strengthened. Then, before she knew what he was about, he put his hand under her chin and tilted it—and kissed her. It was a feather-light kiss, quickly over, and why it had the capacity to make her feel…make her feel…

No. She had to stop thinking about how it made her feel, because that was nonsense. But his hand was still under her chin, forcing her to meet his gaze.

'I will keep you safe,' he said, strongly and surely. 'And Zoe too. You've worked too hard for too long, Elsa Murdoch. Now it's up to Zoe and me to see you have some fun. Just say yes.'

And what else was she to do?

'I guess…yes,' she managed, but she didn't add, Yes, Your Royal Highness. Because that would be agreeing to all of it. The whole royal fairy tale.

Ridiculous.

CHAPTER SIX

Two weeks later they left Australia, luxuriating in first class seats on a direct flight to Athens, to be followed by a smaller plane to Khryseis.

'I'll be on Khryseis to meet you,' Stefanos had said in one of the scores of calls he'd made since then. 'But our people will take care of you all the way.'

They hadn't seen him since that fateful lunch. He'd had to leave. 'Things are chaotic,' he'd said. 'I need to get back to the island straight away but I promise I won't let that disorder touch you.'

It wasn't touching them now. They were in first class airline seats. They had a cocoon each, with every conceivable gadget, including one that turned the seats into beds at the flick of a switch. A hostess had already made Zoe's bed for her, with crisp linen and fluffy duvet, and she was fast asleep.

Elsa was staring out of the window and seeing what was probably Hawaii.

She was trying not to gibber.

She'd been on one overseas flight in her life. To Tasmania. She didn't remember all that many gadgets and duvets and cocoons on that flight. She remembered being served a packet of nuts and a warm beer.

She was about to be a nanny to a princess.

The princess was bone weary. Her little body still wasn't up to strength. The last weeks had been excitement plus, and Elsa had worried about the wisdom of letting her go at all.

'But it's imperative,' Stefanos had said in his deep, grave voice and, dumb or not, she believed him. If Zoe wasn't there he had no power to replace the council. He had no power to stop the corruption he told her was endemic.

So, once again, why rail against something she had no control over? Now, as Zoe snuggled into sleep, she thought with this level of luxury maybe her little charge could enjoy herself.

Maybe *she* could enjoy herself.

Amazingly, her hip wasn't hurting. Normally, sitting for more than a couple of hours made it ache unbearably, but her hip obviously decided it liked first class treatment, thank you very much, and it wasn't only her hip thinking it.

She was on her way to live in a castle. As a nanny. A nanny, she reminded herself. A paid servant. She'd get to eat in the servants' quarters, while Zoe ate in state. She'd use chipped pottery while Zoe swanned round in party dresses, using cut-glass crystal and silverware, attended by butlers and…and whatever else royalty had.

Um…this was Zoe she was talking about. Maybe she couldn't see that happening.

And tucked in her bag was a document, prepared by Stefanos's legal team, read from all angles by her local lawyer and then faxed to a team of international lawyers in Canberra for a final check.

The document said that if, at any time, Zoe seemed so distressed that it was damaging her mental or physical health—and that decision was to be made by a team of independent *Australian* medical experts flown out at Stefanos's expense—then Zoe's fare back to Australia would be paid immediately. And so would hers.

So. Maybe it'd work?

But…she was a marine biologist, not a nanny.

Stefanos had promised her starfish.

Yeah, great. She shoved that thought as far back in her head as she could. She'd like to be rid of it completely—the ache to follow her own dreams.

But Zoe came first. Zoe was more important than dreams. And maybe those dreams could still be resurrected. If Zoe was unhappy they'd come home.

Catch-22. She didn't want Zoe to be unhappy.

'But we can make it a game,' she'd whispered to Zoe as she'd watched her little charge drift towards sleep. 'You being a princess in a castle.'

'With a prince,' Zoe had said sleepily. 'Isn't he nice?'

He is nice, Elsa admitted. Um…all things considered, he's very nice.

Which was why she had to remember that he was a prince and she was a nanny. A nanny with a sliver of a career left as a marine biologist, who could maybe be happy with starfish.

Certainly a nanny with no interest whatsoever in a prince. Even if he was as drop-dead gorgeous as Stefanos.

Especially if he was as drop-dead gorgeous as Stefanos!

She closed her eyes. Two seconds later the hostess was beside her. 'Can I make your bed up for you, ma'am? Here are your pyjamas.'

She handed her a pair of pink silk pyjamas.

There was a well-known Australian politician sitting in the seat diagonally in front of her—she recognised him from the newspapers. He was wearing blue silk pyjamas as he read the financial pages.

What a shame Stefanos wasn't with them, she thought. He'd look really cute in blue pyjamas.

See, she told herself sternly. That's what nannies are paid not to think.

What are nannies paid to think?

Not about lost careers. Not about lost dreams.

And not about drop-dead gorgeous Prince Regents.

Stefanos paced the palace balcony and waited for them, feeling ridiculous. The staff were beside themselves with excitement, so much so that he'd given in and done the dress-up thing again. He'd done it twice now, once in Australia at the formal reception and again today. Hopefully there wouldn't be too many more occasions where he had to feel so ridiculous.

But maybe there would be.

This whole situation was crazy, he told himself, for maybe the thousandth time since he'd heard the news of Christos's death. He was automatically Prince Regent—island ruler until Zoe turned twenty-five—but, although the Regency gave him some powers, the thing he wanted most was denied to him.

He wanted the island to be a democracy, but as Regent he had no power to change the constitution. Democracy would have to wait for Zoe to turn twenty-five.

Since he was a kid he'd dreamed of Khryseis being a great and wonderful place to live. But now…he'd fallen in love with his medicine. He was good at his job. His research was vitally important, and he loved what he did.

What could he do here but tinker round the edges, protect the islanders from the worst of the excesses they'd endured in the past, then—what?—try and remember his general medicine so he could treat the islanders' minor ailments until Zoe came of age? In what, seventeen years?

Then he'd go tamely back to the States and pick up where he'd left off? To a career that was waiting for him?

Yeah, and pigs would fly.

He had no choice. He had to care for the island. He had to care for Zoe.

And Elsa?

She needed care as much as Zoe, he thought. Elsa had stood up to him with the air of a battered warrior, a woman accustomed to having her world shift and accepting those shifts with as much dignity and grace as she could muster. He'd seen how much the thought of losing Zoe terrified her, but once she'd realised how needful it was she'd simply got on with it.

He had the feeling that even if he hadn't offered her a generous salary, she'd still be doing exactly what she was doing. Taking care of Zoe, no matter what life threw at her.

What had life thrown at her?

He needed to find out more about her—and her husband. Why was he no longer on the scene? She still wore a wedding ring.

Um…why was that relevant?

He should have found out. His enquiries had been professional. It had seemed wrong to pry.

But he wanted to know.

He did already know some things. For one… *She seemed loving.* For some dumb reason that phrase had been playing in his head since he'd met her. Her fierce devotion to Zoe was touching something in him that he'd learned to ignore a long time ago.

He didn't do emotion. Since he'd left this island as a teenager he'd been totally committed to his medicine. Yet here he was, not only realising he'd have to abandon the work he was passionate about but, in the stillness of the night, as he lay trying to find a way he could sort all his commitments, Alexandros's idle teasing kept rising up to taunt him.

Wife. Family.

No!

He remembered the horror of his father's death, and his mother's anguish as she'd insisted he take a scholarship to the US to keep him safe. He remembered grief and homesickness, and his mother's death had cemented his knowledge that love caused nothing but pain. Work had been his salvation then, as it could be his salvation now—whether or not it was the work he desperately wanted to do.

'If you please…' A delicate cough sounded behind him and he jumped a foot. The old palace butler moved like a cat. One of these days the old guy was going to give him a heart attack.

He turned and tried to look as if he hadn't had a fright. 'Yes?'

'I believe they've arrived, sir,' the old man said gravely.

He glanced out at the magnificent formal driveway. An ancient Rolls-Royce was proceeding in state down the avenue, the flag of Khryseis flying proudly from the grille.

The butler was beaming with pride and anticipation. That was what this was all about, Stefanos thought grimly. Giving the islanders back their identity.

Which was why he was wearing this ridiculous uniform.

But there were other imperatives hammering at him. Back in New York he had a surgical list still waiting. He couldn't let those kids down. He'd have to return before he could finally commit himself to this place.

The car had pulled to a halt and the driver stepped out. He must be eighty as well—half the retainers in this household were in their dotage—but, like most of the staff, he was also wearing the imposing uniform of the Khryseis royal household.

Since Giorgos's death, since the islanders had discovered they could revert to their own royal family, the excitement had been building. The Isle of Sappheiros now had its own royal family in its palace. So did the Isle of Argyros. Khryseis, the smallest of the islands, was last to revert to rule by its original royal family, and the islanders were looking to Stefanos to make this good.

And they were also looking to this one little girl, coming home. A child who must be protected.

At least he could share that responsibility, he thought, once more feeling grateful for Elsa. Ruling the island might be his duty but with Elsa here he didn't need to commit emotionally. If he kept Zoe safe and her nanny happy, then that was the extent of his obligations.

The Crown Princess was loved by a woman called Elsa. Which meant the love bit could be shelved as not his business.

Elsa and Zoe climbed from the Rolls-Royce and if they weren't quite clutching each other they came awfully close.

'This is really scary,' Zoe whispered, and Elsa couldn't agree more.

It was a palace. A real, honest to goodness palace, vast and ancient. Turrets, battlements, spires and flags, vast entrance steps and Grecian columns, all set against a magical backdrop—sapphire seas, golden beaches, white cliffs with mountains in the background.

Internet pages they'd read had told them that Khryseis was the most impoverished of the three Diamond Isles, but once it had been fabulously wealthy. This palace backed it up. Elsa had never seen a building so fantastic. Or big.

'I hope we don't have to dust and hoover it,' she whispered to Zoe, and Zoe giggled. The tension eased.

Only then Stefanos strode out of the vast front entrance and the tension zoomed back again.

'Ooo er…' Elsa muttered, and Zoe clutched her hand and gave another shaky giggle. Striding down the great granite steps towards them, Stefanos looked like something out of history. Romantic history.

'He's a real prince again. Do you think he wears a sword?' Zoe whispered, awed.

'Hey, he is,' Elsa said as he got closer and they could see the great golden hilt emerging from its scabbard. 'Be good, Zoe.'

'It's only Stefanos. He won't hurt us,' Zoe said, and it was the child who was trying to reassure the adult.

Some nanny she made, Elsa thought. Telling her charge to be scared.

Actually, she wasn't a great nanny at all. She looked down at her scuffed trainers—she'd needed comfy shoes for the flight and these were all she had. For the last four years she'd lived in jeans and sweatshirts. If her royal duties demanded better clothes, they'd need to wait until pay day.

Zoe, however, looked beautiful. In her sparkly new clothes, her dark curls held back with diamanté butterfly clips, her pretty blue sandals adorned with butterflies, she looked every inch a child of royalty.

Underneath her carefully chosen clothes were scars which were still healing, but her new clothes hid them and gave her confidence. As this man coming towards them was giving her excitement.

'I'm going to be a princess,' she whispered.

'And I'm going to be a nanny,' Elsa whispered back.

'Stefanos said we could still look for starfish,' the child said, picking up on her nerves and, amazingly, trying to reassure her.

'He did, didn't he,' Elsa said and fought for a bit more backbone—the courage to pin a cheerful smile in place and turn to greet her employer.

What in the world was she doing here? And why did the sight of the man strolling towards her make her knees feel as if they were turning to jelly?

'Welcome to Khryseis, Princess Zoe.' Stefanos strode towards them and he greeted Zoe first. He took her hands and stooped to kiss her cheeks. It might be a normal Greek greeting but here, now, it seemed a truly royal gesture. Zoe looked suitably amazed.

'I'm not a real princess,' she told him, as if admitting a falsehood.

'You are,' Stefanos said gently. 'Your father was the Crown Prince Christos and you're his daughter. This is where you belong.'

'It's a really big palace.'

'It is.'

'Elsa says we might have to dust and hoover,' she ventured, and Stefanos turned to Elsa and his dark eyes lit with laughter.

'Welcome to you, too,' he said and it was her turn to have her hands grasped and her cheek kissed. Was this the way royalty greeted nannies? 'I promise you no hoovering—and I'm so glad you decided to come.'

Whew. This was a formal gesture, she told herself wildly. He'd kissed her cheek and smiled at her. Why that had the capacity to make her insides melt…

She'd been isolated for too long. She was starting to feel… Like she had no business in the world feeling.

'Zoe was never coming alone,' she managed.

'No,' he said, but something in his tone said that such a

concept wasn't unthinkable. 'She'll be so much happier with you.'

'She…she will.' It was really hard to breathe while he was smiling at her—while he was so close—but she had to start as she meant to go on. 'And thank you for making us feel right at home, by the way.'

'Sorry?'

'By wearing your casual gear,' she said, and managed to smile. 'It makes me feel I'll fit right in.'

His eyes met hers, laughter meeting laughter. But he couldn't respond how he wished. He was aware their conversation was being listened to, even if she wasn't.

There were only three staff members within sight, but every window was open and the palace curtains were inched back enough to allow the servants to hear. He'd deliberately not lined the staff up to meet Zoe, but the islanders' desperate need for a new royal family had to be met.

'Would you like to see your bedrooms?' he asked them both.

'Um…bedrooms,' Elsa said. 'Plural?'

'I want to stay with Elsa,' Zoe said urgently and Stefanos smiled a reassurance.

'I don't blame you. Come and see what we've organised. You'll need to meet a couple of people first. The housekeeper. The butler. We'll leave the rest of the staff for you to meet tomorrow.'

'Oh, goody,' Elsa whispered, and Stefanos smiled in sympathy.

'There's a photo shoot here after lunch,' he added apologetically. 'Christos was well loved on the island and there's huge interest and pleasure that his child is coming home. To ban all photographers would have had cameramen scaling walls, so I've permitted a representative from each of the island's media outlets.'

'You have more than one?' Elsa said, incredulous.

'It's not a complete backwater,' he said gently and she flushed.

'You have multi-media outlets and you have only one doctor?'

'I know—priorities that need fixing. They will be fixed, but I haven't managed everything in two weeks.' He took Zoe's hand and grinned down at her encouragingly. 'You want to see your bedroom? You have a four-poster bed with curtains.'

'Yes, please,' Zoe said breathlessly. She turned with him and they headed up the grand entrance steps.

Leaving Elsa to follow.

I'm the nanny, she told herself, trying not to feel bereft and hopelessly out of her comfort zone. Staying in the background is what I'm supposed to do.

Stefanos and Zoe reached the top step and paused, looking back to her.

They looked fabulous, she thought. Prince Regent and his Crown Princess. Zoe looked lit up like a fairy on top of a Christmas tree, holding her big cousin's hand with confidence.

'Are you coming?' Stefanos said gently. She met his gaze and realised that once again he'd guessed how she was feeling.

Zoe still needed her, she thought wildly. She wasn't being put out to pasture yet.

'I'm coming,' she called. The chauffeur was lifting their bags out of the boot and she grabbed the top one. The heaviest.

'Leave that to the staff,' Stefanos told her.

'I'm the staff,' she said determinedly and, to her amazement, he chuckled.

'I don't think so,' he said. 'I expect the staff to conform to a certain standard in their uniform. I need to tell you that your standard falls a long way short until we can get you outfitted as befits your status…as a friend of the Crown Princess.'

Then his tone became gentle and the laughter faded. 'You've worked hard already,' he said, looking down at her from the top step, and he spoke loudly and clearly enough for his voice to carry into all those open windows. 'You've cared for my little cousin—for our Crown Princess—with all the love at your disposal. It would be my honour to grant you a holiday for as long as you want. Your nominal title is nanny to Zoe, but my command to you personally—to you both—is to have fun.'

CHAPTER SEVEN

THEIR apartments were stunning—two apartments with an adjoining door. Rooms almost big enough to house a tennis court.

'They're built for the Crown Prince and Crown Princess,' Stefanos told them while Zoe and Elsa stared in incredulity.

'This is something out of a museum,' Elsa murmured. 'You know the ones I mean? This is the bed where Charles the First spent the night before the Great Wiggery Foppery of Seventeen Sixty-Two.'

'The Great Wiggery Foppery?' Stefanos asked, bemused.

'Or maybe it was the Great Gunfire Pirouette with Catherine Wheels,' she told him, desperately striving for humour in the face of splendour that was just plain intimidating. 'I'm Australian so my knowledge of royalty is distinctly hazy, but my grandma had a book on Bedrooms of the World. I read it when I was seven and I had chickenpox. They all had descriptions like Queen Anne had dropsy in this very bed and threw up on this very pillow. And no, don't ask me what dropsy is.'

'Are we really going to sleep in here?' While Elsa was covering her nerves with nonsense, Zoe was awed into hushed delight.

'They've changed the sheets since the great dropsy plague,' Stefanos said gravely. 'I think it might be safe to sleep in them again.'

Zoe giggled.

Which was the whole point of the exercise, Elsa reminded herself. If she could keep Zoe giggling…

But for how long?

'We'll sleep in this one,' Zoe said, and proceeded to clamber up onto what was surely intended as the Crown Prince's bed. It was vast, with four golden posts, a golden canopy and rich burgundy curtains drawn back with gold tassels.

'Then Elsa will sleep in the other one,' Stefanos said, motioning through the open door to a bedroom almost as large and a bed almost as luxurious.

The giggling stopped. Zoe's bottom lip trembled.

'No,' she said. 'This is too big by myself. We sleep in the same room at home. Why can't we sleep in the same room here?'

'We can,' Elsa said. 'There's no need to worry Prince Stefanos, though. We'll fix it.'

'You've been sharing a room with Zoe?' Stefanos asked.

'I have.' She met his gaze with open defiance.

'So you had only one bedroom in that little cottage?'

'Zoe has nightmares,' she said. 'Even if we had ten bedrooms we wouldn't use them.'

'I'm not sure the staff will approve of a trundle bed in here. They're wanting Zoe to be real royalty.'

'So Zoe gets the four-poster and I get a trundle.'

'There needs to be some delineation.'

'I'm her friend and her guardian.'

'Yes, and her nanny.'

'So I am,' she said, figuring that here was a line in the sand—her first test. Zoe would not be made to suffer from the demands of royalty. 'So it's back to the trundle. Zoe will not sleep alone.'

'I don't like alone,' Zoe said, relaxing now she was sure Elsa was on her side.

'We'll sort it out,' Stefanos went on in a voice that said this issue wouldn't go away.

'If you think…'

'Leave it,' he said, and she met his gaze head-on. 'Zoe, take a look at the beach.'

Zoe looked—while Elsa met Stefanos's gaze and held. He smiled at her and she thought, Don't you dare. You smile at me and you think you can get away with murder.

The scary thing was that she suspected he could.

'Look at the beach, Elsa,' he said gently, and she tore her gaze away from his and looked.

The palace gardens led down to a wide stretch of golden sand, a cove of shallow water and low, rolling waves.

'Wow,' Zoe breathed. 'Can we swim?'

'As soon as you're settled.' He hesitated, watching Elsa. Who forced her thoughts back to beds.

If he thought he could get his own way simply by smiling… She took a deep breath and started to form a cogent argument about trundle beds, but he'd moved on.

'Lunch is in half an hour,' he told them. 'We'll organise the beds later. Meanwhile, I'll leave you to get settled. The butler will let you know when lunch is ready, and he'll show you the way.'

'Can't we just come down in half an hour?' Elsa asked.

'You'd get lost,' he told her and there was that smile again. 'And now we have you both here we don't intend to lose you. Make yourselves at home and I'll see you at lunch.'

He went out. Elsa was left with confusion, an unaccountable fear and the knowledge that the room was bleaker for his going.

What was it about the man? In his presence she felt about the same age as Zoe.

This was crazy. It was just his uniform, she told herself. The fairy tale bit. He looked so…royal.

'Stefanos said we're getting our photos taken after lunch,' Zoe ventured, looking worried. 'Should I wear something pretty?'

'You look very pretty right now,' she said and gave the little girl a swift hug. A hug she needed just as much as Zoe. 'But maybe we can find you something even prettier. What about your new dress?'

They came down to lunch looking nervous. Zoe was wide-eyed with wonder, clutching Elsa's hand as if it were a lifeline—but she wasn't subdued, Stefanos thought, as he watched them walk down the stairs towards him. She looked like a little girl about to go to a birthday party where she didn't know anyone. It was a bit scary, but it might turn out to be fun.

Elsa, on the other hand, looked nervous in a different way. It was as if she was nervous of her royal surroundings. More. She was nervous of him?

She was still wearing jeans and sweatshirt. Zoe was in the most extravagant of the clothes he'd bought for her—her beautiful party dress. Beside her, Elsa looked subdued. She looked even more subdued when she saw him waiting for them at the foot of the stairs. It was this uniform, he thought regretfully. It was enough to scare *him*. After the media call he could take it off, but until then he had to be a prince.

So. He was a prince. Zoe was a princess. Elsa looked as if she didn't want to be here at all.

And she was still limping. He hadn't noticed when she'd arrived, but watching her coming down the stairs he saw it again. She was holding the balustrade with her spare hand and doing her best to disguise it, but she was being careful. The way she swung her left leg forward... There wasn't full movement in her hip and it looked as if coming downstairs hurt.

Last time he'd seen her he'd seen the faintest trace of a limp. She'd brushed it aside when he'd enquired, and he'd had so much on his mind then that to assume it was a temporary sprain had been the easiest option. Now, though... There was a lot he had to find out about this woman.

Like what was the damage with her leg.

Like why she was coming to lunch and a media call in faded

jeans and sweatshirt. Looking scared. Up until now he would have described her as spirited and feisty. What was it about this place that was sucking the spirited and feisty out of her?

He glanced up at the massive chandelier above his head—two thousand crystals, the housekeeper had told him, and he didn't doubt it for a minute—and he thought, What's oppressive about this?

He smiled at them and Zoe let go of Elsa's hand and bounced down the last few steps to greet him. She gazed up at the chandelier and breathed deeply in small girl satisfaction.

'It's really, really beautiful,' she said.

'So are you,' he told her and she giggled.

He glanced at Elsa—and caught her unawares. There was a wash of pure, unmitigated pain on her face. It was gone as soon as it had come, quickly turned into a smile, but he knew he wasn't mistaken.

'We're hungry,' she said, a trifle too fast, and he thought she was still in defence mode.

'Excellent,' he said. 'In fact, more than excellent when you see what's in front of us.'

He led the way into the dining room and paused at the door, smiling down to Zoe again. 'This is a welcome lunch for you,' he said gently. 'Specially made by everyone who works here.'

And it was—a feast that promised a small girl's heaven. The delicate finger food looked as if it had been designed to tempt and tantalise a little girl's appetite. There were tiny cheesy biscuits in the shape of animals. Finger-sized sausage rolls. Chicken wings with tiny chef-hat wrappers around their tips so a small hand wouldn't get greasy. Strawberries and grapes and slivers of watermelon. Tiny chocolate cakes with a dusting of sugar. Miniature sponge cakes with the tops turned into wings and fixed in place with a mix of red jelly and cream. Petite eclairs with creamy custard filling.

Around them the room was a mass of fresh cut flowers, a wondrous fantasy feast of beauty and pure delight.

Zoe sat down and gazed at the table in awe. 'Elsa won't have to tell me to eat here,' she breathed.

'That's what we hoped,' he said and glanced at Elsa again—and got that look again. Raw pain.

'You don't approve?' he asked and she caught herself and managed to smile. But her smile was strained. She was having trouble disguising how hard it was to summon it at all.

'It's wonderful,' she said.

'So why do you look unhappy?' he asked gently.

'Elsa's a bit sad 'cause she hasn't got any pretty clothes,' Zoe said and popped a strawberry into her mouth—and then looked mortified. She swallowed it manfully and looked even more guilty. 'Is…is it okay to start?'

'Absolutely it's okay to start,' Stefanos said and handed over the sausage rolls. Zoe took two—and then looked at how small they were and took another.

'Thank you very much,' she breathed, and Stefanos glanced at the door. He knew at least six members of staff were behind there, holding their breath that she'd like their offering, that she'd be a kind child, that she could be a princess to be proud of.

She was all of those things, he thought. And it was thanks to Elsa.

Elsa, who didn't have pretty things to wear.

'So you don't have any dresses?' he probed and she cast him a glance that was almost resentful.

'I didn't bring any. And I'm not sad because of that. It's just…I'm just a bit overwhelmed.'

'You mean yesterday there was just you loving Zoe,' he said gently. 'And now there's me and a palace full of staff and an island ready to love her.'

'It's crazy to think like that,' she said, but she did.

'So back to the clothes,' he said gently. 'Can I ask why there's nothing but jeans?'

'I'm a marine biologist. Why would I need dresses?'

There was a loaded silence. Zoe ate two sausage rolls and

a strawberry and then thought about what Elsa had said. And decided she might add her pennyworth.

'Elsa did have pretty clothes,' the child told him, considering an eclair. 'Only she got too skinny and they looked funny on her. We kept them for ages but then she said, "You know what, Zoe, I'm never going to be this size again; they might as well make someone else happy." So we packed them up and took them to a church fair. And Mrs Henniker bought Elsa's prettiest yellow dress and she looked awful in it and Elsa cried.'

'I did not,' Elsa said, fighting for dignity. 'I had hay fever.'

'You only get hay fever when you cry,' Zoe said wisely. 'Giving your clothes away made you really sad.'

The bond between these two was amazing. Up until now he'd thought it was Elsa who did all the giving. Suddenly a new view was opening up.

Zoe was eight going on thirty.

Elsa was…sometimes ninety. Sometimes a kid.

She was trying for indignant here but it wasn't coming off. Zoe had exposed her and she knew she was exposed.

'Why did you lose weight?'

'I stopped eating for a while,' she told him in a voice that said no more questions were welcome. 'I've started again.'

'We might need to buy you some clothes,' he said, and watched as vulnerability disappeared, to be replaced by indignation.

'You don't need to buy me anything. I like my jeans.'

'I like your jeans too,' he said—and he did. They were exceedingly cute. Mind, she could do with a bit more flesh on her frame. She was almost elfin. And that limp…

'What happened to your leg?' he asked, and got another scared look.

'Please…just leave it. I'm here to be with Zoe while she gets to know the country her papa came from. I intend to stay in the background. Can we leave it at that?'

He considered her gravely and shook his head. 'Zoe, what's wrong with Elsa's leg?'

He heard her gasp. He didn't look at her.

This woman had cared for Zoe for four years. If he'd known of Christos's death he would have been there for his little cousin. The responsibility was his, but he hadn't even known of Zoe's existence.

That hurt on all sorts of levels, and one of those levels was the fact that this woman seemed to have put her life on hold for Zoe—and it might be worse than that.

He'd watched her come down the stairs and realised this was no twisted ankle. She was protecting her hip—as she'd been protecting her hip two weeks ago on the beach but he'd been too preoccupied to see it.

'She hurt it when my mama and papa died,' Zoe said, not picking up on the undercurrents. She was back considering food. This meal was a huge success. He could practically hear the chef's sigh of happiness from here.

'Are you going to tell me how badly?' he asked Elsa.

'I broke my hip,' she said discouragingly.

'You were in the car accident with Zoe's parents?'

'Yes.'

'And your husband…' He hadn't put two and two together, but he did now, and he didn't like it.

'Elsa's Matty was killed too,' Zoe said, and she was suddenly grave and mature and factual. 'My mama and papa were in the front seat and Matty and Elsa and me were in the back. A great big truck came round the corner on the wrong side of the road and hit our camper van and our camper van started to burn. Elsa pulled me out but she couldn't pull anyone else out. We were both really, really sad. I was in hospital for a long time—I can hardly remember—but I do remember Elsa coming in a wheelchair to see me. She says my grandma came to see me too, but I can't remember that. I remember being in a bath a lot and crying, but Elsa was always there. And then my grandma got sick so Elsa took me home with her—and now we're living happily ever after.'

She was suddenly back to being a little girl again. Happy

and optimistic. 'Only this is a better place for happy ever after, isn't it, Elsa?'

'There was nothing wrong with my beach,' Elsa said, making an unsuccessful attempt to glower, and Zoe giggled as if she'd said something silly.

'No, but our beach doesn't have cream puffs. These are really good. Can I have another one, please?'

'Be my guest,' Stefanos said and he handed her the plate—but his eyes were on Elsa. 'So why are you still limping?'

And once again it was Zoe who answered. 'Mr Roberts says she should have another operation. Mr Roberts came to see Elsa last time I was in hospital and he said, "When are we going to fix that hip, young lady?" And Elsa said, "When I have the time and the money, and like that's going to happen soon." And Mr Roberts said she had to get her pi…her priorities right and she said she did.'

'Zoe, don't,' Elsa said, looking desperate. 'Please, sweetheart, this is nothing to do with Prince Stefanos.'

'No, but he's nice,' Zoe said, as if that excused everything. 'Can I have one of those cakey things with wings, please?'

What would happen if she just got up from the table, walked right out of here, straight to the ferry, then on a plane back to Australia?

She had a return ticket. That was one of her stipulations about coming.

It was a first class ticket. If she traded it for economy she'd have enough to live on until she could start back to work.

Zoe didn't need her.

Only of course Zoe did. She looked happy and contented but she'd been here for less than a day. She was still clutching her. She was happy because this was exciting and Stefanos was kind. And the rest. Big and too good-looking for his own good—and did he know how sexy he looked in that uniform?

He was doing her head in and her head had to stay intact. She had to stay practical. She needed to find a role for herself here that wasn't tied to Zoe or Stefanos or the palace.

She could do this, she thought. She just had to stay detached from Stefanos and his dangerous charm.

This man was important to her only in his relationship to Zoe. He was good to Zoe. He made the little girl laugh. But he hadn't gained so much trust that Elsa could walk away.

She didn't ever want to walk away. Not from Zoe. The thought hurt on so many levels that the pain in her hip didn't even register in comparison.

'What are you thinking?' Stefanos asked, watching her quizzically from the head of the table. 'To make you look like that?'

'I…nothing.'

'I don't think I've been appropriately sympathetic.'

'I don't know what appropriate sympathy is.'

'Neither do I,' he said softly. 'But if it helped I'd find it for you.'

See, there was the whole problem. She had so much going on in her head—how to fit in here—what she was going to do with herself while Zoe settled—how she was going to make a life for herself after Zoe stopped needing her, as stop she surely would—and across it all was Stefanos's gorgeous smile, the way his dark eyes creased at the corners, the way he seemed to read her mind…

He left them for a while as she drank coffee. Urgent royal business, he said and that made her even more nervous. By the time he returned she was climbing the walls.

'You don't need me for this,' she said and pushed her chair back. 'Zoe, are you okay to do this photo thing with…with your cousin? I'll go up to the bedroom and unpack.'

'No!' Zoe was out of her chair in a flash, darting round the table to grab her hand. 'You have to come with me.'

Not so settled, then. Neither would she be, she thought, if someone told her she had to meet the press.

'I've arranged for Elsa to come with us,' Stefanos told Zoe, and her heart hit her boots.

'Excuse me?'

'I've promised the press they can meet Zoe and you.'

'And me?'

'You're the woman who's been caring for our Crown Princess for the past four years,' he said steadily. 'The islanders would have taken Zoe to them in a heartbeat. All of us owe you a debt that touches our honour.'

He rose and held out a hand to Zoe, and the little girl hesitated for a moment and then gave him hers. It was that sort of gesture. Strong, sure, commanding. Royal.

'If Zoe's brave enough to have her photograph taken, surely you can,' he told her.

'Yes, but Zoe's a princess,' she said on a wail. 'Look at me. I'm not even a proper nanny.'

'You're not,' he agreed. 'You're our friend. And, as our friend…' He hesitated. 'Elsa, giving Zoe clothes seemed appropriate. For you, however, it seems almost insulting and I ask you to accept that it's not my intention to insult you. Nevertheless, I've made some fast phone calls and the owners of our two main dress shops are here already, setting out a selection of clothes. For Zoe's coronation you'll need evening wear and we can't get that here, but for now…it would please me if you could choose something more suitable than jeans and sweatshirt for your introduction to our island.'

She stared at him in stupefaction. 'You want me to buy clothes?'

'I want you to take the clothes that I will buy for you,' he said. 'This will be my pleasure.'

'To dress me?'

His eyes creased involuntarily into laughter. 'I don't think we're quite there yet.'

She stared at him, feeling a tide of colour sweep upward. 'Ex…excuse me?'

'Levity,' he murmured, obviously fighting to get back to being serious. 'You need to excuse me. But this is clothes, Elsa. No big deal.'

'I wear jeans.'

'Zoe says you don't. Not before the accident.'

'I'm a whole new me since the accident.'

'Then is it possible,' he said gently, 'that you can be a whole new you again?'

'I…'

'Please, Elsa.'

She stared down at her battered sneakers, her worn jeans. They were like her skin, she thought, yet another skin she was being asked to change.

Poverty-stricken single mother to royal childminder.

Single woman to wife. Eager student to earnest professional. Married woman to grieving widow.

Skins, skins, skins. She hardly knew who she was any more. What harm could one more change do?

'Fine,' she said.

'Your gratitude is overwhelming,' he murmured, and there it was again—that hint of laughter.

'Did you like it when they told you that you had to wear a sword?' she demanded.

'I…no.'

'Then pay me the compliment of allowing that I feel the same,' she whispered. 'Thank you very much for providing clothes. I accept and I'm grateful. It's just…I've learned from past experience that it hurts to change direction. I'm doing my best to smile while it happens but you'll need to excuse me when my smile falters.'

She chose a simple green sundress. Zoe and Stefanos chose a whole lot more. Presumably the photographers and journalists had been told to wait, for Stefanos refused to hurry and was only satisfied when he—and Zoe—had decided she had enough clothes to make her…pretty.

Pretty was a strange concept. She'd stopped worrying about her appearance four years ago. Now, dressed in a lovely light sundress, with shoestring straps and a skirt that twirled and swished as she walked, she decided there were definite upsides to shedding skins.

She felt…nice. Free. It was a novel experience, but it didn't stop her hanging back as she finally followed Stefanos and Zoe to the palace media centre.

At the door Stefanos stepped back and motioned for Elsa to precede him.

No way.

She shook her head and dropped deliberately further back, and there was no time for him to react. The door was open. Cameras were flashing and questions were flying.

Zoe cast her a panicked backward glance, but Stefanos lifted her up and held her in his arms.

It was the best thing he could do, Elsa thought. Holding her in his arms. Zoe would feel totally protected.

The press was absolutely riveted on Zoe—their princess coming home. Which left her mind free to wander where it willed.

She kind of liked the way she looked in this sundress. And her new sandals were pretty.

Clothes maketh the woman? The man?

Her eyes flew back to Stefanos. She could see why he'd decided to wear his uniform, but it was more than clothes, she thought. He looked confident, sure, in charge. He was assuming the mantle of control of this country.

He had a job to do and he'd do it.

And he held Zoe as if she was his own. His body language was totally protective, and in his arms Zoe felt brave enough to venture shy answers of her own, responses the media loved—responses Elsa knew would go straight to the heart of any islander.

The Prince and his little Princess. She watched them pose together, she watched Stefanos tease Zoe into laughter, and the weird sensations she'd been feeling since the first time she'd seen him standing on her beach were consolidating to something firm and definite and true. Her vision of Matty was fading still further—not disappearing entirely; she knew it could never do that—but fading to a place where he could be mourned without the constant piercing pain that had been with her for years.

She could be pretty. She could change her skin yet again with no betrayal of Matty.

What on earth was she thinking? Crazy, crazy, crazy.

A latecoming journalist jostled past her, nudging her out of her introspection. Hauling her back to reality.

Get back to earth fast, she told herself harshly. This is one of Zoe's fairy tales.

And maybe she ought to listen.

'And may I introduce Dr Elsa Murdoch?' Stefanos was saying, and she was suddenly being looked at by everyone in the room.

Doctor? She hadn't used that title since…

'It's Mrs…' she started but he wasn't allowing her to get a word in.

'Elsa—Dr Murdoch—was in the car crash that claimed Prince Christos's life,' Stefanos said, and his voice was gentle and full of compassion. 'Also killed were Zoe's mother, Amy, and Elsa's husband, Mathew. Zoe still bears the scars, physically as well as mentally, and so does Elsa. Elsa is a world expert on…what did you call starfish, Zoe?'

'Echinoderms,' Zoe volunteered. Stefanos was still holding her tightly and she obviously felt confident enough to answer. 'Or asteroidea,' she added with aplomb.

'That's the one,' Stefanos said encouragingly. 'So, for the last four years, Dr Murdoch and Zoe have been conducting echinoderm—or asteroidea—research while they've gradually healed from their injuries. Dr Murdoch has cared for Zoe with total love and commitment, and for that this country owes her an enormous debt of gratitude.'

'Hey,' she said, startled enough to forget nerves and reply with spirit. 'That sounds like you're about to give me a gold watch and a pension.'

'You deserve much, much more than that,' he said, smiling. 'I'm hoping Dr Murdoch can stay here,' he told the reporters.

'I'm hoping she'll be a constant presence in Zoe's life. I need to be away from the island for a few weeks between now and Christmas—there are ends I need to tie off before I can stay here permanently—but Zoe and, I hope, Elsa, will be happy here for ever.'

And her tingle of humour and enjoyment disappeared, just like that.

Whoa. What was he saying? That she and Zoe would be staying, but he was leaving?

I need to be away from the island...

He was planning on coming and going at will? *While...what had he said?...Zoe and, I hope, Elsa will be happy here for ever.*

She stayed rooted to the spot while more questions were aimed at Stefanos. Was his work still important to him? How committed to the island could he be if he was returning to the States? Exactly how much time would he stay here and would he still play a ceremonial role?

'You know I'm a neurosurgeon,' he was explaining to the press, 'but of course there's work for me to do here now, medical as well as political. However, there are commitments to be honoured in the States before I can take on a permanent role.'

This was never in the contract, she thought wildly. He was leaving?

Stefanos was fielding the final questions. He was saying he'd be here until the coronation, and then he'd return by Christmas. He was intending to get the council sorted within the week...

She was no longer listening.

He was leaving.

He'd organised her to wear a sundress, while he wore a sword. The way she was suddenly feeling...

Maybe she needed a sword as well.

CHAPTER EIGHT

THE media session had taken its toll on Zoe. Jet lag and excitement had finally caught up with her. As the last of the reporters left, the little girl almost visibly drooped.

'Come on, sweetheart, let's get you up to bed,' Elsa said as Stefanos brought Zoe back to her. She carefully didn't look at Stefanos. The things she needed to say to this man couldn't be said in front of Zoe. In fact, maybe they needed a soundproofed room.

'I'm thinking you need a carriage, Your Highness,' Stefanos said grandly and scooped the little girl up again and carried her up the stairs.

Once again Elsa was left to follow. Her anger and bewilderment were building by the minute.

Stefanos was leaving. He was assuming she'd stay and take care of Zoe. In a place she didn't know. In a country she didn't know.

She was furious, but as she limped up the stairs after them her anger receded, leaving her flat and deflated. Like Zoe, she was so tired…

She'd been tired for years, but this was worse. Jet lag? No. It was betrayal, and betrayal hurt.

She stopped at the top stair and thought, I don't want to go on. I don't want to watch Stefanos tuck Zoe into bed and make her smile. I don't want to see Zoe seduced into this life of media attention, of shallowness, of wealth, with only me to protect her.

Royalty had destroyed Christos's childhood—he'd told her that. Stefanos had left the island as well, and he'd left for a reason. How could she possibly assess the risks royalty posed for such a vulnerable child as Zoe?

Regardless, Stefanos was obviously intending that she take on the burden of protecting Zoe. That was what he'd said. For ever?

She didn't follow him into the bedroom. She made it to the top stair and sat. If Zoe needed her, Stefanos would come back for her, she thought, but the way the little girl's eyelids were drooping as he'd carried her, she doubted if she'd notice if Elsa wasn't there. And if she went in now she might explode. That he demand she drop the threads of her life in Australia on command, and yet manipulate her so he could still do what he wanted… That he could return to his old life in Manhattan and leave her to care for Zoe in a place she didn't understand…

There were weary chuckles from the end of the corridor. Stefanos was making Zoe laugh.

Bully for Stefanos.

She felt dizzy, as well as angry and confused and all the rest of it. Her hip hurt. She put her head on her knees and folded her arms over her head. This was jet lag and more. Desolation, homesickness, betrayal. The world could go away…

Footsteps sounded down the hall, approaching her on the stair and pausing. She opened her eyes. A pair of black Hessian boots was in her field of vision.

Stefanos.

'Jet lag too, huh?' he said and he was smiling again. She knew he was smiling. She could hear his smile.

'It's not jet lag,' she said without looking up. 'It's anger and disgust and deception thrown in for good measure. Zoe's your cousin. What do you mean by abandoning her?'

'I'm not abandoning her,' he said, sounding surprised.

'You're going back to Manhattan.'

'Only for a few weeks.'

'Why didn't you tell us?'

There was a pause. And then… Amazingly, an honest answer. 'Because I thought you wouldn't come if I did.'

'How very perceptive.'

He sighed and sat down beside her. 'I'm sorry. I should have told you before, but I have an urgent surgical list to do before Christmas.'

'I had a paper on echinoderms to write up before Christmas,' she retorted. 'Believe it or not, it was important. Someone else is finishing it for me right now.'

'You're saying your echinoderms are more important than my surgical list?'

'You're saying your life is more important than my life?'

He hesitated. 'Elsa, I'm sorry. Of course I don't think that. But you don't understand.'

'So make me understand,' she flashed at him. 'Are there no other surgeons in New York?'

'I can't hand this over.'

'Why not?'

'I can't explain this while you're angry.'

'You don't have a choice,' she said wearily. 'From my point of view, you've conned me into bringing Zoe here. You've seduced the two of us, with your promise of palaces and lovely clothes and happy ever after. But what do I know of this life? How do I know Zoe is safe here? It was your assurance of safety and care that brought us here. How can you calmly say you're going away and leaving us when we've scarcely set foot in the place?'

She was staring downstairs at the massive chandelier below them. Wishing she wasn't in these clothes he'd bought her. Wishing she could wave a magic wand and be home with her beach and her starfish and even her disgusting fish-head cat food—somewhere where she knew the risks and could face them for her small charge; knowing exactly where she stood.

But it seemed that Stefanos wasn't backing down. He was hesitating over what to say to her but she could see that Manhattan was a done deal.

'Just explain,' she said wearily and for a moment she thought he wasn't going to say anything. And then he did.

'I work with overseas aid agencies,' he said slowly into the silence, as if he didn't yet know that he should admit it.

Aid agencies? What sort of aid agencies? What part of this could she believe? 'But you said you work in Manhattan.'

'I do. Patients come to me.'

'How?'

'Aid agencies send them,' he said bluntly, his tone implying he'd decided he might as well tell her and get it over with, whether she believed him or not. 'International aid agencies know what I do and they contact me at need. I intersperse these operations with my normal surgery—that way I can afford it. Mostly I treat people with head injuries from Africa. Neurological stuff. For children especially, as the brain continues to grow, scar tissue causes major problems. I work on techniques to remove the worst of the scar tissue without it reforming. I had to cancel some desperate cases when I realised I needed to find Zoe and get this place sorted. Those kids are still waiting. Now you're here, I need to go back, finish what I've promised and try to hand over my techniques to others to take them forward.'

'You cancelled…' She was staring at him in horror. 'You cancelled them for Zoe?'

'For the welfare of the whole island. If Zoe wasn't back here by the end of next week, then she'd forfeit the throne.'

She frowned, trying to keep up. 'But then you'd inherit.'

'You think I want it? I want to carry on my work.'

She swallowed. Hard. Trying to take this in. 'So… So you really are abandoning us?'

'No,' he said flatly. 'I can't. This place is a mess. Hell, Elsa, there's one doctor on the whole island and that's just the start of it. The local school only takes kids up to sixteen and then there's nothing. There's no infrastructure. The council needs replacing with good, solid people and they'll need support. How can I walk away and leave that to Zoe?'

'I haven't heard about this.'

'I keep it quiet.' He shrugged. 'My wealthy patients come to me in part because of my social position. To be honest, their fees pay for the other work I do, so I have to pander to them.'

'Honestly?'

'Honestly,' he said.

She stared at him. Said nothing. Stared at him still. Why did she believe him?

She did believe him. And if she did believe him…

She took a deep breath, summoned the words she needed and said them. 'I could help,' she said.

There was a loaded silence. He rose and stared down at her, as if she'd suddenly announced the arrival of aliens.

'You're kidding me,' he said at last.

'I don't say what I don't mean,' she said, and rose as well. 'Tell me what you need me to do and I'll do it.' She wasn't feeling very steady. She put her hand on the balustrade to support herself and suddenly Stefanos's hand was over hers.

'You can't,' he said softly.

'I can't help? How do you know I can't?' She tilted her chin. 'Sure, I don't know anything about this place, sure I was angry just then, but I'll get over it. You can teach me. If your work's so important, then I can try.'

The silence extended. She really was exhausted, she thought. If it wasn't for the balustrade and Stefanos's hand…

'Elsa, I'm starting to think there's nothing you can't do,' he said softly into the silence. 'There's no end to your generosity. Zoe's parents die and you abandon your career and take care of her. I arrive and tell you she's needed here and you upend your life and abandon your echinoderms and come with her. And now…your anger turns to an offer of help, just like that. If I said I had to leave tomorrow would you try and handle the council yourself?'

'Maybe I could,' she said and jutted her chin and he laughed, a lovely deep chuckle that had her confused. Veering towards anger again. If only she wasn't so tired.

'No, don't be angry, my lovely Elsa,' he said softly, and

he placed a finger under her chin. 'I'm not laughing at you. Indeed, I never could. But no. Your generosity is amazing. Stunning. And, if I could, maybe I'd be tempted. But the island needs a ruler who knows it. Like it or not, I was raised here. I know the islanders. I know the problems. No, I don't want to rule here. I want to practice my medicine. I won't be able to practice the medicine I want here, but that's a small sacrifice in the scheme of things. I've already started a training scheme back in New York. I just have to hope my work keeps going. If you could bear me to be away for these few weeks it will make all the difference.'

'You should have told me.'

'I should have told you,' he agreed. 'Indeed, I'm starting to think I should have told you many things.' Then, as she pulled slightly away from him, his hands came to rest on her shoulders. 'Thank you, Elsa. I can't believe your generosity, and I will keep you safe. I will keep Zoe safe.'

'I know you will.' Unaccountably, her eyes filled with tears. Dammit, she would not cry. *She would not cry.*

But he was too big and too close and too male.

Matty, she thought, but it was a faint echo of a love that was gone. Only…why did it feel as if she was betraying him now?

'You're as exhausted as Zoe,' Stefanos said softly. She shook her head and tried again to pull away from him—and staggered on the staircase.

But she didn't fall. This man had promised to keep her safe and that was just what he was doing.

'That hip…' he said, holding her steady.

'It's fine.'

'It's not fine. It's on my list to do something about. But not now. Now's for sleeping.' And, before she realised what he intended, she was lifted into his arms and he was striding down the hallway, just the same way he'd carried Zoe. As if her weight was nothing.

'Put… What do you think you're doing? Put me down.'

'In a moment,' he said, not breaking stride. 'You need to go where Zoe's going.'

She wanted to struggle. She really did. But suddenly all the struggle was sucked out of her.

His arms were strong, he was big and capable and he was carrying her like a child. For Elsa, who hadn't been treated as a child since…well, since she was one, the sensation was indescribable.

She could melt into these arms, she thought. She could let herself disappear, stop struggling, let these arms hold her for ever.

Was this what jet lag did to a girl?

He was at her bedroom, pushing open her door with his foot. The interconnecting door to Zoe's room was open and she could see through. Zoe was asleep already.

She suddenly felt inordinately proud of herself, that she was a good guardian, or nanny, or whatever she was supposed to be. She'd checked on her charge, even when she wasn't exactly in control herself.

And then she realised that Stefanos was carrying her through to Zoe's room. And she saw why.

Zoe's vast four-poster bed had been moved closer to the door. Zoe was fast asleep in it. And on the other side of her massive bed was another bed. A matching four-poster. Velvet curtains, a vast canopy, eiderdowns and cushions…

The room had been turned into a twin room, with two beds that were so ridiculously enormous that she gasped with incredulity.

'Wh…'

'I know it's a bit crowded,' Stefanos said, smiling down at her in a dumb, indulgent genie sort of way that for some weird reason had her heart doing backflips. 'You'll just have to slum it.'

Slum it…

Matching four-posters…

'I'm probably going to have to pay out on workers' insurance too,' he said morosely. 'Do you know how much these things weigh? It took eight of us to get it in here.'

'You…you…' She could hardly get it out.

'Idiot?' he suggested, laughing down at her and her heart did another backflip.

'Definitely idiot,' she said, trying for asperity and failing miserably. 'I… Thank you.' She was so far out of her comfort zone that she could hardly make her voice work but there was something else she badly needed to say. 'And…at the press conference…thank you for calling me Doctor.'

'It's what you are.'

'Not since Zoe needed me. I've been her mama since then. If I called myself Doctor, everyone thought I was medical. It just confused things.'

'So you stopped being Doctor and started being Mama. As you'd stop being on holiday and start bossing councillors if I asked it of you. You know, you're one special lady.'

'I am not.'

He grinned and lowered her onto the bed, and when he let her go she was aware of a sharp stab of loss.

'You want some painkillers for your hip?'

'It's not hurting.'

'I'm very sure it is.'

'It's fine!'

'Right, then,' he said and smiled again. She could hear his smile even when she didn't look at him. It was a smile that crept all around her, enveloping her in its sweetness. 'You want help to undress?'

'No,' she said and then, as she reran his question in her head, she found her voice. 'No! And…and don't think I'm not angry any more that you didn't tell me. I still am. It's just got to wait until morning.'

'That's my girl. What if I organise lunch tomorrow so we can talk about it?'

'I don't think…'

'I don't think you can think right now.'

He tugged an eiderdown from the foot of the bed and tucked it around her. 'You'd be more comfortable if you undress but I don't think I can help you there,' he said, his voice suddenly unsteady.

'No,' she said, and then couldn't think why she'd said it. Her voice didn't seem to belong to her.

'You'll be okay,' he said, looking down at her with all the tenderness in the world. As if he cared. As if he really cared.

'You'll be cared for here,' he said, echoing her thoughts. 'You and Zoe will be safe. We'll get that hip fixed. You can play with your starfish and live happily ever after.'

There was a lot to object to in that statement. He seemed to think he was reassuring her.

'I hate starfish,' she muttered.

'You hate starfish?'

'They don't do anything. They just blob. You move 'em and they just blob some more. I hate 'em.'

'You're studying them.'

'Doesn't mean I don't hate 'em.'

'You're done in, sweetheart.'

'I'm not done in. And I'm not your sweetheart.'

'You're not, are you? There's a complication to avoid.'

'Go away.'

'I will,' he said.

But he didn't. He stood gazing down at her and she didn't want him to go. She was half asleep, allowing images from the past—grief, pain, worry, even starfish—to be supplanted by this gorgeous Prince of the Blood.

Prince of the Blood. She wasn't actually sure what the term meant but she knew what it looked like. There was a Prince of the Blood smiling down at her right now, tucking in her eiderdown, looking gorgeous in his fabulous uniform. He was still wearing his sword!

'I love your sword,' she said.

'Don't encourage me,' he said. 'I'm starting to look in mirrors and swagger.'

'So you ought,' she whispered. 'Life should hold a little swagger.'

His smile softened. He stooped so his face was really close to hers and he placed a finger on her lips. To hush her? She didn't know and she didn't much care. It was enough that he was touching her.

It was suddenly incredibly important that he touch her.

'You've lost your swagger,' he said softly, almost as a whisper. 'Life's sucked it right out of you. Let me fix it for you.'

'I don't... You can't.' Matty, she thought desperately, but he'd faded even more. What remained was the memory of how grief felt, how loss felt, how she couldn't afford to fall...

'Elsa...' he said softly and as if in a dream she murmured back.

'Mmm.'

'Is it okay if I kiss you?'

Of course it wasn't. The idea was ridiculous.

But this wasn't real. It was a dream. And in her dream it was okay to kiss a prince. In her dream she could put her arms around his neck, link her hands and tug him downward.

In her dreams she could open her lips and wait for his lips to touch them.

In her dream he kissed her.

He kissed her.

Of all the dumb, stupid, complicating things to do, this must surely be the stupidest.

But she lay in her too-big bed, tucked under the vast eiderdown, looking up at him with eyes that were dreamy and close to sleep.

But not quite. She was watching him. She was smiling at him. And then her hands came up to hold him... He'd have to be inhuman to resist.

She was beautiful.

She was so different from any other woman in his world.

Slight and sexy, her sun-bleached curls were so fine they looked as if they'd float.

Her eyes were gorgeous in her too-thin face. A man could drown in those eyes.

She had eighteen freckles. He'd counted them when?

Maybe the first time he'd seen her. How many times had he recounted? And her lips were so kissable.

What made Elsa's lips more desirable than any other woman's's?

Because they belonged to Elsa?

And because she was responding.

Amazingly, she was tugging him down to her and there was no way he could resist these lips. This mouth. This woman. He sank so he was sitting on the vast bed, and he gathered her into his arms—and he kissed her with all the tenderness in his heart.

She melted into him. What had provoked him to ask permission to kiss her? He didn't know. All he knew was that the desire had become overwhelming. And when his mouth met hers…

He'd kissed women in his time. None like this.

She was warm and tender, close to tears and close to laughter, exhausted by jet lag and by fear of losing Zoe, intimidated beyond belief by her surroundings…and yet she was courageous beyond belief and she was melting into his arms as if she belonged here. She was kissing as well as being kissed. Her lips were demanding, opening, aching for him, and taking him as well as giving herself.

She felt right.

She felt like…home. Home and heart.

There was a ridiculous thought. And, as the acknowledgement of how crazy it was hit home, other realities slammed in.

He did not need to be attracted to this woman. This woman meant family.

He did not do family.

All this flooded through his consciousness like a shock wave, breaking the passion of the kiss, causing his arms to stiffen a little, causing him to break away…

Or maybe it was Elsa who broke away. He hardly knew. All that was certain was that she was still in his arms but the kiss had ended and he felt a flood of regret so deep it threatened to overwhelm him.

And Elsa's eyes were clouding as well, distancing herself from him, her arms untwining themselves from around his neck and pushing against his chest. Pushing him away.

'What…what do you think you're doing?' she whispered and he knew her confusion was at least as great as his.

'What do we both think we're doing?' he said ruefully and looked down into her face and saw fear.

Fear? Where had that come from? Surely she couldn't be afraid of him.

He was a prince in a royal palace and she was…a royal nanny.

He stood up as if she burned, taking a swift step back from the bed. If she could think that…

But… 'You needn't worry,' she whispered. 'I'm not thinking you're about to rape and pillage. I have a scream that can be heard into the middle of next week.'

'Good for you,' he said unsteadily.

'Don't patronise me.'

'I never would.'

She closed her eyes. It was a defence, he knew, but he never doubted for a moment that she'd sleep.

He stood looking down at her for a long moment, trying to think of what to say. Trying to think of how he could take this from here.

'Go away,' she muttered again.

Go away? It was the only sensible thing to do.

Of course it was the sensible thing to do.

Go away, he repeated to himself and it was a direct order, but only he knew how much effort it cost him to turn on his heel and walk out of the door.

If Zoe hadn't been asleep in the next bed…

Maybe it was just as well she was.

CHAPTER NINE

ELSA woke and sunlight was streaming in though the massive French windows of their bedroom. The crystals from the chandelier above her head were sending glittering sparkles across the room.

Zoe was sitting on the end of her bed, fully dressed in another of the lovely outfits Stefanos had bought for her.

She was cuddling a kitten. A small grey kitten with a white nose, white paws and a tiny tip of white on the end of his tail.

'Go say hello to Elsa,' Zoe said, and put the kitten down and watched in satisfaction as the small creature walked along the coverlet, crouched down and put a paw out to tentatively touch Elsa's chin.

'What…where did he come from?' Elsa managed, doing a speedy visual check of the room in case Stefanos was lurking behind the curtains. Not that she was afraid of Stefanos. Not exactly.

But she wouldn't put it past the man to lurk.

'Stefanos gave him to me,' Zoe said with deep satisfaction. 'He said I must be missing my cats at home and he's mine to keep. His name is Buster.'

'Yours to keep…' Elsa said cautiously. This needed thinking about.

There were things like quarantine laws. It was easy enough,

she knew, to get animals from Australia to Europe, but taking them the other way…

She'd just woken up and here was another instance of Stefanos's arrogance. He'd have planned this before last night, she thought. Before she'd known he was leaving. He'd assumed he could talk her round.

He had talked her round.

But something wasn't making sense. Zoe was up and dressed. She'd gone to sleep—what—at five or six p.m.?

She checked her wristwatch.

Eleven.

She sat bolt upright and yelped. Buster bolted for the far end of the bed, where his new mistress scooped him up and held him close.

'You're scaring him,' she said, reproachful.

'I'm scaring myself. How can it be morning already?'

'It's been morning for ages,' Zoe said. 'I woke up and waited and waited but you kept sleeping. And then I opened the door and there was a really nice lady sitting in the corridor and she said her name was Christina and she'd been waiting for me to wake up. She helped me have a bath—it's a really big bath, Elsa, you should see it—and she helped me with my clothes and then she took me down for breakfast and Stefanos was there. So we had a really yummy breakfast—strawberries, Elsa—and then Stefanos took me to the stables and gave me Buster. And I brought him up to show you but you were *still* sleeping, and Stefanos said we had to let you sleep for as long as you needed to, so we've been really quiet only we've just been watching.'

This was just about the longest speech Zoe had ever made. She sat back on the bed and cuddled Buster the kitten, and Elsa smiled at her in pleasure and wonder. The as-yet-not-met Christina must be good to have Zoe smiling after a bath. To be remembering it with pleasure.

But there was another part of her that was saying uh-oh.

Stefanos was truly seducing them, she thought, watching Zoe's face flush with excitement. He'd already seduced her little charge. Zoe might be hugging her kitten but every time she said Stefanos's name her voice took on the hush of hero worship.

He'd given her strawberries for breakfast. He'd given her a kitten.

Bribery, she thought.

And what was he trying on her?

Seduction of another kind.

But…she kind of liked it.

Matty, Matty, Matty, she thought fiercely but it didn't work. Wherever Matty was, however much she'd loved him, he was no longer protection against Stefanos.

'Do you want to get up now?' Zoe said. 'Stefanos wants to take you out to lunch. He said you both need to talk privately about boring stuff, so he asked if I'd mind staying here with Christina and Buster. And Christina thought she might show me the beach. If that's okay with you,' she added, but her tone said Elsa's agreement was never in doubt.

It couldn't be in doubt. Elsa inspected the request from all angles. There was a lot to consider.

Like going out to lunch with Stefanos. He'd suggested it last night. She didn't remember agreeing.

'He said to tell you it's a picnic. He said to tell you shorts are man…mandatory and swords are optional. I don't know what that means.'

'It means Stefanos is being silly,' she said, a bit too abruptly, and Zoe looked at her in astonishment.

'Don't you like Stefanos?'

'No. Yes! I don't know.'

'Do you want Christina to run you a bath?' Zoe said seriously. 'The bath is lovely. It's really, really deep.'

'I believe I can run my own bath,' Elsa said. 'Though I should take a shower. I hope your cousin Stefanos is taking one too. Preferably cold.'

'Why would he want to do that?' Zoe asked, astonished.

'I have no idea,' she said and summoned a grin. 'I know I'm being stupid. But I think it might be me who needs to take a cold shower.'

She went to shower—but then she changed her mind. This wasn't a place for denying oneself.

Her hip would definitely like a bath.

Back home she survived on tank water. Showers had to be fast of necessity.

Here she had a feeling if she wanted to stay in the bath all day, playing with the amazing selection of bottles of luxury…stuff? no one would say a word of protest. So she did. If not for a day, for almost an hour.

She might have used one too many bottles of smelly stuff, she conceded as she soaked on. She was fighting to keep an airway free through bubbles.

Finally, reluctantly, her conscience got the better of her. She wrapped herself in a fabulously fleecy white towel, used several more towels getting rid of the bubbles and padded back to the bedroom.

She opened her wardrobe and gasped. Yesterday she'd accepted two dresses and a couple of shirts and sandals. Some time during the night her selection had been augmented by…well, by enough clothes to keep a girl happy for a year.

This was really intrusive. She should be angry. But… She tugged out a lovely jonquil blouse and a soft pair of linen shorts. She held them up in front of her and any attempt at anger disappeared.

'If you need to change direction, then you might as well enjoy it,' she told herself, and thought she was about to go on a picnic with Stefanos and she had new clothes and she felt terrific and maybe changing direction wasn't bad at all.

He was leaving.

She wouldn't think about that. She'd cope. She always had coped with what life threw at her. And if life was now throwing bubbles and new clothes at her…and lunches with princes…a girl might just manage to survive.

She came down the staircase looking wide-eyed with apprehension, self-conscious in her neat lemony blouse, white shorts and new sandals—and very, very cute. She'd twisted her curls up into a knot. He liked it, he thought. He liked it a lot.

He'd like it better if he could just untwist it…

'Have you been standing there for hours waiting for me?' she demanded as she saw him.

'Hours,' he agreed, and grinned.

Did she have any idea how cute she was? Her eyes were creased a tiny bit from a lifetime spent in the sun, but that was the only sign of wear. Her nose was spattered with her eighteen gorgeous freckles. If he didn't know for sure she must be close to thirty, he'd have pegged her as little more than a teenager.

And she smelled… She smelled…

'Wow,' he said as she came close, and she grinned.

'Lily of the Valley, Sandalwood and Fig and Anise. There would have been lavender in there too, but I couldn't get the bottle open.'

'Thank God for that,' he said faintly and then counted freckles again. 'Um… Don't you believe in cosmetics?'

'Pardon?'

'Most of the women I know wear make-up,' he said lamely, kicking himself for letting his mouth engage before head.

'Well, good for them,' she said encouragingly. 'Do you, too?'

'Do I what?'

'I've spent so much time in doctors' waiting rooms over the last four years that I've read enough cosmetics advertisements to make me a world expert. There's men's cosmetics as well. I'm sure princes use them. Fake tan's the obvious one. Does your tan rub off on your towel?'

'No,' he said, appalled, and she arched her eyebrows in polite disbelief.

'You'll need sunscreen,' he said, sounding lame, and the look she gave him then was almost scornful.

'Go teach your grandmother to suck eggs. I'm Australian. I put sunscreen on before my knickers.'

And then she heard what she'd said—and blushed.

It was some blush. It started at her toes and worked its way up, a tide of pink. She could feel it, he thought, and her knowledge that it was happening made it worse.

He loved it.

'So…so this is royal beachwear,' she managed, moving on with an obvious struggle.

He glanced down at his casual chinos, his linen shirt and his boat shoes. 'What's wrong with this?'

'Looks great for being a prince and lazing on a sixty-foot yacht on the Mediterranean,' she said. 'It's not great for rock pools, though. And that's where I hoped we'd be going. Somewhere rock pooly?'

She was defending by attack, he thought. But she was still blushing.

Last night he'd kissed her. Right now, all he could think of was that kiss. And how he could repeat it.

He may well get his face slapped, he thought. She'd been way out of control last night, exhausted and vulnerable. Right now…her defences were up and, even if he wanted to—okay, he did want to—she'd be sensible enough for both of them.

'The kitchen staff have set us up with a picnic basket,' he told her. 'There's a great little beach I know a few minutes' drive from here. I believe it even has rock pools.'

'What time will we be back?'

'Does it matter?'

'Yes,' she said, definite. 'I want control here. I should even be deciding where we're going.'

'Isn't it usually the guy…?'

'Who gives orders,' she finished for him. 'I'm sure it is, and if it's a prince then it probably works double. But *Sleeping*

Beauty's for wimps. I fight my own battles—and I set up my own defences. Can I tell Zoe four o'clock?'

'If you like.'

'I do like,' she said. 'You're on probation. After that kiss last night… I don't know why you did it but it scared me. I'm happy to have a picnic but let's make it quite clear this relationship is purely business.'

'Of course,' he said courteously but he was aware of a stab of disappointment.

He didn't know what was happening—but what he did know was that he didn't want to be on a business footing with Elsa.

'So why are we going on a picnic?' she asked as they headed out along the coast road. 'Aren't there urgent princely things you should be doing?'

There were urgent princely things he should be doing, but for now… They were ensconced in a Gullwing Mercedes—a 1954 300 SL. A car with doors that opened like wings from the centre. A car that looked like a weird seagull—a crazy, wonderful car. It had belonged to the King, but it had obviously sat in mothballs for the last fifty years. Finding it had been a highlight of the past two dreary weeks.

And now…it felt great. The sun was shining, they were cruising smoothly around the curves of the scenic coast road, the Mercedes' motor was purring as if it was finally allowed to be doing what it should be doing—and for the moment that was how he felt too. As if he'd got it right.

Beside him… A beautiful woman with freckles.

'So we're going to the beach why?' she prodded again and he shook off his preoccupation with Elsa the woman and Gullwing the car and tried to think of what she'd asked.

'I want to be private.'

'Not so you can kiss me again?'

'No,' he said, startled, and then thought actually that wasn't such a bad idea.

'Just as well,' she said, but her voice was strained. He

glanced across at her and thought she'd come close to admitting that last night's kiss had affected her as much as it had him.

'So you want to talk to me,' she ventured.

'We need to depend on each other,' he said, trying to sound suitably grave and princely. 'Maybe it's time we got to find out a bit more about each other.'

'Without kissing.'

'Without kissing.' Hard to sound grave and princely while saying that.

'So you can figure whether I can take on this island?'

'No.' He grew serious then. 'I'm not asking that of you. It's my responsibility. But I did think—even before last night—that you deserve an explanation of who I am—of what's behind the mess of this island. So that while I'm away you have a clear idea of the background.'

He was manoeuvring the car off the main road now, turning onto a dirt track through what was almost coastal jungle. Once upon a time this had been a magnificent garden but that was a long time ago now. He parked the car under the shade of a vast wisteria draping the canopy of a long-strangled tree. As the car's batwings pushed up, the wisteria's soft flowers sent a shower of petals over their heads.

It was right to come here, Stefanos thought. Matters of state had to wait a little. This felt…right.

Elsa was gazing around her with awe and the beginnings of delight. A tiny stone cottage was also covered with wisteria. It looked ramshackle, neglected and unused.

'This looks almost like home,' she breathed. 'Without the termites.'

'You have termites?'

'My house is wood veneer,' she said darkly. 'Veneer over termites. So what's this place?'

'My home,' he said, and she stared.

'Your home? But you live in Manhattan.'

'Now I do. This is where I was brought up.'

She stared around her, puzzled. 'But a prince wouldn't live here.'

'I wasn't raised as a prince. My father scratched a living fishing. He was killed in a boating accident when I was sixteen. Accidents to the island's original royals are littered throughout our history—never anything that could definitely be attributed to the King, but terrifying, regardless. After Papa died my mother insisted I go abroad. She sold everything to get me into school in the States. Christos left soon after, for the same reasons, only Christos's mother had a little more money so she was able to go with him.'

'So you left the island when you were sixteen? Alone?'

'Yes,' he said flatly. 'I had no choice. Mama was terrified every time I set foot on the island so she insisted I didn't return. She died of a heart attack just before I qualified as a doctor, and it's to my eternal regret I wasn't here for her. I hope…I hope she was proud of my medicine. I've always hoped that what I do was worth her sacrifice.' He shrugged awkwardly. 'Who can tell, but there it is.'

'So…' She was eyeing him cautiously. Sympathetic but wary. 'Why are you telling me this?'

'I want to tell you why I left the island and I want to explain how important my medicine is to me.' He hesitated. 'That's all. Dumb, really. But after last night…it seemed important that you know.'

'You can practice medicine here,' she said, still cautious.

'I can,' he said. 'I will. The old doctor here is overjoyed that I'll be joining him.'

'But…not practising neurosurgery?'

'I'd need a population considerably bigger than this island to justify equipment, technology, ancillary staff. So no.'

'You'll be a good family doctor,' she said softly and he smiled.

'I hope so. If I'm not I'm sure you'll tell me. Now… lunch?'

'Yes, please.'

She climbed out of the car and gazed around her. It was a picture-perfect setting, a tiny house nestled in a tranquil little cove. She thought of Stefanos growing up here, using this place as his own private paradise.

He had it all. His career, his title, his good looks, his life.

So why did she feel sorry for him? It wasn't what he'd intended, she thought, glancing at him as he retrieved a picnic basket from the car. But suddenly… Suddenly she thought she hadn't had it too hard at all.

She'd lost Matty but she'd loved him and he'd loved her. Her own parents had died young but her best friend, Amy, had always been close. And then there'd been Zoe.

How hard must it be to walk alone?

How would he react if she told him she felt sorry for him? she wondered, and then she glanced at him again, at the sheer good looks of the man, the way he smiled at her, the teasing laughter behind his eyes.

All this and sympathy too? This man was too dangerous for words!

He suspected it was a picnic to surpass any picnic she'd ever had. Lobster, crunchy bread rolls, butter curls in a Thermos to keep them cool, a salad of mango and avocado and prawns, lemon slivers, strawberries, tiny meringues, a bottle of sparkling white wine…

'This is enough for a small army,' she gasped as he spread a blanket over a sandy knoll overlooking the sea.

'I doubt the royal kitchen appreciates the concept of enough. Do you think you can make a dent in it?'

'I'll do my best,' she said and proceeded to do just that.

She concentrated on eating, as if it was really important. It probably was, he conceded. She'd missed last night's dinner and this morning's breakfast, but she probably didn't need to concentrate quite as hard as she was.

She seemed nervous, and that made two of them. Last night had left him floundering, and quite simply he didn't know how to go forward. This was a woman unlike any other. A widow. A woman with a past, but a woman who was facing the future with courage, with humour and with love.

Quite simply, she left him awed. And now… He felt as if he were treading on eggshells, and he was already sure he was squashing some.

In the end it was Elsa who broke a silence that was starting to seem strained. 'So tell me about the island,' she ventured. She was lying on the rug looking out to sea. She was on one side of the rug, he was on the other and the picnic gear was in between. It was starting to seem a really intrusive arrangement. But it'd be really unwise to change it, he thought. No matter how much he wanted to.

'I'll show you the island,' he told her. 'When you've finished lunch I'll give you a quick tour. It's far too big to see in a day—but I do want to give you some impression of what we're facing.'

'We?'

'Hey, you offered to help,' he said and then smiled at her look of panic. 'But no, Elsa, relax. I meant *we* as in all the islanders.'

She managed a smile in turn. 'Not *we* as in the royal *we*? Not *we* as in, "We are not amused"?'

'No.'

'So there's still nothing for me to do.'

'There is.' He hesitated, trying to figure a way to say what needed to be said. He couldn't. But still it needed to be said.

'There are three things,' he said at last. 'Some time before I go back to Manhattan—before the end of the month—I'd like to take you to Athens. I want you to buy a dress for the coronation.'

It was such an unexpected request that she looked blank. It was left to him to explain—why he'd woken at three this morning and thought he had to do this. He'd fit it into his schedule somehow.

'I want you to have a gown that'll do justice to your role on the island,' he said simply. 'I want you to stand by Zoe's side at the coronation and look royal yourself. You're her guardian. I'll stand by her side as Prince Regent but you're guardian to the Crown Princess. You should be received with equal honour.'

There was a lengthy silence at that. Then, 'A dress,' Elsa said cautiously. 'You mean…not a nice nannyish dress with a starched collar and Nanny embroidered on the breast.'

'I had in mind more a Princess Di dress. Or a Princess Grace dress. Something to make the islanders gasp.'

'Yeah, right,' she said dryly.

'Yeah, right? That would be two positives? That means you agree?'

'That means there's no way I agree.'

'I wish it,' he said.

'Oooh,' she said. 'Is this insubordination?'

'Elsa…'

'Sorry.' She managed a shaky smile. 'It's an amazing offer.' She shook her head, as if shaking off a dream. 'But it's nuts. For one thing, you have way too much to do to be taking me shopping. How could you possibly justify putting off your surgical lists for something so crazy? And second… The clothes you've already arranged for me are bad enough.'

She faltered then, her colour fading as she realised what she'd said. 'I'm sorry,' she said again. 'I mean…they're lovely and I'm very grateful, but…I don't know how to explain. This is me, Stefanos. I might be changing direction but I'm still me. I don't do Princess Di or Princess Grace. Please. Let me keep being Elsa.'

'You can be Elsa in a couture gown.'

'Yeah, right,' she said again. 'But no. So okay, that's sorted. What next? What else did you want to talk to me about?'

'It would give me pleasure to see…'

'No.' Flat. Definite. 'You're royalty and I'm not. Let's move on.'

Uh-oh. He wasn't having much luck here, and the next one was more important. Maybe he should have voiced it first. Except when he'd thought this all through in the middle of the night, the thought of taking her shopping had distracted him. It was still distracting him.

Maybe now, though, he needed to get serious.

'It's not just shopping,' he said softly. 'I'd like you to see an orthopaedic surgeon in Athens. I want you to get your hip repaired.'

'Now?' she said, astounded.

'Now,' he said. 'You're in pain.'

'I'm not.'

'You are. The pin in your hip hasn't held. You need a complete joint replacement.'

Uh-oh, he thought, watching her face. Maybe he'd gone about this the wrong way.

She stood, staggering a little as she put weight on both feet, but she righted herself fast. Her eyes were flashing fire. 'How do you know,' she said, carefully enunciating each syllable, 'that the pin hasn't held?'

'I rang Brisbane.'

'You rang Brisbane.' The fire in her eyes was suddenly looking downright explosive. 'You mean you rang my treating doctor?'

He was suddenly in really dangerous territory. This woman might change direction at will but she was never going to be compliant or boring or…or less than the Elsa he was starting to have enormous respect for.

Respect? Respect didn't begin to cover what he was feeling.

'You wouldn't tell me what's wrong with your hip,' he said, trying to sound reasonable, but he was wrong-footed and he knew it. He'd wanted to sound caring and concerned and…maybe even magnanimous. Instead, suddenly he was feeling unprofessional and interfering and about the size of a rather small bug.

'So you just asked,' she said, and her anger was starting to make her stutter. 'You thought you'd just ask my doctor what was wrong with me. How did you do that? Did you say, "Hi, Doctor, this is a casual acquaintance of one of your patients. Could you tell me what's wrong with her hip?" Or… "This is Prince Stefanos Leandros Antoniadis from Khryseis and I order you to hand over my servant's medical records." Or…'

She paused for breath. 'Or, "This is Doctor Antoniadis and I have a woman here who can't even get up the stairs without limping so can you send me her records—as one professional to another".'

'It wasn't like that. Elsa, I owe you so much.' He'd risen to face her. Now he tried to take her hands, but she wrenched them away as if he were poison ivy.

'You owe me so much that you can't even grant me privacy?' she demanded.

'I have to know what's wrong with you. Zoe depends on you. We need to get it fixed before I leave.'

'Before you leave… It'll take weeks. Months, even. A week in hospital and at least a month in rehabilitation. When you get back from Manhattan, when things are settled, when Zoe's happy, then I'll think about it. Maybe. Possibly. But it's my business. Mine, Stefanos.'

'Zoe will cope…'

'Zoe will not cope. I will not ask it of her. Now, what's the third thing?'

'I don't think it's wise…'

'I don't think any of this is wise,' she said. 'But ask me anyway.'

'It can wait.'

'I might not be speaking to you tomorrow. Tell me now.'

'It was just…' Hell, he'd messed this. He'd messed this so badly. He wanted to back off but she was waiting, breathing too fast, and he knew that not to finish it would make it even worse than it already was. The third request…

'It's none of my business.'

'So tell me and let me decide.'

He hesitated. But he did need to get to know this woman. Even as her employer, he should know her.

'I'd like you to tell me about Matty.'

'Matty.'

'Your husband.'

'You think I don't know who Matty is?' She seemed almost speechless.

'Of course you do. I'm going about this the wrong way but yesterday… I didn't even know how he died. I should have asked you about him and I'm so sorry I didn't. Matty was your husband and you loved him. He must have been really special.'

Speechless didn't begin to describe how she was feeling. What was it with this man? He'd brought her here for a picnic. He'd fed her lobster and wine—and then he'd talked of buying her ball dresses and phoning her doctor and now he wanted to talk about her dead husband.

Her head was hurting. Her hip was hurting.

She wanted to hit him.

Count to ten, she told herself. Come on, Elsa, you can cope with this.

Personally, Stefanos had overstepped the mark. The knowledge that he'd phoned her doctor and found out information was huge—it threatened to overwhelm her. But that was personal.

Asking her about Matty was personal.

This man was her employer. Nothing else.

So why not tell him about Matty?

It was too confusing. How could she tell him about Matty without betraying Matty? Yet how could the act of telling him about Matty be a betrayal? Unless…unless…

It was far too hard.

'Take me back to the palace, Stefanos,' she said wearily. 'I'm sure you have work to do.'

'But…'

'I have work to do too,' she said. 'If I can't help rule your island, then I'll just have to go back to starfish.'

'There are some great starfish…'

'How many times do I have to tell you—I hate starfish,' she snapped bitterly, irrationally, and shoved the picnic basket aside and lifted the picnic rug and shook it. And if the sea breeze just happened to be blowing in the direction of Stefanos…well, the gods must have meant him to get a face full of sand.

But his phone was ringing and he was retrieving it from his pocket. He didn't seem to notice she was throwing sand at him like a two-year-old having a tantrum.

Frustrated, she folded the rug nicely and gathered the gear together and waited for him to finish.

'Of course I can do it. No, you know I promised. From now on, this is what I do.'

'What?' she said as he snapped his phone shut.

'A two-year-old with croup,' he said. 'In the village near here. Would you mind if we stopped on the way back? Though…it'd mean you miss out on your rock pools.'

Okay, enough of the tantrums. She pulled herself together.

'My rock pools can wait. Of course they can. Croup? Are you working already?'

'Our island doctor has more work than he knows what to do with. I've told him I'll start helping at once. We'll get more medical staff here before I leave, but for now… He's stuck in a clinic on the far side of the island and the child's mother has newborn twins at home and isn't well herself. It's probably just reassurance. If you can wait…'

'Of course I can wait,' she said remorsefully. 'I'm not really a brat.'

'I know you're not a brat. You're…' He hesitated. 'No. Let's just go.'

The drive to the village was done in silence. Stefanos was feeling just about as low as it was possible to feel.

This morning it had seemed a good idea—sensible, even—to take Elsa to the beach. He'd decided to show her he wasn't born a prince—that they had more in common than she thought. He'd offer her a beautiful dress, a shopping trip to Athens. He'd have to push to find time to do it but she needed some sort of gesture to show how much he appreciated her care of Zoe. And…it hadn't escaped his mind that watching Elsa buy a beautiful gown might be a whole lot of fun for him too. Time out for both of them.

The other things had been added because they were also

starting to feel urgent. Every time he noticed her limp now he felt bad. And he needed to find out about Matty.

Okay, the last wasn't essential, but it seemed essential to him—more and more. He didn't fully understand why—it was simply the way Elsa was making him feel.

So he'd set his plan in place and, in doing so, he'd alienated her just about as far as he possibly could.

Good one, he told himself, feeling something akin to pond scum. Only pond scum might have more self-respect.

He knew the place he was going. He drove slowly through the nearby village and hesitated. 'Do you want to come with me? Would you mind staying in the car?'

'I'm happier here,' she said, motioning to the village street. 'I'll poke around and talk to people. That looks a nice peaceful little park. If you take hours, don't worry; I'll be under a tree asleep.'

Once again she'd taken his breath away. He thought of the women he'd taken out before—colleagues, New York singles, women who were smart and savvy and stood up for what they wanted.

So did Elsa, he thought, but only when it was needed. Now…she'd made no fuss, she'd released him from any pressure and he knew instinctively that if it took hours she wouldn't fuss at all.

'Thank you,' he said.

'Stefanos?'

'Yes?'

'I might need a bit of money,' she said diffidently. 'I don't have any local currency and it's been so long since lunch… I might need an ice cream.'

And how good was that, he thought as he drove away. Without any more pressure she'd ensured she had enough money for phone calls and help if he really didn't come back for her.

Only she needn't doubt that. He'd definitely come back for her.

* * *

The old doctor was right—the little boy was suffering mild croup, easily handled at home. What was needed was reassurance and his mother got that in spades, just by Stefanos's presence.

'Our Prince,' the young mother said, over and over. 'Here in my kitchen.'

He smiled and cradled one of her twins and shared a cup of tea with her. As the two-year-old slid into sleep, the young father came home, reacted with awe that Stefanos himself had come, decided his wife obviously needed more support if the Prince himself suggested it and, before he knew it, the children's aunt was unpacking a suitcase in the spare room, fast enough to also join the Prince in yet another cup of tea.

There was nothing to this family medicine, Stefanos thought with wry humour, though his house calls might well need to get a bit faster.

Could he be content with family medicine?

It had its own skills. He was out of date. He'd have to brush up on his general medical knowledge, but he would. It could give him satisfaction. If only…if only the work he'd been doing wasn't so imperative.

Elsa wasn't in the park, but he found her easily. She was standing in front of the butcher's shop, happily licking an ice cream cone, reading the literature in the shop window. With her gorgeous bare legs, her flyaway curls, her ice cream, she stood out like a sunbeam.

'Hi,' she said as he climbed out of his car to join her. Maybe he should get himself a less conspicuous car, he thought ruefully. These wings were crazy. The locals were staring at the car and starting to cluster.

'How goes your patient?' she asked.

'All cured.'

'Really?'

'I'm a fabulous doctor,' he said modestly. 'I prescribed one aunt and lo, the problem's solved.'

'Do they sell aunts in bottles?'

'Sure they do. Can we go?'

'Um…maybe. But have you seen this?' she asked, licking her cone with care.

Woman-cum-eight-year-old. She made him feel…

See, that was the trouble. He didn't know how he felt. *This* was something new, something frightening, something he didn't know what to do with.

'Is this beach far?' she asked.

'What beach?'

'Read the poster,' she said with exaggerated constraint.

He read the poster. It was handwritten, big and to the point.

Turtles hatching. Kemp's Ridley. Lagoon Tempio. Urgent assistance needed—now! Helena.

'Do you know where Lagoon Tempio is?'

'I…yes.'

'Can we go?' she asked. She took a final lick of her cone, decided against more and tossed the remainder in a nearby bin.

'You want to go to this beach?' he said cautiously, aware that the eyes of many people were on him.

'Yes.' To his astonishment, she was suddenly deadly serious. She wiped her hands on her hips and faced him square on. 'Please.'

He stared at the sign. It made no sense. 'Who's Kent Ridley?'

'Kemp's Ridley. Lepidochelys kempii. It's the smallest and most endangered of the world's sea turtles. And they breed together. All the females nest on the one night so hatchings are huge. If it's really Kemp's Ridley… I can't imagine it is, but please, Stefanos, I need to go.'

The sudden passion in her voice stunned him. The vibrant excitement. 'Didn't you tell Zoe you'd be back by four?' he said, astounded at the change in her.

'I told you I told Zoe I'd be back by four,' she said impatiently. 'I was scared you meant a spot of seduction. Stefanos, we need to hurry.'

There was a snort from behind them. The onlookers were

close enough to hear. This was a busy shopping street in the middle of the afternoon and every person here knew who he was. Maybe they didn't know who Elsa was—but they were surely interested.

She'd just made them a whole lot more interested. So many people spoke English these days, he thought.

'Elsa…'

'Okay, I know you didn't want to seduce me,' she conceded. 'You just wanted to ask me a whole lot of questions I failed to answer. But I wasn't to know that. So I'm safe but the turtles aren't. If whoever wrote this poster…Helena?'

'Helena's my mother,' a voice volunteered, and Elsa turned with eagerness.

'Your mother?' She'd slipped easily and fluently into Greek. 'Your mother is saving turtles?'

'They started hatching this morning,' a middle-aged man wearing a butcher's apron told her. 'My mother's excited, too. These turtles used to come here in large numbers—the mass nesting is called an arribadas, my mother says—but forty years ago scientists and tourists were coming to see so the King bulldozed the beach. It broke my mother's heart. But this year… This year they've come back. She wants me to help but I have my shop. I put her sign up in my window but it was all I could do.'

'Does she have helpers?'

'I sent my boy down to help her,' the man told her. 'But there are so many birds… My mother can only save a few.'

'Stefanos,' Elsa said and fixed him with a look he was starting to recognise.

'Yes?'

'As far as I know, there's only one known nesting ground and that's in Mexico. To have a Kemp's Ridley hatching ground right here, where I can help… There'll be a million predators feasting on them. Stefanos, we need a royal decree or something.'

'A royal decree?' he said blankly,

'We have to save those turtles.' She took a deep breath. Steadied. 'Stefanos, if you help me save the turtles, then I'll…I'll…I'll even let you buy me a Princess Grace dress.'

There was a ripple of stunned laughter through the crowd. More and more people were clustered around them now, with more arriving every minute. This was their Prince Regent. And the Princess's nanny.

'So what do we need?' he said simply.

'People. Lots of people.'

She was speaking with passion, and she was waiting for him to act.

People.

'The school,' he said.

'What about the school?'

He turned to the crowd. 'Is the school bus available?'

'It'll be taking the schoolchildren home,' someone told him. 'It should be back here in a few minutes.'

'Who's in charge of it?'

'My son,' someone else called.

'Okay,' Stefanos said. 'I'm commandeering the school bus. Can you tell your son that I'll pay him double the going rate to transport any islander and any child to Lagoon Tempio? There's as much ice cream as they can eat for a week for anyone who comes there.' He grinned at the ice cream vendor. 'I'll reimburse you, and I'll also reimburse you for closing the shop now. That goes for anyone who wants to help.' He glanced at the butcher. 'Phillip, can we set up a barbecue on the beach? If we're going to get people there we need to feed them. Can you contact the baker and Marios at the café? I'll reimburse you for anything anyone eats or drinks tonight. Portia…' he turned to another woman standing by a battered Jeep '…can you take Dr Murdoch there now? I'll pay you for your trouble. By the way, everyone, this is Dr Murdoch—a marine biologist who also happens to be the best thing that's happened to this island for a long time. Elsa, I'll organise things here.

I'll phone the palace and ask that Zoe be brought down to join us.'

He smiled at Elsa. She was all fire and pleading and pure adrenalin, wide-eyed with excitement. He put his finger to his lips and then he placed his finger on hers. 'Let's do this together,' he said and he smiled. 'If only because I really want to see you in that dress. And I'm so sorry I upset you. Okay, everybody, let's go save some turtles.'

CHAPTER TEN

IT TOOK half an hour of phone calls and arrangements before he got to the beach himself—and when he did the sight before him almost blew him away.

Lagoon Tempio was a sheltered cove about fifteen minutes from the village. He'd heard stories about turtles hatching here in the past, but he'd only ever known it as a clear felled, barren stretch of land.

But gradually the land had been recovering. The beach was surrounded by thick vegetation again, a horseshoe cove protected from winds and tides, a perfect place for turtles to come to breed.

Because of the clear felling, it had fallen off most of the islanders' radar. Until now.

He looked down to the beach and there were people. There were so many people his heart sank. Uh-oh. Had he been guilty of overkill?

If Elsa was on a turtle saving mission, maybe bringing this many people here was hardly helpful. Maybe he'd done more harm than good.

He'd encouraged every islander to come, thinking some would take up his invitation. Obviously everyone who'd heard of it had come.

But, even as he thought he'd created chaos, he emerged from the narrow track that led onto the beach—a track that looked as if it had just been created this afternoon by people pushing through—and he saw that he hadn't. Or Elsa and Helena hadn't let it happen.

The adults were in lines, forming corridors from the top of the beach to the water. They were standing like sentinels. Or maybe windmills would be a better description.

For overhead were birds. Hundreds of birds, many of which he didn't recognize—ocean feeders, migratory birds, birds who knew that here was a feast for all.

At the top of the beach were sandy mounds, and from each mound came a stream of hatchings. Tiny turtles, two or three inches across, struggling out of their sandy nests and starting gamely towards the water.

With the mass of seabirds above they'd stand no chance. But now… There were corridors of people from each mound.

He recognised Helena—she was in her eighties, one of the island's stalwarts. She didn't sound eighty. She was booming orders in a voice to put a sea captain to shame—but beaming and beaming.

Alone, she couldn't have saved more than a tiny proportion of these hatchings. But now…

Where was Elsa? Where…?

Finally he saw her, up to her waist in water, in the midst of a group of children. Then, as Helena called out to her, she was out of the water, darting up the beach, pulling people from one corridor to start another.

Hatchlings were coming from beyond the trees at the end of the beach. More mounds? Within moments, Elsa had more adults formed into more corridors. There were islanders arriving all the time and she was using them all.

With her new corridors in place she was off again, back into the shallows, whooping and yelling at the birds above and encouraging the kids to do the same.

Amazingly, Zoe was in there with them, whooping as if she was just one of the kids. The little Crown Princess was yelling and laughing and gloriously happy.

And so was Elsa. She was soaking, dripping with water, laughing at something someone said and then flying up the beach to lift a tiny hatchling which had turned the wrong way, lifting it with a base of sand and then setting it safely near the water's edge so it could meet the waves the way it should.

'Are you here to help?' she called out to him, and he realised he'd been spotted.

'Where do you need me?'

'In deep water,' she called. 'If you don't mind getting wet. I can't get protection deep enough. There are so many turtles. For all the mounds to hatch together…'

'We need boats,' he said and lifted his phone.

'Yes, but meanwhile…'

'Meanwhile I'll do it.' He snapped a command into the phone, tugged off his shirt and shoes and headed for the water.

What followed was an extraordinary evening and night, and at the end of it hundreds—maybe thousands—of baby turtles were flippering their way into the deep, thanks to the islanders' turtle saving skills.

Elsa had moved constantly, working her corridor teams in shifts, making sure no one stayed in the water for more than twenty minutes, a miniature drill sergeant in action. She and Helena had formed a formidable team. Helena was frail, though, and she was almost weeping with joy to have this help.

By dusk Elsa had sent Helena home. 'You've done so much,' she'd told the old lady, and Helena had gripped her hands and wept openly.

'This is thanks to you. To you and your prince. I thank you.'

Embarrassed, Elsa had headed back into the water and stayed there.

As the afternoon turned to evening, as Phillip's barbecue faded to cinders, as the mass of turtle hatchling eased and finally it could be left to a dozen people taking turns, he finally dragged her off the beach. He made her dry herself, almost force-fed her a steak and an apple and watched over her while she ate.

'I should be back helping,' she muttered, impatient.

'You can be. But not now. Not until you've had a break.'

Someone had brought a vast mound of pillows and blankets. Zoe and a couple of other island children were lying cocooned in blankets, watching the flames, giggling sleepily to each other. He recognised one of the children as Phillip's daughter—a child about the same age as Zoe. They were lying side by side. It seemed Zoe was making a friend. She looked…happy.

So was Elsa. She was flushed and triumphant and glowing.

The scene was weirdly domestic. Family? In his mind was suddenly a piercing stab of what he'd once had. A longing…

'Did you see them?' Elsa said softly, speaking almost to herself. 'We saved thousands. They face so many dangers in the water but now… Thanks to Helena, they have a chance.'

'Thanks to you.'

'Helena was on her own,' she whispered. 'She's been watching the mounds. If one mound had hatched she would have had a chance to save some. She hadn't realized, or she'd forgotten, that Kemp's Ridley turtles lay their eggs in synchronisation so they all hatch together. There'll be another hatching in twenty-five days—that's set as well. I've worked it out—that's before your coronation so you'll still be here. Kemp's Ridleys lay in synchronisation twenty-five days apart. Isn't that amazing? Aren't we lucky?'

She looked up at him then, and she smiled. 'But it's you,' she said on a note of awe. 'You're a prince. The islanders moved today because you asked them to. If they'd thought about it—if Helena had had the time to individually plead—then maybe she'd have got half a dozen people to help her, but you said come and they came. They came because of you and I can't thank you enough.'

'There's no need for you to thank me.' He was watching her and he was feeling…weird. She was slight and feisty and sand-coated and bedraggled.

He'd hurt her today. He hadn't meant to but he was starting to realise how he'd got it so wrong. And why. She was tugging his heart strings in a way he didn't recognise. Or maybe…in a way he did but until now he'd been afraid to face.

'Do you know how rare these turtles are?' she said softly. 'I can't believe it. They're so endangered. To have a breeding site on this island… I so wish Matt was here.'

That set him back a bit. Pushed what he was thinking to the side.

It didn't completely obliterate it, though.

Even if she didn't tell him about Matty… He could compete with someone who'd died four years ago, he thought, and then realised where his thoughts were taking him and thought who cared; they were going there anyway.

'This is wonderful,' she said softly into the firelight. They had the fire almost to themselves now. The children were nestled in their beds on the far side of the barbecue but the rest of the islanders had either gone home to rest or were back on the beach on their shift. 'I can stay here,' she said. 'I can do so much work here.'

'What about your starfish?'

She looked startled. 'What about my starfish?'

'Have you really lost your enthusiasm?'

She looked at him as if he were a sandwich short of a picnic. 'Enthusiastic about starfish?'

'According to Zoe, it's what you love.'

'I love Zoe.'

'You don't love starfish?'

'As opposed to Kemp's Ridley…' Her voice was awed. 'Kemp's Ridley turtles on an island where my Zoe needs to be. This is awesome.'

'But your research…'

'I can work around that, too,' she said. 'I've already handed over my initial starfish research—there were any number of students just aching to take it on. But if I can do this and keep Zoe happy… There's so much. Helena says there are plans for development of this beach. Something about moving the town's refuse station close by. She's worried.'

'We can protect this beach.' He hesitated. 'And…I hope we can get tourism going. The island's desperate for income.'

'It's hardly touched,' she whispered, looking out through the trees where the lights of a score of torches showed the turtles still had safe passage. 'It could be the best eco resort. Matt and I had such plans...'

There it was again. Matt.

Maybe this was going to be harder than he'd thought.

Maybe what was going to be harder? He knew. More and more, he knew. He watched her face and he thought he wanted this woman so much...

It was too soon. Way too soon. Stupid, even?

'Okay, we have that settled,' she said, not noticing his silence. 'I'll stay here and love Zoe and save turtles. You'll have to figure your own direction, but I have mine.' She rose and wiped her hands on her shorts—a gesture he was starting to recognise. 'Let's move on. If you'll excuse me, I have work to do.'

'I'd be honoured to help,' he said. 'And...I will be here long-term. I will be part of this island. Elsa...' He reached out and took her hands.

She stood, looking down at them in the firelight. The linking of fingers.

'Not a good idea,' she whispered.

'We could work this together.'

'Sorry?'

'It's just a thought.'

'I'm quite happy for you to help with the turtles any time you want,' she said and he knew she was deliberately misunderstanding him. 'But for now... Your patients and the islanders need you, and the turtles need me. Zoe needs me. That's enough for one girl, wouldn't you say, Dr Antoniadis?'

'Steve.'

'Prince Stefanos,' she retorted, still watching their linked hands. 'My employer.'

'I'm not your employer.'

'Why, what else would you be?' she asked and she carefully untangled their fingers. Separated their hands. Took a step back and looked at him with eyes that were carefully watchful. 'I need to go back to the beach. Will you stay here and watch over Zoe?'

'I'll go back to the water. Your hip must be hurting.'

'My turtles are important,' she said. 'They're my job. Let me have that at least,' she retorted and, before he could respond—before he even knew how to respond—she turned and headed back down to the beach.

Leaving him to try and figure where to take things from here.

He stared down at the fire—and then focused. Heading for the flames were three tiny turtles.

How had they made their way back here? They'd built this fire purposely far back from the beach, out of sight of the mounds, so the light couldn't distract the hatchlings from their course. Maybe these three had been distracted by a torch, had deviated from their course and ended up here. He scooped them up before they could get close enough to the fire to harm themselves.

'Elsa?' he called into the night and in seconds she was back. Looking straight to Zoe.

But Zoe slept on. Elsa's face slackened in relief, and he thought how much had she worried? How many infections, dramas had she endured during these four years of getting Zoe back to health?

'It's just turtles,' he said swiftly and she looked down at his hand. He had one hand cupped over the other but tiny flippers were peeking through. They felt weird. A handful of flippering.

'They were just...here,' he said, in case she thought he'd collected them from the beach, done something less than noble, he didn't know what, but he was starting to suspect she thought he wasn't exactly hero material.

Hell, he wished he could be.

'What in the world are they doing here?' she asked, opening his hands and taking them into her smaller ones with all the tenderness in the world. 'Hey, guys, the ocean's this-a-way.'

'I guess, if they walked far enough, the ocean is that-a-way,' he said.

'Yeah, but changing direction's easier,' she whispered. 'I ought to know. Come on, guys, I'll take you where you need to go.'

'What do you mean, changing direction's easier?' he asked.

She looked up at him in the firelight and shook her head. 'If you need to explain it, you can't do it,' she said. 'You just…follow your heart. Thank you, Stefanos, for saving my turtles. And thank you for giving me another direction. I'll make the most of it.'

'Your hip…'

'Has nothing to do with direction,' she said. 'Some things still hurt, no matter what direction you're travelling.'

CHAPTER ELEVEN

FOR the next three weeks she immersed herself in this new life and felt herself…unfurl. That was what it felt like, she thought. As if she was coming to life again.

For the last four years she'd been constantly worried, constantly battling for their survival. Here, Zoe's welfare was more than taken care of. It was Stefanos who inspected the little girl's grafts, who worried about her medically, who even told her to back off a little, she was fussing. Others cooked for her, cleaned… Elsa was an honoured guest, free to do as she wished.

And she was free. Zoe had made a friend her own age, Pip, daughter of Phillip the butcher, granddaughter of Helena, defender of the turtles. She was friends with every one of the castle staff now, she was happy and confident and more than content that Elsa do her own thing.

So Elsa was making her own friends. The turtle breeding grounds was a project which had her waking up every morning aching to get up and go.

The only problem was…in the moments when she'd sit opposite Stefanos at meals and watch his face as the palace secretary outlined what needed to be done that day, she felt…bleak.

He was doing the right thing, the honourable thing. But, for Zoe and for her, this new life promised excitement and freedom. For Stefanos… There was still a conflict that seemed to be tearing him apart.

She didn't know what was happening with his practice in Manhattan. The plan was to leave straight after the coronation and do what needed to be done and return. She tried to talk to him about it, but it was as if after their appalling picnic he'd decided he'd overstepped the boundaries; his life was separate, only overlapping with her need to be with Zoe.

Oh, his bleakness wasn't overt. Outwardly he was cheerful and confident and purposeful. It was only that she seemed to know this man; she seemed to sense how he was feeling.

His trouble was the one cloud on her horizon. Actually, no, sometimes it felt more than that, like a fog she could see rolling in to envelop him, but she had no idea what to do about it. The fact that sometimes she had an urgent desire to take him and hold him and love him… Well, that was just plain dumb.

And…she suspected it might not even help.

Meanwhile, the coronation was almost on them, and she'd made her promise. It was time to buy a dress.

Zoe's coronation dress was exquisite, stitched by hand by a team of dressmakers who smiled all the time they worked, who said what a pleasure it was to be able to do this, what a joy. So, 'Can't I get my gown made here as well?' she asked Stefanos, knowing how stressed he was and how little he could spare the time to be away.

But, 'It's my one bright day,' he said. 'I think I've worked hard enough to earn one free day.'

He surely had. What he'd achieved in these last weeks was little short of miraculous.

The island council had been reformed. Three councillors had been invited to stay on; five had been 'retired'. Stefanos had done it with tact but with an underlying ruthlessness that left her awed.

The governance of the island was now under the control of the council, with ultimate responsibility resting with Stefanos. The royal coffers were being used with a speed that made her blink. Advertisements were already appearing on the mainland, for teachers, for engineers, builders, nurses…

Unemployment on the island had been running at over fifty per cent. No longer. There were schools and hospitals to build, roads to repair, water mains to install, electricity to supply to the inland area…

'Giorgos and his predecessors have held on to our taxes for hundreds of years,' Stefanos told her when she questioned how the island could possibly afford what he was starting. 'Alexandros on Sappheiros has split the royal coffers into three so there's more than enough to get things moving.'

He worked with a ruthless efficiency that left her awed. But still there seemed to be this aching need…

She heard him, late at night. Her balcony overlooked the sea and so did his. She'd walk outside to watch the sea and she'd hear him talking, discussing operations, questioning results, talking to colleagues about cases they needed his help with.

He was needed elsewhere. He was working frantically so he could leave, fitting in as much medicine as he could as well. He'd found a locum to work here while he was away, to leave him free.

And he'd come back. He'd promised that he'd come back. But he didn't want to. She heard it in his voice—that coming back would tear him in two.

And she couldn't help.

But first…her dress.

'I've organised a seaplane to pick us up and take us to Athens for the day,' he'd told her at dinner the day before.

Three weeks ago Zoe would have reacted to this proposal in fear. Now she simply looked up and said, 'Am I coming too?'

She'd been tucking into her dinner as if she had hollow legs. The difference in her health since she had been here was astonishing.

'I've asked Pip's mama if you can stay with Pip for the day,' Stefanos said. 'Is that okay?'

'Ooh, yes,' Zoe said, pleased.

'And Pip's mama says it's okay if Pip comes back here and

sleeps for the night. Christina will look after both of you and you'll have Buster to keep you company. I thought I might take Elsa shopping in Athens for something beautiful to wear to our coronation, and I thought I might take her to dinner afterwards.'

From the start he'd been able to wind his cousin round his little finger and this was no exception.

'Elsa would like that,' Zoe said seriously. 'She says she doesn't like dresses, but she does really. And boys are supposed to take girls out to dinner.'

'Hey,' Elsa said, startled. Half laughing, half horrified. 'I'm here. It's not like you're talking behind my back.' But she was ignored.

'It'll be a date,' Zoe said in satisfaction. 'You have to kiss her on the way home.'

'Who says?' Elsa demanded.

'Pip's big sister went out on a date last week. Pip says when the boy brought her home he kissed her goodnight.'

'Pip's sister is eighteen,' Elsa retorted. 'I'm too old for that nonsense.'

'You're not,' Zoe said seriously. 'You're still quite pretty.'

'Gee, thanks.' She hesitated. 'Stefanos, it really isn't necessary.'

'You promised,' Stefanos pointed out. 'A bargain's a bargain. I've saved your turtles. Twice.'

He had, too. The second hatching, twenty-five days after the first, had been orchestrated so that, as far as they knew, every single hatchling had made it to the water. It was a fraught journey the turtles had before them, the sea was full of dangers, but Stefanos had done everything humanly possible to see they had every chance.

And the price? A snip. An agreement to buy a dress.

'Athens or nothing,' he said. 'It has to be special.'

'All right,' she said grudgingly.

'You're very gracious,' Stefanos said and he was laughing at her. Laughing!

At least the bleakness had lifted for the moment.

That conversation had taken place last night. And now…

Stefanos was waiting in the hall. A car was waiting to take them down to the harbour, to the seaplane.

In minutes she'd be climbing aboard an aeroplane with a prince…

'Are you coming or do I have to come up and carry you down?' he called from below in the entrance hall.

She went.

There was something about this day that made her feel…dizzy. Sitting in the seaplane across from Stefanos, she stared straight ahead.

'Are you okay?' he asked gently, fifteen minutes into the flight, and she nodded but couldn't even find the courage to answer.

This was one day out. A shopping expedition for a dress, followed by a meal.

Why did it feel so overwhelmingly scary?

Stefanos smiled at her and retired to a medical journal. Medicine, she thought. He missed it so much. Or…he missed his own niche of medicine.

He was already busy helping the elderly doctor on the island with his workload. It wasn't the medicine he was trained for, but that was the medicine he was reading up on.

Finally they were there. Athens! It was all she could do not to sit with her nose squashed against the car window.

Athens. The world.

'Not a seasoned traveller?' Stefanos teased, and she flushed.

'Sure I am. I just like looking.' And then, as they swung off the road into a huge car park, she frowned. 'Where are we?'

'It's a hospital,' he said. 'I've arranged an appointment for your hip.'

'Stefanos…' She was almost rigid with shock. 'You've interfered enough.'

'No,' he said. 'Not enough. I know I handled this badly. I

know I should have gained your permission before I accessed your records, but what's done is done. I'm sorry but if I'd told you about this appointment I was afraid you'd refuse to come.'

'You'd be right.'

'Then I'm justified.' He hesitated, but his look was stern. 'Elsa, this is only a doctor's appointment. I'm not chaining you to a bed and operating regardless.' He gave a rueful smile. 'Actually, that might be beyond even my level of intrusion. But I am one of only two doctors on Khryseis and before I go back to New York I need to know you're not doing permanent damage. This man's an orthopaedic surgeon. The best in Athens. You need to see him.'

'You still should have asked me.'

'I'm asking you now. This is my honour, Elsa, and it's also sense,' he said, stern again. 'I know I upset you—obtaining your medical history without permission—but it doesn't stop the need. I need you to do this—for you. It would be childish for you to refuse—no?'

'No.'

'Elsa... You *will* do this.'

She had no choice. He was right—she was being childish but it didn't make it any easier to swallow her temper. She followed him into the hospital, fuming.

He was recognised. Doors opened for him. The receptionist of this best-in-Athens-orthopaedic-surgeon practically genuflected.

'You can go right in, Your Highness. The doctor's expecting you.'

But, to her surprise, Stefanos didn't go in. He simply smiled at her, gave her a gentle push towards the door and settled his long frame into a waiting room chair as if he had all the time in the world.

She stared down at him, stunned.

'What?' he said, looking up. And then, 'He won't bite, Elsa. I thought, as he might want to examine you, I should stay out here. But if you're scared...'

The door was opening behind her. She wheeled round and an elderly doctor was smiling a greeting.

'Dr Murdoch. Come on in.' And then he smiled across at Stefanos. 'Steve. Welcome home. When are you coming home for good, my boy?'

'By Christmas.'

'But not to work in neurosurgery?' the older man said, looking suddenly concerned. 'I've heard you'll let that go. I had this young man working with me for a while as he was training and I was in the States,' he told Elsa. 'It was an honour and a pleasure to work with one so talented.' He turned back to Stefanos. 'But now…to abandon your neurosurgery… There must be some way you can fit that into your new life.'

'There's not,' Stefanos said. 'The island's far too small.'

'Could you work in Athens? There's a need here.'

'No,' Stefanos said abruptly. 'Please…leave it. It's Elsa we're concerned about here. Not me.'

'But what a waste,' he said softly. And then he turned back to Elsa. 'Well, then. What has to be has to be. Meanwhile, come with me, young lady, and let's see what needs to be done about that hip.'

He was, as Stefanos had promised, very good.

He examined her with care and with skill. He already had the X-rays from Brisbane—a fact that made Elsa gasp again with indignation but that shouldn't reflect on this kindly doctor. She let him take his time, carefully assess and then tell her what she wanted to hear.

'You're doing no real harm to the hip itself, but it does need to be repaired and it will give you pain until that happens.'

'So I can wait,' she said thankfully. 'Can you tell that to Stefanos?'

'You want me to call him in?'

'Yes, please,' she said, tugging on her shoes. 'Tell him and let me get on with my life.'

So Stefanos came in. He listened while the doctor outlined exactly what he thought.

'But you know this,' the doctor told Stefanos. 'You've seen the scans.'

'I'm too close to treat Elsa myself.'

'You are,' the doctor said gently. 'And you'd need first rate surgical facilities on that island of yours to be able to do it. You know, that's what you really need. A state-of-the-art suite of operating theatres. Cutting-edge techniques. All the things I hear you're doing in New York.'

'And an island like Khryseis would support that how?'

'I have no idea,' the doctor said sadly, and he turned to Elsa and smiled. 'This man tries to save the world and I wish I could help him. But of course he's right. We can only do what we can do. So let's do that, young lady. We need to get your surgery scheduled. When?'

'But you just said…'

'I said the operation's not urgent. That means it doesn't have to be done as soon as possible. The only way to keep you pain-free is to give you so much opiate as to risk addiction, and I suspect you made the decision some time ago to live with the pain. But, because it's hurting, you're not weight-bearing evenly. That will cause long-term back problems. There's tenderness already in the lower spine and I'm concerned there'll be too much pressure on the muscles around the lower vertebrae. So when can we schedule surgery?'

'We can't,' Elsa gasped.

'I can be back here in seven weeks,' Stefanos said, ignoring her. 'Can we schedule it just after Christmas?'

They left the hospital grounds without speaking. Elsa should have been furious. She tried to dredge up fury all the way to the shops. But instead she simply felt bleak. The cab stopped, Stefanos paid, she got out and looked around her—and she decided there and then to cheer up.

She was here shopping. For a gorgeous dress. This was obviously where the wealthy women of Athens shopped.

Indignation—and bleakness on Stefanos's behalf—would have to wait until later.

'What are we waiting for?' she said. 'Do you have the royal credit card?'

'I believe I do.'

'Then let's not let the little pet get cold,' she said and dived happily into the first shop.

It was as if her visit to the doctor had unleashed something in her that had needed to be unleashed for a long time.

Her exultation—dizzy bordering on hysteria—lasted until she was standing in front of a mass of mirrors wearing a gown that fitted her like a second skin, crimson silk, shimmering and lustrous, flecked with strands of glittering silver. The gown had shoestring straps, the bodice clinging and curving around her lovely body, then falling in generous folds to sweep the floor. She gazed into the mirror in incredulity. She met Stefanos's gaze in the mirror and stared at him as if he were part of the same fairy tale.

Then she seemed to come to earth with a crash. She dragged her gaze from his—and lifted the price tag.

And yelped.

'We'll take it,' Stefanos said, and grinned as her mouth dropped open. He'd obviously put aside his bleakness as well. 'One gown down, half a dozen to go—dear,' he said.

'D…dear?' she spluttered.

'Sorry…' he said, and smiled.

The salesgirl was looking on with incredulous delight. 'You want more?'

'Maybe the others don't need to be quite so formal,' Stefanos decreed. 'But we do want at least three more. And what about some sexy lingerie to go with them?'

'Sexy lingerie!'

'It's in the royal nanny dress code,' he said, straight-faced. 'Don't tell me you haven't read it?'

'But I don't need…'

'You do need.'

'What about your Third World kids?' she demanded. 'Don't you need all your money for them?'

'They're not watching,' he said. 'Quick, buy.'

'Stefanos…'

'Tell you what,' he said with magnanimity. 'For every dollar you spend on your wardrobe I'll donate ten more to my Third World medical network. I can't say fairer than that, now can I? So if you refuse to spend, you're doing an orphan out of medical treatment.'

'Stef…'

'You want to start calling me Steve?' he asked, and suddenly his tone was gentle.

'No,' she said and then, more strongly, 'no. You're Stefanos. Prince Stefanos. And I'm the nanny. But I'm a nanny who won't say no to a dress or two.' Then she blushed. 'Or…or even lingerie. But, Stefanos…'

'Yes?'

'You know when you stayed outside while I saw the doctor?'

'Yes.'

'Step outside, Your Highness,' she said, smiling sweetly. 'In the interest of Third World aid, I need to discuss knickers.'

He'd booked them into a hotel. At first she was incredulous. The taxi dropped them outside the most lavish hotel she could imagine. She stared out at the ancient Grecian columns—how had they incorporated them into a modern hotel?—and then she gazed back at Stefanos.

For a moment she said nothing. And then… 'Ten times the cost to a Third World orphan?'

'You have my word,' he said solemnly. 'My orders are for you to have fun tonight. That's all I ask.'

'I'll wear my second best frock,' she said. And then, more cautiously still, 'I didn't think we were staying the night. I don't have a toothbrush.'

'I believe these things are obtainable for a small fee,' he said. 'Multiplied by ten, of course. And you did buy enough lingerie to keep you respectable—or maybe not respectable—for a month.'

She blushed. 'How did you know I bought…?' He'd been out of the shop. 'How…?'

'You gave me the receipt,' he told her. 'So I could multiply by ten.'

'Right,' she said and blushed some more. Then, 'Okay. So I'll buy a toothbrush.' Then she had another thought and her blush moved from pink to crimson. But somehow she made herself sound stern. 'But it's definitely separate rooms.'

'Separate suites,' he corrected her.

'Oh, of course,' she said and suddenly she giggled. 'This is ridiculous.'

'I have a feeling there hasn't been enough ridiculous in your life.'

'I don't need it.'

'You know, I'm very sure you do,' he said gently. 'And maybe the same goes for me. Maybe we both need a good dose of crazy.'

They ate by candlelight in the hotel restaurant, with a view over all of Athens. A view to die for. Food to die for.

A man to die for.

The set-up was so corny she half expected an orchestra to materialise at any minute and strike up with *Love Me Tender* or something equally soppy. And, just as she thought it, a pianist slipped behind a grand piano and started playing. Not *Love Me Tender*—but close. She was wearing her second best dress, which was a fantasy of Audrey Hepburn proportions. Pale lemon silk with tiny white polka dots. Tiny waist, huge skirt. Cleavage.

She'd twisted her hair into a casual knot, trying for Audrey's look. She thought she looked a bit scruffy for the Audrey look, but Stefanos's long, lingering gaze when he'd come to her room to accompany her downstairs said she didn't look scruffy at all.

She was still nervous. Stupidly nervous.

'Should we be talking politics?' she asked as the waiter brought them plate after plate of food she'd never tasted before but would taste forever in her dreams.

'No politics.'

'About Zoe, then.'

'No children.'

'About your medicine? My turtles?'

'Nothing,' he said softly. 'Just you.'

'Well, there's a boring night,' she said, feeling breathless. 'There's nothing to talk about there.'

'We could dance,' he suggested as the pianist started a soft waltz in the background.

'Right. And my hip?'

'Let me dance for you,' he said. He stood up and held her hands and tugged her to her feet.

'I can't.'

'You can. Take your shoes off and put your feet on mine.'

'That's ridiculous.'

'Not ridiculous at all. Trust me, Elsa. Dance with me.'

Then he took her into his arms—and waltzed.

He moved with the effortless grace of a panther, a dancer who knew every move and who knew how to take her with him.

She hadn't danced since she'd injured her hip. She'd hardly danced before then, but it didn't matter.

Her feet were on his. He was holding her weight so her hip didn't hurt, so she could move with him, as one with him, in this slow and lovely dance, as if she weighed nothing.

How had she got herself here? She'd agreed to buy one dress and now…she was being seduced.

Seduced?

No. This was payola for what she'd agreed to do. He was giving her a very nice time.

And if it was seduction… She didn't care, she thought suddenly. What did it matter if her employer seduced her? Employers did these things. Princes did these things.

Um…no. Elsa Murdoch didn't do these things.

'Did you dance with your husband?' he murmured into her ear…and the fairy tale stopped, right then, right there.

'Pardon?' She froze in his arms. Her feet slipped off his, and she could have cried. She was on solid earth again and the lovely dance had ended.

'I didn't mean…'

'To remind me of Matty? I'm very sure you did.'

But he was looking confused. As if he'd been in a kind of dream as well.

'I did dance with Matty,' she said, jutting her chin. 'We danced very well.'

'You loved Matty?'

'With all my heart.'

'And you grieve for him still?'

'I…yes.' What was a girl to say to that, after all? But something went out as she said it—a light, an intensity in Stefanos's gaze.

And its going meant grief. How could she say she'd loved her husband but she was ready to move on?

How could she think it?

'You'll dance again when your hip's healed,' he was saying softly.

'I won't,' she muttered, coming back to earth with a crash. 'I shouldn't.'

'Elsa…'

'I don't want to think about Matty,' she whispered. 'Not here. Not with you.'

They were alone on the dance floor. There were maybe ten or so tables occupied, but the lights were low, the other two couples who'd danced with them to begin with had left, and there was now just the two of them. The pianist had shifted from waltz music to something soft and dreamlike and wonderful.

There was nothing between them. Only a whisper of breath. Only a whisper of fear.

'Elsa…' he murmured, and her name was a question. His

hands slipped from the lovely waltz hold so they were in the small of her back.

'Elsa,' he said for the third time, and he bent his head…and he kissed her.

It was a long, lingering kiss, deep and wonderful, hot and warm and strong, demanding, caressing, questioning.

It was a kiss like she'd never been kissed before.

She was standing in the middle of a dance floor, her arms around his neck and she was being kissed as she'd always dreamed she could be kissed.

She was being kissed as she'd wanted to be kissed all her life.

Matty…

Stefanos himself had pulled her husband into the equation. He was with her still—maybe he always would be. His kisses had been just as wonderful, but different—so different, another dream, another life. He wasn't stopping her kissing right back.

This was the most wonderful dream. Her hip didn't hurt, her worries about Zoe were ended, she wasn't responsible for anything, for anything, for anything…

He was lifting her so he could deepen the kiss, cradling her, loving her and she thought her heart might well burst, as she realised she was so in love with him.

In love with him.

She, Elsa, was in love with a prince. Wasn't Cinderella only in story books?

And, almost as soon as the thought was with her, the spell was broken. People were…clapping?

She twisted, confused, within the circle of Stefanos's arms and found the tables of diners were all watching them, smiling, applauding.

'It's Prince Stefanos from Khryseis,' someone called out in laughing good humour. 'With the Princess's nanny.'

Oh, right. She pulled back as if she'd been burned and Stefanos let her go to arm's reach. But he was still smiling. Smiling and smiling.

'Not the nanny,' he murmured. 'Elsa.'

'In your dreams,' she muttered and it was so close to what was real that she almost gasped. Not in his dreams. In *her* dreams.

'Stefanos…'

'I'm falling in love with you,' he said, simply and strongly and she gasped again.

'You can't. I'm just…'

'You're just Elsa. You're the most beautiful woman I've ever met.'

'You're kidding me, right?' she demanded. 'I have freckles.'

'Eighteen.'

'Eighteen?'

'Eighteen freckles. I love every one of them. Elsa, I've been trying to figure where we can take this.'

'Where we…'

'If we were to marry,' he said and her world stilled again.

'M…marry?'

'I didn't come prepared,' he said ruefully. 'I should be going down on one knee right now, with a diamond the size of a house in my pocket. But I've only just thought of it. Alexandros said I needed a wife, and he's right.'

'You've had too much champagne.'

'No,' he said and then, more strongly, 'no! I know what I want, Elsa, and I want you.'

'Because Alexandros said.'

'I don't think I did that very well,' he said ruefully. 'Believe it or not, it's far less about Alexandros than about eighteen freckles.'

'Eighteen freckles are hardly a basis for marriage.'

'I believe you're wrong,' he said gravely. 'But we could work on other attractions. Do you possibly think you could love me? I know you loved Matty. I know you still love Matty. I'll always honour that, but…is it possible that I could…grow on you?'

'Like a wart?' she said cautiously.

'Something like that,' he agreed. He smiled and, chuckling, pulled her close.

But… But. This might be the magic she'd longed for but there were buts surfacing in all directions.

'Stefanos, no.' She tugged away again, trouble surfacing in all directions. They were being watched, she knew, but the piano was still playing softly in the background and maybe they were more private here than if they went back to their table.

'Will you be my wife?' he asked, solidly and strongly, and there it was, a proposal to take her breath away.

The *but* was still there. Forcing her hand.

'No,' she said.

'No?'

'I'm not changing direction again.' She stood, mute and troubled. 'Not…not while you don't know where you're going.'

'I do know where I'm going.'

'You don't.' She was frantically trying to think this through. To be sensible when she wanted to be swept away in fantasy. Only fantasy was for fairy tales and this was real. 'Stefanos, the problem is…you've committed yourself to staying on the island and you're making the best of it. But that's not what I want. You making the best of it.'

'It's not such a bad deal,' he said, puzzled. 'If it includes you.'

'I'm not the consolation prize.'

'I would never suggest…'

'No, you wouldn't,' she whispered. 'Of course not. You're too noble and too wonderful and too…' She hesitated. 'Too just plain fabulous. The problem is, Stefanos, that even though I'm falling in love with you—and I am—I can't see you tied even more to the island. Tell me…you're thinking…or you have been thinking…that maybe you can take some slabs of time away. Maybe you can do some teaching. Not when you're needed on the island, of course, but if we can get more doctors, if the politics are settled… You're thinking that, aren't you?'

'Yes, but…'

'But I don't think that'll make you happy,' she said. 'I think that's going to tear you further apart. For you'll lose your skills. You'll see others go where you want to go.' She hesitated. 'Stefanos, when Matty died and I couldn't do what we were doing with coral any more… I know it sounds simplistic and silly in the face of what you're doing but it was important to me and I couldn't just do a little bit. It would have eaten at me. I had to move on.'

'I think,' he said steadily, 'that in marrying you I would be moving on.'

'I won't be the cause,' she said. 'In no way.' She bit her lip. 'Stefanos, do what you have to do and then decide you want to marry me. If you were to do that…'

'I am already.'

'You're not.' She shook her head. 'I can't make you see. I don't even know whether I understand it myself, but in the bottom of my heart it does make sense—that I say no. That I say wait. That I say loving is…for when it's right.' She hesitated. 'Matty and I…'

'Matty?'

'You asked me about Matty,' she said. 'Maybe I do need to tell you. Just as we finished university Matty inherited his father's company. His mother sobbed and said he had to come home and run it. So he did—his entire extended family seemed to depend on him and it seemed the only right thing to do. He loved me so I went with him, but it almost destroyed us. For two years I worked on my research while Matty self-destructed. And in the end he handed the entire company over to his cousins. It left us broke. His family thought he was mad. But, you know what, Stefanos, the one thing I do know… When he was killed I thought of those wasted two years.'

'You're saying…'

'I'm saying I don't want the heartache of those two years again, Stefanos. Oh, I want you. I don't deny I want you—my love for Matty hasn't stopped me feeling more for you than I ever thought I could again. But I will follow my own drum and I won't watch you self-destruct while you follow someone else's.'

'So what do you propose I do?' he said bleakly.

'Work it out,' she said steadily. 'For yourself and for me. Please, Stefanos.'

He didn't understand. He was seeing her distress, but not seeing it either, she thought. Maybe he was only seeing what he wanted to see. The Cinderella bit. The fantasy.

Whereas what she wanted was more. Love at first sight? No. Love for ever.

All at once she felt tired. Weary of the pain in her hip, weary of worry, weary of the pain inside her heart.

It'd be so good to do just what she wanted, she thought. To have the world magically transformed so she could sink into her prince's kisses and let herself have a happy ever after.

Stefanos.

He was fighting to change the world, she thought. He was fighting himself.

She didn't have the courage to stand by his side as he did it.

It was too much. Too soon. Too scary. It was yet another direction, but this one was so big, so terrifying that if she got it wrong it could destroy them all. And if she didn't get it right…if she wasn't sure, if she jumped with her heart before her head said it could follow…where would that leave them all?

Oh, but she wanted to.

She mustn't.

'I need to go to bed,' she whispered. 'You've paid me the most extraordinary compliment…'

'A compliment! It's so much more…'

'It is, isn't it?' she whispered bleakly, and she stood on tiptoe and kissed him lightly on the lips. A feather touch. A kiss he didn't understand. 'I know you don't follow what I'm saying—I hardly understand what I'm saying myself. I only know that…I don't know if I can face your demons with you,

Stefanos. Maybe I need more courage than I have. Goodnight and thank you. And I love you.'

And, before he could respond, she'd turned and fled from the dance floor. She didn't stop until she reached her suite, until she was inside with the door locked behind her.

CHAPTER TWELVE

On a sun-kissed afternoon in early November the Crowns of Khryseis were bestowed on Zoe and on Stefanos.

Crown Princess Zoe of Khryseis was seated on a throne too large for her. Her dress was pure fantasy. She looked adorable. She looked very, very scared.

Only the fact that her cousin was standing right beside her gave her the courage to stay. Stefanos, Prince Regent of Khryseis, the Isle of Gold, had vowed to defend his little cousin, care for her and cherish her and take care of her interests until she reached twenty-five years of age.

Stefanos looked magnificent. Zoe looked exquisite.

Elsa was looking not too bad herself, she conceded, thinking what a waste, why spend all this money on her fabulous gown if her nose was about to turn red? But she was fighting tears, and Crown Princess Lily of Sappheiros glanced sideways at her and smiled and passed over a handkerchief.

'This is dumb,' Elsa whispered, embarrassed. 'I shouldn't be here in the front row with you. I'm not even royalty.'

'Hey, I've only been royalty for a couple of months now,' Lily said. 'And, from what I've heard, you're even closer to Zoe than Stefanos.'

Elsa sniffed. The Archbishop was watching Stefanos sign before his little cousin now. It looked so official. It looked like another world.

She could have been up there. Beaming and waving and being royal too. As Stefanos's wife.

Her reasons for refusing him were sounding weaker and weaker. It was just as well he hadn't proposed again, she thought. Any pressure and she might well cave right in.

'He's gorgeous,' Lily whispered thoughtfully, watching Elsa's face.

'He is.' She looked dubiously at the handkerchief. 'I need to blow my nose.'

'Go right ahead,' Lily said grandly. 'I came supplied with hankies in bulk. They're monogrammed with the royal crest.'

Elsa nearly dropped it. Lily giggled and suddenly Elsa was smiling again, albeit through tears. What was royalty but individuals doing the best they could? The vows that Zoe and Stefanos had just made… They weren't taking them away from her. Or no further than they already were. And she was right not to join them. Her doubts still stood.

The signing was done. The orchestra was starting its triumphant chorus, a blaze of sound proclaiming that Khryseis finally had its own royal family.

Stefanos helped Zoe to her feet. Zoe stood, looking out nervously at the vast audience in front of her.

Stefanos held her hand, stooped and whispered to her.

Zoe stared up at him, then out at the people in front of her. And then, at a signal from Stefanos, the music suddenly died.

Zoe took a deep breath. She turned back to Stefanos, as if for approval of something prearranged, and she looked straight at Elsa.

'I need my Elsa,' she said in a high, clear voice. 'Elsa, can you come up and walk beside me?'

'Quick, blow,' Lily muttered urgently. 'And your nose isn't even red. You're beautiful.'

He walked out of the cathedral behind them. Zoe and Elsa. His little cousin and her beautiful guardian.

Elsa's eyes were looking distinctly watery. He wasn't surprised. His eyes were feeling distinctly watery too.

Elsa should be walking by his side. It felt wrong.

He'd rushed it. He'd pushed her too hard, too fast, ripping her out of her comfort zone, asking the world of her and then asking her to extend that world.

Zoe was happy again. She'd been coached with care and kindness, and she knew exactly what was expected of her today. Elsa had raised her beautifully, he thought. When she'd spoken her responses it had been with the gravity of one twice her age. So much of that was down to Elsa's care, her constant assurances that Zoe was beautiful, that the scars and the pain were only skin deep and what was underneath was beauty and joy.

If he'd got it right he could have been walking down the aisle with Elsa, with Zoe between them.

He'd messed it up—badly.

But he had time, he thought. He could try again.

Only Elsa was right. His doubts about what he was doing were still there.

Khryseis needed him.

His work in Manhattan was still calling.

Elsa had the courage to change direction and move steadily forward. He kept glancing back.

Elsa knew him better than he knew himself. And, knowing him, she had the sense not to want to be his wife.

'Isn't Stefanos beautiful?' Zoe was so close to sleep she could barely form words, but she'd stayed until the last speech had been made, she'd sat attentive and courteous, and Elsa was so proud of her she was close to bursting. But now she'd retired to Elsa's knee for a hug, the hug had turned into a cradling cuddle and it was clear the little girl just wanted to drift off to sleep.

They were watching Stefanos say farewell to the dignitaries. Stefanos as they'd first seen him, only grander.

'I don't have to be scared of being a princess when he's here,' Zoe whispered. 'I wish he wasn't going away.'

'Me, too,' Elsa whispered. For what the heck; there was no point in lying, not even to herself.

'Do you think he'll come and live with you and me for ever and ever?'

'He's said he will. Maybe not with us but near us.'

'That's good,' Zoe whispered, her whisper fading so that Elsa could hardly hear. 'But I'll miss him and miss him. And so will Buster.'

'And so will I,' Elsa told her and watched her close her eyes and drift off into sleep. 'I think I might miss him so much I might have to think about changing direction all over again.'

Only of course there was no time for direction changing. No opportunity. No chance.

A call came through that night. Stefanos needed to be in New York within twenty-four hours.

There were so many things to do, documents to sign, authority to delegate… He moved as fast as he could. Elsa woke at dawn to a light tap on her door and it was Stefanos, come to say goodbye.

She stood at her bedroom door in her lovely new lingerie, feeling shocked, bereft and stupidly frightened.

'You will come back?' she murmured. She must have sounded needy for Stefanos took her hands in his and tugged her into his arms before she could resist.

'Of course I'll be back. I'll be here by Christmas.'

He was as she loved him most, in his casual jeans, an old leather jacket slung over his shoulder, unshaven, a man in a hurry. 'Hell, Elsa, I wish I didn't have to go. But these kids… I can't knock them back.'

'I so wish you could work from here.'

'And we both know that I can't.'

'Of course.' The population of Khryseis could never support the medical facilities this man needed.

'You'll keep Zoe safe. And our turtles. And Buster.'

'I promise.'

'Christmas in Australia's hot, isn't it?' he said. 'You think we can do an Australian Christmas dinner?'

'Amy's Christmas Cake,' she said before she thought about it.

'Amy's cake?'

This was crazy. Standing in her bare feet, talking to a man she loved with all her heart about her best friend's cake.

'It's a berry ice cream cake,' she said. 'Amy was so proud of it—it was a tradition started by the women in her family who couldn't bear a hot Christmas pudding. She'd start a month before Christmas, finding berries, then building layer upon layer of berry ice cream, each layer a different flavour. By Christmas we might have ten layers. Then we'd turn it out and decorate it with more berries. She'd make a berry coulis to pour over. It was so big sometimes it'd last until well into January.'

'So you make it every year?'

'Not…' She hesitated. 'Not since Amy died. Berries are expensive.'

'I see,' he said gravely and took her hands in his. 'Then here's my royal decree. You use the royal card again to buy as many berries as you need—import them, grow them—whatever you have to do to get them, you get them, and make us Amy's Christmas Cake. And we'll eat it well into January.' He was smiling into her eyes and his smile might as well be a kiss. And…she felt like crying.

'Is there anything you want me to bring from New York?' he said, maybe seeing her need to be practical, to get over the emotion. As if she could.

'Come home via Australia and bring me my cats,' she said, trying desperately to joke. 'I miss them.'

'It's a bit of a detour.'

'You're the Prince Regent.'

'So I am,' he said and smiled his crooked, heart-flipping smile, then stood looking down at her for a long, long moment as his smile faded. A door slammed below stairs, someone called to him and he swore.

'I have to go. Will you say goodbye to Zoe for me? I can't wake her yet.'

'Of course I will. Travel safe.' She smiled. 'I was teasing about the cats.'

'I know you were.' He gave an almost imperceptible nod, as though her cats and his safety were inconsequential. As if there was something more important he'd decided to say. 'Elsa…'

'Just go.'

'I will,' he said, but instead he tugged her close and she had neither strength nor will to resist. He pulled her tight into his arms, against his chest, and he kissed her, hard and long and aching with need.

And then he put her away from him.

'G…go,' she managed.

'I love you,' he said, loudly and strongly into the morning.

But still he turned. And he went.

She wanted to sob. Or maybe something louder. She'd actually quite like to stomp a bit. Toss the odd pillow.

Yell.

But Zoe and Buster were fast asleep. She should be, too. What else was she to do?

She needn't worry about breakfast. It would be on the table in a couple of hours, a choice of eight or so dishes, eat what you like and certainly don't worry about the cost.

She was Zoe's friend and guardian, only Zoe already had a friend. After Christmas Zoe would try the little school that stood just by the castle gates. What was a woman to do then?

Research her turtles and don't deviate. Become a world authority. Stay facing in the one direction…

Hope Stefanos could find a direction too, one that could fulfil his dreams, and hope with everything in her heart that his direction matched hers.

She loved him.

There wasn't a lot she could do about it. Flying out of the door wailing, *Wait for me, wait for me,* would hardly be appropriate or sensible or even possible.

So…. Go back to sleep until it's time for the royal day to begin.

Start making Amy's Christmas Cake.

Wait for her prince to come home.

It was a direct flight from Athens to New York. The details of his surgical list had been faxed through to him so he had a mass of reading to do on the way. He leafed through the first case and then the second—and then found himself staring sightlessly ahead. Superimposed on the printed pages was the vision of Elsa's tousled curls, her bare feet, as she'd opened the door to say goodbye.

More than anything else he'd wanted to sweep her into his arms, take her back to her bed and stay with her for ever and ever and ever.

She'd knocked back his proposal of marriage. He was trying to understand her reasons.

He'd spoken too early. One night in Athens hadn't been enough. Her hip had been hurting. He needed to have her healed and then take her away properly—a weekend in Paris, maybe. Or a month in Paris.

Or New York? There was his dream. Manhattan and Elsa. Or…more, he thought. Manhattan and Elsa and Zoe and Buster. His family—something he'd never thought he wanted, but now he had such a hunger for that he couldn't see past it.

But… He had to stay in Khryseis.

And that was the problem, he thought. Elsa knew better than he did that marriage to her would make things better for him. But she'd knocked back his proposal. He had to make things better himself.

'Excuse me, but are you Prince Stefanos of Khryseis?'

The man in the next seat had been glancing at him covertly since take-off. Small, a bit unkempt, wearing half-rimmed glasses and the air of a scholar, he'd been reading notes that looked even more dense than those Stefanos had been studying.

'I am,' Stefanos said warily, because admitting to being royalty was usually asking for trouble.

'So you're the one who seduced our Dr Elsa from her studies.'

'Pardon?' What the hell…? This man looked angry.

'She's brilliant,' the man said, ignoring Stefanos's incredulity. 'She has one of the most brilliant scientific minds in Australia. In the world. She and that husband of hers…the research they did on the preservation of the Great Barrier Reef was groundbreaking. If she'd kept it up it could have made her a professor in any of the most prestigious universities in the world. And then she just hands it over. Hands it over!'

'I don't know what you mean,' Stefanos said.

'Her work,' the man said impatiently, and then suddenly seemed to remember his manners. 'David Hemming,' he said. 'Professor of Marine Studies at… Well, never mind, it doesn't matter. All I know is that I've never seen such a generous act. She had all the research done. All the hard work. She was just starting to see the academic rewards and suddenly a letter arrives out of the blue saying she can no longer go on with her studies but she doesn't want her research wasted so here it is, take it and publish as you see fit, just take it forward. Well, I tell you there's at least eight international experts now who are international experts only because of Dr Langham's generosity.'

'Dr Langham?'

'We could never find her,' he said morosely. 'Only then we started hearing about starfish research—really interesting stuff—and dammit, there she was, only she was calling herself Elsa Murdoch. But, just as we were finding out what she was doing, dammit if she didn't do exactly the same again. Package it all up and pass it on. No honours for her. Just good, solid research that'll mean species will survive that were otherwise facing extinction. And now…'

He'd been building up indignation, incense personified, and Stefanos got poked in the chest with a pencil. 'And now she's off again. But at least it's turtles this time. Kemp's Ridley, by what I hear, and you couldn't get a better woman working on them. You know what? She sees the big picture. Already she's contacting international institutions, trying to broaden our understanding. If she's found this breeding site there must be more. She'll use that to make them safe.'

'How…?'

'Pure energy,' he said, stabbing Stefanos again. 'Only don't you let her give her work away this time. If she settles—if she's allowed to settle—then I'm guaranteeing those blessed turtles will be safe for a thousand years, such is the commitment she generates. So you might have seduced her to your island but you make sure she stays. Or I and half the marine academics in the world will want to know why not.'

And, with a final poke in the chest, he retired back to his notes.

Leaving Stefanos winded.

Stunned.

The vision of Elsa as he'd last seen her was still with him—beautiful, almost ethereal, a freckled imp with her glorious sun-blonded curls. With her face creasing from laughter to gravity, from teasing to earnestness, from joy to…love?

To loss.

If he'd met her when she was twenty, when life was simple, when she was free to fall in love, then maybe he'd have stood a chance. He knew that. For he'd looked into her eyes and what he saw there was a reflection of what he believed himself. That she was falling in love with him as deeply as he was falling in love with her.

Only life had got complicated. He'd thought it was complicated for him. How much more complicated was it for her?

She'd buried a husband. She'd said goodbye to two careers. She'd taken on a child so injured that she'd needed almost a hundred per cent commitment, and that at a time when Elsa was injured herself.

And along came Prince Stefanos, grudgingly changing direction this once. Hating the idea that he'd be handing over his work, his teaching, his skills, watching others take his work forward while he ceased to be able to contribute.

She knew his commitment was grudging. She had so much generosity of spirit herself that she must know it.

He'd enjoy family medicine, he thought, and doing everything else he could to help Khryseis, as a doctor and as the island's Prince Regent. He must. He'd immerse himself into it all, convince Elsa that he was content.

Only she knew him. He couldn't lie to her. And it wasn't entirely the work he wanted to do.

Khryseis wasn't big enough for the medical work he wanted to do.

But…

For some reason, the academic's words stuck. Hit a chord.

You know what? She sees the big picture.

Khryseis was one of three islands. Put together…

He needed to concentrate on these cases. He'd be operating hours after landing. He needed to read his notes.

But there were things happening in his head apart from his most pressing concerns. Major things.

The image came to him of the night he'd held the three tiny turtle hatchlings in his hand.

I guess, if they walked far enough, the ocean is that-a-way, he'd said.

Yeah, but changing direction's easier, she'd whispered. *I ought to know.*

Could he somehow change direction but get to the same place by another route?

There wasn't time to think this through now. Those kids were lined up waiting for him. But he had six weeks to think.

How much did he want Elsa?

And Zoe. And Khryseis. And turtles and cats and Amy's Christmas Cake which, for some weird reason, was becoming a really big thing to look forward to.

How much did he want them all?

He lifted his third set of case notes and tried to read.

But all he saw was Elsa.

CHAPTER THIRTEEN

THEY coped without him.

It was a strange thing, caring for a child who'd been dependent for years but who was finally finding her wings. Zoe couldn't wait to get out of bed in the morning, to meet her new friend, to play with Buster, to be allowed to start school. Medical constraints, always suffered stoically, were now a nuisance to be ignored. She bounced around the palace with growing confidence and pleasure, and by Christmas there wasn't a member of the palace staff who wouldn't have given their right arm for her.

Zoe was gloriously in love with this new life.

So was Elsa. Sort of.

She and Helena were working through the issues with the turtles with cautious exhilaration. There was so much to be done. The turtles' habitat had been destroyed once, and only part of it had regrown. Turtles were crossing roads to dig their nests. There were threats everywhere, and this for a world endangered species. Making them safe was imperative. Extrapolating the research was breathtakingly exciting. She could make a difference.

There were so many things she could do.

But she wanted to be with Stefanos. Every morning she woke rethinking his proposal. Was she crazy? She'd turned down a man she could love with all her heart.

She knew it was more than that, but that was the problem. Her head knew things her heart didn't necessarily agree with.

'Will Stefanos be home for Christmas?' Zoe asked for about the thousandth time since he'd left and, for the thousandth time, she replied.

'He said he would be. He's phoning us as often as he can, sweetheart, and he doesn't seem to be changing his mind. And then he's going to stay with you while I have my hip fixed.'

'I don't want you to go away.'

She didn't want to go away either, but it was organised. The day after New Year she'd fly to Athens and spend a month in hospital.

She should be grateful. She was grateful. Zoe was happy and blooming. There were no money problems. She had work that truly interested her, and her hip was about to be treated.

So why was a part of her so miserable?

Happy Christmas, she told herself fiercely on Christmas Eve, as she helped Zoe hang her stocking in front of the vast fireplace in the great hall. Last year she'd used a sock in front of the fire-stove. This year the housekeeper had hand-stitched Zoe a gold and crimson stocking, with the most beautiful appliquéd Father Christmas and elves and reindeer.

It looked beautiful on the great mantel. But, despite the massive Christmas tree the staff had set up—or maybe because of it—it looked really alone.

'You should have a stocking too,' Zoe said as she'd said every Christmas since they'd been together.

'Stockings are for kids.'

'You never get presents.'

'Stefanos should be home. That'll be a present for both of us.'

'He should be here now,' Zoe said severely. It was almost bedtime on Christmas Eve. She'd counted on her big cousin coming today. 'He said he'd come.'

'Maybe he'll come in the night like Santa Claus,' Elsa said. 'Maybe we won't see him come if we stay up.'

'You think we should go to bed?'

'Why not?' She was weary of waiting, herself. She was

riding an emotional roller coaster and didn't know how to get off. If Stefanos didn't come… He'd promised Zoe.

He'd promised her.

'Okay,' Zoe said, infinitely trusting. She tucked her hand into Elsa's and tugged her towards the stairs. 'Let's go to bed and make it come quicker.'

He had so much to do he felt like Santa Claus, zooming across the world at midnight. Actually he was only flying from Athens to Khryseis on the seaplane, but he did feel a bit like Santa. He had so many gifts in his pack. He sat next to the pilot, gazed out at the blue-black sky and the stars hanging low and lovely in the heavens, and he felt that a little bit of magic was around.

He needed magic. In his pocket was a ring almost worthy of the woman he loved—the ancient ring of Khryseis, plaited gold with three magnificent diamonds embedded in its depths.

She wouldn't take it unless she accepted the rest of his sleigh load, he thought ruefully. A woman of principle was the woman he'd chosen to give his heart.

Would she take it? He'd done so much. If there was anything else he could do… Anything at all…

He had a mad compulsion to tell the pilot to turn the plane around. So much was at stake. The woman he'd chosen as his life's partner had knocked him back because of her principles. If he didn't get it right this time…

What else could he do?

The lights of Khryseis came into view and the plane started its descent. He could see the palace from here, lit up like a fairy palace. That'd be the staff celebrating Christmas, he thought. The whole staff—the whole island—was overjoyed to have their royal family in residence.

Or their royal princess and her nanny, he corrected himself. For a family required more.

Would she accept him now? She must. For years he'd scorned the idea of a family. Now it seemed he couldn't live without it.

He'd met one feisty, beautiful nanny and his world had changed.

'Coming in to land now, sir,' the pilot said, looking ahead at the palace lights. 'Seems someone's keeping the home fires burning.'

'I hope so,' he murmured.

'I think every person on the island hopes so,' the pilot said enigmatically. 'Welcome home, Your Highness.'

'Santa's been and Stefanos is home.'

Elsa woke to find Zoe bouncing up and down on her bed, the long-suffering Buster being bounced with her. 'Come and see, come and see, come and see. Santa's been, Santa's been, Santa's been.'

Despite the tumult of emotions she'd gone to bed with and woken with—*Stefanos is home*—she had to smile. Zoe had been just as excited last year when all she'd been able to give her were a couple of handmade toys she'd bought at a local market. This year should be fun.

Stefanos is home.

'It's humungous,' Zoe was saying. 'You should see. How can Santa have brought it down the chimney?'

Humungous? Nothing she'd stuffed in Zoe's stocking could be described as humungous. And…

Stefanos is home.

'Stefanos…' she said cautiously.

'He got home really late. Christina told me he snuck in after all the staff went to bed—almost morning. Elsa, you have to get up and see what Santa's brought me.'

So Stefanos would be asleep. That gave her breathing space. She'd have time to enjoy Zoe's stocking with her before she needed to face him.

It wasn't that she didn't want to see him, she thought, feeling really confused. Not exactly. There was a big part of her that ached for him.

There was another part of her that was just plain custard.

But he was asleep. Hooray. She threw back the covers, pulled on a robe and padded downstairs.

She'd never get used to the opulence of this place. The staircase was wide enough to fit ten people abreast.

'The king who built this place must have been as fat as a whale,' she told Zoe. 'Or he had ten kids to take by the hand every Christmas morning.' Zoe giggled and they were both still chuckling as Zoe hauled open the double doors to the great hall.

She stopped dead.

How long since she'd believed in Santa Claus?

When they'd gone to bed the Christmas tree was a decorator item, set up by the staff as a tasteful ode to Christmas. Now…whoever had come during the night had turned the tree into an over the top muddle.

The exquisite decorations and silver lights were still under there somewhere, but they were now almost hidden. Hung over the top of them were rows and rows of coloured popcorn, threaded together and hung in vast ribbons of garish colour. There were paper lanterns—every colour of the rainbow. Pictures of cats had been placed in tiny silver frames and hung as ornaments. There was a collection of motley socks hanging everywhere, all bulging.

'The socks have got apples in them,' Zoe said, awed, tugging her towards the tree. 'That one's a football sock and that one has a hole in the toe. And look at my present.'

She was seeing it. Stunned.

It was a trampoline, an eminently bouncy mat, built with a net canopy around it so a child could bounce without fear of falling.

For a child who needed to be encouraged to stretch scar tissue…for a child who loved bouncing…it was the best thing.

'And you have a stocking too,' Zoe said, deeply satisfied. 'Look.'

She looked. On the mantelpiece hung three stockings. Zoe's was bulging with nonsense gifts, a tin whistle, a boomerang—a boomerang?—a clockwork mouse…

More pictures of cats.

And there was a stocking labelled *Elsa*. A small parcel bulged in the toe, a document rolled and tied with a huge red bow was sticking out the end, and there were more pictures of cats.

The stocking labelled *Stefanos* was empty.

'We should have something for Stefanos,' Zoe said anxiously. 'Santa didn't come to him.'

'We have a couple of gifts in our room,' Elsa said uncertainly. 'We could sneak up and put them in his stocking before he wakes.'

'It's too late for sneaking,' said a low gravelly voice and she yelped.

The voice had come from behind the vast Christmas tree. Zoe darted behind in a flash.

'Stefanos,' she shouted. 'He's here. Elsa, he's here, sleeping behind the tree.'

'I always sleep behind the tree,' a sleepy voice murmured, full of laughter. 'For years and years. But I've never yet caught Santa Claus. Has he come?'

'He's come, he's come.' Zoe was squealing with excitement. 'And he's brought crazy socks. Elsa, he's here. Stefanos is here. Come and see.'

There wasn't a choice. She should have at least brushed her hair, she thought desperately, as she tried to organise her smile to be cool and welcoming. She walked cautiously around the tree, and there he was. He'd hauled a mattress downstairs, and a mound of bedding. He was lying back, smiling up at them, his blankets pulled only to his waist. Bare-chested.

Breathtakingly gorgeous.

Buster was on his stomach already, kneading his blankets with her soft paws and purring so hard you'd swear she'd recognised him. Zoe was snuggling down beside him, a little girl with everything she wanted in life.

'You've messed with our Christmas decorations,' she muttered before she could stop herself, and his grin widened.

'I threaded popcorn all the way from New York to Athens,

and I made half my fellow passengers help me. The rest were on lantern duty. And then it still looked a bit empty so Santa had to resort to socks. And a happy Christmas to you too, Mrs Murdoch. Dr Langham. My love.'

There was a bit too much in that statement for Elsa to think about. She opened her mouth to reply and gave up and closed it again.

'No Happy Christmas?' he said, smiling at her evident confusion.

'Happy Christmas,' she managed, sounding winded. 'Why…why aren't you in your own bed?'

'I might have missed present opening. Have you opened your stocking yet?' He rolled out of bed. He'd gone to bed wearing boxer shorts. Only boxer shorts. What more could a girl want for Christmas? she thought as she watched him stretch and yawn; as she thought all sorts of things that surely a nicely brought up girl—a mature widow!—had no business thinking.

Had she opened her stocking? 'N…no,' she managed, annoyed that her voice squeaked. 'It's bad form to open gifts until the family's together.'

'Is the family together now?' he asked gently and he looked at Zoe cradling Buster and then he looked to her with such an expression that her heart did a double backflip. Landed on its back. Refused to start operating again in any mode she considered normal.

'I…I guess,' she muttered.

'No guessing,' he said, suddenly stern. 'You need to be sure. Zoe, I'm assuming you've guessed this very fine trampoline came squeezing down the chimney in the wee small hours especially for you. Would you like to try it out for size?'

'Ooh, yes,' Zoe said and flew with Buster to the trampoline, only to be hauled back by her big cousin.

'Buster,' Stefanos said firmly, removing the long-suffering kitten from her arms, 'stays on the ground.'

Only he didn't. Stefanos handed Buster to Elsa and then, when her hands were safely occupied and she couldn't fend him off, he kissed her. Just the once, but the look in his eyes said there were more where that came from. Just the once, but it was enough to light her world.

'It appears I'm needing to send out a royal decree for mistletoe,' he growled, his lovely crooked smile warming parts of her she hadn't known were cold. 'Honestly. Can't you people be depended on to organise anything?'

She managed a chuckle but it was a pretty wavery chuckle. She was too…thrown.

'Happy Christmas,' he said again, and then obviously decided mistletoe was not absolutely essential and he kissed her again, deeply this time, long and hard and so wonderfully that finally Zoe ceased bouncing, put her hands on her hips and issued a royal decree of her own.

'Yuck,' she said. 'And you're squashing Buster. Stop kissing and open presents.'

'Yes, ma'am,' Stefanos said and swept Elsa—and the slightly squished Buster—into his arms and deposited them both on the settee by the tree. Then he lifted the rolled document out of the top of her stocking and handed it to her, with such gravitas it was as if he was handing over royal title to his land and his kingdom for ever.

She looked up at him, wondering, but he was looking grave and expectant, waiting for her to discover for herself what it was. Slowly she unfastened the ribbon holding the roll of documents together. Buster pounced on the ribbon; she set both ribbon and Buster on the floor and then looked up at Stefanos again, half afraid to go further.

'Well, go on, then,' he said, in the same tone of impatience Zoe had just used. 'Read it.'

She read.

… Transfer of title of Diamond Mine Number Two on the Isle of Argyros, the income from which to be used in perpetuity for the health of all the citizens of the Diamond Isles…

She stared up at him, confused. He smiled back at her, and he didn't look confused in the least.

'I'm changing my direction,' he said softly. 'So I'm hoping…if I head in the same direction as you, can we walk together?'

'I…I don't know what you mean.'

He sat down beside her, took the documents back and set them aside. His face was suddenly grave. 'Elsa, on the plane on the way to New York I met a man who knew you. He told me about your research, and you know what else he said about you? He said… *She sees the big picture.* And he spoke in awe. He meant you don't just look at the turtles on the beach that need saving. You broaden your work; you look at their survival internationally. And I finally figured it out. It was like I'd needed a swipe to the side of the head to wake me up, and I finally got it. That's what I've been guilty of. Seeing only what's before my eyes. Not thinking big. Seeing only my work in Manhattan and how much it means.'

'But your work is important,' she said, confused, struggling to understand.

'It is,' he agreed, still grave, laughter put aside as he tried to make her see. 'Elsa, without conceit, I can say my work changes lives. So when I knew I had to work here I was gutted. I knew I had no choice—the islanders are my people. And then there was a new imperative. You're my people. You're my family, Elsa. You and Zoe. I want you so much—and it was such a shock to realise I ached for a family. I ached for you. I was so committed to what I was feeling for you, and to the needs of the islanders as well, that I'd stopped thinking big. It took one stray remark about how wonderful you were to make me rethink.'

'I don't think I'm following your logic,' she managed cautiously, trying to focus on his words rather than the joy and love she was seeing in his eyes. The joy and love that was building inside her. She didn't know yet what he was talking about but the smile behind his eyes said it was good.

'We're too small.' He had her hands now, holding her tight. 'But now I'm thinking big. Elsa, this document is a plan.'

'Something about a diamond mine?' she ventured. Good one, Elsa. Intelligence wasn't on the agenda this morning—nor was speed reading. All she was seeing was Stefanos.

'Absolutely it's about a diamond mine, my love,' he said and tugged her into his arms and kissed her again. Long and lingering and lovely. But then he set her back from him. There were still things that needed to be said.

There were things she didn't understand, and he had to make her see.

'There are six diamond mines on Argyros,' he said softly while she listened in wonder. 'Argyros is therefore the wealthiest of the Diamond Isles but it has no hospital. Nikos has been talking to me about setting up decent medical facilities there. It's the same on Sappheiros—Alexandros is already making plans for a hospital. And then, on the plane, I made myself see the big picture. Separately we're small islands. We each need good medical facilities but we don't each have the population to set up a major base. But together…'

'Together?'

'It's too big,' he said ruefully. 'To land this on you on Christmas morning. But I can't wait any longer. Elsa, I love you, I want you more than life itself, but I've already asked you to marry me. What I need now is for you to know I've changed. Everything's changed. Except my love for you. So…can I tell you what we've decided? The rulers of the other two islands and me?'

How was a girl to react to that? Her heart was starting to sing. Bubbles of happiness were floating to the surface and filling the room with joy. 'I'm…I'm listening,' she whispered, and suddenly so was Zoe, sitting cross-legged on her trampoline, watching with big, serious eyes. She really was much older than her eight years, Elsa thought, and then she thought that, whatever was coming—and already joy was starting to overwhelm her—it was appropriate that Zoe was here. To bear witness, she thought, and then she thought that was a dumb thing to think but she thought it anyway.

'Earth to Elsa,' Stefanos said, laughing softly and tightening his grip on her hands and she thought, okay, thoughts could come at some other time. Now was the time for listening.

'It's a medical scheme,' he told her, and in his eyes was jubilation, excitement, a man about to embark on a *Boy's Own* adventure. 'A medical centre second to none will be built, here on Khryseis, with satellite hospitals on the other two islands. Fast and easy transfer facilities. Every specialist we need. Together we'll care for the people of the Diamond Isles as they deserve to be cared for. It's what I dreamed of as a kid, as did Alexandros on Sappheiros, and Nikos on Argyros. Three Crowns, Elsa. Three Crowns finally come together to provide care for all.'

'One…one big medical centre?' She was struggling to take it in.

'State-of-the-art. And, with the islands being as lovely as they are, and the salaries we're prepared to pay, we don't expect any trouble staffing them as they should be staffed. We don't see islanders needing to go to Athens for treatment any more. We see mainlanders coming to us.' His hands moved to her shoulders, holding her, desperate for her to share his joy.

'Alex and Nikos flew to New York to work this through with me. For such a project, for something so wonderful for all of us, the diamonds on Argyros will be needed, but none of us can see a better use for them. We envisage offering our medical facilities worldwide. And more. There'll be resorts on each island that are half hotel, half hospital. Come here and be pampered and made well, and support our economy while you do.'

He was so exultant now his excitement was practically blazing. 'We've done the preliminary figures and the guys in suits agree with us,' he told her. 'It *will* work. And here's the tail, Elsa. Here's my huge joy. With the money raised we believe we can still bring people here from Third World countries. I'll be able to operate as I've been doing and I'll be able to teach. So…so what do you think?'

He paused then. He was still holding her by the shoulders, his eyes not leaving hers. But now…his excitement faded a little, giving way to anxiety.

He was asking what she thought? *He was anxious about what she'd think?*

'You'd be here,' she whispered. 'You'd be doing the work you love.'

'I'd be doing all the work I love,' he said, excitement giving way to gravity. 'I'll be ruling this island in Zoe's stead, caring for it as it must be cared for. I'll be doing the medicine I love—I'll be making a difference. And I'll be sharing my life with you.'

'With me.'

'And with Zoe,' he said, his eyes lighting with laughter again. This much joy couldn't be contained for more than a moment. 'And our cats.'

'Cats,' she said cautiously, for she was starting to see a theme here. There were pictures of cats all over the Christmas tree. 'Cats, plural?'

'I made a few calls to Australia,' he said. 'I figured…well, I hoped you might be staying here long term, and the guy feeding your cats now has twenty-three on his list.'

'Twenty-three…' she gasped.

'It seems he's Waratah Cove's answer to the Pied Piper of Hamelin. He's taken them on as his mission in life.'

'Don't tell me you're bringing them here,' she managed.

Zoe said, 'Ooh!'

'That's not an ooh,' Elsa said, torn between laughter and horror. 'It's an Are You Out Of Your Mind?'

'I hoped you might say that,' Stefanos said, smiling into her eyes with such a look that she might, just might, be forced to forgive him twenty-three cats—or anything at all. 'So what I've done is give the guy a job in perpetuity, caring for them all. With one exception.'

'One…'

'A skinny little black one,' he said apologetically. 'I met him that first day when you guys were on the beach and I had to find you. It seems he's been pining for you—he's hardly eaten since you left and, to tell you the truth, I sort of fell for him. So he's on his way here as we speak. My love.'

My love. There was enough in those two words to be perfectly adequate, thank you very much—she hardly wanted more.

Only Zoe was made of sterner stuff. She darted across to the mantelpiece and was flying back, tipping the contents of Elsa's stocking at her feet.

'You have another present and I have six. Maybe I ought to open some of mine first.'

'If you don't mind, Zoe,' Stefanos said and lifted the tiny crimson box from where it had fallen. 'So far Elsa's just had paper. You have a trampoline and this is important.'

'Elsa has a cat,' Zoe said.

'Yes, but he's not here yet. So, as yet, she's giftless.'

'Okay,' Zoe said obligingly, grabbing the long-suffering Buster and squatting beside Elsa. 'But it's really small. Open it fast, Elsa.'

'Open it slow, Elsa,' Stefanos said, and watched as Elsa forgot to breathe and tried to make fumbling fingers operate the catch of the tiny box.

'Let me,' Stefanos said at last, and flicked the clasp. And there, resting on a bed of black velvet, was the most beautiful ring she'd ever seen. It was gnarled and twisted gold, burnished with age and history, with three magnificent diamonds set in its depths—diamonds to take a girl's breath away.

'It's the ancient ring of this island, worn by the ruling Princess of Khryseis for generations,' Stefanos said softly. 'On her marriage. If…if you'd like to be married, that is. If you'd like to be my princess.' He took a deep breath. 'If you'd like to be married to me.'

'It's beeyootiful,' Zoe breathed, but Elsa said nothing at all. She couldn't.

She was so proud of him. She was so in love with him.

He was giving her another chance.

'You can always change it if you don't like it,' Stefanos said, anxious again. 'If you fancy emeralds, or something modern? When Zoe marries she'll inherit it anyway so it'd be good to have a backup. Anything you like, my darling, just say the word. I believe the only thing non-negotiable in this whole deal is who you get to marry.' And he dropped to one knee. 'If it's okay, that is. If you say yes. Elsa, will you marry me?'

She looked up from the ring. He was kneeling before her. Her prince.

'You're proposing in boxer shorts?' Elsa managed.

'I believe I was wearing a suit and tie last time I proposed. Look where that got me. Now I'm trying a different tack.'

'Zoe, if you run and get my camera, I wouldn't mind this moment being documented,' Elsa murmured—weakly—and Stefanos grinned but he didn't shift from where he was kneeling.

Zoe stared at them both as if they were crazy. 'He's asking you to marry him?'

'I believe…I believe he is. I…can you get the camera?'

'Yes,' she yelled and whooped in excitement and headed for the stairs. 'I want to be a bridesmaid,' she called over her shoulder, and continued whooping all the way up the stairs.

'So now,' Stefanos said, starting to look long-suffering. 'Elsa… My love…' But then he had to pause as the butler's long face appeared around the door.

'Good morning, sir,' he said. 'Happy Christmas. Welcome home. Will you be wanting breakfast?'

'Josef,' Stefanos said, in a goaded voice.

'Yes, sir?'

'You're a servant to the royal family, right?'

'Yes, sir,' Josef said, taking in the tableau in front of him and grinning.

'Then you no doubt know about summary beheadings, boiling in oil and the rest.'

'I have read my history.'

'Excellent,' Stefanos said. 'Then I command you to close that door and lean against it and let no one else in, for fear of blood-curdling retribution, for the next ten minutes. At least.'

'Yes, sir,' Josef said, and chuckled and closed the doors.

'Servants,' Stefanos said. 'You can't do anything with them these days. Now, where were we?'

'Exactly where we were two minutes ago, I believe,' she said cautiously. 'You want me to come down on the floor with you?'

'I want you to hush,' he said. 'Elsa.'

'Stefanos.'

'Will you marry me?' he said again, and again the laughter was gone. Only love remained. Only the gravity of a promise to be made for ever.

And what was a girl to say to that? Well, the obvious one for a start.

'Yes.'

He blinked. 'Pardon?'

'Yes.'

'I haven't used all of my very cogent arguments yet.'

'I'm marrying you anyway.'

'And…why would that be?'

'I believe I love you. Are you sure I can't come down there with you?'

'If you must,' he said and tugged her down so they were kneeling face to face under the Christmas tree. 'Elsa, I love you with all my heart.'

'That's exceedingly fortunate because I love you too.'

'Really?'

'Absolutely. Of course I love you more in tassels and with your dress sword and boots, but I'm so far gone I'll even love you in boxer shorts. Are you going to kiss me yet?'

'You don't want to know how much I love you?'

'You can start telling me,' she said, and smiled as an imperious little voice sounded from the other side of the door.

'They want me in there. I've got the camera. They really, truly want me.'

'Well, I guess you can't tell me how much you love me anyway,' she said, smiling and smiling, and maybe even crying a little as well as he tugged her into his arms and held her close. 'Because I don't think we'll know how much we love each other until the end of eternity.'

'Starting now,' Stefanos said. He sighed and called out, 'Okay, let her in, Josef. Let 'em all in. Bring on the world. The Prince and his affianced wife are ready to receive visitors.'

But not quite. As Josef swung the doors wide they were too busy to receive anyone. For Mrs Elsa Murdoch alias Dr Elsa Langham had changed direction yet again.

The future Princess Elsa of Khryseis was kissing her beloved prince as she intended kissing him for the rest of her life.

'Oh, yuck,' Zoe said in deep disapproval as she was finally admitted. She waited and waited and finally looked around for something to distract her. 'And why is Stefanos's stocking empty?' she demanded of Josef. 'Did Santa forget him?'

'I believe His Highness has his Christmas gift,' the butler told her, and smiled at the pair of them. 'I believe His Royal Highness has his family.'

The christening of Christos Mathew Romanos Antoniadis was an occasion of great joy for the island of Khryseis. The celebration was huge, made more so because it coincided with the opening of the Diamond Isles Medical Base, to be celebrated the next day.

The world had come to see, to celebrate this wondrous occasion and to welcome these three islands into the twenty-first century.

For the difference in these islands in the eighteen months since the old King had died and the new generation of royalty had taken power was nigh on unbelievable. Already the islanders were prospering, the glittering Diamond Isles finally succeeding in becoming the magical place to live that they'd always promised.

This medical centre was the icing on the cake—a symbol

of all they hoped to achieve. The staff it was attracting had caused its reputation to go before it, and already there were mainlanders waiting to use it. Already the islanders knew that the network of medical centres could cope with their every need. What was more, the medical centre was only the start of the new order. On every island there was employment, optimism and joy.

And now, on this day, that joy was exemplified by the royal family of Khryseis, and this, the christening of their new little son.

Father Antonio performed the ceremony, and the shaky old priest who'd loved the islanders for all his life blessed this baby with all the love in his heart.

Afterwards Elsa stood on the magnificent lawns of the palace grounds, with her husband by her side, with her baby in her arms and she thought the joy she was feeling right now could never be surpassed.

Only of course it could.

Joy is to come...

Stefanos was standing with his arm round her waist, greeting dignitary after dignitary, accepting their congratulations, smiling with a pride as deep as it was joyful.

There it was again. That word... Joy.

Zoe wasn't with them. She and Pip had slipped away, up to the palace balcony to play with Buster and Spike. Elsa glanced up and saw them, two little girls with two cats, a Zoe who was so confident with her new family that clinging was a thing of the past.

Joy.

'Happy, my love?' Stefanos asked as the line of dignitaries finally came to an end.

'How can you doubt it?'

'So...' he smiled into her eyes '...where do we go from here?'

She smiled back at her beloved husband, and she smiled again at her sleeping son. 'Where, indeed?'

'Another baby?'

'Absolutely,' she whispered, gazing down at the perfection of her little son.

'More turtles?'

'Oh, yes.'

'Another cat or two?'

'Two's enough. I'm thinking of a puppy.'

'Is there room for a puppy with two cats?' Stefanos asked, startled, and she grinned.

'I think there's room for anything in our family,' she said. 'This is the Diamond Isles. Place of miracles. Place of wonder. Home of our hearts, and room for all.'

* * * * *

STEPPING INTO THE PRINCE'S WORLD

MARION LENNOX

For Doug and Natalia.

Wishing you a fabulous wedding and an amazing, fulfilling Happy Ever After. Welcome home.

With grateful thanks to Jennifer Kloester who certainly knows where and how to kick. If Our Jen met a prince on a dark night she'd know what to do. :-)

CHAPTER ONE

You're to take your place as heir to the throne and find yourself a bride.

If Crown Prince Raoul Marcus Louis Ferdinand could cut that last order from his grandmother's letter he would, but he needed to show his commanding officer the letter in its entirety.

He laid the impressive parchment of his grandmother's letter before his commanding officer. Franz noted the grim lines on Raoul's face, picked up the letter and read.

Then he nodded. 'You have no choice,' he told him.

'I don't.' Raoul turned and stared out of the window at the massive mountain overshadowing Tasmania's capital. It was a mere shadow of the mountains of Marétal's alpine region.

He needed to be home.

'I've known my grandfather's health is failing,' he told his commanding officer. 'But I've always thought of the Queen as invincible. This letter might sound commanding, but it's a plea for help.'

'It is.' Franz glanced at the letter again. It was headed by the royal crest of Marétal and it wasn't a letter to be ignored. A royal summons… 'But at least it's timely,' he told Raoul.

Marétal's army had been engaged as part of an international exercise in Tasmania's wilderness for the last couple of months. Raoul's battalion had performed brilliantly, but operations were winding down.

'We can manage without you,' he told him. He hesitated. 'Raoul, you do know…?'

'That it's time I left the army.' Raoul sighed. 'I do know it. But my grandmother effectively runs the kingdom.'

'The Queen's seventy-six.'

'Tell *her* that.' He shook his head at the thought of his

indomitable grandmother. His grandfather, King Marcus, even though officially ruler, hardly emerged from his library. Queen Alicia had more or less run the country since the day she'd married, and she suffered no interference. But she was asking for help now.

'Of course you're right,' he continued. 'My grandparents' chief aide, Henri, has written privately that he's worried about the decisions my grandmother's taking. Or not taking. Our health and legal systems need dragging into this century. More immediately, national security seems to be an issue. Henri tells me of threats which she refuses to take seriously. He suggests increasing the security service, making it a force to be reckoned with, but the Queen sees no need.'

'You're just the man to do it.'

'I've never been permitted to change anything,' Raoul said flatly. 'And now…' He turned back to Franz's desk and stared morosely at the letter. '*This*. She wants me home for the ball to celebrate her fifty years on the throne.'

'It'll be a splendid occasion,' Franz told him. He, too, glanced back at the letter—particularly at the last paragraph—and try as he might he couldn't suppress a grin.

'You think it's *funny*?' Commanding officer or not, Franz copped a glare from Raoul. 'That the Queen decrees I bring a suitable partner or she'll provide me with one herself?'

'She wants to see you married, with an heir to the throne. She fears for you and the monarchy otherwise.'

'She wants me under her thumb, with a nice aristocratic bride to match.'

'You've never been under her thumb before.'

Franz had known Prince Raoul ever since he'd joined the army. Raoul presented to the world as the perfect Prince, the perfect grandson, but Franz knew that underneath his mild exterior Raoul did exactly what he wanted. If the Queen had known half of what her grandson had been doing in the army she'd have called him home long since.

But therein lay the success of their relationship. To his

grandmother, Raoul was a young man who smiled sweetly and seemed to agree with whatever she decreed. *'Yes, Grandmama, I'm sure you're right.'* Raoul never made promises he couldn't keep, but he certainly knew the way to get what he wanted.

'Our people will approve of me in military uniform,' he'd told the Queen when he'd announced his decision to join the army. 'It's a good look, Grandmama—the Crown Prince working for the country rather than playing a purely ceremonial role. With your approval I'll join the Special Forces. Have you seen their berets? It can do the royal image nothing but good.'

His grandmother had had to agree that his military uniform suited him. So had the country's media. At thirty five, with his height, his jet-black hair, his tanned skin and the hooded grey eyes that seemed almost hawk-like, the added 'toughness' of his uniform made the tabloids go wild every time they had the opportunity to photograph him.

'His uniform makes him look larger,' the Queen had told a journalist when Raoul had completed his first overseas posting.

Franz had read the article and thought of the years of gruelling physical training turning Raoul into a honed Special Forces soldier. His admiration for his royal charge had increased with every year he knew him.

Now he came round and gripped his shoulder. Franz had been Raoul's first commanding officer when he'd joined the army fifteen years ago. As Raoul had risen up the ranks so had Franz, and over the years they'd become friends.

'If you were a normal officer you'd be taking my place when I retire next year,' Franz told him. 'The army wouldn't give you a choice and that'd mean desk work. You know you hate desk work. There's so much more you can do working as heir to the throne—and you'll wear a much prettier uniform.'

Raoul told him where he could put his uniform and the older man chuckled.

'Yes, but you'll be wearing tassels, lad, and maybe even a sabre. There's a lot to be said for tassels and sabres. When do you need to leave?'

'The ball's in a month.'

'But you need to leave before that.' Franz glanced at the letter and his lips twitched again. 'According to this you have a spot of courting to do before you get there. First find your bride…'

Raoul rolled his eyes.

'I may have to go home,' he said carefully. 'I may even have to take up the duties of Crown Prince. But there's no way my grandmother can make me marry.'

'Well,' Franz said, and grinned again, 'I know Her Majesty. Good luck.'

Raoul said nothing. Some comments weren't worth wasting breath on.

Franz saw it and moved on to practicalities. 'Let's consider you on leave from now,' he told him. 'We'll work out discharge plans later. You can fly out tonight if you want.'

'I don't want to fly out tonight.'

'What *do* you want?'

'Space,' Raoul told him. 'Space to get my head around what I'm facing. But you're right. I need to go home. My grandparents are failing. I know my country needs me. I *will* go home—but not to find a bride.'

If she edged any closer to the end of the world she might fall off.

Claire Tremaine sat on the very highest cliff on the highest headland of Orcas Island and thumbed her nose in the direction of Sydney. It was Monday morning. In the high-rise offices of Craybourne, Ledger and Smythe, scores of dark-suited legal eagles would be poring over dull documents, checking the ASIC indexes, discussing the Dow Jones, making themselves their fifth or sixth coffee of the morning.

She was so much better off here.

Or not.

She sort of...*missed* it.

Okay, not most of it—but, oh, she missed the coffee.

And she was just ever so frightened of storms. And just a bit isolated.

Would there be a storm? The forecast was saying a weather front was moving well east of Tasmania. There was no mention of it turning towards Orcas Island, but Claire had been on the island for four months now, and was starting to recognise the wisps of cloud formation low on the horizon that spelled trouble.

A storm back in Sydney had meant an umbrella and delays on the way home to her bedsit. A storm on Orcas Island could mean she was shut in the house for days. There was a reason the owners of this island abandoned it for six months of the year. This was a barren, rocky outcrop, halfway between Victoria and Tasmania, and the sea here was the wildest in the world. In the worst of the storms Claire couldn't even stand up in the wind.

'But that's what we put our names down for,' she told Rocky, the stubby little fox terrier she'd picked up on impulse from the animal shelter the day she'd left to come here. 'Six months of isolation to get to know each other and to forget about the rest of the world.'

But the rest of the world had decent coffee.

The supply boat wasn't due for another week, and even then on its last visit they'd substituted her desired brand with a no-name caterers' blend.

Sigh.

'Two more months to go,' she told Rocky, and rose and stared out at the gathering clouds.

To come here had been a spur-of-the-moment decision, and she'd had plenty of time to regret it. She was looking at the rolling clouds and regretting it now.

'I'm sure the weather forecast's wrong,' she told her dog. 'But let's go batten down the hatches, just in case.'

* * *

He should tell someone where he was going.

If he did his bodyguards would join him. That was the deal. When he was working within his army unit his bodyguards backed off. As soon as he wasn't surrounded by soldiers, his competent security section took over.

Only they didn't treat him as a colleague. They treated him as a royal prince who needed to be protected—not only from outside harm but from doing anything that might in any way jeopardise the heir to the throne of Marétal.

Like going sailing on his own.

But he hadn't let them know he was on leave yet. As far as they were concerned he was still on military exercises, so for now he was free of their watch. He'd walked straight from Franz's office down to the docks. He was still wearing his military uniform. In a city full of army personnel, based here for multinational exercises, his uniform gave him some degree of anonymity. That anonymity wouldn't last, he knew. As soon as he shed his uniform, as soon as he went home, he'd be Crown Prince forever.

But *not* married to a woman of his grandmother's choosing, he thought grimly. He knew the women she thought suitable and he shuddered.

And then he reached *Rosebud*, the neat little yacht he'd been heading for, and forgot about choosing a bride.

This was Tom Radley's yacht. Tom was a local army officer and Raoul had met him on the first part of their combined international operation. They'd shared an excellent army exercise, abseiling across 'enemy territory' in some of Tasmania's wildest country. Friendships were forged during such ordeals, and the men had clicked.

'Come sailing with me when we're back in Hobart,' Tom had said, and they'd spent a great afternoon on the water.

But Tom had been due to take leave before the exercises had ended, and a mountain in Nepal had beckoned. Before he'd gone he'd tossed the keys of the yacht to Raoul.

'Use her, if you like, while you're still in Tasmania,' he'd said diffidently. 'I've seen your skill and I know you well enough now to trust you. I also know how surrounded you are. Just slip away and have a sail whenever you can.'

The little yacht wasn't state-of-the-art. She was a solid tub of a wooden yacht, built maybe forty years ago, sensible and sturdy. Three weeks ago he and Tom had put up a bit too much sail for the brisk conditions, and they'd had fun trying to keep her under control.

And now... Conditions on the harbour were bright, with enough sun to warm the early spring air and a breeze springing up from the south. Clouds were scudding on the horizon. It was excellent sailing weather.

He didn't want to go back to base yet. He didn't want to change out of his uniform, pack his kit and head for home.

He should tell someone where he was going.

'It's only an afternoon's sail,' he said out loud. 'And after today I'll have a lifetime of telling people where I'm going.'

He should still tell someone. Common sense dictated it.

But he didn't want his bodyguards.

'I'll tell them tomorrow,' he said. 'For today I owe no duty to the army. I owe no duty to my country. For today I'm on my own.'

Prince Raoul's movements were supposed to be tracked every step of his life. But it drove Raoul nuts.

Even his afternoon's sail with Tom had been tracked. Because he'd been off duty that weekend, his bodyguards had moved into surveillance mode. He and Tom had had a great time, but even Tom had been unsettled by the motorboat cruising casually within helping distance.

'I couldn't bear it,' Tom had said frankly, and Raoul had said nothing because it was just the way things were.

But this afternoon was different. No one knew he was on leave. No one knew he was looking at Tom's boat and thinking, *Duty starts tomorrow.*

No one saw him slip the moorings and sail quietly out of the harbour.

And no one was yet predicting the gathering storm.

'I'm sure it's a storm,' she told Rocky. 'I don't care what the weather men are saying. I trust my nose.'

Clare was working methodically around the outside of the house, closing the great wooden shutters that protected every window. This house was a mansion—a fantastical whim built by a Melbourne-based billionaire financier who'd fancied his own island with its own helicopter pad so he could fly in whenever he wished.

He'd never wish to be here now, Claire thought as she battened down the house. In the worst of the Bass Strait storms, stones that almost qualified as rocks were hurled against the house.

In the early days, Mrs Billionaire had planted a rose garden to the north of the house. It had looked stunning for half of one summer, but then a storm had hit and her rose bushes had last been seen flying towards the Antarctic. It had then been decided that an Italian marble terrace would look just as good, although even that was now pitted from flying debris.

'I hope I'm imagining things,' she told Rocky. Rocky was sniffing for lizards under the carefully arranged rock formations that during summer visits formed a beautiful 'natural' waterfall. 'The forecast's still for calm.'

But then she looked again at those clouds. She'd been caught before.

'If we lose sun for a couple of days we might even lose power. I might do some cooking in case,' she told Rocky.

Rocky looked up at her and his whole body gave a wriggle of delight. He hadn't been with her for two weeks before he'd realised the significance of the word 'cooking'.

She grinned and picked him up. 'Yes, we will,' she told him. 'Rocky, I'm very glad I have you.'

He was all she had.

She'd been totally isolated when she'd left Sydney. There'd been people in the firm she'd thought were her friends, but she'd been contacted by no one. The whispers had been vicious, and who wanted to be stained by association?

Enough.

She closed her eyes and hugged her little dog. 'Choc chip cookies for me and doggy treats for you,' she told him. 'Friends stick together, and that's you and me. That's what this six months is all about. Learning that we need nobody else.'

The wind swept in from the south—a wind so fierce that it took the meteorologists by surprise. It took Tasmania's fishing fleet by surprise, and it stretched the emergency services to the limit. To say it took Raoul's unprepared little yacht by surprise was an understatement.

Raoul was an excellent yachtsman. What his skills needed, though, was a thoroughly seaworthy boat to match them.

He didn't have one.

For a while he used the storm jib, trying to use the wind to keep some semblance of control. Then a massive wave crested and broke right over him, rolling the boat as if it was tumbleweed. The little boat self-righted. Raoul had clipped on lifelines. He was safe—for now—but the sail was shredded.

And that was the end of his illusion of control.

He was tossed wherever the wind and the sea dictated. All he could do was hold on and wait for the weather to abate. And hope it did so before *Rosebud* disintegrated and left him to the mercy of the sea.

CHAPTER TWO

TWO DAYS INTO the worst storm to have hit the island since the start of her stay Claire was going stir-crazy. She hadn't been able to step outside once. The wind was so strong that a couple of times she'd seriously worried that the whole house might be picked up.

'You and me, Rocky,' she'd told him, when he'd whimpered at the sound of the wind roaring across the island. 'Like Dorothy and Toto. When we fly, we'll fly together.'

Thankfully they hadn't flown, and finally the wind was starting to settle. The sun was starting to peep through the clouds and she thought she might just venture out and see the damage.

She quite liked a good storm—as long as it didn't threaten to carry her into the Antarctic.

So she rugged up, and made Rocky wear the dinky little dog coat that he hated but she thought looked cute, and they headed out together.

As soon as she opened the door she thought about retreating, but Rocky was tearing out into the wind, joyful at being allowed outside, heading for his favourite place in the world. The beach.

The sea would look fantastic. She just had to get close enough to the beach to see it. The sea mist was so heavy she could scarcely see through it—or was it foam blasted up by the wind? She could scarcely push against it.

But she was outside. The wind wasn't so strong that it was hurling stones. She could put her head down and fight it.

Below the house was a tiny cove—a swimming beach in decent weather. She headed there now, expecting to see massive damage, expecting to see…

A boat?

Or part of a boat.

She stopped, so appalled she almost forgot to breathe. A boat was smashed and part submerged on the rocks just past the headland.

The boat wasn't big. A weekend sailor? It must have been trying to reach the relative safety of the beach, manoeuvring into the narrow channel of deep water, but the seas would have been overwhelming, driving it onto the rocks.

Dear God, was there anyone…?

And almost as soon as she thought it she saw a flash of yellow in the water, far out, between the rocks and the beach. A figure was struggling through the waves breaking around the rocks.

Whoa.

Claire knew these waters, even thoughtshe'd never swum here. She'd skimmed stones and watched the tide in calm weather. She knew there was a rip, starting from the beach and swinging outward.

The swimmer was headed straight into it. If he was to have any chance he had to swim sideways, towards the edge of the cove, then turn and swim beside the rip rather than in it.

But he was too far away to hear if she yelled. The wind was still howling across the clifftops, drowning any hope of her being heard.

Was she a heroine?

'I'm not,' she said out loud. But some things weren't negotiable. She couldn't watch him drown—not when she knew the water. And she was a decent swimmer.

'You know where the dog food is, and the back door's open,' she told Rocky as she hauled off her coat and kicked off her boots. 'If I disappear just chew a hole in the sack. Tell 'em I died trying.'

But she had no intention of dying. She'd stick within

reach of the rocks, where the current was weakest. She was not a heroine.

Her jeans hit the clothes pile, and then her windcheater. *Okay, then—ready, set, go.*

He was making no headway. The current was hauling him out faster than he could swim.

Raoul had been born tough and trained tougher. He hadn't reached where he was in the army without survival skills being piled on to survival skills. He couldn't outswim the current, so he knew he had to let it carry him out until it weakened—and then he had to figure out a way back in again.

The problem was, he was past exhaustion.

By the time he'd reached this island the yacht had been little more than a floating tub. The torn sails were useless. He'd used the motor to try and find some place to land, but the motor hadn't had the strength to fight the surf. Then a wave, bigger than the rest, had hit him broadside.

The boat had landed upside down on the rocks. He'd hit his head. It had taken him too long to get free of the wreck and now the water was freezing.

If he let the current carry him out, would he have the strength to get back in again?

He had no choice. He forced his body to relax and felt the rip take him. For the first time he stopped trying to swim. He raised his head, looking hopelessly towards the shore. He was being carried out again.

There was someone on the beach.

Someone who could help?

Or not.

The figure was slight—a boy? No, it was a woman, her shoulder-length curls flying out around her shoulders in the wind. She had a dog and she was yelling. She was gesticulating to the east of the cove.

She was ripping off her windcheater and running down to the surf. Heading to the far left of the beach.

If this was a local she'd know the water. She was heading to the left and waving at him.

Maybe that was where the rip cut out.

She was running into the water. She shouldn't risk herself.

He tried to yell but he was past it. He was pretty much past anything.

The woman was running through the shallows and then diving into the first wave that was over chest high. Of all the stupid… Of all the brave…

Okay, if she was headed into peril on his behalf the least he could do was help.

He fought for one last burst of energy. He put his head down and tried to swim.

Uh-oh.

There'd been a swimming pool in the basement of the offices of Craybourne, Ledger and Smythe. Some lawyers swam every lunchtime.

Claire had mostly shopped. Or eaten lunch in the park. Or done nothing at all, which had sometimes seemed a pretty good option.

It didn't seem a good option now. She should have used that time to improve her swimming. She needed to be superfit or more. There was no rip where she was swimming, but the downside of keeping close to the rocks at the side of the cove was the rocks themselves. They were sharp, and the waves weren't regular. A couple picked her up and hurled her sideways.

She was having trouble fighting her way out. She was also bone-chillingly cold. The iciness of Bass Strait in early spring was almost enough to give her a heart attack.

And she couldn't see whoever it was she was trying to rescue.

He must be here somewhere, she thought. She just had to fight her way out behind the surf so she could see.

Which meant diving through more waves. Which meant avoiding more rocks. Which meant…

Crashing.

Something hit him—hard.

He'd already hit his head on the rocks. The world was feeling a bit off-balance anyway. The new crack on his head made him reel. He reached out instinctively to grab whatever it was that had hit him—and it was soft and yielding. A woman. Somehow he tugged her to face him. Her chestnut curls were tangled, her green eyes were blurred with water, and she looked almost as dazed as he was.

He'd thumped his head and so had she. She stared at him, and then she fought to speak.

'You'd think…' She was struggling for breath as waves surged around them but she managed to gasp the words. 'You'd think a guy with the whole of Bass Strait to swim in could avoid my head.'

He had hold of her shoulders—not clutching, just linking himself with her so the wash of the waves couldn't push them apart. They were both in deadly peril, and weirdly his first urge was to laugh. She'd reached him and she was *joking*?

Um… Get safe first. Laugh second.

'Revenir à la plage. Je suivrai,' he gasped, and then realised he'd spoken in French, Marétal's official language. Which would be no use at all in Tasmania's icy waters. *Get back to the beach. I'll follow,* he'd wanted to say, and he tried to force his thick tongue to make the words. But it seemed she'd already understood.

'How can you follow? You're drowning.' She'd replied in French, with only a slight haltingness to show French wasn't her first language.

'I'm not.' He had his English together now. And his tongue almost working.

'There's blood on your head,' she managed.

'I'm okay. You've shown me the way. Put your head down and swim. I'm following.'

'Is there anyone…?' The indignation and her attempt at humour had gone from her voice and fear had replaced it. She was gasping between waves. 'Is there anyone else in the boat?'

Anyone else to save? She'd dived into the water to save him and was now proposing to head out further and save others?

This was pure grit. His army instructors would be proud of her.

She didn't have a lifejacket on and he did.

'No one,' he growled. 'Get back to the beach.'

'You're sure?'

'I'm sure. Go.' He should make *her* wear the life jacket, but the effort of taking the thing off was beyond him.

'Don't you dare drown. I've taken too much trouble.'

'I won't drown,' he managed, and then a wave caught her and flung her sideways.

She hit the closest rock and disappeared. He tried to grab her but she was under water—gone.

Hell…

He dived, adrenalin surging, giving him energy when he'd thought he had none. And then he grabbed and caught something…

A wisp of lace. He tugged and she was free of the rocks, back in his arms, dazed into limpness.

He fought back from the rocks and tried to steady while she fought to recover.

'W…wow,' she gasped at last. 'Sorry. I…you can let go now.'

'I'm not letting go.' But he shifted his grip. He'd realised what he'd been holding were her knickers. He now had hold of her by her bra!

'We surf in together,' he gasped. 'I have a lifejacket. I'm not letting go.'

'You…can't…'

He heard pain in her voice.

'You're hurt.'

'There's no way I can put a sticking plaster on out here,' she gasped. 'Go.'

'We go together.'

'You'll stretch my bra,' she gasped, and once again he was caught by the sheer guts of the woman. She was hurt, she was in deadly peril, and she was trying to make him smile.

'Yeah,' he told her. 'And if it stretches too far I'll get an eyeful—but not until we're safe on the beach. Just turn and kick.'

'I'll try,' she managed, and then there was no room for more words. There was only room to try and live.

She couldn't actually swim.

There was something wrong with her arm. Or her shoulder? Or her chest? She wasn't sure where the pain was radiating from, but it was surely radiating. It was the arm furthest from him—if he'd been holding her bra on that side she might have screamed. If she *could* scream without swallowing a bucket of seawater. Unlikely, she thought, and then wondered if she was making sense. She decided she wasn't but she didn't care.

She had to kick. There was no way she'd go under. She'd risked her life to save this guy and now it seemed he didn't need saving. Her drowning would be a complete waste.

Some people would be pleased.

And there was a thought to make her put her head down, hold her injured arm to her side as much as she could and try to kick her way through the surf.

She had help. The guy still had his hand through her bra, holding fast. His kick was more powerful than hers could ever be. But he still didn't know this beach.

'Keep close to the rocks,' she gasped during a break in the waves. 'If you don't stay close you'll be caught in the rip.'

'Got it,' he told her. 'Now, shut up and kick.'

And then another wave caught them and she had the sense to put her head down and kick, even if the pain in her shoulder was pretty close to knocking her out. And he kicked too, and they surged in, and suddenly she was on sand. The wave was ripping back out again but the guy was on his feet, tugging her up through the shallows.

'We're here,' he gasped. 'Come on, lady, six feet to go. You can do it.'

And she'd done it. Rocky was tearing down the beach to meet them, barking hysterically at the stranger.

Enough. She subsided onto the sand, grabbed Rocky with her good arm, held him tight and burst into tears.

For a good while neither of them moved.

She lay on the wet sand and hugged her dog and thought vaguely that she had to make an effort. She had to get into dry clothes. She was freezing. And shouldn't she try to see if something was wrong with the guy beside her? He'd slumped down on the sand, too. She could see his chest rise and fall. He was alive, but his eyes were closed. The weak sunshine was on his unshaven face and he seemed to be drinking it up.

Who was he?

He was wearing army issue camouflage gear. It was the standard work wear of a soldier, though maybe slightly different from the Australian uniform.

He was missing his boots.

Why notice that?

She was noticing his face, too. Well, why not? Even the pain in her shoulder didn't stop her noticing his face.

There was a trickle of blood mixing with the seawater dripping from his head.

He was beautiful.

It was the strongest face she'd ever seen. His features

were lean, aquiline…aristocratic? He had dark hair—deep black. It was cropped into an army cut, but no style apart from a complete shave could disguise its tendency to curl. His grey eyes were deep-set and shadowed and he was wearing a couple of days' stubble. He looked beyond exhausted.

She guessed he was in his mid-thirties, and she thought he looked mean.

Mean?

Mean in the trained sense, she corrected herself. Mean as in a lean, mean fighting machine.

She thought, weirdly, of a kid she'd gone to school with. Andy had been a friend with the same ambitions she'd had: to get away from Kunamungle and *be* someone.

'I'll join the army and be a lean, mean fighting machine,' he'd told her.

Last she'd heard, Andy was married with three kids, running the stock and station agents in Kunamungle. He was yet another kid who'd tried to leave his roots and failed.

Her thoughts were drifting in a weird kind of consciousness that was somehow about blocking pain. Something had happened to her arm. Something bad. She didn't want to look. She just wanted to stay still for a moment longer and hold Rocky and think about anything other than what would happen when she had to move.

'Tell me what's wrong?'

He'd stirred. He was pushing himself up, looking down at her in concern.

'H…hi,' she managed, and his eyes narrowed.

Um…where was her bra? It was down around her waist, that was where it was, but she didn't seem to have the energy to do anything about it. She hugged Rocky a bit closer, thinking he'd do as camouflage. If he didn't, she didn't have the strength to care.

'Your arm,' he said carefully, as if he didn't want to scare her.

She thought about that for a bit. Her arm…

'There…there does seem to be a problem. I hit the rocks. I guess I don't make the grade as a lifesaver, huh?'

'If you hadn't come out I'd be dead,' he told her. 'I couldn't fight the rip and I didn't know where it ended.'

'I was trying to signal but I didn't know if you'd seen me.' She was still having trouble getting her voice to work but it seemed he was, too. His lilting accent—French?—was husky, and she could hear exhaustion behind it. He had been in peril, she thought. Maybe she *had* saved him. It was small consolation for the way her arm felt, but at least it was something.

'Where can I go to get help?' he asked, cautious now, as if he wasn't sure he wanted to know the answer.

'Help?'

'The charts say this island is uninhabited.'

'It's not,' she told him.

'No?'

'There's Rocky and me, and now there's you.'

'Rocky?'

'I'm holding him.'

Silence. Although it wasn't exactly silence. The waves were pounding the sand and the wind was whistling around the cliffs. A stray piece of seaweed whipped past her face like a physical slap.

What was wrong with her arm? She tried a tentative wiggle and decided she wouldn't do *that* again in a hurry.

'Do you live here?'

'I caretake,' she said, enunciating every syllable with care because it seemed important.

'You caretake the island?'

'The house.'

'There's a house?'

'A big house.'

'Excellent,' he told her.

He rose and stared round the beach, then left her with

Rocky. Two minutes later he was back, holding her pile of discarded clothes.

'Let's get you warm. You need to put these on.'

'You're wet, too' she told him.

'Yeah, but I don't have a set of dry clothes on the beach. Let's cope with one lot of hypothermia instead of two. Tug your knickers off and I'll help you on with your jeans and windcheater.

'I'm not taking my knickers off!'

'They're soaked and you're freezing.'

'I have my dignity.'

'And I'm not putting up with misplaced modesty on my watch.' He was holding up her windcheater. 'Over your head with this. Don't try and put your arm in it.'

He slid the windcheater over her head. It was long enough to give her a semblance of respectability as she kicked off her soggy knickers—but not much. She should be wearing wisps of sexy silk, she thought, but she was on an island in winter for six months with no expected company. Her knickers were good solid knickers, bought for warmth, with just a touch of lace.

'My granny once told me to always wear good knickers in case I'm hit by a bus,' she managed. Her teeth were chattering. She had her good arm on his shoulder while he was holding her jeans for her to step into.

'Sensible Granny.'

'I think she meant G-strings with French lace,' she told him. 'Granny had visions of me marrying a doctor. Or similar.'

'Still sensible Granny.' He was hauling her jeans up as if this was something he did every day of the week. Which he surely didn't. He was definitely wearing army issue camouflage. It was soaking. One sleeve was ripped but it still looked serviceable.

He looked capable. Capable of hauling her jeans up and not looking?

Don't go there.

'Why…? Why sensible?' she managed.

'Because we could use a doctor right now,' he told her. 'Your arm…'

'My arm will be fine. I must have wrenched it.' She stared down. He was holding her boots. He must have unlaced them. She'd hauled them off and run.

She took the greatest care to put her feet into them, one after the other, and then tried not to be self-conscious as he tied the laces for her.

She was an awesome lifesaver, she thought ruefully. *Not.*

'Now,' he said, and he took her good arm under the elbow. Rocky was turning crazy circles around them, totally unaware of drama, knowing only that he was out of the house and free. 'Let's get to this house. Is it far?'

'A hundred yards as the crow flies,' she told him. 'Sadly we don't have wings.'

'You mean it's up?'

'It's up.'

'I'm sorry.' For the first time his voice faltered. 'I don't think I can carry you.'

'Well, there's a relief,' she managed. 'Because I might have been forced to let you help me dress, but that's as far as it goes. You're carrying me nowhere.'

It had been two days since he'd set off from Hobart, and to say he was exhausted was an understatement. The storm had blown up from nowhere and the boat's engine hadn't been big enough to fight it. Sails had been impossible. He'd been forced to simply ride it out, trying to use the storm jib to keep clear of land, letting the elements take him where they willed.

And no one knew where he was.

His first inkling of the storm had been a faint black streak on the horizon. The streak had turned into a mass with frightening speed. He'd been a good couple of hours out. As soon as he'd noticed it he'd headed for port, but the storm had overwhelmed him.

And he'd been stupidly unprepared. He'd had his phone, but the first massive wave breaking over the bow had soaked him and rendered his phone useless. He'd kicked himself for not putting it in a waterproof container and headed below to Tom's radio. And found it useless. Out of order.

Raoul had thought then how great Tom's devil-may-care attitude had seemed when he and Tom had done their Sunday afternoon sail with his bodyguard in the background, and how dumb it seemed now. And where was the EPIRB? The emergency position indicating radio beacon all boats should carry to alert the authorities if they were in distress and send an automatic location beacon? Did Tom even own one?

Apparently not.

Dumb was the word to describe what he'd done. He'd set out to sea because he was fed up with the world and wanted some time to himself to reflect. But he wasn't so fed up that he wanted to die, and with no one knowing where he was, and no reliable method of communication, he'd stood every chance of ending up that way.

He'd been lucky to end up here.

He'd put this woman's life at risk.

He was helping her up the cliff now. He'd kicked his boots off in the water, which meant he was only wearing socks. The shale on the steep cliff was biting in, but that was the least of his worries. He'd been in the water for a couple of hours, trying to fight his way to shore, and he'd spent two days fighting the sea. He was freezing, and he was so tired all he wanted to do was sleep.

But the woman by his side was rigid with pain. She wasn't complaining, but when he'd put his arm around her waist and held her, supporting her as she walked, she hadn't pulled away. She wasn't big—five-four, five-five or so—and was slight with it. She had a smattering of freckles on her face, her chestnut curls clung wetly to her too-pale skin and her mouth was set in determination.

He just knew this woman didn't accept help unless there was a need.

'How far from the top of the cliff?' he asked, and she took a couple of deep breaths and managed to climb a few more feet before replying.

'Close. You want to go ahead? The back door's open.'

'Are you kidding?' His arm tightened around her. He was on her good side, aware that her left arm was useless and radiating pain. 'You're the lifesaver. Without you I'm a dead man.'

'Rocky will show you…where the pantry is…' She was talking in gasps. 'And the dog food. You'll survive.'

'I need *you* to show me where the pantry is. I think we're almost up now.'

'You'd know that how…?'

'I wouldn't,' he agreed humbly. 'I was just saying it to make you feel better.'

'Thank you,' she whispered.

'No, thank *you*,' he said, and held her tighter and put one foot after another and kept going.

And then they reached the top and he saw the house.

The island was a rocky outcrop, seeming almost to burst from the water in the midst of Bass Strait. He'd aimed for it simply because he'd had no choice—the boat had been taking on water and it had been the only land mass on the map—but from the sea it had seemed stark and inhospitable, with high cliffs looming out of the water. The small bay had seemed the only possible place to land, and even that had proved disastrous. What kind of a house could possibly be built *here*?

He reached the top of the cliff and saw a mansion.

Quite simply, it was extraordinary.

It was almost as if it was part of the island itself, long

and low across the plateau, built of the same stone. In one sense it was an uncompromising fortress. In another sense it was pure fantasy.

Celtic columns faced the sea, supporting a vast pergola, with massive stone terraces underneath. Stone was stacked on stone, massive structures creating an impression of awe and wonder. There were sculptures everywhere—artworks built to withstand the elements. And the house itself… Huge French windows looked out over the sea. They were shuttered now, making the house look even more like a fortress. There was a vast swimming pool, carved to look like a natural rock pool. In this bleak weather it was covered by a solid mat.

He wouldn't be swimming for a while yet, he thought, but he looked at the house and thought he'd never seen anything more fantastic.

If he was being honest a one-room wooden hut would have looked good now, he conceded. But this…

'Safe,' he said, and the woman in his arms wilted a little. Her effort to climb the cliff had been huge.

'B… Back door…out of the wind,' she managed, and her voice was thready.

She'd fought to reach him in the water. She'd been injured trying to save him and now she'd managed to get up the cliff. He hadn't thought he had any strength left in him, but it was amazing what a body was capable of. His army instructors had told him that.

'No matter how dire, there's always another level of adrenalin. You'll never know it's there until you need it.'

He'd needed it once in a sticky situation in West Africa. He felt the woman slump beside him and needed it now. He stopped and turned her, and then swept her up into his arms.

She didn't protest. She was past protesting.

The little dog tore on ahead, showing him the way to the rear door, and in the end it was easy. Two minutes later he had her in the house and they were safe.

CHAPTER THREE

THE FIRST THING he had to do was get himself warm.

It seemed selfish, but he was so cold he couldn't function. And he needed to stay switched on for a while yet.

He laid his lifesaver on a vast settee in front of an open fire—miraculously it was lit, and the house was warm. She was back in her dry clothes and after her exertion on the cliff she wasn't shivering.

He was. His feet and hands were almost completely numb. He'd been in cold water for too long.

She knew it. She gripped his hand as he set her down and winced. 'Bathroom. Thataway,' she told him. 'You'll find clothes in the dressing room beside it.'

'I'll be fast.'

'Stay under water until you're warm,' she ordered, and now the urgent need had passed he knew she was right.

He'd been fighting to get his feet to work on the way up the cliff. He'd also been fighting to get his mind to think straight. Fuzzy images were playing at the edges and he had an almost overwhelming urge to lie by the fire and sleep.

He was trained to recognise hypothermia. He'd been starting to suffer in the water and the physical exertion hadn't been enough to raise his core temperature. He had to get himself warm if he was to be any use to this woman or to himself.

'You'll be okay? Don't move that arm.'

'As if I would. Go.'

So he went, and found a bathroom so sumptuous he might almost be in the palace at home. Any doubts as to how close he'd come to disaster were dispelled by the pain he felt when the warm water touched him.

There was a bench along the length of the shower. Two

shower heads pointed hot water at him from different directions. He slumped on the bench and let the water do its work. Gradually the pain eased. He was battered and bruised, but he'd been more bruised than this after military exercises.

With his core heat back to normal he could almost think straight. Except he needed to sleep. He *really* needed to sleep.

There was a woman who needed him.

He towelled himself dry and moved to the next imperative. Clothes. This was a huge place. Who lived here?

The master bedroom was stunning, and whoever used it had a truly impressive wardrobe. There were over-the-top women's clothes—surely not belonging to the woman who'd saved him? He couldn't see her in flowing rainbow chiffon—but the guy's wardrobe was expansive, too. He found jogging pants that stretched to fit and the T-shirts were okay. There were even socks and sheepskin slippers. And a cardigan just like his grandfather wore.

Exhaustion was still sweeping over him in waves, but at least his head was working. It had to keep working. He was dehydrated and starving and he needed to fix it. He found the kitchen, found a stack of long-life milk in the pantry and drank until the hollow, sick feeling in his stomach receded. Feeling absurdly pleased with himself, he headed back to the living room.

She was lying on her back, her eyes closed. He could see pain radiating out from her in waves.

'Hey,' he said, and she turned and managed a weak smile.

'Hey, yourself,' she managed. 'They look a whole lot better on you than Don.'

'Don?'

'Don and Marigold own this place.'

'Not you?'

'I wish.' She grimaced again. 'Actually, I *don't* wish. I've run out of good coffee.'

'You think it's time for introductions?' he asked, and she winced and tried for a smile.

'Claire. Claire Tremaine. I'm the island caretaker.'

'I'm Raoul,' he told her. 'Raoul de Castelaise.' Now surely wasn't the time for titles and formalities. 'Soldier. I'm pleased to meet you, Claire. In fact I can't begin to tell you *how* pleased. Tell me about your arm.'

'I guess…it's broken.'

'Can I see? I'll need to lift your windcheater.'

'I don't have a bra on.'

'So you don't. You want me to find you a bra?'

'I don't care,' she muttered. 'Look at my arm. Don't look at anything else.'

'No, ma'am.' He sat on the edge of the settee and helped her sit up, then carefully tugged off her windcheater. She only had her good arm in it, so it came off easily.

She'd ordered him not to look at anything else. That was a big ask.

Too big.

She was beautiful, he thought. She looked almost like an athlete, taut and lean. Her chestnut curls were wisping onto her naked shoulders.

She looked vulnerable and scared.

He headed back to the bathroom and brought out a towel, wrapping the fluffy whiteness around her so she was almost respectable but her arm was still exposed.

She hugged the towel to her as if she needed its comfort. The bravado she'd shown since the moment he'd met her in the water seemed to have disappeared.

She *was* scared?

Yeah. He was a big guy. Apart from the dog, she seemed to be in this house alone. She was semi-naked and injured.

Why *wouldn't* she be scared?

'Can I tell you that my grandmother thinks I'm trustworthy?' he told her, tucking in the edges of the towel so it made an almost secure sarong. 'She tells the world what a good boy I am, and I'm not about to mess with her beliefs. I *am* trustworthy, Claire. I promise. If only because my grandmother's presence seems to spend a lot of time sitting on my shoulder. You're safe with me.'

And she managed a smile that was almost genuine.

'Scary Granny, huh.'

'You'd better believe it. But I can handle her.'

'And you love her?'

'You can believe that, too.'

And her smile softened, as if she really did believe him. As if somehow his words really had made her feel safe.

'Are you French?' she asked.

'I'm from Marétal. It's a small land-locked country near…'

'I know it,' she said, in an exclamation of surprise. 'Your army's taking part in the international army exercises in Tasmania. I looked it up.'

'You looked it up?'

'I get bored,' she admitted. Her voice was still tight, but she was making a huge effort to sound normal. 'I was listening to the Tasmanian news on the radio. They listed the countries taking part. I didn't know where Marétal was. So you're part of that exercise.' And then her voice grew tighter. 'Are there…are there any other soldiers lost overboard?'

'Only me—and it wasn't an army exercise,' he said ruefully. 'Despite the camouflage, I'm off duty. I took a friend's boat out from Hobart and got caught in the storm. I had two days being flung about Bass Strait, finally made it to the lee of your island and you know the rest. But my friend—the guy who owns *Rosebud*—is in Nepal. He doesn't know I took his boat and I didn't tell anyone I was going. It was a spur-of-the-moment decision. I broke all the rules and the army would agree that I've been an idiot.'

'You've paid the price.

'It could have been a whole lot higher.'

He was watching her arm while they talked. She was supporting it with her good hand, holding it slightly away from her body. Her shoulder looked odd. Squared off.

'Idiot or not, you might need to trust me with your arm,' he suggested. 'Can I touch it?'

'If you don't mind me screaming.'

'I'll be gentle,' he told her, and lightly ran his fingers down the front of her shoulder joint, thinking back to his first-aid courses. Thinking of anatomy.

'It feels dislocated,' he told her.

'It feels broken.'

'It probably feels worse than if it was broken.'

He put his fingers on her wrist and checked her pulse, then did it again at the elbow.

'You look like you know what you're doing,' she managed.

'I've been in the army for years. I'm a first-aider for my unit.'

'You put on sticking plasters?'

'Sometimes it's more than that. When we're out of range of medical help this is what I do.'

'Like now?'

'I hope we're not out of range. You said you have a radio. Two-way? We must be within an hour's journey for a chopper coming from the mainland. Tell me where it is and I'll radio now.'

'Or not,' she said.

'Not?'

'No.' She winced. 'I know this sounds appalling… We have a radio—a big one. We also have back-up—a decent hand-held thing that's capable of sending signals to Hobart. But last time he was here Don—the owner—was messing around with it and dropped his beer into its workings. And the main radio seems to have been wiped out in the storm.'

'He dropped his beer…?'

'Yeah,' she said. 'If it had been Marigold it would have

been a martini.' She closed her eyes. 'There's a first-aid kit in the kitchen,' she told him. 'I think I need it.'

'I doubt aspirin will help.'

'Marigold is allergic to pain. *Very* allergic. She's been known to demand morphine and a helicopter transfer to the mainland for a torn toenail. I'm thinking there'll be something decent in there.'

There was. He found enough painkillers to knock out an elephant. Also muscle relaxant, and a dosage list that seemed to be made out for the Flying Doctor—Australia's remote medical service. The list didn't actually say *This much for a dislocated shoulder*, but he had enough experience to figure the dose. He made her hot, sweet tea—plus one for himself—then watched her take the pills he gave her.

'Stay still until that works,' he told her.

He found a blanket and covered her, and watched her curl into an almost foetal position on the settee. Rocky nestled on the floor by her side.

He tried to think of a plan.

Plans were thin on the ground and he was still having trouble thinking straight.

The drugs would ease her pain, he thought, but he also knew that the longer the shoulder stayed dislocated, the higher the chance of long-term damage.

In the Middle East he'd had a mate who had…

Um, no. He wasn't going there.

He did a further tour and found the radio in a truly impressive study. Claire had been right: there was no transmission. He headed outside and saw a wooden building blasted to splinters. A huge radio antenna lay smashed among the timber.

No joy there.

'You're on your own,' he muttered, and pushed away the waves of exhaustion and headed back to the living room.

She was still lying where he'd left her, but her rigidity seemed to have lessened.

He knelt beside her. 'Better?'

'Better,' she whispered. 'Just leave me be.'

'I can't do that. Claire, we're going to have to get that arm back into position.'

'My arm wants to stay really still.'

'And I'm going to have to hurt you,' he told her. 'But if I don't hurt you now you may have long-term damage.'

'How do I know it's not broken?'

'You don't. I don't. So I'm using basic first aid, and the first rule is *Do no harm*. We were taught a method which only sometimes works, but its huge advantage is that it won't hurt a fracture. If there's a fracture the arm will scream at you and you'll scream at me and we'll stop.' He hoped. 'Claire, I need you to lie on your front and let your arm hang down. We'll put a few cushions under you so your arm is high enough to hang freely. Then I'm going to gradually weight your arm, using sticking plaster to attach things like cans of beans...'

'Beans?'

'Anything I can find.' He smiled. 'In an emergency, anything goes. My first-aid trainer said if I ask you to grip the cans then your arm will tense, so I just need to stick them on you as dead weights. Then we'll let the nice drugs do their work. You'll lie back and think of England, and the tins of beans will tug your arm down, and if you relax completely then I'm hoping it'll pop back in.'

'Think of England?'

'Or sunbeams,' he told her. 'Anything to take your mind off your arm.'

She appeared to think about that for a moment, maybe choosing from a list of options. And then she opened her eyes and glanced up at him, taking in his appearance. From head to toe.

'Nice,' she whispered. 'I think I'll think about *you*. If you knew how different you look to Don... Don fills his T-shirt up with beer belly. You fill it up with...you.'

'Me?'

'Muscles.'

Right. It was the drugs talking, he thought. He needed to stop looking into her eyes and quit smiling at her like an idiot and think of her as a patient. As one of the guys in his unit, injured in the field. *Work.*

Nothing personal at all.

But he needed to get her relaxed. He knelt beside her and pushed a damp curl from her eyes. She was little and dark and feisty, and her freckles were very, very cute. Her hair was still damp from her soaking. He would have liked to get her completely dry, but he was working through a list of imperatives. Arm first.

'H… How does this work?' she muttered.

'The socket's like a cup,' he told her. 'I think your arm's slipped out of the cup, but it still has muscles that want it to go back in. If we weight it, and you're relaxed, then your muscles have a chance to pull it back into place.'

That was the theory, anyway. *If* it worked. *If* the arm wasn't broken. But the weighting method was the only safe course of action. To pull on a broken arm could mean disaster. Gradual weighting was the only way, but she had to trust him.

And it seemed she did.

'Do it,' she said, and smiled up at him. 'Only we don't have baked beans. How about tins of caviar?'

'You're kidding?'

'No. But there are tinned tomatoes as well.' Then she appeared to brighten. 'And we have tins of truly appalling instant coffee. It'd be great if they could be useful for something.'

She smiled up at him and he thought of the pain she was suffering, and the sheer courage she was showing, and the fact that she was smiling to make *him* smile…

And he smiled back at her and backed away—because a

man had to back away fast from a smile like that—and went to find some truly useful cans of coffee.

Somehow he stayed businesslike. Professional. Somehow he followed the instructions in his head from first-aid training in the field. He taped on the weights. He watched for her to react from too much pain, but although she winced as he weighted her arm she didn't make a murmur.

He put on as much weight as he thought she could tolerate and then he sat beside her and waited.

'What do we do now?' she asked.

'Relax. Forget the arm. Tell you what,' he said. 'I'll tell you a story.'

'What sort of story?'

He thought about it. He needed a story that would make her almost soporific so the arm would totally relax.

'How about *Goldilocks and the Three Bears*?' he suggested, and she choked.

'Really?'

'Has anyone ever read it to you?'

'I guess…not for a very long time.'

'Same for me,' he told her. 'So correct me if I get the bears muddled. Okay, here goes.'

And he sat by the couch and stroked her hair and told her the story of the three bears. It was a simple story—not long enough—so he had to embellish it. He had Goldilocks as a modern-day Bond girl, escaping from villains. He had his bears trying to figure the villains from the good guys, and he put in a bit of drama for good measure.

In other words he had fun, blocking the fuzziness in his own head with the need to keep her attention. And as Baby Bear found Goldilocks, and good guys and baddies were sorted, and baddies were dispatched with buckets of Mama Bear's too-hot porridge, and they all settled down for toast and marmalade, Claire's arm did what he'd desperately hoped it would do. It clicked back into its socket.

In the silence of the room, between breaks in the very exciting narrative, they actually heard it pop.

The relief did his head in.

It was almost as if he hadn't realised what stress he'd been under until the arm clicked back into place. The sound was like an off switch, clicking in his brain.

For the first time in his life he felt as if he was going to faint. He put his head between his knees—because it was either that or keel over. And Claire's fingers touched his hair, running through the still damp strands. Caressing.

'It's done,' she whispered. 'Thank you.'

'Thank *you*,' he managed. 'I couldn't have borne it if you'd suffered permanent damage saving me. Claire, I need to fix you a sling.'

'Raoul… First… Lie here,' she whispered. 'Please… Just…hold me.'

He'd been in deadly peril for two days. For a few hours earlier today he'd been sure he'd drown.

He was past exhaustion. He was past anything. Maybe Claire knew it. Maybe Claire felt the same.

'Sling first,' he muttered, and managed to tie her arm so it wouldn't slip, but then he was done.

'I need to sleep,' Claire murmured. 'The drugs… My arm… It's all okay, but… Raoul, stay with me.'

She was lying on the huge settee, tousled, part-wrapped in a fleecy towel, part-covered by the huge blanket he'd found. The fire was putting out a gentle warmth.

He fought for sense but he was losing. He managed to toss more logs on the fire and then he stared into the flames thinking…*nothing*. Goldilocks and the three bears seemed very far away. Everything seemed very far away.

But Claire was edging sideways to give him room to lie with her.

There was no choice. He sat down on the settee and she put her hand up and touched his face.

'We're safe,' she whispered. 'Nice. Stay.'

He lay down, but the sofa wasn't big enough to avoid touching. And it seemed the most natural thing in the world that he put his arms around her.

She curled into him with a sleepy murmur.

'Nice,' she said again. 'Sleep.'

He woke and it was still daylight. Was it late afternoon or was it the next day? For now he didn't know and didn't care.

He was still on the settee. The room was warm. *He* was warm. The fire was a mass of glowing embers.

He was holding Claire.

There were aches in his body, just waiting to make themselves known. He could feel them lurking. They'd make themselves known if he moved.

But for now he had no intention of moving. He lay with the warmth of the woman beside him: a gentle, amazing comfort. Her towel had slipped. He was lying on her uninjured side. Her naked body was against his chest and he was cradling her to him. She was using his chest as a pillow.

He had a T-shirt on but it didn't feel like it. Her warmth made it feel as if she was almost a part of him.

He could feel her heartbeat. Her hair had dried and was tumbling across his chest, and her breathing was deep and even.

After the perils, the fear, the exhaustion of the last two days, he was filled with a sense of peace so great it threatened to overwhelm him.

He'd been in dangerous situations before. He'd had moments when he'd ended up sleeping tight with other members of his unit, some of them women. He'd held people when they'd been in mutual danger.

But he'd never felt like this, he thought. As if this woman was *right*.

As if this woman was part of him.

That was a crazy thought, he decided, and he hadn't even taken any drugs. What was going on?

He must have moved a little, because Claire stirred and opened her eyes and shifted a fraction. She didn't move far, though. She was still cradled against him.

Her heartbeat was still his.

'Nice,' she said, as she'd said before she'd slept, and it was like a blessing.

'Nice?'

'The wind's died.'

It had, too. He hadn't noticed.

He had sensory overload.He couldn't get past the feeling of the woman in his arms.

'Pain?' he asked, and she seemed to think about it.

'Nope,' she said at last. 'Not if I lie really still.'

That suited him. They lay really still. Rocky was snuffling under the settee. Maybe that was what had woken them.

Or other, more mundane things.

'I need the bathroom,' she murmured, and he conceded that he did, too. And the fire needed more logs. And, to tell the truth, he was so hungry he could eat a horse—the milk and tea had barely hit the sides—but he was prepared to ignore everything if she'd stay where she was. But now Rocky had his paws up on the settee and was looking at them with bright, expectant eyes.

'That's his "feed me" look,' Claire murmured, and she moved a little so she could scratch behind his ear with her good hand. And then she said, in a different voice, 'I've lost my towel.'

'So you have.' It was hard not to sound complacent.

She tugged back, hauled the blanket up across her breasts and tried a glare. It wasn't a very big glare. Those drugs must have packed a fair punch, he thought. She still looked dazed.

Actually…*beautifully* dazed. She had wide green eyes that seemed to be struggling to focus. She had skin that seemed almost translucent. Her lashes were long and curled a little, and her nose was ever so slightly snubbed.

'You noticed,' she said accusingly, and he shook his head.

'No, ma'am. I've been looking at Rocky all the time.'

'Liar.'

'Yes, ma'am.'

She grinned, and he thought that if she'd had two good hands she might have punched him. But one was still pretty much tied up. He was safe.

'Life,' she said.

'Sorry?'

'We fought to keep it. We might as well get on with it.'

'You mean we need to feed the fire, go to the bathroom, feed the dog, find something to eat ourselves...'

'And think of some way to contact the mainland.' Her smile faded. 'Will people be looking for you?'

He thought of his minders. At midday, when he'd spoken to Franz, he had been supposed to be with his unit. His minders had therefore been off duty. At six that night they'd have rung to check his itinerary for the following day.

He'd have been expected to be back well before six. They'd have rung and someone would have told them he was off duty. Then they'd have contacted Franz. 'He's off duty as of this morning. I believe he's planning on returning home,' he would have told them, and then someone would have been sent to check his kit and discovered it was still where it was supposed to be.

It would have taken his minders about thirty seconds after that to panic.

'What is it?' she said, and pushed herself up, wincing a bit as she moved her arm.

'What?'

'Your face. Someone's looking for you right now. Someone's terrified. Your wife? Partner? Family?'

'I don't have a wife or partner.'

'Family? Parents?'

'My parents died when I was five, but I do have grandparents.'

'Back in Marétal?'

'Yes.' He closed his eyes, thinking of the fuss when his grandparents discovered he was missing. Then he thought of how long he'd been gone. After all this time it wouldn't be fuss. It would be horror. 'I imagine they'll know I'm missing.'

She was sitting up now, blanket tucked to her chin, concentrating on the problem at hand. 'Don't worry too much,' she told him. 'The wind's died. I suspect you'll be mortified, but the Australian Air Sea Rescue services are good. They can probably track the wind and the currents and get a fair idea of your direction. If I was them I'd be checking the islands first. There's only about ten. Any minute now we'll have choppers overhead, searching for one lost soldier.'

He felt sick.

'Don't worry,' Claire said again. 'I imagine it's embarrassing, getting rescued twice, once even by a girl, but you'll just have to cop it.'

'I won't,' he told her.

'Are you going to tell me how you can avoid it?'

'I already *have* avoided it,' he said, goaded. 'I didn't tell anyone I was going sailing. What's more, I took my friend's boat. My friend's currently trying to climb Annapurna Two in Nepal. He won't know I'm missing and he won't know his boat's missing. No one knows I went to sea. I could be anywhere and my...my grandparents will be devastated.'

His grandparents?

This wasn't just about his grandparents, he thought. His bodyguard consisted of two skilled, decent men who'd feel as if they'd failed. The top brass of the army would be mortified. His friends would be appalled. And, back home, the media would be in a feeding frenzy. *Heir to the Throne Disappears!* It didn't bear thinking about.

He would have groaned if it would do any good.

It wouldn't.

'Raoul...'

'Mmm?'

'We all do dumb things,' she told him, and put her good hand on his knee. 'Some dumber than others. But, hey, you've lived to be embarrassed. The supply boat's due next Monday. You'll climb aboard, they'll let everyone know, and by the time you reach Hobart the fuss will have died down. You might need to apologise to a few people and go home and hug your grandparents, but it's no big deal. So one soldier's gone AWOL? If they don't think you've drowned then they'll probably assume you're in a bar somewhere. Or with a woman.'

And then she had the temerity to grin.

'Actually, they're both true. You're very much with a woman, and if you go through that door there's a truly excellent bar.'

'I think I need it,' he said, and she chuckled and tried to stand.

She wobbled a bit and he rose to steady her.

'What did you give me?' she demanded. 'I feel like I've had enough drugs to down an elephant.'

'Or to not scream when your arm went back in. You were very brave.'

'I was, wasn't I?' she said smugly. 'So I'm brave and you're lost. And my arm's back to where it belongs. They're the givens. For the rest...we just have to get on with it.'

'I really can't get off this place until next Monday?'

'We can try and fix the transmitter,' she told him. 'Are you any good with electronics?'

'No.'

'Then I'm vetoing that as a plan straight away,' she told him. 'I have no intention of saving you twice. Now, Raoul...?'

'Yes?'

'Put some logs on the fire while I feed Rocky. We have life to get on with.'

'Yes, ma'am,' he said, because there was nothing else to say. Nothing at all.

CHAPTER FOUR

THIS MORNING SHE'D been bored.

This morning her entire desire in life had been a decent cup of coffee.

She was not bored now, and her desire was taking a new and entirely inappropriate direction.

Maybe she should be nervous. This guy was seriously big. He had the brawn and build of a well-honed military machine. Even washed up on the beach he'd looked awesome.

She stood under the shower and let the hot water run over her battered body as she let her mind drift where it willed.

It willed straight to Raoul.

She was alone on this island with a guy she didn't know. A seriously big guy. A seriously good-looking guy. He was dark-haired and tanned and his grey eyes were creased at the edges. Was the weathering on his face from years of military exercises in tough conditions? She wasn't sure if she was right, but she guessed she was.

He was kind. He was also skilled. He'd managed to get her arm back into place and the relief had been enormous. He was also worried about his grandparents. She could see that. One lone soldier AWOL from the army wouldn't cause a fuss, but she'd seen that he was distressed. Of course the army would contact his family, and of course it distressed Raoul that his grandparents would worry. Because he was…a good guy.

Raoul. Nice name, she thought. Nice guy. And a seriously sexy accent. Almost French, with something else in the mix.

Sexy.

And there lay the rub. There lay the reason why she should stop thinking about Raoul right now.

'Are you okay in there?'

His voice almost made her jump out of her skin and when she landed she had to fight to get her voice in order.

'F… Fine.'

'Dinner's ready when you are. I already ate, but I'm ready to eat again.'

'You already *ate*?'

'Your refrigerator's amazing. Or should I say refrigerators, plural. Wow. I opened one to check and three eggs almost fell into my hand. So I ate them. You do realise eating's been low on my priority list over the last few days? Having had my pre-dinner boiled egg snack, I'm now serious about making dinner proper. But first I'm here to towel my lady's back, if she wants it towelled, because it's occurred to me that one-arm towelling might be hard.'

There were things there for a woman to consider. A lot of things. She was alone on the island with this guy. Every sensible part of her said she shouldn't accept his help.

Raoul had put a plastic outdoor chair in the shower before he'd let her into the bathroom. He'd fussed, but she'd assured him she was okay. She'd been able to kick off her salty clothes herself, and sitting under the hot water had been easy. She'd even managed to shampoo her hair with one hand.

But now… The wussy part of her said she didn't know how she *could* towel herself with one arm, especially as the painkillers were still making her feel a bit fuzzy. And there was a tiny part of her—a really dangerous part—that was saying she wouldn't mind being towelled by this guy.

She was twenty-eight years old. She was hardly a prude. He was…

Yeah, enough.

But she had three voices in her head now. One saying, *Safe*, one saying, *Sensible*, the other saying, *Yes!*

She had an internal vote and *Safe* and *Sensible* were outvoted by about a hundred to two.

'Yes,' she whispered, but he didn't hear.

'Claire? Are you okay?'

'I'm fine,' she said. 'And, yes, please—I think I *do* need help to get dry.'

It wasn't a bad feeling.

Okay, it was an incredible feeling. He had his hands full of lush white towel and he was carefully towelling Claire Tremaine dry.

She was beautiful. Every inch of her was beautiful. She'd emerged naked from the shower. She'd stood with rivulets of warm water streaming down her body and he'd never seen anything more beautiful in his life.

If he hadn't spent the last two days having cold shower after cold shower, he might have seriously thought of taking one now. Instead of which he had to get his thoughts under control and do what he was here for—get the lady dry.

She'd grabbed a towel, too, but with only one good hand she could do little. She dried her face and rubbed her front, which was okay because that meant he didn't have to dry her breasts. Which would have been hard. But he did have to towel her hair. He did have to run the towel down the smooth contours of her back. He did need to stoop to dry her gorgeous legs.

She was a small woman, but her legs seemed to go on forever. How did *that* happen?

She was gorgeous.

When he'd knocked on the bathroom door he'd just put steak in the microwave to defrost and until he'd entered the bathroom that steak had been pretty much uppermost in his thoughts.

Not now. The steak could turn into dust for all he cared. Every sense was tuned to this woman.

Every part of his body…

'I think I'm dry,' she said, in a voice that was shaky, but not shaky in a pained kind of way. It was shaky in a way that told him she was as aware of him as he was of her.

He could gather her up right now…

Yeah, like *that* could happen. This woman had hauled him out of the water and let him into her home. She'd been injured on his behalf. She was still slightly drug-affected. No, make that a *lot* drug-affected. He'd given her more pain-killers before she'd gone to shower.

Hitting on her now would be all sorts of wrong.

But she was looking at him with huge eyes, slightly dazed, and her fingers were touching his hair as he stooped to dry her legs.

'Raoul…' she whispered, and he rose and stepped away fast.

'Yeah. You're done,' he told her. 'Where can I find you some clothes? Something sensible.'

He spoke too loud, too emphatically, and the emphasis on the last word was like a slap to them both. *Sensible.* That was the way to go.

'I… My bedroom… It's right next door. There's a jogging suit in the third drawer of the dresser. Knickers in the top drawer. I'm ditching the idea of a bra. But I can get them.'

'Stay where you are,' he said roughly, and backed away fast.

Because it might be sensible to help her into the bedroom and help her get dressed, but there was a bed in the bed-room, and a man had limits, and his were already stretched close to breaking.

So he headed into the bedroom and found the jogging suit, and then he opened the knicker drawer and had to take a deep breath before he felt sensible again. He picked up the first pair of knickers that came to hand and practically slammed the drawer shut. A pair of sheepskin bootees stood beside the bed. Excellent. They weren't sexy in the least.

He headed back to the bathroom, thought about helping her, then decided it might be hard but she should be able to cope herself and it would be far, far safer if he stayed on his side of the door.

He knocked and slipped the clothes around the door, without opening it wide enough for him to see her. They needed barriers, he thought. Big barriers. Preferably barriers with locks on them.

He stepped away from the door as if it was red-hot.

'Steak in ten minutes,' he said. 'If you're up to it. If the painkillers aren't making you too dizzy?'

'The painkillers aren't making me too dizzy,' she told him, and then she stopped.

And he thought he knew what she was about to say because he was feeling the same.

The *painkillers* weren't making her dizzy, but something else was.

The same something that was doing his head in?

She dressed, and replaced the basic sling Raoul had fashioned for her.

Her arm was still painful, but it was a steady, bruised ache, not the searing pain she'd experienced when it was dislocated.

She was dry, she was warm, and she was dressed. She hauled a comb through her curls and thought she looked almost presentable. Almost respectable. *Yeah.* She looked at herself in the mirror. Her jogging suit was baggy and old. She had on her huge sheepskin boots. Her hair was combed but still damp and she didn't have the energy to dry it. There was no way she had the energy for make-up, either.

'It's take me as I am,' she said out loud, and then winced. *Take me?*

What was she thinking?

Rocky was sitting at her feet. He looked up at her quizzically, as if guessing her thoughts, and she gave him a rueful smile.

'You and I have been alone too long,' she told him. 'Four months and one lone guy enters our world…'

One *gorgeous* guy. A guy with an accent to make a girl's

toes curl. A guy who was gentle and kind. A guy who'd lost his parents, who knew what being alone felt like.

A kindred spirit?

'Yeah, those drugs are really doing something to you,' she muttered, and adjusted her sling a bit—not because she needed to, but because adjusting it caused her arm to twinge and she felt she needed a little bit of pain right now.

Pain equalled reality. Reality was good.

Reality was getting this guy off her island and going back to her stint of self-imposed exile.

She could smell steak. And onions. Raoul was cooking for her.

'It needed only that,' she muttered, and took a last moment to try and grasp at a reality that was looking more and more elusive.

And then she went to find Raoul.

'Hey.' Raoul turned as she entered the kitchen.

He smiled at her, his eyes raking her from her toes to the top of her head, and his smile said he approved. Of the saggy jogging suit. Of everything. That smile was enough to do a girl's head in.

'Well done. Feel better?'

'I…yes.' Of course she did. A thousand times better. She was clean and she was warm and she was about to be fed. What else could a woman want?

Who else?

'I feel great,' she said, a bit too heartily, and then blinked as he tugged a chair out for her. All this and manners, too?

'You don't need to do this,' she told him. 'I'm the servant here, remember?'

'The servant?'

'Don and Marigold own the island, but they never come here in winter. They needed a caretaker. Rocky and I applied for the job.'

'Just Rocky and you?' He turned to flip the steaks. 'That's hardly safe.'

'There's also supposed to be a handyman-cum-gardener. What they didn't tell me was that he'd quit. He left on the boat I arrived on, and Don and Marigold headed to Europe without finding a replacement.'

He was organising chips on plates. *Chips!* Yeah, they were the frozen oven variety, but she totally approved. Steak and chips and onions. And baby peas, and slivered carrots sautéed in butter. *Wow,* she thought. *Turn back the rescue boats. I'm keeping him.*

Um…*not.*

Drugs, she reminded herself. She really had had a lot of them.

'Don and Marigold need to wake up,' he told her, organising the plates to his satisfaction.

He flipped the steak and veggies on, then carried them to the table, sitting down before her as if this was something they did every day of the week. Then he looked at her sling and leaned over and chopped up her steak. The sensation of being cared for was almost indescribable.

Yeah, maybe she was bordering on delusional…

'They're breaking every rule in the Occupational Safety Code,' he told her, sitting back down again and turning his attention to his own meal. 'Leaving someone in such isolation. Or don't they have those rules in Australia?'

'They do.'

'So why are you still on the island? Come to think about it, why were you here in the first place?'

She didn't answer for a while. She didn't need to. The steak was excellent, as were the accompaniments. She hadn't eaten since breakfast and she'd had a swim and a shock. She could be excused for making food her priority.

But the question hung. *'Why were you here in the first place?'*

It wasn't his business, she thought. But a tiny voice in the back of her mind said, *Why not tell him? Why not say it like it is?*

She hadn't told anyone. She'd simply fled.

'I've been accused of fraud,' she said.

He said nothing.

So what had she expected? Fireworks? Shock? Horror? At least a token of dismay? Instead he concentrated on his second piece of steak as if it was the most important thing in the world. And, because there was nothing else to do, she focused on her food, too. She ate a few more chips and her world settled a little and she felt better.

Lighter.

It was as if the elephant was in the room, but at least it was no longer inside her.

'It couldn't have been a very big fraud,' he said at last, eying the near empty bowl of chips with due consideration.

'What? Why?'

'You're not in jail and you've taken a job as a caretaker in one of the most inhospitable places on the earth. This might be a great house, but you're not living in luxury. So it was either a very small fraud or you've cleverly stacked what you've defrauded away so you can be a billionaire in your old age.'

'I could have paid it back.'

'I suspect if you'd paid it back you wouldn't be on this island. Do you want to tell me about it?'

No, she thought. And then she thought, *Okay, the elephant's out.* But it was still a very big elephant. Regardless of how trivial this guy made it sound.

'It was big,' she told him. 'Something like seven million Australian dollars.'

He shook his head in disbelief. 'Ma'am, if you're hiding that kind of cash you shouldn't let strange men rifle through your knicker drawer.'

And she chuckled. She couldn't help herself.

She laughed, and then she thought, *That's the first time I've laughed since...since...*

She couldn't remember.

'I didn't do it,' she said, and her desire to laugh died. Her thoughts went back to that last day, standing in her boss's office, white with shock. *I didn't do it.*

He hadn't believed her. Why would he?

'So?' Raoul said encouragingly. 'I believe you. You didn't do it, so…the butler?'

She choked again, and he smiled and took another chip and handed it across the table to her.

She took it and ate it, and he kept smiling at her, and his smile was doing something to her insides…

'That's it,' he told her. 'Nice, greasy carbohydrates. Best thing in the world for trauma. Like telling me all about the butler. Jam doughnuts would be better, but for now we're stuck with chips. If not the butler, who?'

'Felicity,' she whispered, and he nodded.

'Of course. I should have guessed. I was lacking a few clues, though. So tell me about Felicity.'

'She's perfect.'

'You mean she probably has the seven million?'

'I guess.'

'Yep, she's perfect, then. Pretty, too, I'll bet.'

And Claire thought of pretty, perfect Felicity and found it hard not to start shaking. But suddenly Raoul's hand was over hers—big, comforting, warm. Joking was put aside.

'Tell me,' he said, and so she did.

From the beginning. All of it.

Of the tiny town where she was raised, of her single mum, of being treated like trash. Of her mum's death when she was fifteen. Of the scholarship and her determination to get out. Of law school and commerce, a double degree. Of academic brilliance and sheer hard work.

Once she'd graduated she'd taken a job in Legal Assistance. It had been a great organisation—helping the underprivileged with legal advice and representation when they couldn't afford it. She'd enjoyed it. Then she'd won a huge legal case that had received national headlines, and she'd been head-hunted by one of the most prestigious law firms in Australia. She had been stupid enough to accept.

Only she hadn't been *one of them*.

'I was the odd one out,' she told him. 'An experiment. They select their lawyers on the basis of family and connections, but one of the senior partners had the noble idea that they should try something else—hire someone on merit. They broke their rules when they hired me. Three others were hired at the same time, on the old system. They'd gone to the same school and the same universities. They were the best of friends. But there was a fourth, and because of me he missed out on a job. So they hated me from day one. I tried not to care. I put my head down and worked. But the more I got ahead the more they hated me.'

'And then?'

'Then there was a problem,' she said, talking almost to herself. 'Insider trading, they call it. Someone in the firm knew something and passed the information on. There was a deal. Someone outside the company made seven million dollars and the media started asking questions. The company had to point the finger at someone.'

'Was there evidence?'

'Of course there was evidence,' she told him. 'A paper trail leading straight back to me. So I was called into the office of the managing director. I had a choice, he said. I could resign and the company's insurer would repay costs, cover the fiasco and keep the company's name clean and out of the courts. Or I could go to jail.' She shrugged. 'They had the best legal team in Australia covering their backs and I was a nobody. I *had* nobody. It didn't seem like much of a choice.'

'But if it wasn't you...?'

She sighed. 'A week after I left Felicity left. For Paris. I have no proof of anything, but Felicity's partner just happens to be the nephew of the managing director, and Felicity had the desk next to mine. So here I am. I haven't been charged with anything, but the legal fraternity in Australia is tight.

My time as a corporate lawyer is over. I might be able to get back into Legal Assistance, but even there I'm now tainted. I took this job to take some time and think through my options, but I don't have many.'

'You could sue,' he said. 'You could fight.'

'Yeah?' She shrugged, and then gave a rueful smile. 'Maybe I could,' she said. 'But it'd cost a fortune. I'd risk debt, or worse, and I'd also risk…'

'Risk what?'

'Attention,' she whispered. 'The media would be all over it. Ever since I was a kid I knew to keep my head down. To stay unnoticed. It's always been safest.' She took a deep breath. 'When I left to go to university our local publican said, "You'll be back, girl. A girl like you…raised in the gutter…you've got airs if you think you'll ever get rid of the stink." But I gave myself airs and this is where it's left me.'

'I wish you'd punched him.'

And the thought suddenly cheered her. She thought back to the smirking publican and wished, quite fiercely, that she'd had the skills then that she had now.

'I could have,' she said, attempting to lighten her voice. 'I have a black belt in karate. I may like keeping myself to myself, but physically if you mess with me you're in trouble. Even if I'm one-handed.'

He looked at her in astonishment. 'You're kidding?'

'Like the publican said, you can take the girl out of the gutter, but you can never take the gutter out of the girl. I learned karate, and the gym I went to taught me base moves as well. I can fight clean or I can fight dirty.'

'That sounds like a warning.'

She grinned. 'If you like. Rocky knows to treat me with respect.' Her smile faded. 'But respect for me is a bit thin on the ground. Bob Maker was a bully and a drunk, but he did get one thing right. Trying to move away from my roots was a mistake. I'll never try it again.'

'So you won't fight? You'll calmly go back where you came from?'

She smiled again at that, but ruefully. 'I wouldn't fit,' she said. 'Legal Assistance is my first love. It's a fantastic organisation. They helped me when Mum died and I was trying to prove I could live independently, but I'm not sure I can go back there. That's what this is all about. Rocky and I are taking six months to think about it. So what about you?'

'What do you mean?'

'Meaning you don't have a mum and dad. I assume your grandparents raised you? Was joining the army a big step?'

He thought about it for a moment. For a long moment. She'd told him so much about herself. It was only fair to explain his background.

But a part of him...*couldn't.* She was sitting opposite him with total trust. She was relaxed, eating her chips, smiling, and she'd just explained how social class had destroyed her career.

Over the years Raoul had watched the almost grotesque change in people's attitudes when his royal title was revealed. Sometimes people fawned. Sometimes people backed away.

With her background, with her recent hurt and with her desire to stay in the background, he suspected Claire would back away fast, and he didn't want that. An urgent voice in his head was starting to say, *This is important. Give it time. Get to know her on equal terms.*

Had his joining the army been a big step?

'I guess it was,' he said at last. 'I'm an officer. I had to fight to get where I was, and to be accepted.'

And wasn't that the truth? Of course he'd been seen as different. It had taken him years to break down barriers, and every now and then the barriers would rise back up.

Like now. If a normal soldier went AWOL questions would be asked, but unless there was a suggestion of foul play the army usually adopted a policy of wait and see. After weeks of tough field exercise some men got drunk, found women, got themselves into places that took them a while to get out of. No one would put out an international alert on *their* disappearance.

Whereas for him…

He had no doubts about the scale of the hue and cry that would be happening. *Heir to the throne of Marétal disappears.* He closed his eyes, thinking of the distress. The fuss. He'd been so stupid.

'You're still tired,' Claire told him, and he thought about explaining and decided again that he didn't want to. Not yet.

He *was* tired. 'I guess…'

'Let's both sleep,' she told him. 'Leave the dishes. They'll wait until morning. I'm beat.'

'The drugs will still be making you dozy.'

'And being tossed around in a bathtub for two days and almost drowned will be making *you* dozy,' she told him. She rose and took a glass of water. 'Pick a bedroom. Any bedroom but mine. Marigold leaves toiletries for her guests—there'll be razors and toothbrushes…everything you need. Raoul, thank you for the meal. Thank you for everything. I'm going to bed.'

She headed for the door. He watched her go. Then… 'Claire?'

She paused and looked back at him. 'Yes?'

'Thank you,' he said softly. 'Thank you for saving my life and thank you…for just being you. And if I ever meet the appalling Felicity it'll be more than karate that comes into play. It would be my privilege to fight for you.'

She smiled, but absently. 'Thank you, but don't get your hopes up,' she told him. 'It's money and power that keeps the Felicitys of this world out of trouble, and neither of us have even close to what *they* have. But there are compensations. That was an awesome steak.'

And then she raised her glass, as if in a toast.

'Here's to what we *do* have,' she told him. 'And here's to

never aspiring to more.' She gave a rueful smile and turned and disappeared.

He didn't follow. Yes, he'd been battered, but he had already slept and there was no way he could sleep now.

He washed the dishes, because that was what you did. Once upon a time he hadn't known what a dishcloth was, but years of roughing it in army camps had knocked that out of him.

Then he figured he should check the damage to the radio transmitter. He'd look pretty stupid if it was just a case of the antenna falling over. And he also needed something to occupy his mind that wasn't Claire.

That was a hard ask. She'd gone to bed, but in a way she was still with him.

She'd told a stark tale and it had hurt her to tell it. He'd been able to tell by the way her face had set as she'd told it. By the way she'd laughed afterwards. He had just been able to…*tell.*

She was right under his skin.

He wanted to find the unknown Felicity and send her to the gutter in Claire's place. He wanted to ruin the entire firm she'd worked for.

He could. Maybe he would.

He thought of what he had—the resources, the power—and thought he should tell her.

Why? What good would it possibly do for Claire to know now what power he could wield?

She was treating him as a companion. He had no doubt that her dreadful little story wouldn't have been told if he'd first appeared to her in royal regalia. But he'd been in army gear, and she'd have had no way of recognising the discreet crown emblazoned on the sleeve. To her he was just a soldier—someone who'd come up through the ranks. A kid with no parents.

She thought he was the same as she was, and he didn't mind her thinking it. No, he *wanted* her to think it.

Why? Tired as he was, the warning bells that seemed to have been installed in his brain since his parents' death were suddenly jangling. He'd been a loner since then—or maybe even earlier. The royal household was always full of people, but whenever he needed comfort he never knew who it was who'd do the comforting. Whose job it was that week…

He'd learned not to need comfort. People came and went. He didn't get attached.

Why was he suddenly thinking of this in relation to Claire?

He shook his head, trying to rid himself of thoughts that were jumbling. He was overtired, he thought, still battered, still not thinking straight. He needed to be practical.

First things first. He didn't intend to spend the rest of his time here wearing Don's clothes. He found the laundry and put his and Claire's salt-laden clothes in the washing machine.

But that was weirdly intimate, too. He shoved them in without looking at them, but as he closed the machine door and the clothes started to tumble he saw Claire's wispy bra tangling with his army gear.

Maybe he should have hand-washed it, he thought, but then again…maybe not.

He turned his back on the laundry, thinking as he did that it was over the top—a vast wet room with every machine a laundry could ever hold.

How was it all powered? There was no mains power here, and if there had been it would have surely been knocked out by the storm.

He did a quick reconnaissance of the house, avoiding the passage to Claire's self-contained apartment. Claire's apartment was sparsely furnished, but the rest of the house not so much. Every room was enormous. Every room was lavish. He had a choice of bedrooms, all made up and ready. The unknown Don and Marigold might obviously sweep in at a moment's notice with a bevy of guests.

The refrigerators would cope.

But the power…?

He ended up in the basement and found his answer. Here was a vast bank of batteries, presumably linked to solar panels. This explained why the house was still warm, the refrigerators still operating.

It still wasn't safe for Claire to be here, he thought. Not alone.

Which led to figuring out the radio. He'd found the second transmitter in the study. It was huge and it was useless.

Frustrated, he found a torch and ventured outside. The wind was still up, catching him in its icy chill, but he'd been in conditions far worse than this during his service. The antenna had been attached to one of the outbuildings and it had crashed down during the storm. It lay smashed across the rocks, and with it lay the remains of a satellite dish.

This had been some communications system. A much smaller one would have been far less prone to damage.

Someone had wanted the best—so they could tune into a football game in Outer Mongolia if they wished. He stared bitterly at the over-the-top equipment and thought they could even have used this to talk to Mars if there had been anyone on Mars to hear.

But not now. A small radio might have been within his power to fix. This, he hadn't a hope of fixing.

In this day and age surely there must be *some* method of communicating with the mainland.

Smoke signals?

Right.

He'd seen the maps. This island was far away from normal shipping channels. There might be the odd fishing trawler around, but after the storm the sea would be churned for days. Fishing fleets would stay in port until things settled.

He thought of his grandparents and felt ill.

There was nothing he could do about their distress. *Nothing.*

He could go to bed and worry about it there.

He did go to bed—in the smallest of the over-the-top bedrooms. He lay in the dark and decided that worrying achieved nothing. He should turn his mind off tomorrow and simply appreciate that he was in a warm bed, his world had stopped rocking and he was safe.

He did manage to turn his mind off worrying.

He didn't quite succeed in turning his mind off Claire.

CHAPTER FIVE

SHE WOKE AND the sun was streaming into her little bedroom. She was safe in her own bed, Rocky was asleep on her feet—and she was sore.

Very sore. She shifted a little and her arm protested in no uncertain terms.

She opened her eyes and saw a note propped against a glass of water.

Pills, it said. *Pain. When you wake take these. Don't try and move until they take effect.*

That seemed like great advice. She took the pills that were magically laid out beside the glass and forced herself to relax. If she lay very still it didn't hurt.

Some time during the night Raoul had come into her bedroom and left the pills. He'd checked on her.

Maybe it was creepy.

Maybe it was…safe.

She let the thought drift and found it comforting. No, it was more than that, she thought. He *cared.*

For Claire, the concept of care was almost foreign. She'd been an unwanted baby. Her mother had done her best by her, but there'd been little affection—her mother had been too stressed taking care of the basics. Claire had been a latchkey kid from the time she could first remember, getting home to an empty house, getting herself dinner, going to bed telling herself stories to keep the dark at bay.

She'd gone to bed last night aching and sore and battered, but so had Raoul. She'd seen the bruises. She was under no illusion that he was hurting almost as much as she was, and he must be far more traumatised.

And yet he'd taken the time to check on her during the

night. He'd thought about her waking in pain and he'd done something about it.

'I'm a sad woman,' she said out loud. 'One act of kindness and I turn to mush. And he owes me. I saved his life. Or I think I did.'

'You did.'

The voice outside the door made her jump.

'Can I come in?'

'I…yes.'

She tugged the bedcovers up to her chin and Rocky assumed the defensive position—right behind the hump of her thigh, so he could look like a watch dog but had Claire between him and any enemy.

And he could be an enemy, she conceded as he pushed open the door. He was back in his army gear. It was a bit battered and torn but it was still decent. He was wearing khaki camouflage pants and a shirt. His shirt was unbuttoned at the neck, his sleeves were rolled back to make him a soldier at ease, but he still looked every inch a soldier. He was shaved and clean and neat, but he still looked…*dangerous*.

He was carrying juice.

'You have great refrigerators,' he told her, and the image of a lean and dangerous soldier receded to be replaced by… just Raoul. The guy with the smile. 'I poured myself some juice and then thought I might check if you were awake. It seems presumptuous to forage in the fridge without my hostess's consent.'

'Forage away,' she said. 'You gave me drugs.'

'They're *your* drugs.'

'They're Marigold's drugs,' she told him. 'But I'm taking them anyway.' She struggled to sit up, and found with one arm it was tricky. But then she had help. The juice was set on the bedside table as Raoul stooped and put an arm around her, pushing a pillow underneath.

He was so close. He smelled clean. He felt…

Yeah, don't go there.

'How sore? Scale of one to ten?' he asked, withdrawing a little.

And she hated him withdrawing, even though it was really dumb to want him to stay. To want him to keep holding her.

How sore? Less since he'd walked into the room, she thought. How could a woman focus on her arm when *he* was there?

'Maybe five,' she managed. 'Compared to about nine last night. Five's manageable.'

'It'll ease. The pills will take off the edge.'

'How do you know?' she asked curiously, and he shrugged.

'I'm in the army. Accidents happen.'

'And sometimes…not accidents?'

'Mostly accidents,' he told her, and gave that lopsided smile that was half-mocking, half-fun.

She liked that smile, she decided. She liked it a lot.

'I've been in the army for fifteen years and never had to put a single sticking plaster on a bullet hole. But broken legs and dislocated shoulders, cuts and bruises, stubbed toes and hangovers…as first-aid officer for my unit I've coped with them all. Actually, make that especially hangovers.'

'Why did you join the army?' She was propped up now. She'd taken her pills. Maybe she should settle down and sleep again until the pills worked, but Raoul was here, and she hadn't seen anyone for four months—surely that was a good enough reason for wanting him to stay? It surely wasn't anything to do with how good he looked in his uniform. And how that smile twisted something she hadn't known could be twisted.

'Lots of reasons,' he told her. 'The army's been good for me.'

'Good *to* you or good *for* you?'

'Both. Has this island been good for *you*?'

'I guess.' She thought about it for a moment and then shook her head. 'Maybe not. Six months is a long time. You just heard me talking to myself. I do that a lot. I guess I'm starting to go stir-crazy.'

'The least your employers could do is give you a decent bedroom,' he told her, looking round at her bare little room in disgust. 'You have bedrooms here that are so opulent they could house a family of six and not be squashed, and you're in something out of *Jane Eyre*.'

'Hey, I have my own bathroom. I bet Jane never had that.' She smiled, the pain in her arm receding with every second—and it had nothing to do with the drugs, she thought. It had everything to do with the way this man was smiling at her. 'But every now and then I do sneak into one of the guest bedrooms,' she conceded. 'They all have fantastic views. Rocky and I read romance novels and pretend we're who we're not all over again. But I'm here to get my life back to normal, not indulge in fantasy.'

'You can't stay here,' he told her.

She took a couple of sips of juice and thought about it. 'I have a contract.'

'The contract doesn't hold water. It's unsafe to leave you here alone for six months and now the radio's smashed.'

'I can get a new one.'

'Which could get smashed, too. When we figure out a way to evacuate me, you need to come, too.'

'I can't just walk out.'

'I assume you can contact Don and Marigold?'

'I...yes. When I get satellite connection again.'

'Or when you get to the mainland and email or phone them. You've been injured. You have no reliable means of communication. Any lawyer in the land will tell you you're within your rights to terminate your contract. And,' he said, and grinned, 'I happen to know a lawyer right here, right now. Don't be a doormat, Claire Tremaine.'

'I'm not a doormat.'

'I know that,' he told her.

And here came that smile again. *Oh, that smile...*

'I had proof of that yesterday,' he continued. 'But for today you're allowed to be as doormat-like as you want. And speaking of wants…would you like breakfast in bed?'

'No!'

'Just asking,' he said, and grinned and put up his hands as in self-defence. 'Don't throw the porridge at me.'

'Porridge?'

'I found oats,' he told her. 'And maple syrup. It's a marriage made in heaven. It's on the stove now.'

'I thought you said you weren't going to forage without my permission.'

'I didn't need to forage for these guys. Like the eggs last night, they jumped right out at me. Want to share?'

'I…' She stared at that smile, at those crinkly eyes, at that magnetic twinkle, and there was only one answer. 'Yes, please,' she told him. And then she added: 'But not in bed.'

Because breakfast in bed with this guy around… Some things seemed too dangerous to be considered.

The transmitter was indeed useless.

They stood in the ruins of the radio shack and stared at the shambles and Raoul said, 'What on earth was he thinking? He could have had half of this set up in the safety of the house.'

'But it would have been only half of this set-up.'

Claire was dressed and breakfasted. The painkillers were working; indeed they might not be needed as much as she'd feared, for with her arm held safe in the sling the throbbing had eased to almost nothing. She'd walked outside with him to see the damage. The wind had ceased. The shack holding the radio transmitter was a splintered mess, debris covered the terracing, but the storm was over.

'He wanted to take over one of the rooms in the house,' she told Raoul. 'But Marigold wouldn't have it—a nasty, messy radio transmitter in her beautiful house. So he planned to build proper housing, but of course he wanted it straight away, so he was forced to use this.' She looked ruefully at the mess. 'This was an old whaler's cottage, but it's been a long time since any whaler came near the place.'

'Or anyone else?'

'The supply boat comes once a week. They didn't come this Monday because of the storm. I expect they'll come next week, unless the weather's bad. That's why we have decent supplies.'

'Fishing boats?' he said, without much hope, and she shook her head.

'I've never seen any. I see an occasional small plane, out sightseeing.' She hesitated. 'You're thinking of rescue. Are you sure your friends won't realise you were on a boat and be searching?'

'I'm sure,' he said grimly. 'There were reasons I wanted to be alone. I seem to have succeeded better than I imagined.'

'Hey,' she said, and she touched his shoulder lightly, a feather touch. 'Not completely,' she said. 'You're stuck with Rocky and me. Want to come to the beach?'

'Why?'

'To see if anything's been washed in from your boat.'

'You need to rest.'

'I've had four months of resting,' she retorted. 'Come on, soldier—or can't those bootees make it?'

He was wearing Don's sheepskin bootees. He stared down at his feet and then stared at Claire.

She smiled her most encouraging smile and turned towards the cliff path. Maybe she should be resting, she thought, but there was a reason she was pushing him to come with her.

While Raoul had been in charge—while there'd been things to do—Raoul's smile had been constant. He'd buoyed her mood. He'd given her courage. But now, standing in the ruins of the only way to get messages to and from the island, his smile had disappeared. She'd heard bleakness and self-blame in his voice.

He'd helped her, so the least she could do was help him back. Maybe she should dislocate the other shoulder. She grinned, and he caught up with her and glanced across and saw the grin.

'What? What do you have to laugh about?'

'You,' she said. 'I might need to put a training regime in place if you're not to get miserable. You're stuck here for at least five days...'

'I can't stay for five days.'

'Five days until the supply boat's due,' she said inexorably. 'But Marigold has a whole library of romance novels, and Don has fishing magazines, so cheer up. Meanwhile, let's go see if anything's left of your boat.'

Rosebud was an ex-boat.

The last time he'd seen Tom's boat she'd been upturned in the surf. Now she was nothing more than a pile of splintered debris on the storm-washed beach.

The radio shack and *Rosebud* had held his only links to the mainland and both were smashed. He looked out at the still churning sea and knew he had a lot to be thankful for—but at what cost?

'Will your friend be very upset?' Claire asked in a small voice.

He thought of Tom, and thought of the new boat he could buy him, and he thought Tom would give him heaps of flak and enjoy buying a new boat very much.

'I guess,' he said.

'Is it insured?'

He hadn't even thought of insurance. 'Probably. I don't know.'

'Will you have to cover the cost? Oh, Raoul...'

And she slipped her hand into his with such easy sympathy that it was impossible for him to say, *No, it's okay, the cost of this yacht is hardly a drop in the ocean of my fortune.*

Why would he say that when she was holding his hand and looking up at him with concern?

Um…because otherwise it was dishonest?

Maybe it was, he thought, but she held his hand and he liked it, and he thought if he was to be stuck here for days then he wouldn't mind being treated as an equal.

Time enough to be treated as a royal when he got home.

And the thought struck again. His grandparents… They'd have heard by now. They'd be grief-stricken, appalled and terrified.

Something must have shown on his face, because the hold on his hand tightened.

'It's okay, Raoul,' she said softly. 'You can't help any of this.'

'I could have.'

'Yeah, but that's in the past. You can't do a thing about that now. Focus on the future.'

'Like you have? Should I go find me a rock to sit on for six months?'

'You can have this one if you like,' she told him. 'I'm over it. Hey, is that a boot?'

It was. Rocky had found it. He was standing over it, wagging every bit of him in excitement. Raoul let go Claire's hand—reluctantly—and went to see.'

One boot. It was half hidden under a clump of seaweed.

'Let's see if we can find more,' Claire told him, and they hunted at the high tide mark and found the other, washed in after he'd kicked it off in the water. It was dumb, but their find made him feel a whole lot better.

Could a guy with boots walk home? Maybe not, but when they were cleaned and dried he wouldn't be dependent on Don's slippers. And when he was finally taken off this rock…

'You'll look very nice for the journalists,' Claire told him, and he looked at her sharply.

'Journalists?'

'You think if someone finds you that you'll slip back into Hobart unnoticed? Storm…wrecked yacht…marooned in the middle of Bass Strait…' She brightened. 'Hey, maybe you could sell it to the tabloids. All it needs is a sex angle and you could maybe make enough to pay for your friend's yacht.'

A sex angle...

The comment had been flippant. Off the cuff. It had been all about tabloid newspapers and what sold. It wasn't anything to do with what was happening to them.

So why did it seem to stand out? Why did the words seem to echo?'

What *was* it about this woman that was making his senses tune in to nuances that shouldn't be there? She was injured, vulnerable, alone. He had no business thinking of her in any way other than as someone who'd saved his life and was stuck on this barren, rocky outcrop with him until help arrived.

Think of something else—fast.

He bent and picked up a battered piece of timber, the painted registration number of *Rosebud*, and tried to think of a way he could get a message to the mainland. A way he could get a message to his grandparents.

He tried not to think of the woman beside him, of how she made him feel.

'Chuck a message in a bottle?' she asked.

He looked sharply up at her. She'd better not be able to read his mind, he thought. His thoughts were too tangled, and somewhere in there was the vision of Claire as he'd first seen her, struggling in the water towards him, holding him, her lovely chestnut curls tangled wetly around her face.

Claire...

Yeah, empty the mind fast, he told himself. What had she said? A message in a bottle?

'I suspect your supply boat might be faster,' he said, and she grimaced.

'You're right. Your grandparents will be very frightened?'

'They'll know I won't have gone AWOL.' *As will half the world.* He thought of the rumours that would be circulating. His country had had recent threats centred on the throne. The current thinking was that they had come from a crazy fringe organisation with no resources. Marétal was a small player on the world stage, but his disappearance followed by silence would have the media in a frenzy. His grandparents would be beside themselves.

No boat for almost a week…

'If we had the internet we could try and make a crystal radio set,' Claire said thoughtfully. 'I had a friend who made one once.'

'Good idea,' he told her. 'Except we *don't* have the internet and crystal sets receive but don't send. But if we had the internet we could email.'

'Oh.'

'But good thinking.'

'Don't patronise me,' she muttered.

He grinned. She really was extraordinary. 'I guess we could always burn the place down,' he said, deciding to join her in the planning department. 'If the fire was big enough and we did it during the day the smoke would be seen for miles.'

'Yeah, and if it wasn't noticed…?'

'Is there a cave in any of these cliffs?'

'I don't know about you, soldier,' she told him. 'But Rocky and I don't take kindly to caves. We like our comfy beds. And how would I explain a fire to Marigold? I'm caretaker for this place. Burning it down doesn't exactly come into my job description.'

'It was just a suggestion,' he said hastily.

'A bad one.'

'Okay, a bad one.'

'Hmmph.'

They stared at the sea some more. She was so close, Raoul thought. She was obviously thinking.

He should be doing some thinking. He *was* thinking. It was just that the woman beside him was taking up a whole lot of his thinking room.

'What about an SOS in the middle of the island?' she said, and he hauled his thoughts back to sense when his thoughts really didn't want to go.

'SOS...?'

'We could do it in rocks,' she said. 'There's a flat plateau behind the house. It's strewn with small rocks. We could organise them into an SOS. I'm thinking by tomorrow sightseeing flights might start again from Hobart. A plane might fly across.'

'Do they always fly across?'

'There aren't many,' she told him. 'It's winter. Tourists who pay money for flights will be thin on the ground and we don't have a weather forecast so it might be a lot of effort for nothing.'

He thought about it. SOS. The universal cry for help. Was it justified?

They were both well. They had enough supplies to keep them fed for as long as they were stranded and the house was more than comfortable.

'It'd be for your grandparents' sake,' Claire said, watching him. 'And you might get charged for the cost of the rescue.'

He might.

The cost would be negligible compared to the costs his country would be facing trying to locate the heir to the throne.

Claire was watching him thoughtfully. 'Is it just for your grandparents?' she asked, and he thought about telling her.

I'm royal and there'll be a worldwide search...

Not yet. For some unknown reason a voice in the back of his head was pleading, *Not yet.* She thought he was an equal. A soldier, nothing more.

She'd been battered by people who'd treated her as trash. She was feisty and brave but she'd retreated to this island, hurt.

He didn't want her retreating from *him*. He knew he'd have to tell her, but now the voice was almost yelling.

Not yet. Not yet.

'There'll be a fuss and a half when I get off this island,' he told her. 'Part of me thinks I should just stay. But the fuss has to be faced some time, and my grandparents…they'll be pushing for a search, no matter what the cost.'

And that was the truth, he thought. When he thought of the resources they'd be throwing at it… At *him*… And his two bodyguards… They'd be being vilified and it wasn't their fault. Short of burning down the house, he had to try everything.

'Let's do it,' he said shortly, without answering her question, and she looked at him curiously.

'There's stuff you're not telling me.'

'I'm ashamed of myself.'

'Would the army rescue you?'

'Yes.' That would be the best outcome, he thought. If the army could slip in and take him off the island…

'An SOS seen by sightseers is going to hit the media,' she told him. 'Are you prepared to have your picture taken?'

'I guess it'll be both of us.'

'Not me,' she told him. 'Not in a million years. I'm hiding, remember? If you get taken off by a crew of SAS forces abseiling down with parachutes and stun guns I'll be hiding in Don's basement. Tell them you were taken in by a hermit with a beard down to his ankles who fires at the sight of a camera. Better still…' She hesitated. 'Better still, just wait for the supply boat.'

'I don't think I can.'

'Really?'

'Really.'

She looked at him long and hard. Then she sighed and picked up his waterlogged boots.

'Okay, then,' she told him. 'Let's go dry some boots and organise some rocks.'

* * *

He organised rocks. Claire sat on a rocky ledge at the edge of the plateau and watched.

It was kind of peaceful. The wind had died completely. The weak winter sun was warm on her face. Today was one of the few days she'd had here when the weather made her think this was a wonderful place to stay.

Or maybe it was the company. Maybe it was because the ache in her arm was fading. Maybe it was because she and Rocky were safe and yesterday had made her realise how wonderful 'safe' was.

Maybe it was because she was watching Raoul work.

He worked…like a soldier. He'd decided a small SOS wouldn't cut it—he needed to work big. So first off he'd cleared an area the size of a tennis court. That alone had been huge. Now, the rocks he was heaving weren't small. One-handed, Claire couldn't have begun to help, but even if she'd been two-handed it would have been a big ask.

Raoul had simply set to work, heaving rock after rock. After the first half hour he'd stripped to his waist. He sweated a bit as he worked. His body glistened in the sunlight.

A girl could waste a lot of hours watching that body, Claire thought, and as there was little she could do to help she might as well enjoy it.

She did enjoy it.

She'd spent four solitary months here. She'd only seen the guys on the supply boat—two guys in their sixties, salt-encrusted to their toenails, bearded, weathered, cracking up at their own jokes as they tossed her supplies onto the beach and left her to cart them up to the house.

They hardly talked to her—they were men in a hurry, trying to get their run done and get back to Hobart and the pub. They couldn't know how important they'd become to her—two harried boatmen and fifteen minutes' terse conversation, mostly about the weather.

And now she had her very own guy here, to look at all she wanted, and who could blame her if she was enjoying it very much indeed?

'You're making it very big,' she ventured, and he tossed a few more rocks and wiped the sweat from his forehead with the back of his hand. He was magnificently tanned, she thought, or maybe he was permanently bronzed.

He was gorgeous.

'Last S,' he said, and headed to a pile of rocks that loomed over the plateau. He climbed the rocks as if he'd been bred on cliffs, sure and steady on the shale. This was the high point of the island. He gazed down at his efforts and gave her the thumbs-up.

'Want to see?'

'I don't think I can.' She couldn't get the full effects of his artwork from ground level, but climbing the loose rocks with one arm would be asking for trouble.

'That's what I'm here for.' He slid down the slope, reached her and held out his hand. 'Your servant, ma'am.'

'I'm very sure you're not,' she said a bit breathlessly, and he smiled.

'You saved my life. You've taken me in and fed me. Believe me, Claire, I'm your servant for life.'

And he drew her upright and she was too close. But then he turned and started up the shale again.

A part of her didn't want to be tugged up the shale. It wanted to stop exactly where it was and be held.

But that wasn't Sensible Claire thinking. It was Dumb Claire. And hadn't she made a vow to be Sensible Claire forever?

Tomorrow, she told herself. Or the next day. Whenever the SOS worked. Then she'd be alone again and she could be as sensible as she wanted.

But Raoul was tugging her up the rocks, holding her tight, making sure she didn't slip, and the feeling of him holding her was making Sensible Claire disappear entirely.

Sense would have to be left to the soldier.

'What do you think?'

They'd reached the top. He turned and held her at the waist—in case she slipped?—and she forced herself to stop focusing on the feel of his hands and look down at his handiwork.

He'd cleared the plateau. The rocks he'd used were seriously big. No one could fly over and miss the message he'd made.

He could be rescued today, she thought. A plane could fly over right now and within an hour a rescue chopper could arrive from the mainland. He'd be gone.

She shivered.

'You're cold,' he said, and curved his arm around her as if he could keep her warm just by holding her.

As indeed he could, she thought ruefully. Even hot.

'I've been doing manual work. You should have stayed inside.'

'But I love hard work,' she managed. 'I can sit and watch people do it for hours.'

Wrong, she thought. *I can sit and watch you...*

'Inside now, though,' he told her. 'You need to rest.'

'You're the one who was battered for two days.'

'So I was. So we both need to rest. And then… Do you have any movies on that very impressive entertainment system?'

'Indeed we do.' She thought for a bit, which was kind of hard, because he was holding her and he was really close and his chest was bare and his skin felt…

Um…what was she trying to think of? Movies. Movies would be excellent.

'Actually, they're mostly on the net,' she told him. 'And we have no net with the communications down. But we do have a few oldies but goodies on DVD.'

'I'm all for oldies but goodies. Popcorn?'

'Possibly not. Potato chips and nuts?'

'My favourite. You want me to help you down from this rock or would you like me to carry you?'

And what was a girl to say to that?

Luckily Sensible Claire hadn't completely disappeared. Luckily Sensible Claire said that this guy had had a physical battering and carrying a load—*her*—down the loose rocks would run every risk of disaster.

'I'll walk,' she said, and Dumb Claire almost cried.

CHAPTER SIX

THEY BOTH HAD a sleep. Then Raoul foraged in Don's cellar while Claire cooked a simple pasta dish.

He showed her what wine he'd chosen and she pretty near had kittens. 'Do you know how much that's worth?'

'No.' Then he looked at the dusty label and grinned. 'Though I can guess.'

'Raoul, it'll be half a week's salary.'

'But I could be dead. And Don owes you. He's stranded an employee with no back-up on a deserted island. Hey, and you're a lawyer. We're safe.'

'Right,' she said dryly, but she stopped arguing. Who could argue with that smile?

They curled upon the sofa and ate dinner, and Claire found chocolate, and the wine was truly excellent.

There were three settees in front of the vast TV screen, but two were elegant and only one was squishy and right in front, so it seemed foolish not to share.

They watched *African Queen* and then *Casablanca*. The wine was still amazing. The fire crackled in the hearth. Rocky snoozed by the fireside. They hadn't bothered with lights as the day faded to night. The television and the fire gave enough light.

And then the movie ended and they were left with the glowing embers of the fire.

'Another one?' Raoul asked as Humphrey Bogart walked away in the fog.

Claire was too busy sniffing to answer.

'I guess not,' Raoul said thoughtfully, and produced a handkerchief and dried her cheeks.

And she had enough sense left—*just*—to recognise the linen.

'That's one of Don's monogrammed handkerchiefs.'

'There goes another week's salary,' he said, and smiled into her eyes. 'I can't think of a worthier cause.'

'Raoul…' She should pull back, but he didn't. He traced the track of her last tear and suddenly things intensified. Or maybe they'd been intensifying all day and now they were too aware of each other, too warm and safe, too…*aware*?

Wrong word. There must be another, but Claire couldn't think of one. Actually, she couldn't think of anything but Raoul and how close he was.

She put her own hand up and touched his face—the bronzed skin, the creases at the corners of his eyes, the raw strength she saw there. And something inside her wanted. Badly wanted.

'Raoul,' she whispered again, and her body seemed to move of its own accord. Closer.

'Claire…'

'Raoul…'

Raoul's smile had faded but his hands were still tracing her cheeks. When he spoke his voice sounded ragged. 'I'm aware, my amazing Claire, that you're alone on this island apart from Rocky, and that Rocky doesn't seem to be standing guard right now. Don deserves to be tossed in jail for leaving you defenceless, and I will not take advantage. But…' He hesitated. 'I *would* like to kiss you. So, in the cold light of day…'

'It's night.'

'In the warm glow of night,' he continued, and put his finger under her chin and raised her face to his. 'Would you like to be kissed?'

'You ask me that after *Casablanca*?'

'I know I don't rate beside Humphrey.'

'*How* do you know?'

'Just guessing.'

And she managed a smile back. Sort of. 'I'd have to see.'

'Have you ever kissed Humphrey?'

'No, but I've watched him kiss. He's pretty good. It's no small order to try and match him.'

'You're asking me to try?'

'No,' she said, and her voice was pretty much a whisper. She was feeling melty. Warm. Safe. Loved?

It was a dumb feeling—a mockery, a lie. How could she feel so deeply so soon? But it was there just the same, and there was no way she could ignore it.

'No,' she said again. 'I'm not asking. I'm ordering.'

And then there was nothing to be said. Nothing at all. Because he was taking her into his arms—gently, because of her injured arm. Or maybe gently because there was no way this man would force himself where he wasn't wanted. She knew him hardly at all, but she knew that about him at least.

And she knew more. She knew how he'd taste. She knew how he'd feel. She knew how her body would respond as their lips met, as the heat passed from one to another, as her whole body seemed to melt into his.

She didn't know how she knew, but she did. It was as if her whole life had been building to this moment. It was as if he was the other half of her whole, and finally—finally—they'd come together.

It was a dumb thought. Theirs was a fleeting encounter, she thought, with what little of her mind she had left to think. This man was a stranger.

Except right now he wasn't. For this moment, on this island, he was everything she needed and more.

And caution was nowhere.

He kissed...but what a kiss.

He hadn't expected to be blown away.

He'd expected a kiss he'd enjoy. He'd expected—or hoped for—warmth, arousal, passion.

He hadn't expected his world to shift.

It did.

Was it shock?

Was it the fear of the last few days?

Was it that Claire had rescued him?

Who could say? But somehow being with this woman had changed something inside him, and whatever it was it felt huge.

He'd been in the army for years. He'd worked with feisty women—women with intelligence and honour and courage. Back home in Marétal he'd met some of the most beautiful women in the world. Society darlings. Aristocracy and royalty.

Beauty and intelligence weren't mutually exclusive. He'd dated many of those women and most he still called friends.

Not one of them made him feel like Claire was making him feel now.

He'd known her for less than two days. This was just a kiss.

So how did it feel as if breaking apart from her would break something inside him?

And, amazingly, she seemed to feel the same. Her body was moulding to his and her hands cupped his face, deepening the kiss. She was warm and strong and wonderful, and the feel of her mouth under his was making his body desire as he'd never felt desire.

This wasn't just a kiss. It could never be just a kiss. This was the sealing of a promise that was unvoiced but seemed to have been made the moment she'd crashed into him out in the water.

Claire.

If she wanted to pull back now he'd let her. Of course he would. He must, because this was a woman to be honoured.

Honour.

With that thought came another, and it was a jolt of reality that left him reeling.

This woman had saved his life. She'd been injured, battered, drugged, all to save his sorry hide, and now she was sharing her place of refuge with him.

Right now he wanted her more than anything he'd ever wanted in his life, but…

But. The word was like a hammer blow in his brain.

But he was a man of honour…

A prince…

He hadn't even told her who he was. If this went further she'd wake up tomorrow and know she'd been bedded by the heir to the throne of Marétal.

There'd be consequences, and consequences had been drilled into him since birth.

Bedding a woman he'd just met…

But how could he think of consequences? He was kissing Claire and she was kissing him back. How could he think past it?

How could he draw away?

She wasn't sure how long the kiss lasted. How did she measure such a thing? How could she think of trying to measure? All she knew was that she was kissing and being kissed and she never wanted it to end.

His arms were around her, tugging her body to him. Her breasts were crushed against his chest.

It felt so right. It felt as if she'd found her home.

Raoul. Her head was singing it—an ode to joy. *Raoul.*

Was it just that she'd been stuck alone on an island for four months? Was this some sort of Robinson Crusoe syndrome?

Their passion was pretty much overwhelming her. She seemed to have too many clothes on. Raoul definitely had too many clothes on.

Almost involuntarily her hands moved to the front of his shirt, tugging…

And his hands caught hers and held them.

He put her away from him and it nearly killed him. Every nerve-ending was warring with the caution that had been instilled in him since birth.

But he wasn't only fighting that caution. There was also

a voice hammering inside, pounding out the fact that this was uncharted territory. This woman was special.

This woman had the means to slice through the carefully constructed armour he'd developed ever since his parents died. He didn't need anyone. He'd learned that early. And yet when Claire had surged through the surf to save his life… Yes, he had needed her, and somehow with every moment his body was telling him he needed her more.

But honour demanded that he step away. Honour and the need to rebuild that armour.

And was there a touch of fear in there as well?

No!

She wanted to scream it.

Don't stop. Please don't stop. I want to get close. So close...

But he was putting her back from him. She could see passion in his eyes, a desire that matched hers, but she could also see an almost desperate control.

'Claire… We can't.'

'Why not?'

'It's too soon.' His voice was almost a groan. 'Hell, I want to—I'd be inhuman not to—but you've been injured. You're still shocked and so am I. You're on this island by yourself. I won't take advantage.'

'What are you talking about? You wouldn't be taking advantage. We're both adults.'

'If we'd known each other for such a short time on the mainland…' He had her shoulders, was searching her eyes. 'Claire, would you be sleeping with me tonight or would you be saying wait a little?'

'I don't believe this.'

'I don't believe I'm saying it either. Claire, more than anything in the world I want to take you to my bed right now. But I won't. It's not just honour. It's sense. In the army—'

'What's this got to do with the army?'

'Everything,' he told her. 'And nothing. But in the aftermath of battle there's often emotional meltdown. What we've been through is the equivalent. We can't take this further until you're sure.'

And his words made her stop.

I'm sure.

She wanted to scream it from one end of the island to the other, but all of a sudden she wasn't.

He was being sensible. She hated him for it, but he was right.

If the weather blew up again they could be marooned together for weeks. Sense said that she had to keep her emotions under control.

She didn't want to be sensible.

She drew back, feeling foolish, emotional and, yes, if she was honest, humiliated. And he saw it. He reached out and touched her face again, but this time his touch was different. It was a feather touch. It was a caress all on its own.

'Don't feel like that,' he told her. 'Claire, I'm trained to recognise my emotions. I'm trained for sense.'

'And I'm not?'

'I don't know,' he told her. 'All I know is that the way I'm feeling about you is scaring the heck out of me.'

'So you'll run?'

'Only as far as another movie.'

'Raoul…'

'Claire.' He touched her lips. 'You are truly beautiful. You are truly wanted. But we both know that sense should have us building six-foot walls.'

'I guess…' she whispered, and he smiled at her, that smile that undid every single thing he said about sense.

'I *know*,' he said, and it nearly killed her that he was right.

Somehow she slept that night. Somehow she made it to breakfast. Somehow she swallowed her humiliation and got on with getting on.

But she didn't know whether she wanted a plane to come or not.

At dawn she was already tuned in to the sound of engines, but it was midwinter and the storm would still be fresh in people's minds. That storm had swung up from the Antarctic seemingly with no warning. Tourists would therefore be delaying or cancelling their sightseeing flights, so a plane was unlikely.

Somehow she had to figure a way to get through this without going nuts. She needed a way of facing Raoul and not wanting him…

After breakfast—a meal full of things unsaid, of loaded silences—she decided to cook. Cooking had been a comfort to her forever, so why not now?

'Muffins,' she told Raoul.

'Muffins?' He'd been distant over breakfast. He was obviously finding the going as hard as she was. It seemed up to her to find a way through it.

'If you want fresh food on this island you need to cook,' she told him. 'And I even have frozen herbs. So if we want muffins for lunch…'

There was a silence, and then, 'Do you have apples?'

'Tinned.'

'Hmm.' He considered. 'That might be a challenge, but I'm up for it. You make your muffins. I'll make *tarte tatin*.'

'*Tarte tatin?* With tinned apples?'

'I'm a camp cook extraordinaire.'

'Wow!' She stared at him. He was back in Don's pants and the T-shirt that stretched too tight. They'd showered before breakfast. His hair was still damp. He was still a bit…rumpled.

The man could cook.

So they cooked, but if she'd thought it would make things easier between them she had been dead wrong.

She watched as he made pastry from scratch, his long,

strong fingers rubbing butter into flour as if he'd been doing it all his life.

Wanting him was killing her.

'Who taught you to cook?' she managed. 'Your grandmother? If your mother died when you were so young…'

'Many people taught me to cook,' he told her. 'I was never neglected.'

'It sounds like you came from a wonderful community.'

'I did,' he said, but his answer was curt. Maybe it hurt to go there. 'And you?'

'I taught myself to cook.'

'Not your mother?'

'Mum was on her own. I was an accident when she was eighteen and she had a hard time keeping me. She struggled with depression but she did her best. Early on I learned I could make her smile by having something yummy ready when she got home. She used to clean at the local hair salon and she brought home magazines that had got too tatty. I learned to cook from those magazines. It took me ages to accept that some ingredients were too expensive. I'd write a list, and get fed up when she'd come home with cheddar cheese rather than camembert—but she tried.'

'You both sound…courageous.'

'We weren't courageous. We just survived. Until…'

'Until?'

She shrugged. 'Until Mum couldn't survive any more. When I was fifteen she lost the fight.' She dredged up a smile. 'But by then I could cook—and cook well. I could look out for myself, and I was pretty intent on a career where I could afford good cheese.'

'So you became a lawyer?'

'As you say. I pushed myself hard and libraries were my friend. Study was my friend.'

'Hence the French?' She'd spoken French in the water. He'd hardly remembered, but he remembered now.

'What else was there to do when the nights were lonely?'

she asked. 'Italian. French. Chinese. And cooking—which seemed the most important of the lot.'

'You speak Italian, French and Chinese?'

'Doesn't everyone?' She cocked her head to one side. 'Soldier?'

He couldn't resist. *'Was ist Deutch?'* he demanded. *What about German?*

'Ich spreche Deutsch. Aber ich kann nur verstehen wenn langsam gesprochen wird.'

I speak German but I can only understand if people speak slowly.

'Sie sind eine erstaunliche Frau,' he said.

You are an amazing woman.

She grinned. 'Well, I can understand that. You're not bad yourself. German, French, English… Any more?'

'There might be,' he admitted. 'I have smatterings of a lot. Marétal's official language is French, but it's pretty multilingual, plus years in the army means I've travelled. Want to go head to head with how many languages we can swear in?'

She chuckled. 'No way. Rocky would be shocked. Besides, if we're competing I'd rather cook. Your *tarte tatin* against my muffins?'

'Who gets to judge?'

'Rocky, of course,' she told him. 'And he's a very satisfactory judge. If it's edible he'll give it ten out of ten every time.'

The wind was getting up again. Whitecaps topped the ocean. It was becoming more and more unlikely that there'd be any joy flights over the island today, so therefore why not relax and have a cook-off?

It was an unlikely pastime. If anyone had told him three days ago that he'd be marooned on a rocky outcrop, cooking *tarte tatin* beside a woman he was trying not to go to bed with, he'd have thought they had rocks in their head.

But that was what was happening.

He cooked, but a good half of his attention was on the

woman beside him. She was struggling a little, sparing her bad arm. He'd told her she should rest, that she could watch *him* cook, and she'd reacted as if he'd said she had two heads.

'And let you lord it over me when your *tarte* comes out of the oven? In your dreams, soldier. This is battle!'

It was hardly a grim battlefield. They were watching what each other was doing. Learning. Pausing to watch the tricky bits. And finally they were relaxing.

They were talking about the island and her four months here. The things she'd seen. Her personal quest to rid the island of every bit of fishing line that had ever been washed up there—*'Do you know what damage tangled line can do to wildlife?'* The books she'd read. The story of Rocky—how she'd chosen him from the rescue shelter the day before she'd left for the island and how she'd spent the first month trying to persuade him to come out from under her bed.

She talked of her childhood. She talked of her admiration for the legal assistance organisation she'd worked for and how she never should have left. She talked of its scope and its power. She talked of the disaster of her time in Sydney.

She tried to get him to talk to her.

'Is it the army that's making you silent?' she asked at last. 'They say returned soldiers are often too traumatised to speak. Is that you?'

'That's a blunt question.'

'Hey, I had a mother with depression. I learned early not to sugarcoat things. "Mum, how bad are you feeling? Scale of one to ten." That's what I learned to ask. So there you go, Raoul. How traumatised are you—scale of one to ten?'

'I don't think I'm traumatised.' Though that wasn't exactly true. There had been engagements that he didn't want to think about, and she must have seen it in his face.

'You don't want to go there?' she asked, and he shook his head.

'No.'

'And when your boat turned upside down…?'

'I was too busy surviving to be traumatised. And then along came a mermaid.'

'How very fortuitous,' she said primly. She'd finished her muffins—they were baking nicely—and she'd started on a lasagne for dinner. She was feeding pasta dough into a machine, watching with satisfaction as the sheets stretched thinner. 'So what about your childhood?'

'I don't think I'm traumatised.'

'Not even by your parents' death.'

'I was very young. I can hardly remember them, and my grandparents took over.'

'But you don't want to talk about it?'

'No.'

'Fair enough,' she said, and went back to her lasagne.

He thought she wouldn't press. She didn't sound in the least resentful that she'd just told him all about her and he wasn't returning the compliment.

He *should* tell her about himself.

It would change things, though. Of course it would. The decision not to go to bed with her had been the right one, he thought. Claire could be…his friend?

So if she was just his friend why not throw his background out there and see how it altered things?

He could say… *The reason I wasn't traumatised by my parents' death is that I hardly saw them. They were socialite royals. They had a good time while their child stayed home with the servants. Even after they died my grandparents were distant. The reason I cook is that I spent much of my childhood in the kitchens. The head cook called me* 'mon petit chou' *and hugged me as I licked cake mixture from a spoon. The kitchen was my security.*

But he didn't say it. To admit to being royalty was huge, and what was between them seemed strange, tenuous, uncharted territory. Their friendship had happened so suddenly he didn't know how to take it. He only knew that this woman seemed like a miracle. She'd appeared in the water when he was about to drown. She'd given him life. But then, on land, she'd turned out to be…different. As different a woman as he'd ever met.

A woman who made him feel…vulnerable?

A woman he wanted to protect.

So he said nothing. He fell back into silence as they cooked and Claire was silent, too. She was restful, he thought. She was a woman he could come home to.

Or not leave?

A woman he could stay with for the rest of his life.

Whoa. Where had *that* come from? How crazy a thought was that?

Far too crazy. He needed to get away from here and rebuild his armour—fast. He was a loner—wasn't he?

'Done,' she said, popping her lasagne into the oven and closing the door with a satisfactory click. 'That's timed for dinner.'

'Time for a rest?'

'Why would I want a rest?'

'Your shoulder,' he said tentatively. 'Doesn't it hurt?'

'Only when it jerks, and I'm not jerking. And I don't feel like a rest.'

'Then how about a walk?' More than anything else he wanted to take this woman into his arms and carry her to bed, but there was still a part of him that was rigidly holding back. If a plane arrived now and he was airlifted off the island—what then? What next?

He had to go home.

He could take her home with him.

The thought came again from left field, mind-blowing in its craziness. What was he *thinking*? He'd known this woman for *how* long? *Take it easy,* his sensible self was ordering, and he had to listen, even if it almost killed him.

'A walk would be good.'

She was eyeing him speculatively and he wondered if

she'd guessed what he was thinking. Probably she had, he thought. She seemed…almost fey.

No. In some weird way she seemed almost an extension of himself. She'd know what he was thinking.

And maybe she agreed. If she was indeed some deep-linked connection to himself then she'd be as wary as he was. And as off-balance. And she'd understand his need to rebuild his armour.

'We could go and see the seals,' she suggested, and he tried to haul his thoughts back into order and believe a walk to the seals would be good. It was a poor second to what he'd prefer, but it had advantages.

They were full of muffins. *Tarte tatin* and lasagne were waiting in the wings for dinner. The wind had died a little and Rocky was looking hopeful. A man had to be practical instead of emotional.

But it nearly killed him to nod and agree.

'Excellent idea. Let's go see some seals.'

The seals were on the far side of the island. By the time they reached them Raoul was counting his blessings that he'd found his boots and they were clean and dry enough to be useful.

Claire, on the other hand, was wearing light trainers and was leaping from rock to rock like a mountain goat. Okay, not quite like a mountain goat, he conceded as he watched her. With her arm firmly in its sling, as long as they were off the slippery gravel she was as lithe and agile as a fawn.

'You've been practising,' he told her, and she looked back at him and grinned.

The wind was making her curls fly around her face. She looked young and free and…happy. Something had lifted, he thought, remembering her face two days ago. Yes, she'd been in pain, but there'd been other things going on behind the façade. Things he didn't know yet.

Things he might never know?

How had his presence lifted them?

'I've had four months to practise,' she told him. 'Rock-hopping has become my principal skill.'

'Do you regret coming here?' If he was honest he was struggling to keep up with her. It wasn't strength that was needed here, it was agility—and she had it in spades.

'Yes,' she said honestly. 'I was battered and my pride was in tatters and I wanted to escape. But next time I want to escape, please tell me to choose a tropical island with cabana boys and drinks with little umbrellas.'

'The weather's got you down?'

'The isolation. Rocky's an appalling conversationalist.'

'So will you leave now?'

'How can I leave?' She surveyed a large rock ahead of her, checked it out for footholds and took a jump that had him catching his breath. But she was up on top without even using her hands. Maybe the mountain goat analogy was appropriate after all.

'Because it's not safe,' he told her. 'You're not safe here.'

'I'm safer than walking through King's Cross at three in the morning. That's the red light district of Sydney.'

'So there's another place you oughtn't to be.'

'My chances of getting mugged here are practically zero.'

'And your chances of slipping on a rock and falling and being stuck out here alone, with no one to find you…'

'And being eaten by the seagulls,' she finished for him. 'I thought of that. I'm very careful.'

He watched her tackle another rock. 'Define "careful".'

'I'm safe.'

'You're not safe.'

'You think I should stay in the house and read and cook for the entire time?'

'Don shouldn't have left you out here alone. You shouldn't have come.'

'Okay, I shouldn't have come,' she told him. 'It was a whim when I was feeling black, and, yes, Don told me there was another guy here. I talked to him via radio before I came. He seemed decent. He didn't tell me he intended leaving.'

'And now you're alone with no radio.'

'I can get it fixed. I have the authority.'

'It's smashed. It'll take weeks. Claire, you need to come off the island with me.'

There was silence at that. She paused on the top of the rock she'd reached, looked at him for a long moment and then shook her head.

'Not with you. I'll think about it. But I guess I agree about leaving. Without a radio it's not safe, but the supply boat can take me off. I can stay in Hobart until it's fixed.'

'It's still not safe.'

She turned and started climbing again. 'Define "safe". I thought I was safe in a nice lawyerly job in Sydney and I almost ended up in jail. How safe's *that*? And how safe are *you*? Where's your next assignment? War zones in the Middle East? Do you want to pull out of *them* because they're not "safe"?'

'I'm no longer in the army.'

She stopped then, and turned and stared at him. 'No?'

'No.'

'So the uniform…?'

'Probably needs to be returned—though it does have a few rips. My last pay might be docked.'

'I thought you were AWOL.'

'I'm not. I'm on indefinite leave until I can be discharged. That's why I was out in the boat. I had a last talk to my commanding officer and then went down to the harbour to think things through.'

'So they might not even be worried about you?'

'They'll be worried.'

She nodded, surveying his face. There was a long silence.

'You're not happy about leaving the army?' she said and he shrugged.

'No.'

'But you're safe?'

'Yes.'

'You don't want to be safe?'

'It's time I went home.'

'Because…?'

'My grandfather's in his eighties and he's getting frail. My grandmother worries. They need help.' How simplistic a way was *that* of saying what was facing him?

'Oh, Raoul…'

The wind caught her hair, making her curls toss across her face. She brushed them away with impatience, as if the way it impeded her view of him was important. She was watching his face. She was asking questions she wasn't voicing.

'It's tearing you in two to leave the army,' she said softly, and there was nothing to say to that but the truth.

'Yes.'

'What will you do?' she asked at last, and he shook his head.

'I'm not sure yet. There will be things…that have to be done.'

'Things you don't want to think about?'

'Maybe.'

'Like me when I leave this island.'

'The army's been good to me,' he said. 'This island hasn't been all that good to *you*.'

'Hey, it's taught me rock-climbing skills. It can't be all bad.' She smiled at him—a gentle smile that somehow had all the understanding in the world in it. 'Maybe we're alike,' she said. 'Maybe we just need to figure where our place is in the world and settle. Stop fighting to be something we're not.'

'Like you…'

'A corporate lawyer? Rising above my station? I don't think so. As I said, I'm thinking of getting my job back doing legal assistance, working for the socially disadvantaged. I fit there.'

'That sounds bitter.'

'It's not meant to be.' She took a deep breath and turned to face out to sea. 'I know I'm not socially disadvantaged any more,' she said. 'But I also know where I don't fit. I tried to take a big step from my background and failed. I know where my boundaries are.'

'So if someone asked you to take a huge step...?' Why had he asked that? But he had. It was somehow out there—hanging.

'Like what?' She looked at him curiously. 'Like Don offering me this job? That was pretty crazy.'

'I don't know. Something adventurous. Something fun. All jobs don't have crevices waiting for you to fall into.'

'No,' she said thoughtfully. 'They don't. But it behoves a woman to look for crevices. It behoves a woman to be careful.'

And she turned and leaped lightly to the next rock.

He stood watching her for a moment, thinking of crevices.

Thinking of the royal family of Marétal.

Thinking that Claire Tremaine would think—like him—that royal life might well be one huge crevice.

CHAPTER SEVEN

THE SEALS WERE AMAZING—once you got over the smell. Claire had been there often enough not to be blown away by the aroma, but she watched Raoul's reaction and grinned.

It was a rocky inlet, far too dangerous to swim in or beach a boat, but the seals loved it. The rocks were covered by a mass of seals, mostly pups, basking in the weak afternoon sunlight or bobbing in the sea. A couple of massive bull seals were sitting at either end of the cove, watching over the nursery with brooding power.

'Those guys fight a lot,' she told Raoul. 'They think they're great, but when they're busy fighting I've seen younger males pop in and take advantage. Power doesn't always outweigh brains.'

'You've noticed that?' He shook his head and went back to screwing up his nose at the stink. 'You'd have thought these guys would have sorted a sewerage system.'

'Maybe they don't have a sense of smell. Trust an ex-soldier to go all sensitive on me. Next time we'll pack some air freshener. But come and see.'

This was her favourite place on the island. Her favourite thing to do. The young seals were being joyous, tumbling in and out of the water, practising their diving, sleek and beautiful under the translucent sea and bouncing and boisterous on the rocks. The best vantage place was further round—a rocky outcrop where she could see straight down into the depths. She wanted to take Raoul's hand and tug him to where she intended to stand, but she managed to hold herself back.

She had no right to tug him anywhere, she thought. He was being sensible and she must be, too.

She thought suddenly of the young bull seals, charging

in when their elders were fighting, taking their fill of the females and then leaving. That was what men did, she reminded herself.

But not Raoul. Raoul was different?

Or not different. Just...kind? Not leading her anywhere he didn't intend to follow?

So she didn't take his hand. She headed up to the outcrop herself and willed him to follow. As, of course, he did.

Despite his sense, he was a young bull at heart, she told herself, but she couldn't quite believe it. He was so like her. He was a soldier, a kid with no parents, a man with courage and with strength.

Maybe she could turn and touch his face...

'What's happening?' Raoul asked sharply, and she hauled her attention from thinking about Raoul to the surface of the water.

All the seals were suddenly gone. The water, filled moments ago with tumbling pups, was suddenly clear.

And as they stared a crimson smear bloomed up to the surface. A silver-grey mass swirled underneath and then was gone.

Even the seals out on the rocks stilled. The world seemed to hold its breath.

'Shark,' Raoul said, and his hand slid into hers.

Shark.

She watched the crimson stain spread on the water. She thought of the seal pup, its life over almost before it had begun.

She thought of Raoul in the water two days ago and shuddered.

'You don't swim while you're alone here?' Raoul asked, almost casually, and she shook her head.

'No.'

'I mean...not on this whole island?'

'Only...only when I'm pulling dumb sailors out of trouble.'

'Have you seen this happen before?' His tone was still casual.

'I...yes.' Of course she had. Seal breeding areas were a natural feeding ground for sharks.

'The island's not very big. So there are sharks...*everywhere*?'

'Obviously not where *you* fell in,' she retorted, trying to make her tone light.

'But you knew...?'

'No biggie. My lasagne will be cooked. You want to go back and have dinner?'

'Half my kingdom,' he said, and now he'd forgotten to be casual. His voice was thick with passion. 'It's yours. My life... You swam into these waters to give me that.'

'Seeing as you've already spent more than half your kingdom, drinking Don's wine and smashing your friend's boat, that's not much of an offer.'

'Whatever it is, I mean it. Claire...'

'No biggie,' she said again. 'Leave it, Raoul. I might even have done the same for Felicity.

'You're kidding?'

'Well, I might have swum slower,' she admitted. 'I might not have minded if her toes had been a bit nibbled. But, yeah, I'm pretty certain I would have had to do it for Felicity. Not that I'd have enjoyed it.'

'Like you enjoyed rescuing me?'

She gave him a long, assessing look and she grinned. 'I did,' she admitted. 'There are aspects of rescuing you that I enjoyed very much indeed. But I'm putting them on the back burner. You've decreed we be sensible, and sensible we shall be. Home to lasagne, soldier, and then bed. Alone.'

They ate lasagne and Raoul's truly excellent *tarte tatin*. They watched *National Velvet* and *The Sting*. They were excellent movies. They had trouble paying them the attention they deserved, but they had staying power.

At some time during one of the movies they edged together on the settee. There was only one blanket, and the snacks had to be within reach of both of them. It was only sensible to stay close.

The movies came to an end and they followed them with a nature documentary. Birds in Africa. Raoul thought he should abandon the television and head to his separate bed, but he didn't want to break the moment, and it seemed neither did Claire.

So they both pretended the birds were riveting. She was leaning against his shoulder, nestled against him. His chin was on her curls. She fitted into the curve of his arm.

She felt…*right.*

And he had to tell her.

Somehow he'd found himself with someone who must surely be the most wonderful woman in the world. Though that was a crazy thought, he decided. There must be other wonderful women.

But he'd met many women. His grandmother had pushed many at him, many had launched themselves at him, and he'd even pursued some himself.

None came near this woman. None made him feel like this.

But he'd been acting on a lie. Oh, he'd *told* no lies, but this relationship was moving fast, moving hard, moving to places he'd never been before and it was based on trust.

Claire thought he was a soldier. Claire thought he was a kid with no parents.

That much was true.

Claire thought his background wasn't so different from hers, and he'd let her think that.

He sat with Claire nestled against him and let things drift. He was savouring the feel of her, the silence, the peace of this place. He knew what was waiting for him in the outside world. The palace would be frantic. There'd be a worldwide hunt. The media would go nuts when he reappeared.

He'd like to hurl the SOS stones from the plateau and stay here forever, holding this woman in his arms. But his responsibilities were unavoidable. He'd walked from the barracks and climbed on board *Rosebud* because he'd felt overwhelmed by the responsibilities facing him, and those responsibilities hadn't disappeared.

His country needed him.

And Claire?

She had him confused. The armour he'd so carefully constructed didn't seem to be working against her.

He was a loner. He had to walk away from her—a plane might arrive tomorrow—but when he left he didn't want her to think these few days had been a lie.

She needed honesty.

He touched her cheek and she stirred and smiled—a smile that was so intimate it almost tore his heart.

He knew he made her smile. She made *him* smile.

'Claire…?'

'Mmm…'

All he wanted was to take her into his arms, make love to her and block out the outside world. Put it off. Take every moment of this time and let Claire find out when finally she must.

But *must* was now if she was ever to trust him.

'Claire,' he said softly, and traced her cheek with his forefinger. 'Let me tell you who I really am.'

Royal.

The word was drumming a savage beat all through her body.

Royal.

She should have known.

How *could* she have known? She couldn't possibly. It wasn't as if he'd come out of the surf wearing a crown or something.

She choked on a sound that might have been laughter but

wasn't. Raoul's hold on her tightened, but he didn't say anything. After telling her he was simply holding her, waiting for her to take it in.

And Raoul holding her was part of the dream, too.

This whole thing had been a dream.

Hauling a soldier out of the water, the deadly peril, the lifesaving stuff, being carried up to the house, her shoulder being righted, the care, the comfort and then the kiss. The beginnings of love? That was what it had felt like, she acknowledged, but of course it had been an illusion. A two-day fantasy that had culminated in the greatest fantasy of all.

A prince!

She felt very close to hysterics and her thoughts were all over the place. It was frogs who were supposed to turn into princes. Not gorgeous half-drowned soldiers who were perfect just the way they were.

'I never should have kissed you,' she managed, because she had to say something. Somehow she had to move forward from this moment.

'Because…?'

'Because then you'd still be a frog. And I liked my frog.' She took a deep breath and pushed herself up. She sat and looked at him in the firelight. He gazed calmly back—her soldier, the man she'd felt seeping into her heart, the man she'd thought was within her orbit.

'If we're talking fairytales…'

'*Cinderella*'s another one,' she said. 'And I never understood that story. She got to change rags for tiaras, but everyone would always know there were rags underneath.'

'You're not in rags. And tiaras aren't compulsory.'

And suddenly the conversation had changed. It was all about them. It was all about a future neither had even dared to consider until this moment. A nebulous, embryonic future which suddenly seemed terrifying.

'I shouldn't believe you,' she said at last. 'Why *do* I believe you?'

'Because in telling you I risk losing you,' he said.

He wasn't moving. He was leaning back on Marigold's sumptuous cushions, watching her, giving her the space she didn't want but desperately needed.

'And the last thing in the world I want to do is lose you.'

'You never had me.'

'No,' he told her. 'But, Claire… I'm starting to think that what we have might be…possible…'

And she snorted. How did she feel? Humiliated, she thought. And lost. As if she'd lost something she'd never had.

'After two days?' she managed. 'I don't think so.'

'It's true. If I hadn't told you then you'd be still lying in my arms, and that's all I want. But I had to tell you some time. Claire, does it have to make a difference?'

'A difference to what?' Although she knew.

'A difference to me seeing you again, off the island. A difference to taking this friendship further.'

'You're kidding me, right? A kid from Kunamungle? A baby with no known father? A kid brought up on the wrong side of the tracks—and even though Kunamungle's small, believe me, there *is* a wrong side of the tracks? A woman who couldn't even get accepted in a legal firm? A lawyer with no background, no money, no aspirations, and now with the stigma of fraud hanging over her head? You're telling me you're heir to the throne of Marétal and asking if it makes a difference to a possible friendship? *Yes*, Your Highness…'

'Don't call me that.'

'Yes, Your Highness, it *does* make a difference.'

'Why?' he said evenly. 'Claire, nothing has changed. I still feel—'

'It doesn't matter how you feel,' she snapped. 'Haven't I always known that? It doesn't matter how you feel or what you want or what you hope for. It's what you *are* that matters.'

The night was too long. The house was too big. Their bedrooms were too far apart and Raoul knew he had to leave her be. Claire had retired to a place he couldn't reach, and after breakfast the next morning—another silent breakfast—she headed off for a long walk with Rocky.

'If a plane comes I'll come back,' she told him. 'Otherwise I could be some time.'

'Like Oates of the Antarctic, heading out into the snow for the last time?'

'Hardly,' she snapped. 'I'm not about to die in the snow because of one prince.'

And she stomped off towards the cliffs.

He was left thinking that he really wanted to go with her. But he had deceived her. The least he could do was give her space. This would probably be their last day together. Surely a plane would come soon. Followed by a chopper to take him off the island. Followed by the rest of his life.

It was his last day with Claire and she'd left.

He couldn't blame her. Swapping roles, he might have walked himself, he thought. And then he really thought about it. If he'd been a soldier and only a soldier, and she'd been heiress to a throne, how would he have reacted?

He wouldn't have walked. He'd have run.

Even if it had been Claire?

Maybe.

He didn't do ties, and royalty would have terrified him too.

Maybe Claire was right, he conceded. *Cinderella* was a sexist fantasy. Put a woman in a beautiful gown, give her a tiara and a palace and expect her to live happily ever after? It wouldn't work for him—although the gown and tiara analogy had to change—so why would it work for Claire?

It wouldn't.

So that was the end of that.

But at the back of his mind was a harsh, unbendable wish. The end? It couldn't be. It mustn't be because he wanted her.

So soon?

And there was another problem. With the threat of a plane

arriving at any minute emotions seemed to have become condensed. He was so unsure where this was going. He felt as if his armour had been cracked, and it scared him, but the more he saw of Claire, the more he was prepared to risk.

Too much was happening, too fast. The responsibilities he faced back in Marétal were enormous. The adjustment he was facing made him feel ill. He didn't need emotions messing with what was ahead of him.

He didn't need Claire.

So if a plane arrived today he might well never see her again. A prince from Marétal and an Australian lawyer? How many chances would they have to meet?

Never.

He thought suddenly of his grandmother's demand that he bring a woman to the Royal Anniversary Ball.

Claire?

Polite society would have her for breakfast, he thought. His grandmother alone would be appalled.

Impossible. The whole situation was crazy.

The house was empty, echoing. He found himself straining for the sound of a far-off engine, a plane, the signal of the end of something that had barely started.

Surely it didn't have to end yet.

He abandoned the house and headed down to the cove where Claire had swum to save him. The water was calm today, but the beach was littered with debris from the storm and from the battered *Rosebud*. The yacht was now little more than matchsticks. He searched the beach, looking for anything he could salvage for Tom, but he was doing it more to distract himself rather than because Tom would want anything. Tom was free, off climbing his mountains.

Two weeks ago Raoul had said goodbye and had been consumed with regret. He'd wanted that kind of freedom.

He couldn't have it. And now he couldn't have even a friendship with Claire.

Unless he didn't treat her as Cinderella.

His thoughts were flying tangentially, and all the while he was distracted by the thought that a plane could arrive at any minute. Finally he climbed along the side of the cove, where the waves from the open sea crashed against the cliffs and he couldn't see the sky from the south. If he couldn't see the plane it didn't exist, he told himself, and he almost smiled. It was a game he'd played when he was a child, when he'd been forced to sit through interminable royal events. He'd worked out how to look interested and still disappear inside his head, dreaming of where he'd rather be.

He had no choice as to where he'd be.

Did he have a choice in who he'd be with?

Claire...

She was a beautiful woman and she made him feel as he'd never felt before. Yes, it was too soon to think about the future, but his head wasn't giving him any leeway. He wanted her.

She was an intelligent, courageous woman who was street-smart. She was a woman who spoke Italian and French, and he had no doubt she was fluent. The phrase he'd flung at her in the water had been gasped, yet she'd understood it without hesitation.

Marétal's official language was French, but natives spoke a mix of Italian and French with some of their own words.

Claire was smart. She'd pick it up.

She didn't want to be Cinderella. Who would?

And he... What did *he* want?

Besides Claire.

He forced himself to think sideways, to think of the life he wanted as a royal.

He wanted to make a difference.

Claire would never want a job that involved tiara-wearing and nothing else. Well, neither did he. If he had to go home—and he did—then he needed to make something of it.

With Claire?

Don't think down that route, he told himself. *Don't even think about hoping.*

But the ball… He had no doubt his grandmother would still insist it go ahead. He also knew that if he didn't organise a partner his grandmother would attempt to do it for him, and the thought was suddenly so claustrophobic it almost choked him.

Claire was still front and centre. He thought of her as she could be. Someone not royal from birth but truly royal as she deserved to be. Why *shouldn't* the woman who'd saved his life be his partner at the ball? Even if nothing came of it, it would be a night of fantasy. A night he'd never forget.

She'd never agree. Why would she?

She needed a job to do. She needed to be needed.

Something colourful caught his eye, caught on a pile of seaweed. He stooped and picked it up.

It was a tiny plastic building brick figure. It was a miniature construction worker, complete with a hard hat and a spanner in his hand.

He'd noticed it on the shelf above Tom's bunk, taped fast to stop it falling. He'd commented on it on their first day's sailing and Tom had grinned, a bit embarrassed.

'That's Herbert. I've had Herbert since I was six years old. He's my good luck talisman. Where I go, he goes.'

He'd noticed him when he'd gone aboard again five days ago and thought of Tom, gone to climb mountains without Herbert.

He had Tom's good luck talisman.

And imperceptibly, ridiculously, his spirits lifted. 'Sorry, Tom,' he told his absent friend. 'Take care on those mountains, because Herbert's about to work for *me*.'

Maybe…

He dusted the sand from Herbert and tucked him carefully into his pocket.

'Come on, then, Herbert,' he told him. 'I'll send you on

to Tom when you've done your job here. But now *I* have need of you. Let's see what happens if we offer a lady a job.'

'A job.'

Claire had walked her legs off. She'd been tired, her arm had ached, and finally she'd turned back. She'd known she had to face him some time. She might as well get it over with.

She'd found Raoul in the kitchen, flipping corn hotcakes. He had smiled at her as if nothing had changed. He'd asked politely about her walk and then watched in satisfaction as she'd eaten his hotcakes. Okay, she was discombobulated, but a woman could be discombobulated *and* hungry.

And then he'd said he wanted to offer her a job.

She stared at him, all six feet of gorgeous Prince, and felt herself cringe. What was he saying?

'I don't think royal mistress has ever been one of my career choices,' she said carefully.

'Who said anything about you being a royal mistress?'

'I kissed you. I know it's dumb, but now it makes me feel smutty.'

'You could never be smutty.'

He reached over the table to touch her face but she flinched.

'Don't.'

'Touching's out of order?'

'Until I get my head around this, yes.

'Claire, you're my friend. You're the woman who saved my life. You're also the woman who attracts me in a way I don't understand yet.'

'You lied.'

'I didn't lie,' he said evenly. 'But neither did I tell you the truth. Why would I? It would have made a difference. If we'd lain exhausted on the sand after you helped me out of the water and I'd said, *By the way, I'm a prince,* wouldn't it have changed…everything?'

'Yes.' She might as well be honest.

'Well, maybe that was what my dumb attempt to sail in dangerous weather conditions was all about. For the last fifteen years I've been in the army. Working in a tight-knit unit with men and women focused on a common mission. I've been one of many. But the moment I return to Marétal—the moment I step out of army uniform—things will change. As they would have changed if I'd told you.'

'I thought you were like *me*.'

'How could I be like you? You're beautiful.'

She flushed. 'Don't, Raoul.' She closed her eyes and he could see her trying to tear her thoughts away from the personal. 'The SOS…' she said. 'Your grandparents…'

'They're the ruling monarchs. The King and Queen.'

'So the heir to the throne is missing, presumed drowned?'

'Probably presumed kidnapped,' he said grimly. 'There have been threats. We haven't taken them too seriously—my country seems too small to attract terrorist interest—but now I'm missing they'll be being taken very seriously indeed. I can't imagine the resources being thrown into searching for me.'

'But they won't think of here.'

'They won't think I'm dumb enough to take out a boat without letting anyone know, and Tom doesn't know his boat is missing. I'll have a lot of humble pie to eat when I get home.'

'So you're hoping a plane will come today?'

'Yes,' he said gently, and made an involuntary move of his hand towards hers. And then he pulled back again. 'I have to hope that—if just to stop the anguish of my grandparents and the money being spent on searching for me. But when I'm rescued… Claire, I'm asking if you'll come with me.'

'To this job?'

'Yes. Can I tell you about it?'

'Oh, for heaven's sake…' She got up and filled the kettle, then took a long time to organise cups for coffee. 'I must have been banged on the head. This isn't real.'

'It *is* real. Claire, I can't leave you here. This place is unsafe. You have no radio transmission, and as far as I can see it could take weeks to get technicians here to fix the system.'

'I can order a smaller unit…'

'Which will come by the next supply boat—which might or might not arrive depending on the weather. And you'll still be alone. If you slipped on the rocks… If you swam…'

'I won't swim. Are you crazy? The water's just above freezing.'

'You're quibbling. It's not safe for you to be here and you know it. Don should know it. If you don't tell him then I will.'

'Okay.' She turned to face him, tucking her hands behind her back like an errant child facing a stern teacher. 'I shouldn't have come here,' she conceded. 'Like you, I made a spur-of-the-moment decision and I accept it's not safe. So, yes, I'll lock up and go to Hobart—but that's as far as I'm going. You head back to your royal fantasy. And I'll…'

'You'll what? Look for a job? I'm offering you one.'

'Raoul…'

'I won't let this go,' he said, steadily and surely. 'Claire, this thing between us… I've never felt anything like it and I can't walk away. But I've scared you silly. Plus, it's too soon. We've been thrown together in extraordinary circumstances. If you were Sleeping Beauty I'd see you for the first time, fall in love with you on the spot and carry you away to my castle for happy-ever-after. But that story's always worried me. After the initial rush of passion, what if she turns out to have a fetish for watching infomercial television? Or women's wrestling? What if she insists on a life devoted to macramé?'

'I don't know what macramé is,' she said faintly.

'Exactly. And therein lies the brilliance of my plan.'

'The job?'

'The job,' he agreed. 'Claire, I have a problem. I've upset my grandparents enormously. In three weeks there's a ball to celebrate their fifty years on the throne. I imagine that right now it's been cancelled, but as soon as I turn up alive my grandmother will resurrect it. She's indomitable.'

He paused. Claire handed him a mug of coffee. He took a sip and grimaced, as they both did when they tasted this coffee. There was nothing like caterers' blend to make you rethink your caffeine addiction. But even the truly awful coffee wasn't enough to distract him from what seemed such a nebulous plan.

'And…?' she prodded.

She really shouldn't talk to him of the future, she thought. He was a royal prince. He had nothing to do with her.

Except she'd kissed him and she'd wanted him. Her body still did want him, regardless of what her mind was telling her. Was desire an excuse for keeping on talking?

'I'm expected to have a partner for the ball,' he said in a goaded voice, and she decided she needed to stop wanting straight away.

'So you're going to ask me?' she managed. 'Cinderella.'

'I told you—I don't buy into Cinderella.'

'And I don't buy into balls. Or royalty. Or—on a basic level—being surrounded by people who think they've been born better than me.'

'I would *never* think that.'

'You don't need to. It's bred into your genes. You look down your aristocratic nose…'

'That's insulting,' he said, suddenly exasperated. 'Can you get off your high horse and listen to a perfectly good job offer?'

She thought about it, or tried to think about it, and then decided the only way to think about anything was not to look at Raoul. *Prince* Raoul, she reminded herself savagely, and she plonked her cup hard on the table, spilling about a quarter of the contents, and stared into what remained.

'Shoot.'

'Shoot?'

'Go ahead. Tell me about your job so I can refuse and get on with my life.'

'Claire…'

'Talk,' she ordered. 'I'm listening, but not for very long.'

CHAPTER EIGHT

BUT IN THE end she did listen.

In the end it sounded almost reasonable.

'A couple of years ago one of the Australian soldiers I was on an exercise with told me about his son,' he told her. 'The boy was faced with a lengthy jail term for being immature, gullible and in the wrong place at the wrong time. It seems the legal assistance service you worked for helped him escape conviction and gave him another chance. To my shame I'd forgotten it until you mentioned it, but I know we don't have such a service at home—legal help for those who can't afford lawyers. Claire, if I'm to return as more than a figurehead I'd like to institute a few reforms—reforms long overdue. I've never had the authority to make those changes, but maybe it's time for a line in the sand.'

'A line...?'

'You'd be the beginning of my line,' he told her.

She dared a glance at him and discovered he was smiling. She went back to her coffee fast. 'What do you mean?'

'I mean you would accompany me back to Marétal. You'd be greeted by my grandparents as the woman who saved the life of the heir to the throne. And I'll say I've offered you a job—investigating the need for such a service in our country.'

He held up his hand to prevent her instinctive protest.

'Claire, hear me out. My idea is that you'd spend a month talking to our public services, talking to the people high up in the judicial system, assessing whether our system is similar enough to the Australian system for something like legal assistance to work. Given you'll have access via me to whoever you want to speak to, a month should be sufficient to give you an overview. And then you'd go home.'

She did raise her eyes then. She stared up at him in astonishment. 'I'd go home?' she managed.

'Once you've spoken to my people I'd ask—through diplomatic channels—that you have the same access to yours. Then I'd ask that you put forward a proposal for Marétal. It might be six months' work to put together such a proposal, but that six months…' He hesitated. 'Claire, we could use it. We could just…see.'

'See what?' She was having trouble speaking.

'See where we are at the end of six months,' he told her. 'See if we feel the same as we do now. See whether this relationship has legs.'

'Legs…' she muttered, and managed a sort of smile. 'Slang in how many languages?'

'How many do *you* know?' He shrugged. 'Claire, you're smart, you're strong, you have solid legal training and you know enough about the needs of low-income earners to be empathic. You're what our country needs.'

'Others could do the job.'

'I want you.'

And there it was, out in the open, staring at them like a two-headed monster.

I want you.

She could say the same.

She couldn't.

'The ball…' she muttered, and he gave a slightly shamefaced grin.

'That's the pay-off,' he told her. 'A favour, if you like. Claire, I can't pretend there's nothing between us. There is. We both know it. If you come back to Marétal I won't deny there's an attraction.'

'You think I'd move into your palace? Not in a pink fit.'

He grinned. 'How did I know you'd say that? But my plan's more practical. We could find you a nice little apartment in the legal quarter of the city. You'd start work. There'll be a flare of publicity when we arrive, but it'll settle. It'll be suspected that we have a relationship, so there will be media interest, but it won't be over the top.' His grin turned a bit lop-sided. 'I *have* had girlfriends before.'

She tried not to smile back. She tried really hard.

She failed.

'Really?'

'Really.' And then he did reach out and take her hand, and she knew she should pull back, but she couldn't. Not when it was Raoul.

'And thus we come to the brilliance of my plan,' he told her, and she blinked.

'Brilliance?'

'I could escort you to the ball. My grandmother couldn't object because you're the woman who saved my life. She'll stop throwing society darlings at me for a while. She and my grandfather will have a wonderful ball, which they'll thoroughly enjoy, without my grandmother watching me every minute of the night to see who I'm dancing with. You'll get to wear a very beautiful dress—did I tell you I owe you at least a gown? And then you could go home.'

She stared at him blankly. 'Home. To Australia. I don't get it.'

'You should,' he said gently, and his hold on her hand tightened. 'Claire, I think I'm falling for you,' he said. 'But after this short time of course I can't be sure. To be honest, relationships have always scared me. I've been a loner all my life and I'm not sure I can stop being a loner. If you're feeling the least bit like I am you'll be feeling just as uncertain. Plus, the thought of royalty scares you. I'm not surprised—it still scares *me*. But this scheme gives us time. By the night of the ball you'll have had weeks in the country. Then there'll be the ball, which will be royalty at its most splendid. Afterwards you'll get on a plane and you'll spend a few paid months back in Australia investigating the intricacies of legal assistance on Marétal's behalf. And thinking about me—us.'

'Thinking about you…us?'

'That's my hope,' he said, and threw her one of those gorgeous grins that made her heart twist.

Oh, my... Where were her thoughts? They were all over the place. *Think,* she told herself. *Stop sounding like a parrot and get real.*

'The whole idea's crazy,' she managed.

'Tell me why.'

'If you want to find out about our legal assistance scheme you should send one of your own people out here to see how it's done.'

'I could,' he agreed. 'But if I gave the job to any of my senior people they'd come with prejudices. They'd think they'd be doing the old school lawyers out of jobs, and the younger staff wouldn't have the clout to ask the right questions. Claire, you wouldn't be changing anything. All you'd be doing at the end of six months would be handing over a concept that our people could work with.'

Our people. How had he suddenly transformed into a royal? she thought. Last night he'd been a soldier and her friend. Okay, being honest, he'd also—almost—been her embryo lover. Being honest with *herself,* if he'd taken her to bed she would have gone and gone willingly.

But today…

'If I gave the job to any of my senior people...'

He was speaking as a prince. He *was* a prince. He was as far from her as the sun was from the earth.

He was holding her hand.

'But why? Why me?' she demanded. 'And why now? Surely this legal assistance scheme isn't a priority?'

'It's not a priority,' he agreed. 'But it is a real need, and it's my need, too. And I hope yours. Claire, it's not safe for you to stay on this island. You must see that. Soon we'll be taken off. When we do the eyes of the world will be on us. I'm sorry, but I can't stop that. In Australia I can't protect you from media hype. In my country I can—to an extent.

The palace can call in favours. Yes, there'll be speculation, but we can live with that. The line is that I met you, I was impressed with your legal credentials…'

'You don't know anything about my legal credentials.'

'I do,' he told her. 'How can I doubt that they're impeccable? Not only do I trust you, I can ensure the world will, too. Two minutes after we land in Hobart there'll be a legal suppression order thumped on the appalling Felicity and her friends. If one whisper of improper conduct comes out, your ex-firm will be faced with a libel suit so massive it'll make their eyes water. Claire, what I'm proposing is sensible, but it's not sense I'm talking. It's desire. This way you come back to my country. I won't be able to spend much time with you between now and the ball, but you'll see enough of me—and I'll see enough of you—to decide if we have the courage to take this thing forward.'

'Courage…'

'It *would* take courage,' he told her.

His fingers were kneading hers gently, erotically, making her feel as if she wanted to stop talking this minute and head to the bedroom while there was still time. But of course she couldn't. Raoul was talking sense and she had to listen.

Sense? To fly to the other side of the world with a royal prince? *Her?* Claire Tremaine?

Her head was spinning. The only thing grounding her seemed to be Raoul's hold on her hand, and surely she shouldn't trust that.

'It would take courage,' he said again, as if he'd realised her mind was having trouble hearing, much less taking anything in. 'But what I'm suggesting takes the pressure off as far as I can figure how to do that. You'd stay in my country until the ball. You'd dance with me as my partner.'

He gave another of his lopsided grins and she wished he hadn't. It made her… Well, it made it a lot harder for her to take anything in.

'It would be a favour to me,' he told her. 'It would take the pressure from me. It would make my grandparents happy…'

'That you're dancing with a nobody?'

'They can hardly think you're a nobody when you saved my life.'

'Don't you believe it.'

'Claire, stop quibbling,' he said, firmly now. 'Because straight after the ball you'll have a return ticket to Australia. Ostensibly to research a legal assistance system on our behalf. No—*really* to research a legal assistance system. That will give you time to come to terms with everything you've seen and with how you feel about me. It will give us both time. You can return to Australia with a job to do and we can both take stock of how we feel. No pressure. Your call.'

No pressure.

No pressure?

Her head felt as if it was caving in.

'You don't know what you're asking,' she managed, and he took both her hands then, tugging her so she was looking straight at him. What had happened to their coffee? Obviously that was what happened when you used caterers' blend, she thought tangentially. You got distracted by…*a prince*.

'I *do* know what I'm asking,' he told her. 'And it's a shock. To you, though—not to me. Claire, I knew the moment you pulled me from the water that your life had changed. You don't save royal princes and then get marooned on deserted islands with them for days without media hype. You *will* get media hype, and I'm sorry. But there's also this thing between us—this thing which I'm not prepared to let go. With my plan… I'm trying to rewrite the *Cinderella* story. I'm trying to figure how to get through this with your dignity as top priority. This way you'll come to the palace, you'll meet my grandparents, you'll see things as they are. Then you'll come to the ball as an honoured guest. And, yes, I'll dance with you—a lot—but in real life the Prince has to dance with others, because feelings can't be hurt. And you'll dance with others, too, because men will be lining up. And at midnight…'

'Where's my glass slipper?' she said shakily, and tried to smile.

He smiled back. 'That's where the plot changes to what it should be. At the end of the ball I'll put you back into your carriage, which won't turn back into a pumpkin, your luggage will be waiting and you'll take your return ticket back to Australia. I won't come hunting for you. You're your own person, Claire. If you take this job then you have months of secure employment, doing work my country needs. And then you can work out if you have the courage to return.'

'Why…why would I return?'

'Because, fast as this is, and even though I've known you such a short time, I suspect I'll be waiting for you.'

'But no promises?' she said, fast and breathlessly, and he nodded.

'No promises from either of us,' he told her. 'Both of us know that. But this is a chance…our only chance…to wait and see. If you have the courage, my Claire.'

'I'm not your Claire.'

'No,' he agreed. 'You're *your* Claire and the decision is yours. Will you come home with me and give us a chance?'

And what was a woman to say to that?

How could she look into those eyes and say no?

She might have courage, but her knees felt as if they'd sagged under her—and she wasn't even standing.

'Claire?' he said softly, and put a finger under her chin and raised her face so her gaze met his. 'Will you come with me?'

'Yes,' she whispered, because there was no other response. 'Yes, I will.'

And then the world broke in.

At two that afternoon a small plane swooped low over the island.

After four months of isolation the pilots of such planes, like the captains of the supply boats, seemed to have become Claire's friends. They weren't really. They were people doing their job. She couldn't talk to them, and she didn't even know their names, but she usually walked outside and waved. Sometimes they flew low enough so she could see people waving back.

They'd just finished lunch, a mostly silent meal during which too much seemed to be happening in their heads for talk to be possible. Raoul had talked of practicalities and Claire had listened, but mostly her head was full of one huge question.

What had she agreed to do?

The sound of the plane was almost a relief. She glanced out of the window and hesitated. 'If I go outside and wave they'll think I'm okay,' she told him. 'They might not even see the SOS.'

'No one can miss my SOS,' Raoul told her. 'And if you *don't* go outside we'll have people thinking you might be wounded. I didn't have enough rocks to write a detailed explanation of the problem underneath. Claire, we need to be seen. Together. I assume they know you're usually alone here? They'll see us. The wreckage from *Rosebud* on the beach is self-explanatory. Let's go.'

So he led her outside, and they stood on Marigold's Italian terrace, and Claire waved and Raoul stood silently by her side.

He seemed grim.

And as she waved for the first time it struck her. What he was asking of her was huge, but what he was facing himself was even bigger. He'd been in the army for fifteen years—a rugged life, dangerous, challenging, but obviously something he felt deeply about. He was back in his army uniform now, having decided he wouldn't risk facing the world in Don's gear. But it was more than that, she thought. In his army gear he knew who he was.

She glanced at the set lines on his face and thought again of the reasons he'd walked down to his friend's boat and set out to sea.

This was an ending for him. And end of being who he wanted to be.

The start of his royal life.

'You'll be brilliant,' she said, and he looked down at her, startled.

'What…?'

'As a prince. You'll be amazing. Look at you now—you've had three days lying around here and you could have… I don't know…rested on your laurels, played the royal Prince, ordered me around like anything…'

'As if I would.'

'Exactly,' she said. 'Instead you taught me how to make *tarte tatin*, and if nothing else ever comes of this then I thank you. You've assessed this whole situation. You came over all bossy when you told me I need to leave. But more…you thought of the legal assistance thing—and, Raoul, I know that's partly for us, but it's also for your country. You're thinking of what it needs. If you start that way you'll be brilliant. I know you will.'

'Not unless…' And then he stopped. 'No. I won't blackmail you.'

'Excellent,' she said as the plane swooped low, did a one-eighty-degree turn and swooped again, right over the centre of the island where Raoul's SOS stood out like a beacon. 'Because we both have enough pressure on us already. All we can do is face forward and get on with it.'

CHAPTER NINE

THREE WEEKS LATER, in an apartment in Marétal's secure legal precinct, she woke where she wanted to spend the rest of her life.

She woke in Raoul's arms.

'Let me not move.' She murmured the words to herself, not daring to whisper, hardly daring to breathe. 'Let me hold this fantasy as truth.'

For this *was* a fantasy. This was where Cinderella could have her fairytale, she thought. In the arms of her Prince.

No. She wasn't in the arms of her Prince. She was in the arms of the man she loved.

And almost as she thought it Raoul woke, and the arms that had held her even in sleep tightened. Her body was spooned against his. Her skin was against his. The sensation was almost unbearably erotic. The sensation was pure… fantasy.

'I can't believe it's only weeks since I first kissed you,' he murmured into her hair. 'It feels like months. Or years.'

They'd been businesslike, as planned, even though it had almost killed them. But they'd had to be. They'd travelled back to Marétal together, but as soon as their plane had landed Raoul had been absorbed back into the royal family.

Claire was being treated as an honoured guest. The story was that she'd rescued him and he'd been fortunate enough to persuade this skilled lawyer to take an outsider's look at the country's legal system.

There'd been mutterings from the legal fraternity—'Why do we need such an overview?'—but she was young and non-threatening and the royal sanction was enough to keep the peace.

There'd been more than murmurs from the media—of

course there had: *Prince trapped on remote island with glamorous Australian lawyer.* But Raoul had organised her clothes to be couriered from Sydney. She'd taken pains to appear in the prim clothes she customarily wore for work.

There'd been a lavish dinner held by the royal family to thank her formally for her heroism, and Raoul had sat by her side, but she'd deliberately dressed plainly, with little make-up and her hair arranged in a severe knot. Raoul had been charmingly attentive, but he'd carefully been charmingly attentive to the woman on his other side too, and the rumours had faded.

The media would have killed to listen in on the phone calls Raoul made to her every night, the calls she held out for, but the apartment he'd organised for her was in a secure part of the legal district where privacy was paramount.

'If I so much as smile at you in the way I want to smile at you you'll be overwhelmed,' Raoul had told her, and she'd agreed.

This was the plan. She was here to do a job—wasn't she? Nothing more. And Raoul's calls… They were those of a friend.

Except she knew in her heart they were much more. She should stop them, she thought, but she couldn't bear to.

And the calls were a mere fraction of her day. For the rest of the time she could tell herself they weren't important. She'd buried herself in the work she was here to do, and somewhat to her surprise had found it incredibly interesting. There *was* a need. She could do something useful. Paths had been opened to her through Raoul, and through the interest in her background. She'd learned a lot, fast.

What she'd also learned was how constricted Raoul's life was. He could go nowhere without the eyes of the world following.

But finally, last night, Raoul's promise to keep his distance had cracked. A plain black Jeep had driven up to her apartment and paused for maybe five seconds, no longer. A soldier had stepped out and he'd been inside her apartment before the Jeep had disappeared from sight.

If anyone had been watching—which they probably hadn't, because interest had died down—they'd simply have seen a shadow, and that shadow had disappeared so fast they could never have photographed it.

The shadow had finally risked coming.

And Claire should have greeted him formally, as a friend—no, as an employer—but it had been three long weeks, and the phone calls had become more and more the centre of her day.

And, sensible or not, she'd walked straight into his arms and stayed.

The shadow was now holding her. He was running his lovely hands over the smoothness of her belly. He was kissing the nape of her neck. He was sending the most erotic of messages to every nerve-ending in her body.

Raoul. Her fantasy lover.

Her Prince.

'How long can you stay?' she whispered to him now. She scarcely dared to breathe the question but it had to be asked. This night had been so unwise but it would have to stop. Was this all there was? One night of passion, maybe two, before she returned to Australia?

It had to be—she knew that.

Because she needed to return. She'd known that from day one, when she'd seen the sea of photographers pointing their cameras at her. Raoul was royalty and he lived in the media glare, and even if she was ever deemed suitable for him she had no wish to join him.

Except for the way he held her.

Except for the way she felt about him.

Except for now.

Last night… It had been as if two halves had found their whole. She'd walked into his arms and she'd felt complete in a way she'd never felt before.

Raoul had warned her he was coming and she'd made dinner. Dinner had been forgotten.

Dinner had turned into all night.

Dinner had turned into perfect.

'I'm taking all day,' he murmured into her hair, holding her closer. 'Imperatives be damned. You can't believe how much I've missed you. Holding you feels like it's making something in me complete. My Claire. My heart.'

'I can't be your Claire, Raoul. It's taken you three weeks to find an opportunity to come.'

She didn't say it as a reproach. It was simply fact. She'd learned by now how much his country needed him. But he wanted to explain.

He rolled over, propping himself above her so he could look down into her eyes. 'Claire, you know why. You didn't want to come to this country as my lover. Neither of us wanted that. We had to let the media interest die. But we can't go on this way. Maybe it's time to let the world know what's between us.'

He kissed her then, lightly on the lips. Or he meant to. His kiss deepened, and when it was done he pulled back and the smile was gone from his eyes.

'I want you,' he told her. 'I've never wanted a woman as I've wanted you. I've never needed a woman. Claire, every time we talk I'm falling deeper and deeper in love with you. My days have been a nightmare, a jumble of pressing needs, but every night I've called you, and that's what holds me together. Claire, I know it's early. I know I said you're free to go—and you are. But if you could bear to stay for longer… If you could bear to be seen by my side…'

And the world stilled.

She loved him. She knew she did. Their time on the island had been the embryo of their loving. The flight back to Marétal had made it grow. The long calls every night… The sight of him in the newspapers, discussing the needs of his country, shouldering a responsibility she knew was far too heavy for one man…

But to announce their love to the world? To let the media in?

'You could face that?' She said it as a breathless whisper and he smiled then—that smile that did her head in, the smile that wanted her to agree to anything he suggested.

Anything? Such as walking out onto the balcony and shouting to the world that they were lovers?

Staying with Raoul seemed right. But the rest… It did her head in.

'Still too soon?' he asked, sounding rueful. 'Claire, I've known you for less than a month and yet I'm sure.'

'But…' she managed, and he sighed and closed his eyes, almost as if he was in pain.

'But,' he agreed. 'I live in a goldfish bowl. It's a privileged goldfish bowl, but that's what it is.'

'You're doing your best to improve your bowl,' she told him, striving for lightness.

Striving to keep the underlying question at bay. Or the underlying answer. The answer she knew she'd have to give.

'The news is full of reports of the discussions you've been having with your grandparents and parliament,' she told him. 'They say you're dragging Marétal into the twenty-first century. You want parliament to have more power. You want the people to have more say. And yet the Queen is arguing.'

'My grandparents have held the rule of this country for fifty years,' he told her, following her lead, maybe realising how much she needed to play for time. 'They've wanted me to share that rule. It's come to the crunch now, though—they *need* me to share rather than *want* me to. I hadn't realised quite how frail my grandfather is and how much my grandmother depends on him. So they need me. But I've told them that if I'm to inherit the throne I'll do it on my terms. Or walk away.'

'*Could* you walk away?'

He'd hugged her around so they were face to face on the pillows—the most intimate of positions. His nose was four inches from her nose. His hands still held her waist. They were talking of something as mundane as…inheriting a throne.

'If they won't agree then I might not have a choice,' he told her. He sighed. 'She's fighting me every inch of the way. Even security for the ball… Our security service is tiny, but it should *be* there. She refuses to have officers in the ballroom. But with so many dignitaries from so many places how can we check? The ball is for my grandparents and she insists on having her way.'

'And if she keeps insisting?' She couldn't help it, a tiny flicker of hope kindled and flared. If he could abandon the throne… If he could just be what he once had been… Raoul. Soldier. Sailor.

Lover.

'I don't know,' he said bleakly. 'I'm trying to think of a path but there's no one else to take it on. I have no cousins, and the constitution states that the country reverts to being a republic if the throne has no heir.'

'Is that a problem?'

'After so many years under a monarchy parliament's weak. Anything could happen.'

'So you're stuck?'

'I think I am.'

The flicker of hope faded. Raoul smoothed her face with his beautiful hands and kissed her on the eyelids.

'Don't look so sad, *ma mie*.' He hesitated. 'Is it possible…?' He drew back a little so he could look directly into her eyes. 'Is it possible that you've already decided you can't be with me?'

How to make him see…? 'Raoul, you know I'd stay—but three weeks…and this is the first time…'

'Because of caution. With no caution I'd have had you in my bed every night.'

'And have the whole world looking down on me?'

'Is that courage speaking?' An edge of anger came into his voice. 'Are you *so* afraid of what people will think?'

'Your grandmother made it quite clear… My dog…'

He managed a smile at that. The Queen had asked Claire to be brought to her straight from the airport. Rocky had just been released from his crate. The royal couple had been on the palace steps to greet their heir's saviour.

'It was me who dropped the leash,' Raoul said ruefully. 'After twenty-four hours in a cage he did what any dog would do. She'll warm to him.'

'He's not remotely pedigree. Like me.'

'What's the reverse of a snob? Someone who's proud of her convict ancestors? That should be you. *I'm* proud of your ancestors,' he told her. 'They produced *you*.'

She managed to smile, but the knot of pain within was killing her. The thought of what he was asking was huge. To stand beside him in the glare of publicity… To pretend to be something she could never be…

'Raoul, I can't do this. I need to go home.'

His smile faded.

'I know you do,' he said softly. 'I did know, even from the start, that asking such a thing of you was grossly unfair. I think I've always known what your answer would be. In your place my answer would be the same.'

He sighed then, and kissed her once more, his lovely hands caressing her body, making every sense cry out that here was her place. But it wasn't. It never could be.

'Don't be sad.' He kissed her eyelids again, and maybe there was the beginning of tears there for him to kiss. 'Let's pretend. Grant ourselves a little more time for fantasy. The ball is on Friday. You need to come to the palace to be fitted for a ball gown. I'm being fitted for my own uniform today. So—a fantasy afternoon with swords and tassels and tiaras and lace. Can you have fun with me? My grandparents are in the country, so we'll have the place to ourselves.' He grimaced. 'Well, that's if you don't count a hundred-odd staff, but we pay them well to be discreet. And afterwards...a picnic in the palace grounds? Out of sight of prying lenses? Rocky's more than welcome. What do you say, my Claire? A day of fantasy and fun before we accept reality?'

How should she respond? She glanced across the room to where her severe black jacket hung on the back of a chair—her legal uniform, her life after this time-out.

Her time with Raoul.

'We should end it now,' she whispered, because she had to. Because how was it fair on Raoul to keep him loving her one minute longer?

'Do you want to?' he asked, and his hands caressed her body, and he touched her lips and smiled. 'Now?'

'Raoul...'

'Another week,' he told her.

'Of one-night stands?'

'I'll take what you give me, my love,' he told her. 'Because the rest of my life is a very long time.'

So there were undertones of impending sadness and inevitability, but at some time during the next few hours Claire gave herself up to the idea of enjoying this short sweet time, taking what she could and walking away with memories.

At least that was what she told herself in the sensible part of her brain. But most of her brain was taken up with simply being with Raoul. The future was some grey, barren nothing. For now there was only Raoul—only the way he held her, the way he smiled at her, the way he loved her.

At midday another Jeep arrived discreetly at her apartment and Claire and her shadow soldier—and Rocky—slipped into the back. Then the Jeep made a circuitous journey to the royal palace, and Claire and her dog and her shadow were in Raoul's world.

They drove past the grand entrance, where the King and

Queen had watched down their noses as she'd stumbled through formal greetings.

The palace was a storybook fantasy—a concoction of white stone, turrets, battlements, and heraldic banners floating from spires. The palace scared her half to death. This time, though, they drove around to the back, winding through formal gardens into a place that seemed almost a secret wilderness. The driveway curved onto gravel, accentuating the sense of country, and the Jeep finally came to a halt at a far less intimidating entrance, built between stables and a massive conservatory.

A servant did come down the back steps to greet them, but he was dressed in smart-casual. He was in his sixties, white-haired and dignified, and his smile was warmly welcoming.

'We're happy to have you back, miss,' he told her, and his tone said he meant it.

'Claire, this is Henri Perceaux—my grandparents' chief advisor,' Raoul told her. 'Anything you need to know about this country, ask Henri. On top of everything else, he's my friend. He taught me how to ride a horse when I was six.'

'That's something I've always longed to do,' Claire told him, and both men stared at her as if she'd grown two heads.

'You're Australian and you don't ride?' Raoul demanded.

'Nor do I pat kangaroos as they hop down the main street of Sydney,' she retorted. She shook her head. 'Stereotypes… Just because I'm Australian…'

'Apologies,' Raoul said, and then fixed her with a look. 'But you *can* surf, right?'

'Um…yes.'

'Then you can still be an Australian. Even if we're about to fit you with a tiara.'

'You're about to fit me with a *tiara*?'

'I've a team of dressmakers organised to discuss what you'd like to wear to the royal ball,' Henri said, sounding apologetic. 'If it's satisfactory with you, miss?'

She took a deep breath. Where was a fairy godmother when she needed one? she thought. One wave of her wand and Cinderella had a dress to die for. Cinders never had to face a team of dressmakers.

'Anything you want, they will construct,' Raoul told her. 'Let your imagination go.'

'My imagination's frozen. I don't know much besides black and jeans.'

'Then let yourself have fun,' Henri interspersed. He cast a covert glance at Raoul. 'That's a lesson that needs to be learned. You can still be royal *and* have fun.'

'Says you,' Raoul retorted.

'If I may be so bold,' Henri told him, 'I've watched your grandparents for many years, and within the constraints of their royal roles they do indeed enjoy themselves.'

'They do,' Raoul said tightly. 'But they have each other. They've been lucky.'

The palace was amazing. Over the top. Splendid. When Raoul would have taken her through the palace grounds first, thinking maybe she'd find the fabulous gardens less intimidating, the little girl in Claire made her pause.

'First things first. I'm in a palace. I need to see a chandelier.'

'They're all in the reception rooms and formal living areas,' he told her, bemused. 'Oh, my grandmother has one in her bedroom—no, make that two—but that's because she likes a bit of bling.'

'Will you show me?'

'My grandmother's bling?' he demanded, startled, and she stopped dead.

'No, Raoul, not your grandmother's bling. Your grandmother scares me. But a chandelier, none the less.'

'Which one?'

'Don't be obtuse. *Any* one.'

'Why?' he asked, curious.

'Because the only chandelier I've seen is a plastic travesty my friend Sophie hangs in her bathroom. And even though Sophie's cut me off because of my dubious legal status, one day I may meet her again and I'd love to be able to raise my brows in scorn because I've met a chandelier bigger than hers.'

'You've truly never met a chandelier?'

'I told you—I come from the other side of the tracks, Your Highness,' she retorted.

He looked down at her for a long moment, as if considering all the things he should say—he wanted to say. But finally he sighed and shrugged and managed a lop-sided smile. 'One chandelier coming up,' he told her. 'But if we're going to do this then we'll do it properly. The ballroom.'

'There won't be people?'

'It'll be empty. Cross my heart. Who goes into a ballroom unless there's a ball?'

'Someone to polish the chandelier?'

'It's the weekend. Chandelier-polishers are nine-to-five guys, Monday to Friday.'

'You know that how...?'

'It's in the "*Boys' Own Almanac of What Princes Need to Know*". Trust me.'

'Why should I trust you?'

'Because I'm a Prince of the Blood and I love you,' he told her, and before she could think of a retort he handed Rocky to Henri to take to the stables for a romp with the palace dogs—*'I'll take good care of him, miss.'* Then he took her hand and towed her through a maze of more and more breathtaking passages until they came to a vast hall with massive double doors beyond.

'Behold, my lady,' he said, and tugged the doors open.

If she only saw one chandelier in her life, this was the one to see. It was breathtaking.

Raoul flicked on the lights as he pulled open the doors

and the chandelier sprang to life. Once upon a time it must have been fitted with candles, but the lighting was now instant, with each individual crystal sparkling and twinkling its heart out.

And there were hundreds of crystals. Maybe thousands. The chandelier was a massive art form, a work of a bygone era when such things had been made by skilled artisans funded by the very richest in the land. This was a work of joy.

She'd never seen such a thing. She stood in the cavernous, deserted ballroom and she gaped.

'It's enormous,' she managed at last.

'There are bigger,' he told her. 'If you're interested, the world's largest is in the Dolmabahçe Palace in Istanbul. It has over seven hundred lamps, it weighs over four tons, and they have a staircase with balusters of Baccarat crystal to match.'

She thought about that for a moment and finally decided to confess. 'I don't know what a baluster is.'

'You know what?' He grinned. 'Neither do I. But that's what our guidebook says. We include the information so we sound modest.'

She looked up again at the glittering creation and shook her head. 'Modest? I don't think so. How can you come from living in the army to living in a place like this?'

'How do you know I didn't have a wee chandelier in my rucksack?' he said.

But he suddenly sounded strained and she thought it had been the wrong question. Chandelier or not, he wasn't where he wanted to be. But then he smiled, and she knew he was hauling himself back to reality. Putting regret aside.

He tugged her around to face her and his smile was a caress all by itself. 'Claire, I refuse to let you be intimidated by a chandelier. They're useful things and that's all.'

'Useful for what?'

'For dancing under. How are your dancing skills? I'm demanding to be your partner for at least one waltz.'

'Only one?' she asked, before she could stop herself.

'It depends,' he told her. 'If I dance with you more than twice the media will have me married to you and be conjecturing on how many children we'll have. I'm not objecting, but…'

'Two dances only, then,' she said hurriedly, because she had to. 'Raoul, we need to be sensible.'

There was a moment's pause. She saw his face close again, but then it was gone. Put away. He was back under control.

'As you say,' he said tightly. 'But the waltz… Claire, the eyes of the world will be on us. Do you need a fast lesson?'

'I can waltz!' She said it with some indignation, but then relented. 'Okay, I don't move in circles where the waltz is common, but my mum could dance and she taught me.'

'I'll feel different to your mum.'

'You think?'

'Try me,' he said, and held out his arms, waltz hold ready.

And she hesitated, because more and more she wanted to melt into those arms and more and more she knew she didn't fit there. But Raoul was asking her to dance under what surely must be the second biggest chandelier in the world and he was holding out his arms…

And this was Raoul.

She smiled up at him—a smile full of uncertainty and fear, a smile that said she was falling—had fallen—so deeply in love there was no going back. A smile that said she knew the pain of separation was inevitable but for now she was so in love she couldn't help herself.

She stepped forward into his arms. He took her in the classic waltz hold, lightly, but as if she was the most precious creature in the world.

They danced.

She melted.

There was no music—of course there was no music—

but the beat was right there in her heart. In his heart. She knew it. She felt it.

He held her and their feet scarcely touched the ground. He moved and she moved with him, in perfect synchronisation. How they did it she would never afterwards be able to tell.

It was as if this man had been her partner for years.

For life.

They danced in the great empty ballroom, under the vast chandelier that had seen centuries of love bloom under its sparkling lights, and that was now seeing a Prince of the Blood fall deeper and deeper in love.

And when the dance drew to an end, as dances inevitably did, the lights continued to glitter and sparkle as Raoul tilted his lady's chin and kissed her.

And as he did so a youth appeared in the doorway. He wasn't a palace employee but an apprentice to the master electrician who checked the chandelier at regular intervals.

The electrician didn't work nine to five—not when there was something as major as a ball coming up. Not when every guest room had to be checked and every facet of palace life had to be seen to work splendidly for this state occasion.

He'd finished checking the chandelier lights that morning, but was missing a spool of wire. 'Check the ballroom,' he'd told his lad. 'Make it fast.'

So the lad had slipped into the room—and stopped short.

He knew the Prince—of course he did. And the girl… This woman had been on the front pages of the newspapers for a couple of days. She'd rescued the Prince. She was here for a royal reception and to do some legal something or other. The media had reported sadly that there appeared to be no romantic attachment.

And yet here they were.

The apprentice might not be the smartest kid on the block, but he knew an opportunity when he saw it. He raised his phone and with one click it was done. Photographed. Safe.

Then he went back to report sadly to his boss that the spool of wire was nowhere to be found.

The kiss ended. They were left gazing at each other in some confusion.

I could let myself stay in these arms, Claire thought. *I could just...try.*

And if it failed? If *she* failed? This wasn't some minor fling. Breaking the Prince's heart would make her seem like a villain the world over. But the alternative…to live in a gilded cage and be judged…

She shuddered, and Raoul saw the shudder and touched her face.

'No,' he said, strongly and surely. 'Today we don't let the future mar what we have. You know what I'd like to do now?'

'What?'

'Take you to the gymnasium and let you show me your karate skills. You did say you were good.'

'I did,' she said, because why use false modesty here? Raoul might admit that his was only the second biggest chandelier, but her karate skills were okay.

'So prove it,' he told her.

She knew what he was doing. The kiss had been intense, passionate—a kiss that claimed—and she'd stepped away in fear. She was falling so hard, so fast. How to keep her sensible self working?

But Raoul must have seen the flash of fear and suddenly emotion was taking a back seat to challenge. Karate. 'I bet you can't throw me,' he told her.

'I bet you I can. Do you really have a gymnasium?'

'Yes.'

'Just for you?'

'The staff use it, too,' he told her. 'This is a large palace and we look after our employees. But I can block out any time I want it to myself. Usually I don't, but today I took the precaution…'

'Because you want me to prove myself?'

'Claire, you don't need to prove a thing,' he told her, his voice gentling. 'You've already proved you're the woman—'

'Not another word,' she interjected, suddenly breathless. 'Not one more word, Your Highness. But, okay, let's head to this gymnasium and see if I can throw you.'

She could throw him.

He lay on his back, stunned, and looked up at the diminutive woman above him with incredulity.

At her first approach he'd allowed her to throw him. He'd learned some martial arts himself—it had formed part of his army training. Then, bemused by Claire's claim to skill, he'd performed a token block—because he suspected that, yes, she really could throw, but he was large and skilled himself, and he didn't want to hurt her pride.

That thought had lasted all of twenty seconds, which was the time Claire had needed to move in, feign an amateurish movement, change swiftly to a move that was anything but amateurish and have him flat on the mat.

She grinned down at him. 'You'll have to do better than that, soldier.'

Soldier. For a moment she'd lost the Prince thing. She was having fun, smiling down at him, laughing at the ego that had had him misjudging her.

So then he got serious. He rose and circled and thought about everything his martial arts sergeant had told him.

As a soldier Raoul was trained to work with any number of different weapons. He could work on tactics, set up a battalion for attack, retreat, advance, camouflage, exist on meagre rations, survive with bush craft...

He could do this.

He moved in to attack, thinking how best to throw her without hurting her.

The next moment he was on his back again, and he didn't have a clue how he'd got there. *Whump!* He lay, winded, on the mat, and she was smiling down at him with the same patronising smile that said this throw had been no harder than the first.

'What the…?'

'I told you I was good,' she said, with not a hint of false modesty about her. 'Believe me?'

'Teach me that throw.'

'Really?'

'Please,' he said humbly, and she put down a hand to help him up.

He gazed at it with incredulity, and then grinned and put his hand in hers. She tugged him up, and he let her pull, and the feeling was amazing. He wanted to kiss her again—very, very badly—but she was in full martial arts mode. She was *sensei* to his pupil and she was serious.

They had an hour during which he learned almost more than in the entire time the military had devoted to teaching hand-to-hand combat. And at the end he still didn't know a fraction of what this woman could do.

Karate was fun.

Dressmakers were scary.

The appointment was for two. Showered in the lavish gymnasium bathrooms, dressed again and with make-up newly applied, she should be ready for anything.

She wasn't.

Henri had come to find them. Raoul had left her for his own fittings and Henri had escorted her to a massive bedchamber on the second floor.

He swung the door wide and four women were waiting for her, all in black, all with faces carefully impassive.

'You'll take care of Miss Tremaine,' Henri said.

'Of course,' the oldest woman said smoothly, and closed the door on Henri and turned to appraise Claire.

She was a woman whose age was impossible to guess—slim, elegant, timeless. She also seemed deeply intimidating. Her gaze was surely a dressmaker's appraisal—nothing more. Claire shouldn't take it personally. But it was hard not to as every inch of her body was assessed and while the other three women stood back, silent, probably doing the same thing.

'Excellent,' the woman said at last. 'I'm Louise Dupont. These women are Marie, Belle and Fleur. Our job is to provide you with whatever you need for the grand ball and for the preceding official engagements which we're informed you're invited to attend. Belle has a list of the requirements. Would you like to tell us your ideas first, so we have an idea where we're going?'

'Simple.' It was as much as Claire could do to get the word out. 'I'm not royal, and I'm not accustomed to such events. If I could, I'd wear a little black dress…'

'A little black dress to a royal ball…?' Louise's expressionless face almost showed a flinch, and the women behind her gasped.

'I know I can't do that, but I'd like something that won't make me stand out.'

Certainly, *mademoiselle*,' Louise said woodenly, and swathes of cloth produced, and sketches, and a part of Claire was thinking, *What a coward*.

Among the swathes of cloth were brocades, sequins, tulle, lace of every description. But sense was sense. She chose beige for one of the anniversary dinners and a soft green for the other. Matching accessories. Deeply conservative. Then the ball dress…

'I really can't have black?'

'Their Majesties would consider it an insult,' Louise told her, and so Claire fingered the silver tulle for just a moment and then chose a muted sensible navy in a simple sheath design.

It will look elegant, she told herself, and the way the women set about fitting the cloth to her figure she knew it would.

And then Raoul arrived. One of the women answered the door to his tap. Whatever he'd tried on, he'd tried on fast. He was back in his casual trousers and open-necked shirt, but he stood in the doorway looking every inch a prince. He stared at the pinned sheath of navy cloth covering Claire and groaned.

'I *knew* it. Get it off.'

'I beg your pardon?' Louise turned and saw who it was, but her attitude hardly changed when she did. 'I beg your pardon—Your Highness.'

'Do you really think that's suitable for a royal ball?'

'It's what Miss Tremaine wishes.'

'Miss Tremaine wishes for the fairytale—don't you, Miss Tremaine?' He shook his head in exasperation. 'Louise, Miss Tremaine is returning to Australia after the ball, to life as a country lawyer. This ball is a ball to be remembered all her life.'

He strode across to where the remaining bolts of fabric lay and lifted some white lace shot with silver.

'This, I think. Something amazing, Louise. Something that makes the world look at Claire and know her for the beauty she is. She'll be wearing my mother's tiara...'

'Raoul!' She should have used his formal title but she was too gobsmacked. 'I don't want to stand out. Plain is good—and I'm not wearing a tiara.'

'You saved my life. If that's not a reason to lend you my mother's tiara I don't know what is. She'd be proud to have you wear it. You need a dress to match. Something magnificent, Louise. Something fairytale.'

'Would you like us to set up screens so you can supervise?'

'No!' Claire retorted.

Raoul grinned. 'What? No screens?'

'Go away!'

The women stared at her in astonishment—a commoner giving orders to royalty?—but Raoul was still smiling.

'Only if you promise to indulge in the fairytale. The full fantasy, Claire. Remember what Henri said? Have fun. Louise, can you do fairytale?'

'Certainly, Your Highness,' Louise told him, sounding intrigued.

'Then fairytale it is,' Raoul told her. 'Get rid of that navy blue.'

'Raoul…'

'I'm leaving,' he said, still smiling at her, and his smile was enough to have every woman in the room trying to hide a gasp. 'But you *will* have fun.'

'I will have fun,' she said grimly.

'That's my brave Claire. Go for it.'

And in the end she did have fun. Raoul left and she had two choices—she could try and incorporate a bit of bling into her image of plain or she could go for it.

With the women's blatant encouragement she went for it.

'I *do* like a bit of fairytale,' Louise admitted, letting her dour exterior drop.

Raoul had suggested the white lace shot with silver, and after a little thought that was what Louise recommended. The design she suggested was a gown of true princess splendour, with a low-cut sweetheart neckline and tiny slivers of silver just off the shoulders to hold the bodice in place. A vast skirt billowed and shimmered from a cinched waist, and a soft satin underskirt of the palest blue made the whole dress seem to light up.

That was the vision. For now it was only draped fabric, held together with pins, but Claire gazed at herself in the mirror and thought, *What am I doing here?*

She needed to ground herself. She needed to find Rocky and go home, she told herself as more and more of the shimmering silver was applied. To Australia. This fairytale was sucking her further and further in.

But she couldn't leave until after the ball.

At last the interminable measuring was done. 'You'll do our Prince proud,' Louise told her, permitting herself a tiny smile, and Claire tugged on her jeans and blouse as fast as she could and wondered how her presence could possibly do anyone proud. She felt a fraud.

Raoul was in the hallway, calmly reading, clearly waiting for her. He had Rocky on his knee. Rocky bounced across to greet her with canine delight and Raoul smiled—and she was in so much trouble.

'Hungry?' he asked. 'Picnic in the grounds?'

'Raoul, I should…'

'There's a whole lot of *I shoulds* waiting for us in the wings,' he said gently. 'For now, though, let's put them aside and focus on the *I wills*.'

CHAPTER TEN

RAOUL DIDN'T RETURN to her apartment that night, and neither did she stay in the palace. It had been a risk for one night; another night would be pushing things past reasonable limits if they were to keep the media treating their relationship as platonic. As they must.

Claire slept fitfully in her sparse apartment. She woke early, eager to throw herself back into work, which was far less confusing than being with Raoul. She was due to meet the head of Raoul's fledgling social services department. She drank coffee and read her notes from the previous week, trying to block out the fantasy of the weekend. Then, still with time before the car came to collect her, she retrieved the newspapers Raoul had organised to have delivered to her door.

She opened the first one and froze.

The page was entirely taken up with a photograph. Claire and Raoul, underneath the chandelier. The moment their waltz had ended. That kiss. The photograph had been blown up to the extent that the images were grainy, but there was no mistaking the passion.

This was no mere kiss. This was a kiss between two lovers. This was a man and a woman who were deeply in love.

She gasped and backed into the hallway, as if burned, dropping the paper on the floor. She stared down at it in horror.

The headline…

Roturière Australienne Pièges Notre Prince.
Commoner Australian Traps Our Prince.

Scarcely breathing, she picked it up again.

The first article she read had been hurriedly but deeply researched.

When she'd first arrived in Marétal the press had given their readers a brief background of the woman who'd rescued their Prince.

Lawyer taking time out from successful career to caretake an island...

It had sounded vaguely romantic, and the description had been superficial.

There was nothing superficial about *this*. Overnight someone had been in touch with an Australian journalist, who must have travelled fast to the tiny Outback town of Kunamungle. There was an exposé of her childhood poverty and scandal, even a nasty jibe from the publican—'*She always thought she was better than us—she was dragged up in the gutter but ambition was her middle name...*'

More coming! the article promised, and Claire thought of the fraud allegations and what might come out—what *would* come out—and she felt ill.

This was sensationalist journalism and it cheapened everything. She felt smutty and used and infinitely weary.

She flicked to the next paper.

Prince Désire Paysanne...
Prince Desires Peasant.

The phone rang. It was Raoul. He spoke, but she couldn't make herself reply. She leant against the wall, feeling she needed its support. The papers were limp in her hands. She dropped them again and felt as if she wanted to drop herself.

'Claire, talk to me.'

'There's nothing to say,' she whispered. 'I knew this would happen. So did you.'

'I need to see you.' He groaned. 'But I can't. The media have staked out the palace gates. I'll be followed if I come to you and it'll make things worse.' He paused. 'Unless you want to face them down together?'

Together? With all that implied? 'No!'

Somehow she hauled herself together. She was here to do a job and she would do it.

'I have an appointment with the head of your social services department in half an hour,' she told him. 'In this precinct. I imagine the media can't get in here?'

'They can't. You'll still do that?'

'I promised,' she whispered. 'It's what I came here for.'

'You came here for so much more.'

'No,' she said, and anger came to her aid now—fury plain and simple. 'I didn't. I agreed to take on a job. If I go home now then your papers will say that every single thing they've printed is true. That I came here to trap you…'

'We both know that's a lie.'

'I bet that's what they said about Cinderella.'

'We're not basing our relationship on a fairytale.'

'You said it,' she said wearily. 'Raoul, it's impossible. This is real life. We had…we *could* have had…something amazing…but amazing doesn't solve real-life problems. You know I'm not good enough for you.'

And he swore—an expletive so strong she almost dropped the phone.

'Um…' she said at last. 'My translation isn't that good.'

'Claire, I *will* see you.'

'No,' she told him. 'It does neither of us any good.'

'You did promise you'd come to the ball.'

She fell silent then. The ball… She *had* promised. And there was the dress. And there was Raoul. And he'd be in his gorgeous regimental uniform.

Cinderella had *her* midnight, she thought ruefully. Maybe she, too, could have her ball and her midnight. There'd be no glass slipper afterwards, because happy-ever-after only happened in fairytales, but the ball would be something she could remember all her life.

She shouldn't. The sensible part of her brain was screaming at her: *Don't, don't, don't!*

But there was still another part of her—the part that remembered Raoul holding her in the waltz, the part that remembered a dress of shimmering silver, the part that knew for the rest of her life she'd remember one night…

And she had to finish what she'd come here to do. She'd do her work, she'd have her ball and she'd go home.

'Okay,' she whispered.

'Okay, what? Claire…'

'I will come to the ball,' she told him. 'As long as…as long as you don't attempt to see me before then. I won't come to the receptions. Just the ball. And I'll finish the work I'm here to do this week so I can go home straight afterwards.'

'It doesn't make any kind of sense'

'It does,' she said sadly. 'It makes all kinds of sense. It's anything else that's just plain lunacy.'

Raoul read the papers from cover to cover.

They were tearing Claire to pieces. No mercy… This woman wasn't good enough to be the future Queen. The papers said so.

A fury was building inside him—a rage so cold, so hard, that it was all he could do not to smash things. The palace was full of excellent things to smash. Priceless china, artwork that still had the power to take his breath away, precious carpets and furnishings…

Right now he wanted to put a match to the lot of it and watch it burn.

Instead he forced himself to keep reading as he knew that Claire, when her work for the day was done, would read.

Together they could face them all down, he thought. This wasn't insurmountable. In time they'd see…

But she wouldn't let that happen. He knew that with a dull, unrelenting certainty. Claire's self-image had been battered from birth, and the ghastly Felicity and her cronies had smashed it to nothing. He knew how wonderful she was, but she'd never let herself believe it. She'd be miserable here, knowing everyone was looking down at her. Her self-image wouldn't let her go past it.

The whole situation was impossible. He slammed his fist down on his desk, causing his coffee to jump and topple and spill onto the priceless Persian rug.

Excellent. A good start.

There was a faint knock on the door.

'Come in,' he snapped, and Henri was at the door, looking grave.

'I am so sorry, Your Highness,' he told him.

'So am I.' He hesitated, and then thought, *Why not say it like it is?* 'The paper's right. I love her.'

Henri stilled. 'Truly?'

'What do *you* think?'

'This criticism will pass.'

'She doesn't think she's good enough, but she's better than all of us put together. What am I going to do? I can't demand she stay. I can't insist she subject herself to this sort of filth.' He picked up the top newspaper and tossed it down onto the pool of spilled coffee.

'She'd like to learn to ride,' Henri said weakly. 'Maybe you could ask her to come here for a lesson.'

'You think that would be an enticement for her to stay?'

'I…no.'

The two men stared at each other for a long moment. Raoul didn't even try to hide his pain. This man had known him since childhood. It was no use trying to hide.

'She must be really special,' Henri said at last.

'She saved my life,' Raoul said simply. He stared down at the spilled coffee and his mouth twisted. 'She saved *me*.'

'So how can you save her back?'

Raoul shrugged. 'I know the answer to that. I need to let her go.'

'There must be another way.'

'If you can think of one…' He lifted the newspaper he'd tossed and screwed it up. 'If you think the media will quit with this… It's relentless.'

'I'm so sorry,' Henri said gently. 'You know, the palace could put out a rebuttal…'

'Everything they say is true. They're crucifying her for things she had no hand in. They're crucifying her for her birth.'

'Are you thinking of marrying her?' Henri asked. 'Are you really thinking she's worthy of the throne?'

The question made Raoul pause. He thought of the years of isolation, of the armour he'd built around himself. He thought of his relentless quest not to need people. Not to love.

He thought of Claire.

'Are you really thinking she's worthy of the throne?'

She surely was. Of course she was. And then he thought of the throne without Claire and he was suddenly face to face with what he must have known for weeks.

'Of course I am,' he said bleakly. 'She's the woman I need beside me for the rest of my life.'

'Will she agree?'

'No,' he said bleakly. 'She won't, and I don't blame her.'

Claire spent the week working harder than she'd worked in her life. She'd been working to a plan and now she simply continued with the plan—except she worked faster.

She was interviewing as many of the country's movers and shakers in the justice system as she could. She was also talking to the police, prison officers, parole officers, small-time lawyers who worked at the fringe of the system—and to people who'd found themselves in court themselves. People who'd failed to find legal help when they'd needed it most. People whom legal assistance was designed to help.

As an outsider she could never have done this work alone, but Raoul had set it up for her. The people he and his staff had chosen for her to talk to were extraordinary, and to her relief almost none of them had backed out of the interviews because of the photograph and the lurid exposé of her past.

'I thought you wouldn't be here,' a lawyer she'd talked to that first morning had said. 'The papers say your legal work is just a smokescreen for you staying with the Prince.'

'It's not. My legal work is the reason His Highness persuaded me to come.'

'So you and the Prince…?' he'd probed, and she'd managed to smile.

'Legal work is dull. A woman has a right to a little fun on the side,' she'd told him, somehow managing to smile.

He'd stared at her in astonishment and then he'd laughed, and they'd got on with their interview.

So that was how she was managing it—laughing it off as best she could as a bit of fun, pretending it had nothing to do with her work and ignoring Raoul.

He still rang every night, and she answered his calls. She talked determinedly about the work she was doing—there was so much that could be done for his country and her report would be comprehensive—but she refused to talk about anything personal.

'Personal's a mistake,' she told him when he pressed her. 'You know that. And who knows who's listening in on this conversation?'

'No one is.'

'You can't be sure.'

'Claire…'

'I'll come to the ball and then I'm out of here,' she told him. 'My work will be done by then.'

'You know I want you to stay.'

'And it's totally unsuitable that I stay. Raoul, find yourself a princess. I'm just Claire.'

And each night she disconnected from his call with a firmness she didn't feel. She punched the pillows into the small hours and even made them a bit soggy, but there was no way she was relenting.

She had to do what she had to do and then leave.

* * *

Raoul also had to do what *he* had to do. As the week went on he became more and more sure that his decision was the right one. He needed her.

Need…

The knowledge made him feel exposed as he'd never been exposed before. It was terrifying and it was exhilarating and it was inarguable.

He'd lost his parents when he was so young he barely remembered them. His grandparents had been kind, but remote. He'd been raised by servants and then he'd found himself in the army—a place where teamwork was valued but individual emotional strength was everything.

He'd learned to be a loner. He'd thought he could be a loner all his life.

He'd been wrong, and the knowledge left him with no choice. Meeting Claire had made something inside him break and it couldn't be repaired.

A part of him said that was weak, but there was nothing he could do about it. Rejecting her felt like tearing himself apart.

He'd faced the worst of conflicts in the Middle East, but he'd joined the army for a reason. He'd spent a solitary childhood when life had seemed bleak to the point of misery. He thought of that solitude now. He had thought he'd trained himself to accept it.

He hadn't.

Two days before the ball he went to see his grandparents. Their discussion was intense, personal, a far cry from their usual formality, but at the end he knew his decision was the right one.

The King had said little, just looked grave.

The Queen had been appalled. 'You *can't*.'

'I might not be able to but I intend to try. Grandmama, it's the only way I can stay sane.'

'She's not worth it. A commoner…'

'She's worth it.'

'Raoul, think of what you're risking,' she'd wailed, and he'd shaken his head.

'I think of what I'm gaining, Grandmama. We can do this if we work together.'

'You're not giving us a choice.'

'No,' he'd said, and he had glanced at the side table where the morning newspapers were, full of even more vituperative stories about his Claire. 'No, I'm not. The country's condemned Claire and in doing so it's refused the best thing that's ever happened to it. And it's rejected the best thing that's ever happened to *me*.'

Cinderella had her coach at midnight. Claire had her plane tickets. Her flight back to Australia was booked for early in the morning after the ball.

'It's the same thing, except I won't be leaving any glass slippers behind,' she told herself.

She was standing before the full-length mirror in her apartment, staring at herself in awe. She'd been invited to dress at the palace but she'd refused, so Henri had organised a dresser, a hairstylist and a make-up artist to come to her. She therefore had three women fussing about her. A chauffeur was standing by with a limousine in the courtyard.

For this night she was deemed royalty.

One night before the rest of her life…

She stood in front of the mirror and knew exactly how Cinderella had felt.

This wasn't her. This was truly a princess.

Her reflection left her feeling stunned. She looked taller, slimmer, glowing. She looked regal. Her curls were loosely caught up, deceptively casual, so they framed her face, tumbled artfully to her shoulders. They were caught back within a glittering tiara so some curls hid the diamonds and some diamonds sparkled through.

The tiara alone had made her catch her breath in wonder, but there was also a matching necklet and earrings.

'They haven't been worn since the Prince's mother died,' the dresser said now, sniffing faintly in disapproval. 'I'm astonished that he thinks it's suitable to bring them out today.'

And there it was—the whole reason this wouldn't work. This woman had read the tabloids. She knew just how unsuitable Claire was.

'I guess it's a final thank-you gift before I go home,' Claire said, managing to keep her voice light, as she'd fought to keep it light all week. 'And it *is* just a loan…'

'But for him to lend it…'

'Well, *I* think it's lovely,' the hairstylist said stoutly. 'Perfect. And I loved the picture of you and His Highness in the paper, miss. So romantic. Wouldn't it be lovely if it was real?'

'I think I might regret it if it was real,' Claire managed. 'Do I absolutely need to wear this corset?'

'Hourglass figures need hourglass corsets,' the dresser snapped. 'The women I normally dress don't complain. You must make sacrifices for a decent figure'

'You have a lovely figure already,' the hairstylist declared. 'Don't listen to her, miss.'

And Claire wasn't listening. This week had been all about not listening.

She stared once more into the mirror at the sparkling vision in silver and white, at the way her skirts shimmered and swung, at the beautiful white slippers—not glass!—peeping from under her skirts. At her hair, which had surely never been lovelier. At the carefully applied make-up, which made it look as if she was wearing no make-up at all and yet made her complexion glow. At the diamonds and the sparkle and everything in life which didn't represent Claire Tremaine.

'Okay,' she whispered. 'Bring on my pumpkin.'

'Your car's ready, miss,' the stylist breathed. 'Oh, miss, you'll break your Prince's heart tonight.'

'He's not my Prince,' Claire told her, gathering her skirts and her courage. 'He's never been my Prince and he never will be.'

The ball was an hour old when Claire arrived.

Raoul was half afraid that she'd got cold feet and wouldn't show at all, but at this late stage there was little he could do about it. As heir to the throne he opened the ball with a waltz with the Queen of a neighbouring country. Then there were others he needed to dance with. He had obligations to fulfil and there was no way he could disappear quietly to phone her.

All he could do was dance on with the list of notables Henri had told him were compulsory, and hope that she'd find the courage to come.

Finally he was rewarded when a stir from the entrance announced her arrival.

'Miss Claire Tremaine,' the footman announced in stentorian tones.

The ball was well under way. The announcement of new arrivals had become a muted background to the night—no one was listening—but somehow all ears caught this.

The attention of the entire ballroom seemed to swing to Claire.

She was stunning. Breathtaking.

Henri must have orchestrated this late entrance, he thought. Henri was in charge of Claire's travel arrangements. Raoul wouldn't put it past him to have staged Claire's entrance so she had maximum attention.

As she did. She stood in the entrance looking slightly unsure—no, make that *very* unsure. She looked so lovely the entire ballroom seemed to hold its breath.

His grandmother was by his side and her hand clutched his arm. 'You don't need to go straight to her,' she hissed. 'The way she looks…others will dance with her. This is nonsense, Raoul. See sense.'

'I *am* seeing sense,' he told her. 'Grandmama, you know what I must do.'

'Not tonight,' she urged. 'You need to accompany us onto the dais for the speech. You need to be seen as royal. Stay with us.'

'Only if you acknowledge Claire.'

'I'll acknowledge her as the woman who saved your life, nothing more.'

'Then I'll be in the crowd, watching. If you expect me to be an onlooker, so be it. But meanwhile…' He gently disengaged her arm. 'Meanwhile I need to welcome the woman I love.'

It might as well have been a fairytale. For as she stood, uncertain, alone, Raoul made his way through the crowd and quite literally took her breath away.

The ballroom itself was enough to take her breath away. It was transformed by the lights from the great chandelier, by a thousand flowers, by an orchestra playing music that soared, by the throng of nobility in attire that was truly splendid.

But the most splendid of all was Raoul.

He was truly a prince of dreams. He was in full royal regalia, a superbly cut suit with a wide blue sash, medals, epaulettes, glittering adornments of royal blood and military might.

His jet-black hair was immaculate. His height, his build, his dress—he looked every inch a prince at the peak of his power. He was the total antithesis of the man she'd helped from the water.

He was magnificent.

He was smiling as he broke through the throng, and he held his hand out to her well before he reached her.

'Miss Tremaine,' he said as he reached her. 'You are very welcome.'

And her response was something that stunned even herself. She sank into a curtsy—a full gesture that she hadn't known how to make until she'd done it.

He took her hand and raised her fingers to his lips, his eyes dancing with laughter.

'What have I done to deserve this?'

'I've watched too many romantic movies,' she told him. 'In this outfit nothing else seems appropriate.'

'Claire, stay...' The laughter died and his voice was low and urgent.

'For tonight,' she whispered. 'For now.'

If tonight was all he had then he intended to use it. How to hold this woman in his arms, how to dance with her, how to feel her melting against him and know that she willed it to end?

But he knew why. All around them were eyes raised, looks askance, the occasional snigger, the odd snort of outrage. *This* was the woman who would steal their royal Prince. He knew Claire could feel it, and there was nothing he could do but hold her and know there must be a future for them.

A future at a cost...

But he couldn't think of that tonight. He couldn't think of anything but the woman in his arms.

As they danced the titters and the whispers fell away. He held her and her beautiful gown swirled against his legs, and her breasts moulded to his chest and he felt...

He felt as if he was flying.

She loved him. How could she let him hold her like this and know that she had to leave? If she let herself think past midnight then her mind simply shut down.

All she was capable of was dancing with the man she loved. Of holding him to her.

Of loving...

Only, of course, the night wasn't all about dancing. There were formalities scheduled. After the next set the King and Queen were to make their anniversary speech. And as they made their way to the stage they paused by the couple in the midst of the dance floor.

'You should stand by us, Raoul,' the Queen told him, but she said it in the tone of one who knew she was already beaten.

'You know my decision,' Raoul said softly. 'I stand by Claire.'

'Raoul—go,' Claire told him.

'Will we come to the stage as a couple, Grandmama?' Raoul asked, but the Queen shook her head.

'No! This is *not* what I planned.'

'I'm staying here,' Raoul told her.

'Then come onto the stage with us yourself, young woman,' the King told Claire unexpectedly, suddenly urgent. As if he'd somehow emerged from his books and was seeing Raoul's firmness for what it was. 'This country's treating you shabbily and I won't have it.' He put a hand on her arm. 'Come with us. Please.'

'As a couple,' Raoul said.

'No!' The Queen was vehement.

'Then come to assist an old man onto the stage,' the King told Claire. 'Raoul, assist your grandmother.' And he took Claire's arm and held it.

So in the end there was no choice. They made their way to the stage, but not as a couple. The King was escorted up first, leaning heavily on Claire as if he did indeed need her help.

Raoul escorted his grandmother up the stairs as well. But then, as she made to tug at him, to stand beside her on the far side of the stage from Claire, he shook his head.

'Claire, our place isn't here.'

The noise from the ballroom had faded. Attention was riveted on the stage. To reach Raoul, to leave the stage, Claire would have to walk right in front of both King and Queen.

Raoul was on the far side of the stage, waiting for her to return to him. She sent him an almost imperceptible shake of her head and backed into the wings. The curtains hid her.

This was her rightful place, she thought. Out of sight. She was in the wings with the workers, with the people handling the curtains, the workers associated with the orchestra.

Where she belonged.

She leaned heavily against the nearest wall and hoped Raoul wouldn't follow.

Fantasy was over. The King was preparing to speak.

Somewhere below was Raoul. He needed to listen to his grandparents' speech but she didn't need to be beside him.

She couldn't need him at all.

If there was one thing King Marcus had been known for during his long reign it was his long speeches—and he didn't disappoint now. He'd prepared a very meaningful, very erudite, very lengthy speech and the crowd settled down to listen. This was their King. The country was fond enough of their Queen, but King Marcus was seldom seen in public and they were prepared to indulge him when he was.

After a moment's hesitation Raoul backed away from the stage, stepping down into the main hall. He didn't want any attention to play on him. After all, this was his grandparents' night, and he even found it within him to be grateful that Claire had backed into the wings, out of sight. The focus was on his grandparents—as it should be. The time for him to claim Claire would follow.

Around him the guests were listening with polite attention, laughing when the King meant them to laugh, applauding when it was appropriate. The men and woman in the orchestra behind the King were all attentive too. They were giving this pair of beloved monarchs their due.

He had a sudden vision of himself and Claire in fifty years, doing the same thing.

It wasn't going to happen.

He glanced at his grandmother and found she was staring straight at him. He winced and turned his attention elsewhere. To the orchestra on the raised platform behind the royals. Men and women in demure black, riveted to the King's words.

Except one. A young man seated behind the drums. The man seemed to be searching the crowd. Looking for someone?

His attention caught, Raoul followed his gaze and saw the man's eyes meet one of the guests. A man in his mid-forties was standing not far from Raoul. He was formally dressed, as a foreign diplomat, and he was standing alone. There was nothing to make him stand out from so many similar guests.

But the man was watching the drummer, not the King, and as the drummer's gaze met his he gave his head an almost imperceptible nod. Then casually—oh, so casually—he reached down as if to adjust his shoelace.

And then he straightened, his arm outstretched…

A glint of metal…

Years of military training had made Raoul's reactions lightning-fast. Act first—ask questions later. That was the training instilled for when lives were at stake.

Raoul, ten feet from the man in question, dived like lightning and brought him down in a tackle that pinned him to the floor.

The pistol in the man's hand discharged—straight into the polished floor. But that wasn't the only threat. He knew it wasn't. He held the man, pinned him down hard, and looked desperately up at the stage as he yelled. 'Security! Drummer on stage!'

And as the dark-suited security officers streamed in from the foyer, where they'd been banished, he was remembering a letter. It had been pointed out to him by Henri. It had been addressed to the Queen…

If you don't follow our orders we'll kill the King and take you as our prisoner for ransom. You might as well pay the money now. It'll save you grief...

There'd been a similar threat—and a tragedy—in another country a couple of years back. Their security chief had been worried enough to talk to the Queen, asking permission to bolster his team. He'd wanted to increase the royal security presence within the ballroom.

'You can do what you want *after* the ball,' the Queen had said fretfully. 'I won't have my ball marred by a room full of bodyguards.'

He'd then shared his concerns with Henri, who'd come to Raoul. 'Please...talk to your grandmother,' Henri had told him, and Raoul had. But with no success.

'You're not in charge yet,' the Queen had told him. 'This is *our* ball. You won't bring a woman of our choice. We won't have your bodyguards.'

'They're not *my* bodyguards, Grandmama. They're yours—to keep you safe.'

'There is no threat in *my* kingdom.'

But of course there was—and it was here. It was real. A diplomat wouldn't have faced a body-search. He'd have been able to conceal a gun.

We'll kill the King and take you as our prisoner...

There were two threats here, and he'd only disarmed one.

'The drummer on stage!' he yelled again to the men approaching.

'Nobody move!' a voice shouted out—icy, cold, vicious.

And Raoul twisted and stared up at the stage.

The drummer had launched himself in from the wings and grabbed the Queen. She'd been standing beside the dais while her husband spoke. The man dragged her back towards the wings, and at her throat he held a vicious, stiletto-type knife that looked as if it might have been concealed in a drumstick.

And Claire was there as well. At the sound of the gunshot and Raoul's sharp command she'd edged out from the wings.

She was right behind the drummer.

The three of them might well have been alone on stage. The men and women in the orchestra were slightly removed from the main players. The King was standing stunned on his dais.

There was the Queen and her assailant—and Claire.

The drummer was hauling the Queen further back, and as he did so he glanced behind him. He saw Claire.

He flicked her a glance that took in the swirl of her amazing skirts, her low-cut neckline and the gorgeous tiara set in beautifully coiffured curls. His glance was contemptuous—a momentary summing-up that said she was nothing of importance. She was the dirt the media had been speaking of. She was something to be safely ignored.

He had his knife to Queen Alicia's throat and was tugging her backwards.

For the moment Queen Alicia was refusing to move, digging in her toes, dragging passively, surprisingly fierce for someone so elderly. 'Let me go,' she ordered, in a voice as imperious as her regalia.

'Shut up!' the drummer snarled, and then as the appalled hiss from the ballroom faded to stunned silence he raised his voice. 'One move from anyone and I'll kill your Queen. If she's so precious, stay where you are. She's coming with me. And *you...*' He turned to Raoul. 'Let my friend go.'

Raoul was at the far end of the ballroom. He was with the security forces. They had the diplomat in their grip.

Raoul had the gun in his hand. The sound of its explosion was still reverberating through the horrified throng. He raised the gun and then lowered it, watched helplessly as the security officers did the same.

The drummer was holding the Queen hard in front of him. To shoot risked killing her. There was nothing he could do.

'Let him go!' the drummer snarled again, talking directly to Raoul. 'Now!'

There was no choice. Raoul gave a nod and the security officers let the man go. The man started to move up through the crowded ballroom, shoving stunned aristocracy aside.

And Claire's mind was racing. In a minute she'd have two of them on the dais, she thought. In a minute they'd have the Queen outside, in their hold. Raoul was powerless.

A minute…

She needed a second.

And the voice of her *sensei*…

She glanced out at Raoul, one sweeping glance in which their eyes met for just a fraction of a second but the message she gave him was powerful.

And then she had to ignore him. She had to move.

Now.

She kicked off her ridiculously high, ridiculously beautiful shoes and in almost the same movement lifted her voluminous skirts high. She raised her gartered knee as high as she could and with the heel of her bare foot slammed a *yoko geri* side-kick with lethal force into the back of the assailant's knee.

She'd only ever done this in training. She'd only ever known it as practice, and she'd certainly never done it while dressed in a corset and ballgown.

'Do this and you'll rip ligaments, or worse,' her *sensei* had told her. 'The first rule of Karate is not to be present. Where there is trouble, you are not. But if you're ever trapped in a life-or-death situation this will cause extreme pain and do enough serious damage to give you time to escape.'

And there was no doubt that was exactly what she'd done. The guy screamed and started to drop.

There was still the knife. He could kill the Queen if he dragged her with him, but years of training, years of knowledge and practice were flooding to her aid. What followed was almost a reflex action. Even as the guy buckled she had his knife arm by the wrist and was pulling it back, her other hand pressed against his elbow, pushing forward. She pressed hard with both hands and the guy screeched in pain.

'Drop it,' she bit out as his knees hit the floor.

Queen Alicia was crumbling with them, unbalanced by

the change of pressure. The combined mass of royal skirts was making the entire scene surreal—where were crisp karate uniforms when she needed them?—but she was totally focused on her assailant.

The guy's hand jerked, still holding the knife. 'You slut…'

'I'm not a slut,' she said calmly. 'But I *am* a Third Dan Karate Black Belt. Drop the knife or I'll break your arm.' And she applied more pressure. Not so much as required to break it—at least she didn't think so—but enough to have him screaming again.

Enough to have the knife clattering harmlessly to the floor.

She fielded it and kicked it under Alicia's skirts—because who knew who was out there in the ballroom if she kicked it off the dais?

And she kept on holding the guy's arm, pushing him flat to the floor, with his arm still held behind him, because she didn't know if the knife was all he had. And then she didn't have to hold him, because Raoul was leaping up onto the dais with her.

She glanced out over the ballroom and realised he'd got her silent message. The security officers had moved, obviously at Raoul's command. The man he'd had to release had been grasped again.

They had them.

Security was suddenly everywhere. Control was theirs.

The guy was underneath her. The last threat. And Raoul was with her.

It was over.

CHAPTER ELEVEN

AT FIVE THE next morning Claire boarded her plane.

Why not?

There was no reason why not. The ball had ended in disarray. The security team hadn't been prepared to let it continue. Who knew what else had been planned?

The guests had dispersed, vetted as they left, their credentials finally minutely inspected.

The Queen had collapsed in hysterics. Raoul had been taken up with security concerns, with coping with the ruffled feathers and nerves of the invited dignitaries, with the calming of his distraught grandparents.

Apart from one brief, hard embrace when they'd realised the danger was past, Claire hadn't seen him. She'd been whisked outside by the security people and Henri had appeared at her side and asked her if she'd like to use a salon in the palace to wait for Raoul.

'I'd like to go home,' she'd told him, and he'd nodded gravely and organised a car to take her back to her apartment. Because that was what he thought home meant.

An hour later a slim figure in jeans and a windcheater had slipped out of her apartment, carrying her own baggage to the taxi she herself had arranged.

And now she was on the plane, staring fixedly forward while she waited for take-off. White-faced but determined. What a way to end it. Maybe she should have waited, but her ticket was for this morning and there was no point. What had to be said had been said.

Marétal to London. London to Sydney. In twenty-four hours she'd be back in the apartment she hadn't been near for almost six months.

She had work to do—she'd come to Marétal on a contract and she'd fulfil her obligations. The next few months would be busy. But she wouldn't return to Marétal. Her report would be emailed. Raoul and his staff could use it or not.

She felt ill.

'Orange juice?' A steward was moving down the aisle, offering refreshments. 'I'm sorry, but there's a slight delay in take-off. It shouldn't be more than half an hour.'

She closed her eyes. Half an hour. The beginning of the rest of her life.

Raoul. How could she leave him?

How could she not?

She should be exhausted. She should sleep. But of course sleep was nowhere. She was still wired, still filled with adrenalin, still seeing Raoul heading towards the stage to help her. Still seeing the fear on his face.

He loved her. She knew he loved her. And to be loved by such a man…

Such an impossible man.

There was a stir among the passengers and she opened her eyes and glanced out of the window. There were two dark limousines, their windows tinted to anonymity in the dawn light, driving onto the tarmac. They stopped and a security contingent emerged from the second car—suited men, armed, dangerous.

Where had they been last night?

And then the door of the first car opened and out stepped…

Raoul.

Raoul in jeans and T-shirt, carrying a rough canvas duffel. Raoul looking every inch *not* a royal.

There was fierce talk between the men—remonstrance? But Raoul simply shook each man's hand and then turned and looked up at the plane.

She shrank back. If he was here to take her off the plane…

She wouldn't go. She couldn't.

She sat head down, scarcely daring to breathe, but nothing happened. She couldn't see the door from where she sat. There was a murmur of interest from the passengers forward of her and then nothing.

'Prepare for take-off…'

Nothing more was said. She ventured a peek out of the window. The cars were gone.

The plane turned its big nose ponderously out to the runway, the taxiing complete.

She closed her eyes as the plane gathered speed and then they were in the air.

Marétal was left behind.

'Would you like a facecloth?' An attendant was moving down the aisle, doing her normal thing, business as usual.

She offered the facecloth to Claire and Claire buried her face in it.

'Hi,' said a voice behind the attendant—a voice she knew so well. 'Do you think that when you're all washed up you can cope with a visitor?'

The seat next to hers was empty. Of course it was.

That couldn't just be a coincidence, she thought as Raoul sank down beside her, and amazingly she even found space to be indignant. The plane was almost full. How had he managed this?

He was royal. Being royal opened doors.

'Very nice,' Raoul said approvingly as he sank into the business class seat. 'I'm back in cattle class. I had to be ever so charming to the staff to be allowed up here.'

'You're in Economy?' As a first statement it was pretty dumb, but then dumb was how she was feeling right now.

'*Your* travel is funded by the Royal Family of Marétal,' he told her. 'I'm funded by me. And I'm unemployed. We unemployed people need to watch every cent.'

It was too much to take in. 'Why…why are you here?' she managed, and for answer he simply took her hand.

'You saved the life of the Queen of Marétal. Someone

has to thank you. I got busy, and when I had time to look around you were gone.'

'I had a plane ticket.'

'So you did.' His hold on her hand tightened. 'As it happened, so did I.'

'You...?'

'You don't think I'd let you go all the way to Australia without me?'

'Of course I do,' she snapped. She was tired, confused, and starting to be angry. 'Raoul, this was never the plan. Go away.'

'It's a bit hard to go away now,' he said, peering out of the window to the night sky. They were now thousands of feet high. 'I believe I've burned my bridges. Henri's cleaning up the loose ends in Marétal. I'm here with you.'

'Henri...'

'He's good,' Raoul told her. 'He's the new administrator of the country. I'm unemployed.'

Unemployed...

He took her breath away. He was looking endearingly casual, in jeans and a tight T-shirt that showed every muscle his army life had toned. He was starting to look a bit unshaven. The difference between now and when she'd last seen him was extraordinary.

Unemployed?

'I've quit,' he told her, settling in. 'This is very nice indeed. How long do you think they'll let me sit here?'

'As long as you want. You're the Prince,' she snapped.

He shook his head. 'Nope. I need a new title. I've been Prince Raoul. I've been Lieutenant Colonel de Castelaise. Now I need to be just plain mister. Mr de Castelaise? That sounds wrong. *Monsieur?* Yes, but I intend to be an Aussie. Any suggestions?'

She had no suggestions at all. She could only stare. If she went back behind her facecloth again would he disappear? This felt surreal.

She was starting to feel as Cinders must have felt when her coach had turned back into a pumpkin. In the middle of the road surrounded by orange pulp. Stranded.

Hornswoggled.

'You can't…just resign,' she managed at last, and Raoul nodded, thoughtful.

'That's what I thought. I couldn't see how I could. But when it got closer to losing you I didn't see how I *couldn't*.'

'Your country needs you.' Her voice was scarcely a whisper.

'That's what I believed, too,' he told her. 'But over the last few weeks I've been looking hard at how our country's run and seeing things in a different light.'

'I don't understand.'

'I'm not sure I do either,' he told her. 'Not fully. But what I *do* know is that my grandfather wasn't born to rule. Yes, he was the heir to the throne, but his head was always in his books. His parents despaired of him. His country despaired of him. But then he did something amazing. He met and married my grandmother. She wasn't what you might call a commoner—she was Lady Alicia Todd—but she was just the daughter of a country squire and she had no pretensions to royalty. But she married my grandfather, she took up the reins of the country, and she's been a superb monarch. She's fading now. She's ceased to move with the times, but she's still awesome. She's still the Queen.'

'She needs help. You said yourself…'

'I know she does. But when I was thinking this through I wondered… All those years ago, what would my grandfather have done if someone had told him—as I believe many people did—that Alicia wasn't fit to be Queen? And the answer was obvious. He would have abdicated rather than lose her.'

'You're not threatening…?' Still she was having trouble getting her voice to work. 'You're not threatening to abdicate?'

'I haven't threatened anything,' he told her. 'I've left.'

'You've walked out?'

'Hey, I'm honourable,' he told her, sounding wounded. 'How could I just walk out?'

'You tell me. Words of one syllable,' she said, trying hard to glare. 'What have you done?'

'Moved the Crown into administration.' He thought about it for a moment and reconsidered. 'That's a three-syllable word. Thrown the reins to Henri? Henri's still two syllables, but he's the best I can do. This whole situation is the best I can do.'

'Raoul...'

'You see, Henri doesn't want it,' Raoul told her. 'In fact he's still trying to talk me out of it. But we're organising good people around him. It'll take time, and I will have to return to get things into final shape, but we'll make it work. We don't have a choice.'

'But you're *needed*,' she said, flabbergasted. 'Raoul, you know you are.'

'And I intend to stay hands-on,' he told her. 'I'll return every so often, for as long as they need me. If my grandfather's health declines further, then those visits might end up being long, but that's all they will be. Visits.'

'How can you *do* that? They need you all the time.'

'And there's the problem,' he told her. 'I need *you* all the time.'

That took her breath away. She wasn't sure how she could make herself breathe, much less talk, but somehow she must.

'Isn't that...?' She could hardly make herself say it, but it had to be said. 'Isn't that selfish? Your country needs you. Even on so short a visit I could see the difference you'd make.'

There was a moment's silence. His face set, and she knew suddenly that what he was proposing was no whim. What he was saying was the end of some bitter internal battle, and even now the outcome hurt.

'I could make a difference,' he agreed at last. 'I know I

could. But, Claire, the more I see of you the more I know I couldn't.'

'I don't understand…'

'Last week, after that appalling photograph and the ensuing fuss, I went to see my grandparents,' he told her. 'I talked to both of them and I asked them honestly if they could have ruled for so long and for so well if they hadn't had each other. My grandfather, the King, was the first to answer and he was blunt. He said Alicia was his strength, and that he'd never have been able to do it alone. That's what I expected. But then my grandmother decided to be honest as well. She told me that, strong as she appeared, my grandfather was her spine. That without him she believed she'd collapse like a house of cards. That her love for him was what sustained her. And she conceded more. That royalty was a massive privilege but also a massive burden. And she said that, disapprove of you—*and* your dog—as she surely did, if I truly loved you then she understood. She'd fight me all the way to the altar—she would *not* support me marrying someone so patently unsuitable—but she understood.'

'Oh, Raoul…' Where was the facecloth when she needed it?

But Raoul had her fingers under her chin, forcing her gaze to meet his. 'So it's Henri,' he told her. 'It's Henri and our staff, and my grandparents, and me working from the sidelines. In time the country will become a democracy and they'll see they don't really need a monarch. We'll work something out. We must.'

'But *you*?' It was almost a wail. 'Raoul, it'll take years to make Marétal a democracy, and even then the monarchy could stay in place. You'd make a wonderful king.'

'Not without you.'

'That's crazy. I could never be royal. Your whole country thinks I'm a piece of dirt.'

'So my whole country can think we're *both* pieces of dirt,' he told her. 'I dare say they will when they wake up

tomorrow. *Prince Absconds With the Love of His Life*. I hop
that's the headline.'

'After the events at the ball it could be *Prince's Sense Blown to Pieces*.'

'The Prince's senses are indeed blown,' Raoul said.

He was still tilting her face, and his eyes were now smil ing. His appalling decision to leave the succession was pu aside. What mattered now was them.

'They've been blown apart by one green girl. Claire, I'n coming to Australia with you, whether you will it or not Where you go, I go. Your home is my home. I'm not exactl sure what I'll do yet—I'm thinking maybe a job in secu rity? A bouncer at a pub? What do you think? Your caree prospects are so much better than mine right now, but re gardless...unemployed or not... Claire Tremaine, will yo marry me?'

And there was the end of breathing. Who needed t breathe? Who could even *think* of breathing?

'I can't,' she managed at last. She was struggling betwee tears and laughter. 'Raoul, you know I can't.'

'Why not? Are you too good to marry a bouncer?'

'Raoul, you're a *prince*.'

'I can't be a prince without a princess. I thought I could I was an idiot.'

'You can't throw it all away.'

'I already have. I booked this flight days ago, and the last night you showed me your *yoko geri* side-kick—that' what our security chief tells me it was—and any last nig gles of doubt were gone. My brave girl. My heroine. My heart's yours, Claire Tremaine. I'm your faithful shadow You can be a lawyer wherever you want and I'll be righ there beside you.'

Then suddenly he paused, as if struck by inspiration.

'Wait. I have it. You and I could be a team. We could trai Rocky to be our killer attack dog. Attack Dog Security—how does that sound as a family business?'

'Right…'

'It *is* right, though, isn't it?' Laughter faded. Everything faded. 'Claire, I'd give up the world for you. Indeed, I don't have a choice—because you *are* my world. Marry me, my love, and somehow we'll make a future together.'

'Raoul…' But she couldn't say more.

He tugged her into his arms and kissed her and she let herself be kissed. She even melted into the kiss. But when the kiss drew to an end and she managed to tug away her eyes were still troubled.

'I don't know what to do,' she whispered.

'I do,' he told her. 'Marry me.'

'But the future…'

'Will fall into place. It must because it doesn't have a choice. Marry me, my love. My Claire. Please.'

And what was a woman to say to that, when Raoul was looking at her with such a look?

Heart on his sleeve… She'd heard the expression so many times…wearing your heart on your sleeve…and she'd thought nothing of it.

But it was true. Raoul was hanging his heart on his sleeve right now. He was caressing her with his eyes, loving her, wanting her.

What did the future hold for both of them? She didn't know. But sitting beside him in the quiet of the plane, looking steadily into eyes that loved her, she knew she had only one answer to give.

'Yes, my love,' she whispered. 'Come what may, I guess… I'll marry you.'

They stopped to change to another flight in London, sat in the airport lounge and barely spoke. None of the passengers from the Marétal flight seemed to be going on to Australia, so no one knew them.

Claire leant on Raoul's chest and slept.

He sat and held her and felt his world shift and shift again. *What had he done?*

He'd set things up as best he could at home. Henri was in charge. With the army manoeuvres finished, the best of Marétal's army was home again, so Franz himself could investigate the aftermath of the events of the ball.

His grandparents had been devastated at his decision to leave, but at least they understood.

He was free to hold this woman forever.

But he wasn't quite free.

A niggle of doubt still troubled him. He knew sometimes that niggle would become a shout, but still… To take the throne without her… He'd self-destruct—he knew he would. These last weeks had become a tangle of introspection, of self-questioning, and in the end he'd come up with what he knew was the absolute truth. He wasn't a loner, and the throne was essentially one of the loneliest places in the world.

Was it weak to say he knew he'd self-destruct? A lifetime on the throne without Claire? He'd looked long and hard at himself and known he couldn't face it.

He loved her.

He held her in his arms while she slept. His chin rested on her hair. She was trusting in sleep, her mouth curved into a faint, loving smile. He had the woman he loved most in the world right here in his arms and nothing else could matter.

He'd do everything in his power to keep Marétal safe, to see it into a prosperous future, but he couldn't give up Claire. This woman was his and he was hers.

The future stretched ahead in all its uncertainty, but for now… He was with Claire and that was all that could matter.

She shouldn't let him do it. For Raoul to abdicate…for *her*…

He mustn't.

She knew he mustn't but she'd said yes.

How selfish was that?

It was impossible, and yet she couldn't let herself think of impossibility. Soon she'd wake up to reality, she thought as she lay nestled in Raoul's arms, half asleep.

Soon she'd wake up—but not yet. Please, not yet.

Sydney, Australia.

'We can't go to my apartment,' Claire had told him as they landed. 'Firstly it's a shoebox, and won't fit us both, and secondly I've sublet it. I…*we* need to find something else. I meant to go to a hostel…'

'Hostels mean dormitories,' he'd said, and had taken charge.

She woke up after a glorious twelve hours' sleep to find herself cocooned in Raoul's arms, sunlight streaming in through the windows of their hotel room and a view of Sydney Harbour that was truly breathtaking.

'So…so much for being unemployed,' she managed as Raoul stirred with her. 'Five-star luxury… We need to say goodbye to all this.'

'Not this morning, woman,' he growled, holding her to him. 'Not until I'm over jet lag—and I hear jet lag lasts a long time. And there's only one cure. Come here and I'll show you.'

And the spectre of unemployment went right out of the window as she turned within his arms and smiled at her beloved, and then melted as she surely must. *Oh, Raoul...*

They loved and loved, and for the moment the cares of the world were put firmly aside in their joy with each other.

But finally the world had to intrude—of course it did. Hunger had a habit of asserting itself even in the most fabulous of settings.

They made themselves decent—sort of—and ordered breakfast, and Claire gasped when she saw it.

'We can't do this. You've said you're an unemployed bouncer. Champagne for breakfast?'

'If I'm not mistaken you've just agreed to marry me There are some occasions when even unemployed bouncers require the best.'

And who was arguing this morning? Just for today sh could put doubts aside and drink her lovely champagne an eat her gorgeous croissants and look lovingly at this gorgeous prince-cum-bouncer as he finished his own croissar and reached lazily for the newspapers that had been delivered with the breakfast tray.

She watched his face change.

'What?' she said, and rose and went to stand beside him

They were in the breakfast nook—a curved bay windo overlooking the sparkling waters of Sydney Harbour. The were both dressed in the towelling robes provided by th hotel. It was the most beautiful, most intimate of settings—a breakfast to remember—and yet as she watched him sh saw the dreamlike quality fall away and reality set in.

'Problems?'

'No,' he told her. 'It's just… I didn't think it'd make th news here. You're going to be hounded again.'

And there it was—a front-page spread—and once agai she was in the centre. Claire in her Cinderella dress. Claire i the moments after Raoul had reached the stage, the attacker disarmed. Raoul leading her to safety. Raoul in his beautifu prince's clothes, his arm around her, curved in protection.

And the headlines…

Australian Woman Saves Queen…
Assassination Attempt Foiled…

'I might have known,' Raoul said. 'All media's parochia Your press will have picked up that there was an Australian in the middle of it and gone with that angle. Claire I'm sorry.'

'I can live with a few days' media attention,' she said

and managed a smile. 'Especially if we can stay here. Hunker down. Let the world forget us.'

'We might be able to manage that.' He tugged her down onto his knee. 'That's what you want? For the world to forget us?'

And she thought, *Did she?*

For herself? Definitely. Since when did publicity mean anything good? As a child she'd hated anyone looking at her. The taunts. The active discrimination against the child of a single mum…

Yes, she'd hated it and feared it. And the whole lawsuit thing had terrified her even more.

Raoul had had a lifetime of attention being trained on him. Surely he must hate it, too.

She knew he did, but now he was fetching his laptop from his bag, logging in to the internet.

'I need to see what the papers are saying at home,' he told her.

And she thought, *Home? Home is where?*

He was sitting on the bed and she went to join him. He put the laptop where they could both see.

There'd been two mornings in Marétal since they'd left. Two lots of newspapers.

The first newspapers they read were those published in the immediate aftermath of the drama. There were photographs of the white-faced King and Queen, dignified but clearly shaken. There were fuzzy photographs of the attackers being led away by Security. There were photographs of the King and Queen, and of Raoul and Claire.

Saved by Our Prince! the headline screamed, and Raoul winced.

'That's hardly fair.'

'You stopped him firing.'

'And if it wasn't for you the Queen would have been taken and held for ransom,' Raoul told her, and flicked through to the next day's headlines.

Which were different.

The reporters had had time to figure out the details of what had happened.

There was a photograph of Alicia with the knife at her throat, being hauled back towards the wings.

There was a photograph, slightly blurred, of a make-believe princess, her dress hiked up, her legs bare, her shoes kicked off. The moment her foot had come into contact with the assailant's knee. A second photograph of her grip on his arm.

The third photograph was of Raoul, launching himself onto the stage to help her hold.

And the headlines?

The Woman We Called Commoner...
The Princess We Need.

She didn't say anything. She simply sat as Raoul read out the stark article underneath.

Our Prince and the woman he loves saved our King and Queen. This woman we've condemned has done our country a service we can scarcely comprehend. This newspaper wishes to unreservedly apologise...

And then there was a photograph of a shadowy Raoul being escorted to the plane. And another headline.

Bring Her Home, Raoul.
We need her.

'Is that why you're really here?' Claire asked in a small voice. 'To...to bring me back?'

And Raoul set his laptop aside and turned to hold her. 'No,' he said, firmly and surely. 'The media's fickle. They might now have decided they love you, but *I* fell in love with you approximately two minutes after I met you, and I'm not fickle. Claire, I booked my plane ticket almost a week ago. What I'm doing has nothing to do with how my country's reacting to you now. It's all about loving you.'

'They think you're here persuading me to return.'

'That's because we haven't released a statement yet,' he told her. 'Henri made me wait until I was here, until I'd had time to ask you to marry me, before we made an official statement. He said—and he may be right—that if you told me to go to the devil then I might well decide to head back to Marétal with my tail between my legs.'

'And be a solitary prince forever?'

'Probably.' But he hugged her tighter. 'Luckily that's not an option. You've agreed. Do you think we could sneak out today and buy a ring?'

'Sneak out?'

'We could go out the back way. Get one of those nice tinted limos. Go somewhere innocuous and buy a diamond.'

She thought about it. There was a lot to be said for it.

'We could go out the back way. Get one of those nice tinted limos. Go somewhere innocuous...'

Coward.

The word slammed into her head and stayed.

Coward.

She looked at Raoul—really looked at him. He was her soldier, her lover, her Prince.

He'd offered to give up his world for her.

He'd asked her to marry him and she'd said yes.

But had she said yes to Prince Raoul or had she said yes to the man she'd like him to be? A man disappearing into the shadows because she didn't have the courage to stand beside him?

She thought suddenly of that appalling time almost six months ago, when she'd been hounded by the thought of wrongful fraud charges. Running to Orcas Island.

Becoming a shadow.

She thought of the taunts of her childhood and how she'd hidden in her books. Keeping her head down. Being nothing. Hoping no one would notice.

She thought of her workplace, wearing black or beige. Making no waves. Cringing as she waited for criticism.

Coward.

'Raoul,' she said, in a voice that must belong to her but she barely recognised it. It was another woman's voice. Something inside her had shifted. Or come together.

Raoul met her gaze and she thought it was this man who'd changed her. Raoul had given her this. And she'd take it, she thought with sudden determination. Raoul loved her. What sort of gift was that? What was she about, continuing to run?

'Yes?'

He sensed something had changed. He knew her, this man. He knew her so well.

They could stand side by side forever.

'Would you help me bring Felicity to justice?' she asked, and he blinked.

'Felicity?' He looked confused—as well he might.

'She stole money from my law firm,' she said, clearly now, because suddenly her way was defined and there was no way she could deviate. 'I was blamed, but with decent lawyers I could prove it wasn't me. I chose not to make a fuss. That was partly because I didn't have the funds to fight, but I could have borrowed to do it. I chose not to. I chose to disappear. Felicity and her nasty friends counted on it. But suddenly… Raoul, I don't want to disappear any more, and I don't want an accusation of fraud hanging over my head. Even though they've hushed it up I won't accept it. Will you help me?'

'I…yes. Of course I will. Though maybe you should wait a little. For the next couple of weeks you'll be the target of media.'

'Then media might be able to help me. If an accusation is

made, I'll defend myself.' She took a deep breath. 'If you're by my side.'

'You know I will be.'

'As the proprietor of Attack Dog Security?'

He smiled at that. 'We need to get Rocky out of quarantine first.'

It was harder to get Rocky back into Australia than it had been to get him to Marétal. He was currently one day into a hefty quarantine period.

'That's another thing,' she said diffidently. 'I don't want my dog locked up any more.'

'Australian quarantine is stringent,' he said, cautious now, not sure where she was going.

'But if we decided to get back on a plane tomorrow, to return to Marétal, then he'd spend only two more days in a cage.'

What followed was a moment's silence. No, make that more than a moment. It was long and it was filled with questions and it stretched on forever.

'We?' Raoul asked, and his voice sounded strange. 'If *we* decided?'

'I'm not sending Rocky back without me.' She hesitated, and then she placed the computer carefully out of the way, so there was nothing between them. Nothing at all. She took his hands in hers and held them tight. 'And I won't go back without you. But I will go back.'

'Why?' His voice was laced with strain.

'Because it's right,' she whispered. 'Because I know it's right. Because your place is there and my place is at your side.'

'Claire, there'll be...'

'Media. Intrusion. Lack of privacy. But, hey...' She suddenly cheered up. 'There'll also be an awesome hairstylist. She's lovely, and I bet as a princess I can have her do my hair every time we have a state occasion.'

'She can do it every day,' he said grandly. 'But, love...'

'Mmm?' She'd moved on. She was starting to think about personal hairstylists. And the palace gardens, which surely beat the rocks of Orcas Island. And a library. And chandeliers…

'What are you thinking?' he asked uneasily, and she grinned.

'If the Queen can have a chandelier in her bedroom I don't see why I can't have one.'

'You can have ten.' And then he reconsidered. 'But not as big as the one in the ballroom?'

'No?' She sounded gutted, and he laughed, and then he drew her to him and his face grew serious.

'Claire, what are you saying? You know I love you, but this is huge. You're a private person. You'll be in a goldfish bowl.'

'We can buy curtains.'

'Claire…'

'I just figured it out,' she said, cupping his face in her hands, holding him, loving him. 'It's taken me a while, but I have it. This courage thing… Do you remember in the water? I saved you and you saved me right back? As a team, imagine how much more we could save. Imagine how we could save each other.'

'We could do it here,' he said urgently. 'With our Killer Attack—'

'Don't tempt me.' She put a finger on his mouth, shushing him. 'I've been an idiot. If I have you beside me why do I need privacy? Why do I need anything but you? And you… Raoul, you're needed in Marétal. You know you are. I'll never forget that you've given me this choice, but if you stay here you'll worry about your country. You'll worry about your grandparents. You'll worry about security and whether your people can get legal assistance and proper education and healthcare. And, as much as I know that the Attack Dog Security team could do some vital work, keeping the citizens of Australia safe, I suspect that we could do more in Marétal. If we work together.'

There was another pause—a pause so long she didn't know how to break it.

Raoul's hands gripped hers so tightly they hurt.

'You'd do that?' he asked her in a voice choked with emotion. 'For me?'

'No.' She shook her head. 'I've been stupid. I've been a coward. And I didn't see I'd be doing it for *us*. I'm even thinking Cinders had a point, accepting her Prince's hand on the basis of one glass slipper—though I have to think that she was a wuss, staying in the kitchen waiting for him. I won't wait for you, Raoul. I want you *now*. I want you forever.'

How had things changed so fast? She didn't know. She would never afterwards be able to tell. But all she knew was that they had.

She wasn't a coward. She wasn't the illegitimate kid—the one dressed in secondhand clothes, trying to claw her way up through poverty. She wasn't anyone the Felicitys of this world could stomp over.

She was Claire, and she was loved by Raoul, she thought. She was loved by her man.

And then she forgot to think, because she was being kissed—kissed as she needed to be kissed, as she deserved to be kissed—and she kissed him back. And there was nothing else to be said for a very long time.

And afterwards—when the kiss was finally done, when there was room again for words between them—Raoul pushed her back and his dark eyes gleamed.

'Diamonds,' he told her, with all the authority of the Royal House of Marétal behind him. 'This very afternoon. Do you still want the back way and tinted limousines?'

'Not on your life,' she told him. 'I want a chariot or six. Where do you think we can find a pumpkin, a few mice and a fairy godmother?'

CHAPTER TWELVE

THEY WERE MARRIED six months later, with all the pomp and ceremony Queen Alicia could manage. She had decreed that a royal wedding must be a showcase of splendour, and so it was. Every dignitary in the land was there, plus as many of Europe's aristocracy as she'd been able to summon.

But no one had needed much summoning. This was a day of joy, and the world was waiting and willing to share.

The bride arrived at the cathedral in a magnificent, horse-drawn coach, with the Horseguards of Marétal parading before her. By Claire's side was King Marcus.

'A girl has to have someone to give her away,' Marcus had said, emerging from his library to give a decree of his own. 'You've almost single-handedly saved the royal family of Marétal. Unless there's someone else at hand to do it, it would be my very great honour to assist.'

And Claire had joyfully agreed.

Marcus was her future father-in-law.

Marcus was the King of Marétal.

Marcus was her ally and her friend.

She seemed to have lots of friends now, she thought, though she was still dubious about many. There'd even been a fawning letter from one of the associates at her old law firm…

You always seemed such a loner, but I was thinking... we did enjoy shopping together. And I've always been on your side, even though I couldn't say. I needed my job too much. If you need a bridesmaid...

Claire most definitely didn't. That appalling time was best forgotten.

Thanks to Raoul's intervention, Felicity and her partner were now facing a hefty jail sentence, and there'd been an 'undisclosed' amount of compensation paid into Claire's bank account. There'd been media coverage of the entire case.

So now it could be forgotten—and today of all days who would think of it?

There were crowds lining the streets, smiling and cheering.

'Wave,' Marcus told her, and she thought of how anonymous she'd always wanted to be.

But she managed to wave, and Marcus waved, too, and she thought, *We're two of a kind. Two introverts in the royal spotlight.*

And then she stopped thinking, for they'd reached the cathedral. Henri was handing her down from the coach. Henri, too, had become a true friend, as had her gorgeous hairstylist, who was currently fussing over her train.

And then it was time.

The doors to the cathedral were flung wide. The sound of trumpets rose triumphantly to the skies.

'Ready?' Marcus asked.

She took a deep breath and nodded. They trod regally—as she'd practised—up the great steps, in through the nave.

The cathedral opened up before them, magnificent in its age and beauty. It was filled with every dignitary in the land, plus so many people who were Raoul's friends and who were becoming her friends.

Raoul stood at the altar. Beside him was Tom, owner of *Rosebud*—because Raoul had thought, Who else could be his best man? The soldier who'd lent him his unseaworthy boat, which had led to him being saved by Claire, was the obvious choice.

But Raoul had saved her back, Claire thought mistily as the sound of trumpets filled the cathedral, as the congregation rose to its feet, and as Raoul turned and smiled at her.

Raoul's smile…

That was what had got her into this mess, she thought. That was the whole trouble.

That was the whole joy.

He smiled, and the over-the-top setting was forgotten. She'd practised walking in this amazing dress, with its vast train, with its priceless adornments. She'd practised keeping step with Marcus. She'd even practised her vows.

But who could think of any of those things when Raoul was standing at the end of the aisle waiting for her?

Raoul. Her heart. Her destiny.

He was in full royal regalia. He looked magnificent, but she wasn't seeing the uniform. She was only seeing Raoul.

Theirs wouldn't be a marriage like that of Marcus and Alicia, she thought mistily. Raoul wanted—needed—her to share his kingdom and of course she would.

For she wasn't unequal. She was loved. She and Raoul were meant to be forever and ever, she thought, and she managed a tremulous smile back at the man she loved with all her heart.

'You can do this,' Marcus whispered at her side, and she managed to smile at the old man, the King of Marétal.

'Of course I can,' she whispered back, and then there was nothing left to be said.

She made her way down the aisle to be married.

Surely there'd never been a more beautiful royal bride, Raoul thought as he watched Claire and his grandfather walk steadily along the aisle towards him. Even the Queen's eyes were misting with tears.

His beautiful Claire was coming to wed him.

By Raoul's feet sat Rocky. Claire had tried to train him to be the ring-bearer, but in rehearsals he'd proved unreliable to say the least.

'But he needs to be there,' Claire had said.

So they'd organised a velvet cushion to be placed front and centre. Claire had trained and trained him, and this morning a footman had taken him on a run that should exhaust the most exuberant dog. So he now lay by Raoul's side, looking as if butter wouldn't melt in his mouth.

But he was also watching Claire approach, and he wasn't totally to be trusted.

'Stay,' Raoul murmured as he stirred, and he looked up at Raoul and thankfully subsided. He wouldn't jump up on the royal bride.

'She's exquisite,' Tom breathed as Claire grew nearer. 'You lucky man.'

And that reminded Raoul of the final thing he had to do.

In his pocket was the tiny figure made of plastic building blocks. Herbert. Tom's good luck charm.

He hadn't admitted to Tom that he'd found him, but now it was time.

'This is yours,' he told Tom. He handed him over but his gaze didn't leave Claire.

'You found Herbert?' Tom stared down at the tiny figure in astonishment. 'My good luck Herbert?'

'I've had him and I've used him,' he told him. 'But as of today he's all yours. Use him wisely, my friend.'

Tom looked at him in bemusement, and then pocketed Herbert safely beside the royal wedding rings. There were things he wanted to ask, but now wasn't the time.

For Claire had reached her Raoul, and Claire was smiling and smiling, and even a tough Special Forces soldier like Tom was finding it hard not to choke up.

'My Claire,' Raoul whispered, taking her hands and drawing her forward. 'My love. Are you ready to be married?'

And Claire's smile softened to a tenderness that must melt the hardest of hearts.

'How can you doubt it, my love?' she whispered. 'Indeed I am.'

* * *

Marétal's first legal assistance office was opened six months later. A small, nondescript building, set in the part of the capital where it was most needed, it seemed a bizarre setting for the fanfare that went with the opening. For not only were the King and Queen present, but so were His Royal Highness Crown Prince Raoul and his beautiful wife the Princess Claire.

Claire wore a turquoise and white dress from one of Australia's leading designers. For this she was criticised in the media the following day—*Support Our Industries!*

The article beside it also wondered why the royal family was always accompanied by a nondescript fox terrier, when everyone knew the royal dog of Marétal should be the Marétal Spaniel.

Claire read those articles early. For once she'd woken before Raoul and had fetched the papers to read in bed. She smiled when she read them. She then hugged the dog she'd graciously admitted to the royal bedroom—because a woman needed some company before her husband woke.

She thought briefly about the articles and decided that she liked her turquoise and white designer frock very much, regardless of who had designed it. And she loved her dog.

And then she forgot all about them.

For her days were too busy for her to be bothered with criticism. She had better things to be doing than worrying about the day's press.

Things like lying in the arms of her husband. Things like living happily-ever-after.

Finally he was waking.

'What are you doing, woman?'

Raoul's voice was a sleepy murmur as he tugged her down against him. Passion was never far away. Love was for always.

'I'm thinking I might get my toenails painted,' she told him, kissing him with all the tenderness he deserved. 'Louise knows someone who can paint intricate designs on individual toes. Does that seem a good idea?'

There was a moment's pause, and then a fast rearrangement of the bedding while the toes in question were examined.

'They seem good to me now,' he told her at last. 'I like them as they are.'

'They seem like a bare canvas.'

'What would you like on them?'

'Storks,' she said complacently. 'I'm wearing open-toed sandals to my next three functions. I'm wondering if the media will pick it up.'

There was another pause. A longer one.

'Storks?' he said at last, and she chuckled.

'Yep. Mind you, if I do it today I'll need to fit the appointment in well before my meeting with the Chief Justice. It wouldn't do to appear before His Lordship with not-yet-dried toes.'

'I guess it wouldn't.'

But Raoul had ceased his toe inspection. He sat up and gazed at her in bemusement.

Claire smiled at him and thought she'd never seen him look sexier. Mind, it could be the early-morning sun reflected from the crystal chandelier above her head.

No, she thought dreamily. He'd looked just as wonderful back on Orcas Island. Her soldier. Her sailor. Her love.

'Are we by any chance going to have a baby?' Raoul demanded at last, in a voice that was just a tiny bit strangled.

'We might be.'

If she sounded like the cat that had got the cream, who could blame her?

'You're pregnant!'

'Only a bit.'

Ten weeks. It was time she told him—probably more than time—but life was busy, and he'd fuss, and they were so gloriously happy how could anything make them *more* happy?

But she was wrong. What crossed Raoul's face was a flash of joy so profound she felt her eyes welling with emotion. With love.

'Claire…'

'Papa,' she said, and then she could say no more.

She was gathered into his arms and held.

So in the end she had to delay having her toes painted with little storks, and she was sadly late for her meeting with the Chief Justice.

'There's no use being royal if I can't issue a royal decree,' Raoul declared. 'And this morning I decree that my wife will lie in my arms until she's listened to every reason why she's cherished. Are there any objections?'

'No, Your Highness,' she whispered as he folded her into him. 'I can't think of a single one.'

* * * * *